Prologue

The young man stood up and then slowly walked over to the large oak tree next to the bench. He leant his shoulder against the trunk and stared out across the park. As he spoke, he remained standing with his back to the girl who he was talking to.

"There are people dying in this world because their country doesn't have enough money to spend on medical equipment and the drugs they need to stay alive." He slowly shook his head and frowned. "Yet those same countries spend billions a year on weapons of destruction just to kill other people."

The young man turned around to face the girl with a look of torment in his light blue eyes. His expression was solemn and he held his head low in a morose manner. As he carried on talking, he walked over to stand in front of the bench.

"There are terrible wars going on all the time around the world just because of religion, greed or any number of other pointless reasons. People are dying of diseases, hunger and all kinds of illnesses simply because there's not enough done to get the cures they need to survive." He lowered himself down and squatted in front of her. "How can I just go on living my life as if everything is alright when I know that such things are going on all around me? All I want is to make the world a better place."

The girl had sat with her eyes lowered throughout the time that her lover had been talking, but now she found herself looking directly into his gaze. She knew that what he was saying was true, even if she did not like to hear it. As she spoke, she leant forward and tried her best not to look displeased.

"I know the world's not perfect..." She paused and took in a deep breath. "But why does it have to be you on this righteous crusade, like some kind of messiah? Why should you suffer? Why should you have to go through pain for others?"

"There is no reason why I *have* to do it." The young man lightly took hold of her hands. "But I want to. I know I'm capable of becoming a pioneering doctor, a leading scientist or even a respected politician. There's so much I want to do."

The girl nodded her head in an understanding manner.

The silence was broken by the squeak of the door as it swung open on its worn hinges. A dark outline of a medium sized man partially covered the doorway as he stood in a tired posture. His hand clumsily moved towards the light switch and with a flick of his finger the room was illuminated. As he pulled the coat off of his shoulders he uneasily made his way to stand by the window at the other end of the room.

Doctor Peter Elster wore a nervous expression upon his face as he looked out across the twilight sky. A peaceful orange glow from the setting sun rested above the lights of the city creating a palette of warm and soothing colours. This restful scenario was not, unfortunately, a reflection of the state of his troubled mind.

Peter's office was on the tenth and top floor of Starrow Town hospital and the lofty view from the window to the ground below did very little to help his fragile nerves. Being one of the newer doctors he was, regrettably, not given the choice of which office he would like to have had. No doubt, if it had have been his decision, he would have chosen one very near to the bottom floor due to his acute affliction to vertigo. Although he found the view uncomfortable, it was not just his phobia of heights that caused his discomfort.

Doctor Elster was of average build and had a dark thick moustache that seemed to underline his large red nose. He was a kind man and was always willing to give up the time to converse with his patients. This was the part of the job that he enjoyed most. The healing of people and the satisfaction that came with it.

Peter had made the choice of a career in medicine at a very young age and he had pursued his goal of becoming a doctor ever since he had been at secondary school. From a teenager to an adult he had passed all of the necessary exams and had become a well-respected member of the medical profession. He had set his target and he had hit the mark.

Although Peter had gained a lot of experience over the years it could not have prepared him for what happened just over twelve months ago. This was the dark part of his life of which the memories had been deliberately placed well back into the depths of his mind. It was the reoccurrence of these thoughts that were once again making him nervous this evening.

Fourteen months ago on the outskirts of the town of Starrow a new chemical plant had been built by a Japanese company called Tarbon Incorporated. It produced all kinds of manufacturing materials that were mostly quite harmless, but there were also some that were dangerously toxic. For safety reasons these more hazardous chemicals were stored in storage tanks made out of reinforced metal in a secured area of the plant.

Being a new business in Starrow, Tarbon Incorporated offered new employment for a lot of the town's people. Administration clerks, warehouse workers and chemical truck drivers were all employed by the plant taking a big slice out of the town's unemployment figures. Everyone was happy with the new increase in the town's prosperity, until disaster struck.

One of the fork lift truck drivers was carrying some empty barrels through the warehouse when he went across puddle of spilt oil and instantly span out of control. He was only going at a slow speed, but the weight of the heavy vehicle sent him skidding towards the brick wall of the secured toxic chemical area. All he could do was sit helplessly as he slid uncontrollably towards a big sign that read; 'DANGER! Life Threatening Chemicals'.

The forks were the first part of the truck to hit the wall. It was almost as if the bricks were made out of paper as the iron prongs stabbed straight through them into one of the metal chemical tanks behind them. Flashing lights and screeching sirens instantly went off all around the plant and mayhem erupted.

Just before the accident happened, a young woman called Sylvia Woodley who worked in administration was taking round the monthly pay slips. She was on her way through the warehouse when she heard a big bang and turned around to see a mauve gas seeping from a wall. Within an instant she had breathed it in and had fallen unconscious.

The spilt toxic chemical from the tank was called 'Nasterax', and was a newly developed extra thin liquid used in the making of industrial glue. As soon as it had got out of the secured area its fumes spread out across the warehouse instantaneously knocking several people unconscious. The liquid itself gushed out all over the fork lift truck and the floor around it completely covering the driver and a passing warehouse manager. Their deaths were extremely painful.

All of the other people who had been affected by the fumes were instantly rushed to hospital so that they could receive medical treatment. Most of them were allowed to go home after at least a couple of days, but one of the patients who were kept in was Sylvia Woodley. She was found to be four months pregnant at the time of the accident and tests were being carried out to see if the baby had been affected. It was an agonising wait for her, her husband and the medical staff.

After months of examinations the worst had became apparent. Sylvia Woodley's baby was almost certainly going to be deformed. Her womb was swelling far beyond the usual size and the baby that she was about to give birth to was not going to be normal. Although the painful wait of not knowing was now over, the worst was yet to come.

The day had come when Sylvia Woodley was going to give birth and Peter Elster was on duty. The medical staff knew that there were going to be complications so more than the usual amount of doctors and midwives were present. It was an appalling sight.

Sylvia Woodley had a caesarean birth, but her baby girl did not live beyond an hour of her life. From the shoulders up the child was quite normal, but below that was a massive over swelling of the torso and legs. The baby was so disfigured its lungs were too deformed for it to be able to breathe properly. It just kept making a croaking noise until it stopped altogether.

What should have been the happy occasion of a life being brought into the world had turned out to be a hideous spectacle of the death of a newborn child. It was not just sickening for the mother and distraught father who had held his wife's hand throughout the ordeal, but also the doctors and midwives who had been present at the birth. There was not a person in the delivery room that had not been appalled by what they had witnessed that day.

It had taken Doctor Elster months to get over the trauma and he had even partaken in psychological treatment to help him cope. In his weekly sessions his explanations to the therapist were as graphic as they were horrifying.

"It was the disgusting sounds that the baby kept on making." His nerves would make him twitch uncontrollably on the left-hand side of his face. "I still hear the gurgling when I go to bed at night."

It was a slow process, but Doctor Elster had managed to come out of the shock of what he had encountered and had somehow got on with his life. His training had helped him cope with it and his colleagues had stuck by him when he needed them most. Something like that, however, is never forgotten and it is made even worse when such an occurrence is ever repeated.

Over a year later, as Doctor Elster looked out across the city from his office window, the terrible memories of what had happened that day were again torturing his mind. Just as his life had returned to normal it seemed as though the nightmare was about to happen again.

One of the other workers at the Tarbon chemical plant who had breathed in the fumes was a young married woman called Marilyn Cain. She had received several check ups at the hospital and had been cleared to go home after finding that she had suffered only a few minor effects. It was only when she conceived her first child five months after the accident that an interest had been renewed in her. The doctors instantly carried out examinations of the womb and after fears that the baby was going to be different it was decided that when she gave birth that extra caution should be taken.

The day had finally come for Marilyn to have her baby and it was again on Doctor Elster's shift. He could not believe his luck. His twitch had come back and he nervously rubbed the left-hand side of his face with the palm of his hand. In an act of despair he threw his coat across the room towards the clothes hook on the opposite wall, but he missed by a long way sending it into a heap on the floor. As he wondered what might lay ahead of him on this most foreboding of nights he stood in a desolated manner with a solemn look upon his face.

It was while Doctor Elster was mulling over this all too familiar anguish that he was momentarily startled by a loud knock on the door. When he got a hold of himself he beckoned to the person outside his office to enter.

"Come in!"

The door opened sharply revealing a tall nurse who seemed to be rather out of breath. Her face appeared to be slightly flustered due to her moving at a more than casual pace through the hospital. As she spoke she put her hand to her chest and tried to control her breathing.

"Peter, could you come to the delivery room please?"

Doctor Elster pulled his white coat off of the back of the chair and opened the top draw of his desk to get his stethoscope.

"Is Mrs Cain having her baby?" His voice was laced with the sound of dread.

"Yes, doctor!" The nurse sighed and shook her head. "And things aren't going right."

Doctor Elster involuntarily shuddered at first, but the spasm subsided as quickly as it had come about. After a deep breath he hesitantly paced over to the door and switched off the light as he made his way out. As they quickly paced through the corridor he tried to extract some useful information out of the nurse.

"What are the complications?"

"There seems to be some swelling just like the other Nasterax baby." The nurse closed her eyes in a despairing manner. "The head seems to be too big."

"Too big? But the scans two months ago showed that it was normal."

"Not the latest ones."

Doctor Elster rubbed the twitching side of his face and clumsily put his stethoscope around his neck with his other hand. When they reached the delivery room they immediately heard the sound of people rushing about in an almost frantic manner. He waited a moment before entering.

"The best thing you can do is to..." He paused. "Expect the worst and deal with it."

This piece of advice was more aimed at him than at her and the nurse knew it. As he made his way through the double doors he did not see the look of concern appear upon her face.

The first thing Doctor Elster saw when he entered the delivery room was a huddle of doctors and midwives crowding around a woman who was lying in the birth position. As he approached, a middle aged female doctor turned to face him. She looked slightly harassed, but she whispered to him in a calm and precise manner.

"The part of the baby which is swollen is the head." She seemed to be quite cool considering the circumstances. "It might prove to a bit hard for her to push it out, but she's making as good as progress as could be expected of her."

Doctor Elster nodded and came over to stand by Mrs Cain who was now sucking deep breaths out of an oxygen tank. There did not appear to be a father of the child anywhere

4

around the delivery room. As if things were not bad enough she could at least have done with some close support from her partner. This was just a sad reflection of the world.

Marilyn Cain was only in her mid twenties and this was her first baby. She seemed to be quite a pretty girl with her high cheekbones and long brunette hair. Her face, however, was now quite distorted as she winced due to the pressure that she was putting into trying to deliver her baby.

Peter's mind straight away went back to Sylvia Woodley and the birth of her Nasterax baby. He remembered the look of horror in her eyes as the life faded away from her baby. And worst of all, the sounds.

Marilyn then gave out a groan almost as if she was trying to get Peter's attention. This seemed to do the trick and he suddenly became aware of his duties. In response he tightly grabbed hold of her hand and spoke to her in a determined manner.

"Hello, Mrs Cain. I'm Doctor Elster, and you and I are going to deliver your baby."

Marilyn looked at him straight in the eye and seemed to acknowledge his will power with a slight nod of her head. At that point a large portly looking mid-wife leaned across from the other side of the delivery table to speak to Peter.

"Mrs Cain's tried to push the baby out several times, but we've had no luck yet." She looked at him as if she was questioning his usefulness.

"Forceps?" Peter knew that they had probably already tried his obvious suggestion, but he wanted to make sure.

"Can't! It's not the head that coming out first." The mid-wife spoke in a deep resolute voice. "It turned overnight. I think the best we can do is give it another go at trying to get it out normally and then if that fails we'll go for a caesarean."

Peter could not believe his luck. If he was about to encounter the same experience as he had before he just did not think that he would be able to cope with it. Twice in a lifetime was far too much.

Marilyn then gave her most forceful push yet. She seemed as though she was putting every bit of energy she had into it. Her face turned a dark red hue and her eyes tightly closed. With all the effort that she was putting in it almost seemed as if she was never going to succeed until a shout came from the young nurse who Peter had come in with.

"It's coming!"

The portly mid-wife immediately moved around in between Marilyn's legs knocking one of the other doctors out of her way.

"I can see its feet." She announced eagerly. "Keep pushing!"

Peter carried on looking into Marilyn's eyes as he spoke.

"Keep it up. It won't be long now."

"The stomach's out." The portly mid-wife held onto the baby's legs with one hand and pulled out her umbilical cord scissors with the other. "It's a boy." She announced.

Marilyn then let out a strained groan as she gave her last push to get the remainder of her son out. The strength of the final exertion was just enough to do the job and she felt the new born baby slip out. Then there was silence.

Marilyn had half fainted due to the pain and it was only Peter who kept her partially awake by giving her more oxygen. He could barely hold the mask to her mouth due to most of his concentration being fixed upon her newborn baby.

The butch mid-wife's face was distorted with a frozen look of horror. In her static frame of mind she had unknowingly dropped her scissors next to where the baby was lying on the delivery bed. All of the medical staff just stood staring at the baby boy with pale withdrawn faces. One of the nurses could not help but turn away and lean upon a nearby doctor's shoulder for comfort.

The silence seemed to last for an eternity. No one wanted to say a word. They all just stood there staring at the same thing.

There at the centre of everyone's attention lying on the delivery bed in between Marilyn legs was her son. Alive, silent and deformed. The skin of the new born baby boy was a deathly pale colour all over with just a slight shade of pink, but what was really disturbing was that his head was swollen to the point of being at least twenty percent bigger than a normal baby's cranium.

The deformities, however, did not seem to be causing him any distress whatsoever. He seemed to be the only living being in the room that did not seem to be in any kind of torment. There was nothing but peace within the features of his face.

The baby just lay there with his eyes closed and without shedding a tear. Everyone else in the room was in a state of shock and did not make a move. It was almost as if they were all going to just indefinitely stay where they were, then something suddenly happened. Marilyn Cain's son opened his eyes.

Now there was a new surprise for everyone. The baby's irises were abnormally light crystal blue in colour with the smallest of pupils in the centre. They looked like cut diamonds as the lights from overhead reflected off them with a scintillating sparkle.

Peter could not help but make a surprised remark.

"Jesus!"

But still the baby just lay there calmly breathing and utterly content.

When Marilyn finally came to moments later the portly midwife passed the baby into her arms. Peter was just about to say some words to comfort her, but he did not get the chance. She looked down at what was lying on her chest and saw what she had given birth to. As she looked at her son's deformed head, ghost like skin and his icy coloured eyes staring straight back at her she let out a hideously loud ear-piercing scream. That was certainly not the baby that she had wanted.

David Cain the son of Marilyn Cain was three years old and was deformed. He was aware of the fact and actually did not really care too much about it, but his mother certainly did. From the first moment she had set eyes upon her son she had despised him.

Since David had been born he had received a number medical check-ups a year. His health was perfect, but his appearance was not. At birth his head was considerably bigger above the ears than what was deemed to be normal, but since then its growth in comparison to his body had slowed down. It was currently about fifteen percent too large, but the doctors had predicted it would reduce to about ten percent by puberty. As for the gaunt colour of his skin, that seemed to stand out more, what with his lips being a normal shade of red and due to him inheriting his mother's dark hair. He was not anaemic, but had somehow been poisoned whilst in his mother's womb which had resulted in him looking like he was constantly ill.

Marilyn had cut David's hair short in an attempt to try to hide the deformity of his head, but it was still quite noticeable especially when wet. When his mother was combing his hair he was sometimes sure that he could see a slight sneer cross her face, but he never said anything.

None of David's physical differences ever bothered him. In his own eyes the way he looked simply did not matter. He did, however, sometimes wonder if his mother held her own different opinions.

One thing was for sure, the doctors who carried out the tests on David saw the advantages of his deformities. They did not hold back when describing how special he was. It was while he was in one of the examination rooms at Starrow hospital for yet another one of his check-ups that they made their views clear.

"Your son is gifted, Mrs Cain." The middle aged male doctor who was sitting behind a desk spoke in an overawed manner. "Not only is his brain bigger than a normal child's, but size for size it operates considerably faster as well."

Marilyn just turned to her son and sighed.

"Never mind David! Your head's not that bad." She looked at him with feigned pitiful eyes and sounded quite insincere. "You can always wear a hat."

Another older female doctor who was standing in the corner of the room tried to explain to Marilyn exactly what they meant.

"You don't understand, Mrs Cain!" She spoke slowly so as to make herself as comprehensible as possible. "He's more intelligent than *us*."

David looked at his mother and wondered if she understood what the doctors were saying. She seemed to be more bothered about the way he looked rather than what he was capable of. He knew he was dissimilar from other people in appearance, but he also knew that he was different in the way he used his brain.

Along with all of the medical tests that the doctors had given David the thing they assessed the most was his intelligence. He enjoyed taking these examinations and thought of them as good fun even though he was meant to take them seriously. The doctors had said that the average IQ for a person was meant to be about one hundred, but whenever he asked them what his score was they told him that they had not yet worked it out. He thought it must have had something to do with the questions being so easy.

After David averaging a medical or intelligence test nearly every three months of his life, Marilyn had now come to the conclusion that he had been examined enough. She decided to tell the doctors at the hospital that there were to be no more. When she spoke to them her voice was agitated and bitter.

"I don't care what you think my son is." She pointed her finger at David. "I don't want you testing him anymore. It's like he's one of those monkeys you people do your experiments on."

The male doctor tried to reason with Marilyn.

"It really isn't like that, Mrs Cain." He put his hands flat out on his desk and leant forward. "It's for his good and yours."

The female doctor still tried to explain the entirety of David's mental abilities.

"Most people use just fifteen percent of their brain. We think David might use up to thirty percent." She spoke in a pleading manner. "Your son is very, very clever. In fact he's brilliant. We've just got to find out how brilliant."

Marilyn was not impressed and she made her feelings clear.

"Well, you can't! You're just wasting his time and mine." She got up out of her chair and started to walk towards the door as she spoke. "He's not coming back, ever!"

In her fit of anger Marilyn had forgotten all about David and had walked off into the corridor leaving him sitting on a chair in front of the desk. He sat in a morose manner with his head bowed and his arms crossed. If it had of been up to him he would have kept on taking the tests, but unfortunately it was not. The male doctor leant forward and gave him one last piece of advice.

"Just remember this, David! You're one of a kind. You're not a genius." He spoke in a quiet and wistful tone of voice. "You're a genius, genius, genius!"

David had been quite sure that he knew what the doctor had meant by what he had said and it had made him feel quite pleased with himself. It just appeared as though his mother did not have the same opinion. He sometimes wondered if she had actually made the decision for her own sake rather than his own, but he would never say anything to her about it.

Marilyn watched as her son played on the rug next to the fireplace. She forced a smile at him as he looked up at her to see if she was looking at him. David had built an extremely accurate looking horse out of plastic building bricks and was quite proud of his creation. He did not see his mother's false look of impressiveness disappear as soon as he looked away.

It was Marilyn's wish to have had a baby girl who she could dress up and make a beautiful woman out of. Although she would have been quite happy to have had a boy, she considered what she had got to be a deformed *thing* that she was too embarrassed and ashamed even to show to her family and friends. All of her feelings towards her son were of a sickening contempt.

Due to Marilyn's humiliation she had become a recluse and had isolated herself within the four walls of her home. Over the last three years she had only gone out to buy the shopping or to do anything that was deemed important. She had hid herself and her child from the world. They saw no one and no one saw them.

David was oblivious to his mother's anti-social behaviour due to his lack of awareness of the outside world. Although he had already acquired an extensive vocabulary he still had a lot to learn about life. This was something that only time could teach him.

Marilyn and David had managed to live comfortably for the last three years due to a massive legal payoff from Tarbon Incorporated. The Japanese company was dishonoured by the lack of safety at the plant and had issued each of the effected families a large lump sum of money. This had suited Marilyn entirely, what with her desire to be separated from the outside world and having to live life as a single mother. She had bought her own semi-detached house and lived off of the rest of the money along with state benefits.

As for Marilyn's husband he had left as soon as he had found out that she was pregnant. He was a low earner and they had been finding it hard to cope even before David had been conceived. What with the prospect of an extra mouth to feed and all the responsibilities of being a parent he fled without even a good-bye. Although they were married it appeared as though his own welfare was his greatest concern.

With her embarrassing son and her husband gone Marilyn had fallen into a deep depression. She had not looked at a man for all the years since her David was born and no man had looked at her. That was at least the case up until now.

Whilst Marilyn was shopping at a local supermarket she had met a man by the name of Graham in the queue at the delicatessen counter. He was nice, in his early thirties and had asked her out for dinner. It was all the prompting that she needed to change her ways.

Marilyn had not yet told David about her date and she was not really looking forward to doing it either. She was sure that the subject about his father would be brought up in the conversation and that was something that she would find hard to handle. It still hurt her to talk about the subject and she would cry, get annoyed or ignore her son if he ever mentioned it. So both of them were now sitting in the living room amidst the glow of the fire with a conversation looming that would no doubt lead to at least one of them feeling a certain amount of discomfort.

David had now dismantled his model made out of the plastic bricks and had put them away in a cardboard box. From a plastic bag by his side he pulled out a spinning top and started to push down on the top to make it spin. As it did so the patterns on top swirled around producing a rainbow of revolving hues.

Marilyn had now decided that it was time to tell David about Graham and her impending date. As she got off of her chair and came to sit on the rug next to him in front of the fire the expression upon her face was one of reluctance. She was not looking forward to this for a number of reasons, the main one being that she would have to tell him that tomorrow night he would have to stay at his Aunt Geraldine's and Uncle Raymond's house and this would not please him at all.

David liked his Aunt and Uncle, but he did not quite feel the same way about their daughters. They always seemed to taunt and laugh at him. He knew it was because his head was not quite the same as theirs, but he did not find it amusing like they did. There had been many occasions in the past when he had been on the end of their mockery, so he had long decided that it would be best just to ignore them.

Marilyn hated sending David out of the house, especially to Geraldine and Raymond's. Her sister had two pretty little daughters who were, of course, not deformed. She felt embarrassed that she had not achieved something as simple as giving birth to a normal child. Unfortunately, the only option she had of getting rid of David for tomorrow night was to send him round to her sister's.

Marilyn was now sitting next to her son with a forced smile and was watching him play with the spinning top. She decided it would be best to make some small talk before announcing her date.

"Do you know what makes it stay standing up, David?" She leant round in front of her son to see his face. "It's because it spins."

David looked up at his mother and smiled.

"Yes. It's known as centrifugal force, mum." He looked back at the spinning top. "As it spins around it makes the weight around the circumference equal all the way round keeping it upright."

Marilyn sat back with a confused look on her face.

"Oh!" She slowly nodded her head. "Yes, that's right."

Marilyn did not know what her son was talking about, but tried to hide her ignorance.

David had already started to get bored with the repetitious spinning top so he put it back into its box. His shoulders slumped and he breathed out a bored sigh. Marilyn decided that now would be a good time to tell her son about her date.

"What would you say if I met a man, David?" She moved closer to him and tried her best to explain. "Someone who your mother liked, and who also liked her. You know, like very close friends."

David smiled and looked round his mother. He could see that she was nervous, but he also realised that she wanted a positive answer.

"I think it would be nice, Mum!" He replied.

"You would?" Marilyn sounded surprised.

"Yes! What's his name?"

"Graham."

David spoke in an encouraging manner.

"It would be really good for you to have someone to take you out Mum. You deserve it." He put his arm around his mother's back and rested his head on her chest. "I'm pleased for you."

Marilyn half smiled and half winced.

"Oh Mummy! Why can't big head go to someone else's house?" Wendy stamped her foot on the kitchen floor. "It's not fair."

"Be nice to him girls!" Geraldine tried to reason with her daughters. "He is your cousin."

The two sisters, Wendy and Clare, were seven and nine years old respectively, and if there was one sure thing that they both had in common it was the fact that they both despised David. They would repeatedly tell their mother that the way he looked and the things that he said would scare them and make them feel uncomfortable. Most children have a habit of being quite unforgiving over such things, but these two were especially callous.

9

Geraldine was cooking the dinner in the kitchen whilst her daughters were standing next to her with their hands placed petulantly on their hips. They were both wearing pretty dresses and had colourful bows in their hair, but they also wore scornful looks upon their faces.

"Well, I'm not going to talk to him." Clare frowned.

"And neither am I." Wendy turned to her sister and nodded defiantly.

Geraldine slowly shook her head and watched as her daughters stomped out of the kitchen in a show of disapproval.

"Poor kid." She muttered to herself.

As soon as the doorbell rang, Wendy and Clare instantly turned to each other and sneered. They were sitting upstairs in their room and did not need to look outside to know who had arrived. The passive resistance was about to begin.

Geraldine opened the front door and greeted Marilyn and David who were standing with thick coats on to protect them from the chill of the night.

"Come in you two! You must be freezing." She said it with an exaggerated smile upon her face.

Geraldine looked very similar to her sister. She had brunette coloured hair and a pretty face, but she was slightly shorter and a touch on the plump side. Nevertheless, she still had her fair share of the family's good looks.

Marilyn and David stepped into the hallway and started to take their coats off. As Geraldine closed the door behind them she forwarded some hospitality.

"Would you both like a cup of tea?"

"Yes, please. But I can't be too long though." Marilyn answered quickly then turned to David and spoke to him in an impatient tone. "Well, answer your Aunt!"

"No thank-you." He replied politely.

Geraldine hung their coats on some hooks in the hall and then turned to face Marilyn.

"Well, don't keep me waiting! Come into the kitchen and tell me what he's like!" She winked at her sister and smiled cheekily.

Marilyn smirked back in a similar manner. She was wearing a short skirt with a low cut top and was out for fun tonight. As she turned to walk into the kitchen she excitedly flicked her hair and adopted an exaggerated strut. Geraldine then turned to David and bent down to talk to him.

"The girls are upstairs in their room, David. You can go and play with them if you like?"

Both of the ladies wanted some privacy so that they could have some girls talk, so they were hoping that he would comply. David was quite aware of the nature of the situation and he realised he was not welcome. Not wanting to be a nuisance, he reluctantly turned around and started to make his way towards the stairs with his head sadly bowed. As he wandered off he muttered some words of support to his mother.

"Enjoy yourself, Mum!"

Marilyn just ignored him and followed her sister into the kitchen.

There was a quiet knock on the door even though it was already wide open. Wendy and Clare both turned to see David standing in the doorway with a shy look upon his face. They immediately turned back to what they were doing and blatantly ignored him.

David waited for a few moments and then realised that he was not going to be invited in. He could not stay out on the landing all evening so he shuffled into the girl's bedroom and sat on a chair next to the dressing table.

Wendy huffed.

10

The girl's bedroom was decorated in various soft shades of pink and was very neat and tidy. They had a big selection of dolls spread out across several shelves upon the walls that they were both very proud of. Although they now had company they just continued playing a board game in the middle of the room totally ignoring their unwelcome guest.

David just looked at the clock on the wall and sighed. The time was half-past five. He wondered how long this whole thing might last. There was nothing else he could do but just sit there and wait until bedtime. So, that was just what he did, with his shoulders slumped and a dejected expression upon his face.

"Girls! Bedtime!" Geraldine called out from downstairs.

The sisters were sitting on the floor reading some girls magazines. They both instantly got up and went to the bathroom to prepare to go to bed.

David just looked at the clock on the wall and shook his head in a morose manner. It now said eight o'clock. The time he had spent being bored and ignored had somehow seemed to last a lot longer than two-and-a-half hours.

Throughout the evening David had made several attempts at trying to make conversation with the two sisters even to the point of showing an interest in their dolls, but he had been answered with a stony silence on each occasion. It just did not seem logical to him that they could dislike him as much as they did. He could not see why they found his difference of appearance that offensive.

Geraldine called out some more instructions from the foot of the stairs.

"David you can sleep in the spare bedroom at the end of the landing."

This was followed by the sound of some sly giggles coming from the bathroom. David just sombrely stood up and shuffled off to bed.

As soon as the knock sounded on the front door a broad smile instantly crossed Marilyn's face. A week into her relationship and she had finally brought up the courage to invite her new partner round to her home for dinner. She looked across the living room at David who was reading a newspaper.

"Graham's here." She enthusiastically announced.

David smiled in return and did his utmost to respond to her excitement.

"Good!" He was pleased to see his mother so happy. "I bet he's as nice as you say he is."

Marilyn skipped like an excited schoolgirl into the hall and quickly checked her hair in the mirror before answering the door. She was wearing a new blue dress and matching shoes that she had bought herself to impress the new man in her life. As soon as she had managed to calm herself down she opened the door.

"Hello, Graham!"

"Hello, Marilyn! How are you?"

"Fine, thank-you!"

David smiled to himself and got up out of his armchair. He walked over to stand by the window and was immediately bathed in the warm rays of the sun. He could hear his mother and Graham exchanging more pleasantries and waited patiently to be introduced to her new gentleman friend.

"Come in, Graham! This is..." There was a slight pause in the middle of her introduction as she walked into the room. "My son, David."

Graham walked into the living room and looked around. He was a tall man of about the same age as Marilyn and seemed quite neat and presentable. As he looked at David, who was now standing amidst the haze of the sunlight, he cheerfully smiled.

"Hello, young man!" He put out his hand to offer his greeting. "Nice to meet you!"

David walked out from under the light that was flooding in through the window and responded to the introduction by also putting out his hand. Marilyn closed her eyes and braced herself. This was something she was not looking forward to. She had not told her new date that her son was deformed.

As David emerged from the glow of the sun Graham squinted to see through the haze. When he had first walked into the room all he could see was the outline of the young boy's head and not his deathly pale skin, but now his vision was clear his jaw dropped and his face twisted into a look of shock.

David saw the dramatic change in Graham's expression straight away and he instantly knew the reason why. A feeling of shame and guilt washed over him even though he had done nothing wrong. He had extended his arm out to shake hands, but now gradually lowered it.

Graham seemed almost relieved to see the boy's arm drop. He did not seem to be too pleased about having to touch someone so ill looking. Taking one step back, he put both of his hands deep into his pockets.

Marilyn opened her eyes. She had not needed to see what had just happened to know what had occurred and her face had now turned a bright red. David realised that the best thing that he could do right now was to go upstairs to his bedroom and leave the two of them together. He could not have helped what had happened, but he did feel as though it was somehow his fault.

"I'm sorry Marilyn, but I can't see you anymore." Graham's voice sounded nervous on the other end of the phone. "I just don't think it will work."

"Oh, why? Please, I really do like you." Marilyn was desperate for another chance. "Let's just have one more night together!"

Graham raised his voice in desperation.

"No! I can't do it!" He then lowered it again and began to speak more calmly. "I think you know why."

There was a long pause from both ends of the line, and then the silence was broken.

"Yes! I know why." This was all Marilyn could say.

"Sorry!" Graham sounded sincere, but it was no consolation. "Good-bye!"

The line went dead.

Marilyn was standing in the hallway leaning against the front door. She clumsily put down the phone receiver and slowly moved over to the stairs. As she slouched down on the bottom step David walked in from the lounge and stood over her. He had obviously been listening into the conversation and spoke to his mother in a genuinely concerned tone of voice.

"Are you all right Mum?"

Marilyn just looked up at him with reddened eyes and what appeared to be a sneer.

"Just..." She paused and then bowed her head. "Go away!"

David stood static for a brief moment with the sides of his mouth turned down. All he wanted was for his mother to be happy and he knew that it was his fault that she was not. He almost felt as if he might cry, but he was beaten to it.

Marilyn had now started to sob and a couple of tears fell from her cheeks splashing against her new blue shoes. David decided that he ought to now just leave his mother alone so he instantly turned to make his way into the living room. As he walked off he slowly shook his head in a humbled manner.

Marilyn watched through her tear filled eyes as her son skulked off. The look on her face was one of sorrow, but it also had a tinge of anger. With the thoughts of who was clearly to blame for her being dumped she mouthed out a cruel word which she knew would hurt David deeply.

"Bastard!"

David stopped where he was, paused for a moment and then carried on walking. The remark had cut like a knife, but that was what it was meant to do. There were two people crying now.

Although Marilyn had not seen the expression on David's face she knew that her insult had hit the mark. Her mouth twisted into a sneering smile of satisfaction and she raised her eyebrows in an uncaring manner. That had felt callously good.

"It's the big building next to the doctors." Marilyn turned around from the sink where she was washing the dishes. "Why do you want to go there?"

"It's obvious, isn't it?" David looked at his mother with an excited expression upon his face. "You know I like to read."

"I can't imagine you liking some of the books there."

"Mum, I don't read 'Rupert the Bear' anymore."

Marilyn pulled the towel off of the working top and started to dry her hands. She then looked at her son with a slight frown as she spoke.

"You know, most *normal* children of your age go out to the park and play games. Why don't you go and do that instead of reading boring books in a stuffy old library." She shook her head and gazed out of the window in front of her. "You are six years old, not forty-six."

"I don't like *playing*. Whenever I go to the park all I see is boys kicking footballs, girls skipping or they just ride bikes round in circles." David shrugged his shoulders and raised his eyebrows in an unimpressed manner. "I can't think of anything more boring than that."

"Well, it's up to you I suppose. It's your life." As Marilyn walked past her son she looked at him with a disapproving expression upon her face. "I just think you should try enjoying yourself for once."

David took in a deep breath and then let it out with an exasperated sigh. His mother never seemed to encourage him with anything that he did. It did not really bother him that much, but whenever she put him down it did make him feel rather low.

It had come to the point that when David was doing anything that he enjoyed he never told his mother about it. This would at least mean that he would not be sneered at. He might not have received the positive encouragement that most children of his age might have gained from their parents, but at least he would not get a negative reaction towards his interests.

Unfortunately, on this occasion David had to ask his mother where the town library was because he did not know himself. He knew that she would tell him that there was no point in him going, but he had prepared himself for that. He decided to just listen to what he needed to hear and then disregard the criticising comments.

David picked up his pens and note pad from the kitchen table and put them into a carrier bag. As he went to leave he paused as he reached the front door and called out a farewell to his mother.

"Bye Mum! I'm going to the library now."

Marilyn was sitting in the living room reading a magazine and had to raise her voice so that she could be heard.

"Yeah! I'll see you later." She whispered the next remark. "Don't go and do anything silly, like have a good time!"

David had obviously not heard the last remark and just strolled out of the house content in the knowledge that he was going to do what he wanted to do.

On the front of the library was a metal plate with the inscribed words 'Starrow Public Library - Opened in 1975 by the Town Mayor, Harold Jacobs'. David stood in front of the doors in complete awe at the size of the building. He was expecting a much smaller place with just a mediocre amount of books, but he was more than pleasantly surprised by his findings. This was certainly going to provide the abundance of knowledge that he craved for and more besides.

David rarely came to this part of the town and when he had done he had only passed through on the bus whilst on the way to his Aunt Geraldine's. Although the library was one of the larger buildings in the high street he still had not noticed it due to its almost nondescript front. His only disappointment was that he had never been there before.

As David walked in through the double doors of the entrance and came to stand inside the building he froze to the spot and his jaw dropped in astonishment. It was almost as if the library seemed to be bigger on the inside than it was on the outside. He had almost forgotten that there were another two floors on top of this one. As he looked across all of the isles of books he whispered to himself in a wondrous manner.

"There are millions." He slowly shook his head in disbelief. "Absolutely millions."

To David's right there was an isle with a sign above it which read 'Modern History'. Without wasting another second he sharply made his way towards the shelves looking all around at the other books as he paced along. He knew that he would not be able to read everything here, but he would have a good attempt at trying.

The first book that David pulled off of the shelf was entitled 'The History of Aviation'. It seemed like a good book to start with so he took it over to a table at the end of the isle and sat down to read it. This was certainly going to be time well spent.

It had been quite busy in the town library and a large number of people had come in and out during the course of the day. David had been reading for about three-and-a-half hours and had got through eight books already. As he slid the last one he had read back onto the shelf that he had got it from he pulled out the one next to it. The title of it was 'Photography of Conflicts'. There was no picture on the cover, which seemed rather strange to him, but he thought it might just be worth a read anyway, so he sat back down again and turned to the first page.

One word summed up David's state of mind: Shock.

The first picture David saw made his blood freeze. It took up a two-page spread of a Middle Eastern man being shot in the head by a man with a pistol. Next to the picture was a small amount of print which read 'A Vietnamese police chief shoots a Vietcong officer through the side of the head in the streets of Saigon'. Even the title of the chapter was a sombre testament to what he was seeing.

'Moments of Death'.

David could not believe his eyes. His stuttered remark showed his surprise.

"Oh my goodness!"

The rest of the book did not improve. Although David was appalled by what he was seeing he felt a compulsive urge to just keep turning over each page almost as if to see if the next sadistic image was going to be as horrific as the last. He could not understand how people could bring themselves to do such evil things. Each picture was so graphically appalling that it almost made him feel nauseated.

Halfway through the book David came across a photo of some starving refugee children hours away from needless deaths. He now knew that it was not just adults who suffered, but children also. As he turned over to the next page he came across a picture of a street in Israel which was littered with the bodies of murdered civilians. It now became apparent that he was not just reading about history, but such sickening things were also happening right now.

David winced repeatedly as he in turn studied each photo and read the written description next to it. There was a part of him that did not want to believe that human beings were capable of such acts of immorality, but what he held in his hands was a grim testimony of proof of their tyranny. It almost seemed as if the book was cataloguing the sickest of humanity's crimes. Atrocity after atrocity, brutality after brutality, and yet there was not one

15

picture of a person other than a victim who wore a regretful expression. The people who were committing these heinous acts either had looks of utter hate or, most sickening of all, they seemed to be enjoying themselves.

It was only when David saw the images of the murdered Jews from the Second World War senselessly killed for their religion that he decided to finally close the book. He was only half of the way through it, but he found that he could not read anymore. Every picture he had just laid his eyes upon had filled his mind with abhorrent scenes of death and violence. He wanted to get them out of his head, but he simply could not stop thinking about them.

David now decided that the sooner that he got rid of the book the better. He stood up and walked over to the shelf where he had got it. As he slid it back he quietly spoke to himself in an appalled manner.

"What kind of world have I been born into?" He slowly shook his head. "It's evil, sick..."

David could not even finish his sentence due to his revulsion. He picked his bag up off of the table that he had been sitting at and started to sharply make his way out of the library. As he reached the exit he turned around to face the inside of the large building and quietly spoke to himself in a sickened manner.

"There's something wrong with the people of this world..." He slowly shook his head. "And someone needs to do something about it."

David had seen a lot of confusing scenes already in his short lifetime. He could not understand why people who did not know each other would clearly have some reason to hate one another. On one occasion he had walked past a pub on a Saturday afternoon and had seen two men beating the hell out of each other over a seat in the beer garden. Some people's actions just seemed so ludicrous.

Up until now, David had found that life was very hard to understand. He could not comprehend such concepts as hate, anger, spite or any other emotion that brought about harm to another person. There were times when he had wondered if he would ever be capable of such irrational thoughts and, if so, would he be able to control them.

At eleven years old, David had grown up to be a tall and relatively thin boy. The swelling on the sides and back of his head had slowed down in its growth rate, but due to his meagre frame it was nevertheless quite noticeable. His skin was still a slightly pale colour and his eyes had kept their ice like irises. So, even at his young age he had learnt that all this was enough for the majority of people who he had already met to look beyond his personality and with their shallow minds prejudge him.

Fortunately, David did not care about his appearance or what other people thought of it. He knew that what he had gained because of his deformities was a very special gift and he was more than grateful for his intellectual talents. It was these thoughts which were passing through his mind as he made his way home from his day at primary school.

David had spent the afternoon painting pictures of farm animals and had to learn some brief lines for the school play. These were parts of his curriculum that he had little time for. He could not see the point in wiping paint on a piece paper or pretending to be a pirate, especially when he could see the value in such subjects as mathematics, English literature and the sciences. It was clear to him that he was wasted and wasting time.

Thankfully, David's days at primary school were coming to an end and as far as he was concerned they had not come too soon. When he had first started he had enjoyed learning the basics of the various different subjects, but he had soon learnt all that the teachers had to offer and had quickly grown bored. Although it had been the beginning of his educational life he had still considered it to be a mostly fruitless time for him. He longed for the more advanced curriculum that a comprehensive school would offer.

As David reached his home he stood for a moment and frowned at what he saw. Paint was peeling from the window frames, there were several tiles missing from the roof and the front door was both green and red due to there not being enough paint to finish the job. As he opened the gate at the end of the garden path it scraped across the concrete making an unpleasant high-pitched noise. He winced at the sound and then sighed.

The compensation money that Marilyn had received from the Japanese company who owned the Tarbon chemical plant had run out a good few years ago and she was now only just getting by on state benefits. It had not taken too long for the corrosiveness of time to take its toll upon the house and there was no more money left to make the needed repairs. He knew his mother was finding it hard to cope so he thought it would be for the best if he did not mention the way the house looked to her.

Marilyn had been a single parent for eleven years now and that alone was a hard enough job in itself. She had brought David up as best as she could what with the circumstances. He was clothed, fed and sent to school every day. There may not have been the warm glow of love around the home that most children were been bathed in, but at least he received the bare necessities that he needed to survive.

Just as David went to put his key in the front door it sharply swung open momentarily startling him. After he gained his composure he looked up to see his mother standing in the doorway with a broad grin across her face.

"Hello, David!" Marilyn put her hand on her son's shoulder and led him into the house. "Did you have a good day at school?"

"I suppose it was alright." David spoke in a hesitant manner and was quite confused by his mother's delight at seeing him. "I mean, it was alright in the broadest sense of the word."

Marilyn clearly seemed to be excited about something as she spoke.

"What did you do today?" She quickly started to unbutton his coat. "Tell your Mother what you've been up to!"

After Marilyn had undone all of the buttons on David's coat, he turned around to hang it up on a hook in the hall. By the time he had turned back to face her she was already sitting down in an armchair in the living room looking at him expectantly. This was not like her at all.

As Marilyn spoke she shook her head with excitement.

"Well? What did you do today?"

David was not sure if he liked this. His mother was never this talkative towards him and it made him feel quite nervous. As he reluctantly went to sit down in an armchair opposite her he thought that it would be best to answer her questions simply for the sake of politeness.

"I painted some pictures of pigs and cows and I learnt some lines for the school play." He spoke in an uncomfortable manner and with an uneasy frown upon his face. "That was it really."

"That's nice." Marilyn leant forward to show that she was giving him her full attention. "What play is it?"

"It's not really nice. You know I hate painting and as for acting..." David did not need to finish his sentence.

Marilyn sighed. She realised that her show of attention was not getting her anywhere so she decided that it was time to say exactly what was on her mind.

"David, I've got a job." She smiled broadly.

"Really?" David's surprise was quite evident as he stammered out his words. "Where?"

17

"At the expensive clothes shop in Ferris Street." A proud look crossed Marilyn's face as she completed the description of her job with an air of pompousness. "As a manageress, I'll have you know."

"How did you get it?" David was confused, but it felt surprisingly satisfying. "I didn't even know you were looking for a job."

"I wasn't. Your Aunt Geraldine spoke to a friend of hers who works at the shop and he offered me the job." Marilyn sat back and wistfully looked around the living room. "It'll be nice to get some extra money around here. This place needs some work done to it."

That was an understatement. The living room was just as tatty as the rest of the house. Wallpaper was peeling from the walls, paint was flaking away from the ceiling and the armchairs were riddled with rips and stains.

David smiled at his beaming mother. Now that he had gotten over the surprise he found that he was really quite pleased for her. In an attempt to show some enthusiasm he decided to ask her some more questions about her new job.

"When do you start?"

"Next week." Marilyn looked down at her blouse. "I'll need some new clothes though."

The conversation went on for quite some time. It was rare for the two of them to talk and David wanted to make the most of it. He knew that his mother did not feel the same for him as the other children's parents at his primary school did for them, but *he* loved her anyway.

David had learnt a long time ago to make the most of what he had. He had no friends, he had no brothers or sisters and he had no father. The only person who he could talk to and love was his mother. So, whenever he had the chance to make the most of one of these opportunities he grasped hold of it with the tightest of grips.

Although the conversation between the two of them meant a lot to David it would not last for long. Marilyn's excitement would soon wane and she would become quite bored with her son's constant inquisitive questions. The only reason why she was talking to him was because she also had no one else to talk to about it. She had lost touch with all her old friends and her sister obviously already knew. They really were two lonely souls momentarily grasping at a rare chance at the pleasure of someone to converse with.

The real reason why Marilyn was so excited about the job at the clothes shop was not because she saw it as an opportunity to earn some money or to establish a working future for herself. It was simply because she saw it as a chance to socialise. She needed a man desperately.

There were nights when Marilyn would lay in bed and cry herself to sleep thinking about her loneliness. On a number of occasions she would look at herself in the mirror and wonder if she was ugly or if there was something wrong with the way she acted, but in the end she would always come to the same conclusion. The problem was not a fault with her. It was because of him.

Marilyn blamed David for nearly all of her woes. Since the first time that she had brought a man back to the house she had been terrified of introducing anyone to her son. The look of horror upon the man's face had ripped her heart in two. It was a scenario that she simply did not want to ever repeat again.

Marilyn thought that if she were to ever have a long lasting relationship with a man he would have to know what David looked like from the start. There was no doubt that she would meet men in the clothes shop. She would just have to somehow inform them of her son's disposition beforehand.

These thoughts were, of course, brought about by Marilyn's paranoia of David. His head was larger than normal, but was not as out of proportion as it used to be. He only looked disgusting to his mother and anyone else who could not bear to look upon anyone who was different to them. If she had have adopted any of her son's logic she would have realised that such people were not worth being with anyway.

This was something else that David found to be very confusing. For someone to hate someone because they were not the same as everyone else seemed so illogical to him. He just considered it to be yet another one of society's many faults.

"Are you ready David?" Marilyn called out from the bottom of the stairs. "We haven't got much time."

"I'm now coming." An animated reply.

David ran down the stairs with an excited look upon his face. When he got to the bottom he turned to his mother who was checking her summer hat in the mirror and spoke to her in a cheerful tone of voice.

"What else do they have at funfairs Mum?"

"Oh, loads of things." Marilyn turned around and frowned at her son. "You've asked me this enough times already. I've told you as much as I can."

"Yes I know, but I've never been to a funfair before." David morosely put his hands in his trouser pockets and scuffed the carpet with his feet. "I'm sorry! I didn't mean to be repetitious."

Marilyn opened the front door and waved across the street at Geraldine and her daughters who were waiting in their car on the other side of the road. It was a hot sunny day and there was an aura of excitement throughout the town of Starrow as people made their way to the park. The unmistakable furore of the funfair had captivated everybody.

Geraldine was already going with her daughters and had invited David and Marilyn to join with them in the festivities. Both mother and son had warmly accepted the invitation, even though their motives were quite different.

David had never been to a funfair before and was more than just excited. He had heard of the fun and games that were to be had, as well as some of the prizes to be won on some of the attractions. For five days he had talked about nothing but the carnival and how much he was looking forward to it. His mother had soon grown tired of the constant questions and had on numerous occasions told him to stop going on about it.

What Marilyn did not want David to know was that she was just as excited as him and had been trying her best not to let it show. It was not, however, the games and attractions that appealed to her. She had never liked that sort of thing even when she was young herself. There was another reason for why she was going.

Marilyn had been working at the clothes shop for two weeks now and had already had some close encounters with some of the male customers. It was on the Thursday that had just gone that she had finally met one man who had met her requirements. Only he was not a customer.

On the second week of her being there an electrician had been called in to fix a light socket. He was a big burly man by the name of Norman, and Marilyn had soon struck up a conversation with him. They had talked for quite some time and he seemed to be quite a pleasant person. What with him being single and about the same age as her, she had soon taken a liking to him.

After them talking for a good hour the topic of the funfair had been brought up. It was big news around Starrow due to there being only one every two or three years. Norman had told Marilyn that he would be going with a workmate and that he would like to meet her there. Unfortunately, she did not want to go by herself and she especially did not want to go with just David. She, therefore, told him that she might or might not go depending on whether she was going to be busy.

The day after the conversation with Norman, Marilyn had a phone call from Geraldine with an invitation for her and David to go to the funfair. This was the opportunity that she had needed and she accepted it without hesitation. She immediately told her sister about her reason for wanting to go and the two of them had decided to make it more of a mission than a fun day out.

Marilyn had not told David about why she wanted to go to the funfair. She did not want him messing things up. Although he was a very perceptive person and would normally be able to tell if his mother was hiding something from him, on this occasion he was blinded by his own excitement. So, both of them had eagerly looked forward to this day even though was for their own very different reasons.

The two of them hurried down the garden path and got into the waiting car. Marilyn sat in the front passenger seat next to Geraldine and David sat in the back with Wendy and Clare. He was greeted with the usual sneers and stuck up noses, but he was too cheerful to be bothered about such things on a day like this.

David stood gawping at what stood before him. There were bright colourful flashing lights, fairground rides whizzing around at all kinds of speeds and people everywhere seeming to be having the time of their lives. He was ecstatic with excitement and could not wait to join in.

Just as David took a step forward a worrying thought suddenly crossed his mind and he instantly turned to his mother with an anxious look upon his face.

"Mum..." He was interrupted.

"Yes, I know!" Marilyn reached into her purse and frowned. "Here, have five pounds. But it's all you're getting!"

"Thanks Mum." David was delighted.

The five of them jostled their way through the crowds of people. Whilst the children looked at each ride with expressions of fascination the two grown-ups, unbeknown to the rest of them, were searching for Marilyn's date. After walking around for quite some time they finally found Norman and his friend in the middle of the fairground standing by a stall.

Marilyn immediately became nervous and grabbed hold of her sister's arm.

"What shall I say?" She asked with in worried voice.

"Well, whatever comes into your head." Geraldine replied, shrugging her shoulders.

"Like what?"

"I don't know. What did you say when you first met him?"

Whilst all this was going on David had been listening into their conversation. He had noticed that his mother was pointing at two men who were standing by a stall and she appeared to have some kind of interest in the bigger of the two. With his usual inquisitiveness he kept on concentrating on every word that they were saying

Marilyn started to tell Geraldine the full story.

"I met him in the canteen at work. He was really nice and interesting." She smiled and nudged her sister. "I must admit though, I hoped he would have asked me out to a bit better place than a funfair."

"Maybe he likes a bit of fun." Geraldine cheekily replied. "There's nothing wrong with that."

The two of them giggled for a short while and then Marilyn went back to her nervous demeanour.

"What shall I say though? Oh God! I haven't done this in such a long time." She woefully put the palm of her hand to her forehead. "I don't think I'll be able to go and talk to him."

Geraldine put her arm around her sister's shoulder.

"Let's just hope he comes to you."

David looked over to the two men and gazed at them in a thoughtful manner.

Norman had a large build and was quite tidy in his appearance. His hair was neatly brushed back and he always kept a comb in his back trouser pocket. Although he was quite broad across the shoulders and had a stalwart chest, his stomach protruded out in front of him almost as if it were a constant reminder of the nights of heavy drinking which he had made his body endure over the years.

The expression upon Norman's face seemed to be somewhat permanently frowning. His lips appeared as though they were constantly sneering and his eyes tended to give a person the impression that he was scowling at them. He had a demeanour that suggested that he had gone through some bad times in his life and was keen to let other people know about it.

Norman had been a self-employed electrician for just over ten years and had made a steady living out of it. He was never going to be rich, not just because the pay was not high enough, but because he had never been one for saving. The public houses of the town of Starrow regularly laid claim to a large slice of his wages.

Terry, Norman's friend, had a much smaller build and was not nearly as well dressed. He was wearing paint-splattered dungarees and a tatty blue baseball cap on the back of his head that almost seemed to be glued into position. His most prominent feature though was the condition his face was in. The last twenty years he had spent smoking had taken their toll on him and had caused his cheeks and temples to be extremely sunken in.

Norman had a good reason to dress neatly today, even if Terry did not. He was wearing his favourite black leather jacket, a slightly expensive shirt and new jeans. His inclination for this extra effort was because he was hoping to meet a good-looking woman who he had met at a clothes shop in town during the week. The only reason why he had invited someone else along was in case she did not turn up and, although he would not admit it, he was a bit shy.

Norman and Terry had been standing at an air rifle stall where the object of the game was to shoot the targets to win a prize. After realising that the sights on the guns were spuriously out of aim they had given in and had made their observations more than clear to the worker behind the counter with a number of profane remarks. As they turned around to look for the beer tent they were approached by an odd looking boy who spoke to them both in a worried tone of voice.

"Excuse me. I can't find my mum." The boy looked quite upset. "Could you help me find them please?"

Norman breathed out an unenthusiastic sigh.

"Well she must be around here somewhere." The large man made no attempt to hide his indifference to the situation he had just found himself in. "Where did you see them last?"

"I don't know." The boy looked around as he spoke. "This place is so big I can't tell where I was."

Terry turned to Norman and raised his eyebrows in a conceding manner.

"I suppose we better help him find his mum."

"Yeah, alright." Norman shook his head and then swore under his breath. "Fuck it!"

The odd looking boy smiled and took hold of Norman's hand. As the three of them made their way through the crowds of people neither of the two grownups had any inclination whatsoever that they had been duped by the youngster who was walking with them. David just led them both towards his mother with the knowledge that he had just pulled off his carefully worked out plan to perfection.

21

As Geraldine checked Marilyn's hair she started to give her sister some tips on what to say to Norman.

"Just talk to him about anything. Ask him how he is, tell him he looks nice and..." She paused for thought. "Tell him you like a man with muscles!"

Marilyn grinned at her sister and excitedly raised her eyebrows.

"That comes later." Her eyes opened wide. "But not much later."

Geraldine smiled in return and took a step back to look at Marilyn. She then looked over her sister's shoulder to eye up the target. It was at that point when her face turned to stone.

"Oh no!" She muttered.

"What?"

Marilyn did not like the look on Geraldine's face. She thought at first that maybe Norman was talking to another woman or even that he already had a girlfriend or wife who had just turned up. As she turned around to see what was the matter she realised that the worst possible scenario had taken place. It was not the fact that Norman was now walking towards her, but that her son, David was with him.

"That little bastard!" Marilyn's face twisted into a vicious look of hate. "I'll kill him!"

"Don't be too mad at him, Marilyn!" Geraldine tried to calm her sister down. "He doesn't know any better."

Marilyn started to make her way through the crowd to get to her son. Geraldine grabbed hold of her daughters and followed close behind. The sisters had sensed that something had gone wrong and had a pretty good idea that their archenemy was to blame. Their faces lit up with excitement and eagerness at what was about to unfold.

David could now see that his mother was approaching and immediately smiled in her direction. He had already introduced himself to Norman and his friend Terry, so now he thought it was best for them to meet his mother as well. As she got nearer he turned to the two men.

"Norman, Terry this is my mother." He put his palm out in her direction. "Marilyn."

As Norman looked up to where David was motioning an ambivalent expression of surprise and pleasure crossed his face.

"Marilyn!" He moved closer. "You're David's mother?"

Without making any attempt at a greeting, Marilyn just sheepishly apologised for whatever she thought could have happened.

"I'm sorry, Norman. My son hasn't been any trouble to you has he?"

"No!" Norman patted David on the shoulder. "He was lost and asked me to help him find his mum."

Marilyn was still not sure if this was a good or bad thing.

"Really? And he hasn't been a nuisance?"

"Not at all." Norman suddenly saw an opportunity to sell himself. "Soon as I realised that he was lost I made an effort to help him. Some people don't do things like that, but I don't mind myself."

"Well, that is good of you." Marilyn was more than impressed.

By this time Geraldine and the girls had joined the group and were all keeping a close eye on the proceedings. The sisters were now disappointed to see that their enemy was not in trouble as they had hoped he would be. Instead, it regrettably appeared as though he had somehow managed to do something that was right.

Marilyn smiled at Norman and then looked down at David with a frown as she spoke.

"How could you have got lost?" A fake attempt at affection. "Silly you!"

David's reply was a skilful change of the subject.

"It's sounds as if you two have already met Mum?" This was said with a well-acted out expression of inquisitiveness. "Where was that?"

"We met during the week."

Marilyn half smiled and then looked round at Norman, who did likewise in return. She now realised this was her chance to make an impression. In a soft tone of voice, she forwarded a pleasantry.

"I'm glad you could make it."

"I'm glad *you* could." Norman moved closer.

The two of them then started a conversation which the both of them were quite happy to leave everyone else out of. Terry soon realised that his friend was making some progress so he wondered off to find the beer tent. Wendy and Clare certainly had no interest in what was going on and joined the back of a queue which was leading up to a stall which sold big bags of honeycomb.

David just turned to Geraldine who was watching her sister with wide eyes.

"They like each other, don't they?" He pointed to his mother and Norman. "I thought they did."

"Yes, you're right." Geraldine was confused that David should ask such a question. "How do you know?"

At that, David just smirked knowingly at his Aunt and then walked off to enjoy the rest of the funfair. He had the money that Marilyn had given him and now it was time to spend it. This was going to be an even better outing than he had expected.

Geraldine now understood. She realised that it had been no accident that David had got lost. He had deliberately planned it to help out his mother. She whispered to herself in an awed manner as she watched the gifted young boy confidently stroll off.

"Clever boy!"

David walked down to the foot of the stairs and then looked at himself in a mirror. A proud expression crossed his face as his gaze went from his head to his feet. Today was his first day at secondary school and he could not hide his elation.

Marilyn had bought David his new school uniform and he was now eagerly checking it for any unwanted wrinkles or blemishes. He had black shiny shoes, black trousers, a white shirt and a dark purple tie in the school colours. He was well dressed and well prepared.

Slung over David's shoulder was his new school bag that he had saved up for himself. This was his favourite new necessity, not because he had bought it with his own pocket money, but because it held all of his pens, pencils and rulers. These were truly the tools of a scholar.

David could not wait to start studying. At primary school he had been taught only a limited amount of maths and English, but now he was going to have lessons in chemistry, physics, sociology and much more besides. All he wanted to do was feed his mind. He sometimes thought of his brain as a big hole that simply had to be filled with knowledge.

As David adjusted his tie for the umpteenth time his mother called out from the kitchen.

"Hurry up! Breakfast is ready!" Her voice sounded hurried and impatient. "I don't want it getting cold."

"Coming!" Came the reply.

As David walked into the kitchen he noticed Norman sitting at the breakfast table with a scowling look upon his face. Realising that something was not right he decided to pretend as if he had not noticed anything out of the ordinary and sat down on the opposite side of the table from the large man. He did not even extend his normal morning greeting just so as not to get into a conversation.

Norman had now been living with Marilyn for about a month and had firmly settled himself in. They shared the work around the house and the bills. Money was still quite tight, but they were comfortable enough. Everybody seemed to be getting along well and, most importantly, he seemed to be able to bare the burden of living with her deformed son.

Norman did not talk to David much. He even sometimes seemed to try to avoid him. There had been times when they had brought up discussions about current affairs or politics, but the big man had soon grown bored.

Marilyn broke the stony silence in a false cheerful manner as she put two plates of bacon and eggs on the table.

"Eat up then!"

"Thanks, Mum!" David replied.

Norman just looked at her and sneered.

Marilyn frowned and spoke in a pleading tone of voice.

"Cheer up!" She sat down next to Norman and put her hand on the back of his. "He's got to have the school uniform."

Norman sat back in his chair as he raised his voice in disgust.

"Yeah! But not so bloody much!" He pointed at David across the table. "He's got half of the clothes shop there."

Marilyn tried to reason with him.

"It's the school rules. Everyone has to dress the same."

This did little to sway Norman. As he started to shovel food into his mouth he kept on talking without any attempt at trying to keep any of it from falling back out.

"Second hand!" He wiped his mouth with the back of his knuckles. "He could've had second hand!"

Norman had been outraged by the amount spent on David's new school uniform. He had wanted to use the money to go out to the pub for the night, but Marilyn had insisted on spending it on clothes. They had engaged in many heated discussions about the subject, but he had never let his temper go like this before.

As Marilyn looked at the Norman's fists tighten her face instantly went pale.

"Calm down!" She spoke nervously and with a hint of fear. "Please, calm down!"

David could not help but feel guilty about the fact that all this was because of him. Although he also knew that it was compulsory to wear school uniform he still felt as though there had been a certain amount of extravagance. He watched it all with a worried look upon his face as he ate his breakfast.

Norman was now pointing his knife at Marilyn and was speaking in a threatening manner.

"If I wasn't calm..." He nodded his head and his lips tightened. "You'd know about it."

David looked at his mother who now had a tear running down her cheek. He could see that she was starting to become quite frightened, just as he was. In an attempt to make some damage control he thought he ought to apologise.

"I'm sorry! I'm really sorry!" He looked at them both in turn with wide penitent eyes. "I didn't mean to cause any of this."

As Norman spoke his words were muffled due to his mouth being full of fried bread.

"So you bloody should be! You cost us a fortune!"

Marilyn fearfully agreed with a forced sneer etched into her face.

"Yes! You had to have everything you wanted, as usual!"

This was not actually true. David had gone to the shop with his mother and she had chosen all of the clothes herself due to her seeing this as a chance to make her son look like a normal child for once. Nevertheless, he decided it would not be such a good idea to mention whose decision it was to spend so much under the present circumstances. Marilyn was obviously scared and had found that blaming her son was an easy way of getting out of being under the pressure of Norman's temper. Her son knew this, of course, but was willing ignore the truth on this particular occasion.

That morning when David left for his first day at secondary school no one said good-bye or good luck to him. He just quietly closed the front door behind him and made his way out into the street to wait at the bus stop. When he had left the house he did not hear the remarks made about him behind his back.

"Bastard!"

"Greedy little arsehole!"

When David saw the queue of children at the bus stop his worrying about his mother and Norman was instantly replaced with his original feelings of excitement. He hurried across the road and waited on the edge of the curb. The other pupils all stood in their own groups and although he knew some of them from his last school he did not know any of their names. As he stood there alone none of the children talked to him just as they always had done.

When David was in his infant years some of the children used to tease him about his head, skin colour and eyes. The teachers had soon put a stop to it when they caught them, but it was no consolation. None of the pupils would ever befriend him.

As the years of David's life had gone by he had gotten used to being alone. He had no brothers or sisters, his mother was clearly estranged from him and he had never seemed to be able to make friends with anyone. This did not really bother him as most of the children of his age tended to bore him. They all talked about trains, spaceships and planes, whereas he talked about science, history and social affairs.

There was only one person in David's life that he could really rely on and that person was he himself. Friends were something that he would like to have had, but he would just have to live without them. He was not sure whether he liked the ways things were or not.

"Look at him!" The boy pointed to a lonely figure standing by the edge of the road. "He's a bloody freak."

"Yeah! He looks weird." His friend replied. "His head's like a bloody pumpkin."

"If he looks at me I'll smash his frigging face in." The first boy had a vicious look on his face. "I aint going have him coming nowhere near me."

Martin Dent looked like a bully, sounded like a bully and basically was a bully. Even to a grown-up he looked like a fearsome sight. He had a skinhead, two earrings in his left ear and a big scar on the right side of his forehead. It was obvious that he had already decided on his political views by the way that he wore a bomber jacket with a union jack on the back with badges adorned with far right slogans.

Martin Dent was proud of the reputation that he had earned from the people who knew him and he regularly built on it. He would bully someone for their race, the colour of their hair, the size of their nose and any other reason that he could think of at the time. Like all bullies he ruled with the use of fear. Unfortunately for the children who he chose to pick on he could back it up as well.

As for Martin's friend, he was a different person entirely. Steve Harding was a coward to the very end. When the odds were in his favour he would be the most spiteful bully going, but when there was the slightest competition he would flee as if it were for his

25

life. He went around with Martin for the protection and the image. Being opposed to a member of 'Dent's gang' would send shivers down any boy's spine.

Steve grinned through one side of his mouth as he spoke in his usual sly manner.

"What are you going to do to him, Martin?"

"I'm going to make him regret looking like an alien." Martin nodded to himself and then turned to face his friend. "What do you reckon?"

"Yeah! Let's do it!"

Steve stood to one side to let Martin pass. The thought of him going first into uncharted territory was not an idea he was very fond of. This boy who they were just about torment could have a good right or even a nose-splitting head butt.

The two of them made their way across the pavement and came to stand by the side of David. A few of the other children saw what was happening and immediately cleared space between them and the possible trouble. Martin prodded his victim on the shoulder with an out stretched finger.

"Oi! Weirdo!" He clenched his teeth. "What's wrong with your bloody head then?"

David turned around with a puzzled look on his face and tried to answer the question.

"Well I... It's because..." He could not hide his bewilderment. "Pardon?"

"You heard what I said." Martin's face twisted into an impatient glare. "I don't want to repeat myself."

David did not know what to say. He was not sure how he could answer such a question. In his usual way of doing things he started to take a moment to think about it, but when realised that his lack of haste was annoying the boy who was asking the question even more he quickly came out with an answer.

"I was born this way." It was true, but not very explanatory.

"I know that, you twat!" Martin raised his voice. "I didn't think you'd swallowed a football."

David was by now becoming scared and could not help but lower his head in a cowering manner. He was lost for words. Not even he knew exactly why he was born this way, so he simply did not know how to answer.

"I don't know why my head is like this." It was all he could say. "I really don't know."

Steve had started to sense fear and he made the most of it.

"So you don't know why you're weird?" He pushed David in the chest to show he meant business. "You make me feel sick when I look at you."

"Yeah! You make us feel ill. You freak!" Martin moved closer. "You better watch that you don't come near me or I'll kick your teeth down your throat!"

David was shocked. He did not know what he had done to deserve what he was getting. In the hope that they might just go away he decided just to keep his head lowered and not say a word.

Martin wanted to make sure that he had got his message over so he grabbed hold of his victim's cheek and started to squeeze.

"If I puke because of you..." He moved his face within inches of David's. "I'll smash that thick head of yours into a pulp!"

Steve laughed at the spectacle.

"He's just a wimp." He mused. "Just bloody wimp."

David winced as the pain burnt through the side of his face.

"Ow! Please, let go." He pleaded for clemency. "It hurts."

"I know. It's meant to." Martin gave one last big squeeze and then pushed David away. "And if you don't want any more you better keep away! Alright?"

"Yeah!" Steve agreed. "Keep well away!"

"Alright!" David rubbed the side of his reddened face and erratically nodded his head. "I will! I promise!"

The two bullies laughed as they turned away. David did not even want to look in their direction as they left in case he provoked them and they came back to bully him even more. All of the other children who had been watching what had just happened wisely said and did nothing. They all just turned back to their own groups and carried on ignoring him.

David just wiped a tear from his eye and he muttered to himself soliloquy.

"What is wrong with this world?"

When David got off of the bus most of his enthusiasm for the day had already gone. As he stood on the edge of the schoolyard he felt quite depressed and he breathed out a forlorn sigh. He was hoping that this was going to be a really enjoyable moment in his life, but up until now it had been far from that.

Whilst David was standing staring at his new school a tall boy of about two years older than him barged into his shoulder and immediately shouted at him afterwards.

"Get out of the way!"

David rubbed his shoulder and looked up at the boy with a sad look upon his face.

"Sorry!" He tried to be as apologetic as possible.

"Bloody right as well!" The tall boy scowled at David as he walked away. "You should watch what you're doing, you prat!"

The barge into the shoulder did not hurt, but the abusive remark did. David thought that he ought to start moving in case he got in someone else's way. As he walked across the schoolyard he looked around and noticed that all of the other pupils had friends. They all stood around in their close knit groups and somehow seemed to already know each other.

No one even looked at David. He even wondered if they knew he was there. As he came to stand in the middle of the schoolyard he dropped his bag on the ground and slowly shook his head. There was not a single other pupil within yards of him and there seemed to be a ring of empty space around him. Up until now he did not know what it meant to be really lonely, but this was an abrupt lesson.

The rest of the day had carried on just about the same as the way it had started. At lunchtime a couple of older pupils had decided to make some nasty remarks about David's head. He had ignored them and had walked off to another part of the schoolyard. Although he may have been out of harm's way, he still did not feel safe. Everyone seemed to rebuke him. The children all looked the other way when he came near them and even the teachers did not want to associate themselves with him. He was not really sure why all this was happening, but he wished that it would stop.

David was scared, lonely and very unhappy. All he could do was hope that the rest of his school days were not going to be anything like this. He did, however, have a feeling that that was not going to be the case and that he would have to get used to it.

The school bus pulled away leaving a small crowd of children hovering around the bus stop. David stood in the middle of them all looking very depressed and rejected. As the pupils slowly scattered off in the direction of their homes they left him standing alone on the pavement. None of them said 'goodbye' to him, but that was because none of them had even said 'hello' to him.

David was wondering to himself what he was going to tell his mother about his first day at school. All he had learnt so far was that there was a number of people in this world who found pleasure in making cruel remarks to him about his head and that there were some who would not even acknowledge his presence enough to even do that. He simply could not tell his mother that.

As for the lessons David had had on his first day they were all either boring, uninformative or too easy. He thought his first maths class was going to be a big leap forward for him, but it seemed to be just as simple as it had been at primary school. English, geography and history were not much of an improvement either. They were all just as unproductive.

David hoped that today was just going to be a one off and the years that were to follow were all going to be better for him. He had been looking forward to secondary school for so long, yet it now seemed as though it had all been for nothing. He had gained no extra knowledge and certainly no friends.

After waiting for a while at the bus stop to muse over his day, David finally got on his way and slowly paced across the street towards his home. When he reached the front door he paused and took a deep breath. He was hoping that his mother did not show too much concern about how he had got on. The last thing that he wanted her to do was ask him if he had made any new friends or even worse if he had been bullied.

David opened the front door and stepped nervously into the hallway. As he glanced into the living room he noticed his mother and Norman sitting side by side on the settee. He called out to them in a shy and subdued manner.

"Hello!"

Norman greeted him with just a grunt. Marilyn also seemed as though she was only just aware of his existence.

"Hi! Close the front door after you!"

David just walked into the living room and stood patiently by the side of the settee waiting to be asked about his day at school. After standing there for a short while, he realised that his mother and Norman were both engrossed at the television and seemed to have little time for anything else. It was at this point that he came to the conclusion that he need not have had any fears about being asked about his day.

For the first time in David's life he was glad that his mother was not bothered about him. She simply did not care about his first day at secondary school. At least he would not have to tell her about it now. In an ironic sort of way he was quite pleased.

A small table lamp perched on the edge of David's desk dimly lighted the room. Its narrow band of light illuminated the pages of the eleven year olds book just enough for him to be able to read it comfortably. As he turned the page he leant his head back and yawned.

David was reading the book for a school project which one of his English teachers had given him to due to his own request. He was studying the works of Shakespeare and was in the middle of 'Othello'. After about fifty pages he was almost starting to wish he had not asked for the extra work as he was finding the seventeenth century writer to be rather boring. His yawn, however, was mainly brought about by tiredness.

On the previous night Marilyn and Norman had thrown an all night party to celebrate their surprise engagement. The two of them had been dating now for only a matter of months, but they had decided that they should marry when their time together had reached a year. They both seemed to be very happy with the new turn in their relationship and were now looking forward to their wedding.

David had thought that the surprise engagement had come at just the right time as his mother and her new fiancé seemed to have been having a number of big arguments over the last couple of months. Money was beginning to become a bit of a problem in the household and they were both getting rather worried. Norman was finding it hard to get new contracts in his electrician business and was not bringing in the money which he used to. The announcement of their engagement and the celebration party they had thrown seemed to lift the gloom from the house and put everyone in a much better mood.

The party had gone all the way through to the late hours of the morning and the loud music had kept David awake way past his usual bedtime. Although he would have rather have been asleep he had found the whole thing to be quite intriguing. He considered the way that grownups acted when they were socialising to be quite odd.

Halfway through the night of the party David had heard two men talking outside his bedroom and he had opened his door just enough so he could see and hear them. They seemed to be drunk by the way they were slurring their speech and finding it hard to stand up straight without leaning against the wall. To be quite honest, he thought they both looked rather ill.

David could not understand why people would want to drink alcohol when it so obviously affected their physical and mental state in such a negative way. He had seen men lying unconscious in the middle of the street before now and there had also been other times when people seemed to want to get violent just because they were drunk. Some day he hoped that he might just see the sense in it all.

The two men outside David's room had been talking about politics and one of them seemed to have some very unusual views. He had his head closely shaven and wore a pair of ripped jeans that had braces hanging off of the sides. His friend wore a black leather jacket with metal studs fastened to various parts of it.

"Fucking Pakis! Piss them all off!" The skinhead slurred. "Send the lot of them back."

"Yeah! That's right Charlie." The young man in the leather jacket seemed to just reluctantly agree regardless of what the other one said. "I know what you're saying."

"Eunoch Powell was right when he said 'bollocks'!" The skinhead drunkenly raised his fist. "Rivers of blood!"

"Yeah!" His friend appeared to not quite understand and just forced an unimpressed smile. "Bloody rivers!"

David shook his head and frowned. He could not understand how someone could have such illogical views. As far as he knew everyone was the same. To him no race, religion, sexuality or colour of a person made them better than any other. Life was confusing.

After deciding he did not want to hear anymore of the skinhead's views, David started to go back into his room. Just as he went to close the door he noticed a man and a woman sitting at the top of the stairs. They were kissing frantically and the man's hands were straying into some rather private places.

David's pale skin blushed at the sight. He had always thought that procreation was a thing couples would want to have kept from the eyes of other people.

"Why haven't they got any respect for each other?" He whispered to himself. "They obviously don't love one another."

Life was very confusing.

It seemed as though Marilyn and Norman had not wanted to end their engagement celebrations in just the one night and had decided to go to the pub for further festivities. The time was now coming up to midnight and David had heard them shuffling their way through the front door. By the commotion that they were making it sounded as though they had been drinking heavily.

"Shit! Who left that rug there?" Norman bellowed out his slurred words and then let out a loud unceremonious burp. "That's fucking-well dangerous."

"It's always been there, Norm'." Marilyn replied apologetically. "Sorry about that!"

"Fucking thing's going in the morning, I can tell you!" Norman sounded the more drunk of the two. "Any beer in the fridge?"

"Yes, at the back." Came the reply.

Noises came from the kitchen where Norman was shuffling around in the fridge looking for the beer.

"How can I get at it when it's back there?" His patience appeared as though it was starting to wear thin. "There's all sorts of shit in the way."

The crashing sounds of objects falling from the fridge rang out throughout the house.

"Careful, Norm'! You're making a mess." Marilyn tried to reason with her drunken fiancé. "There's milk everywhere now."

"Shut up, woman! I've got to have some beer, haven't I?" The reply was obviously no compensation for the mess on the kitchen floor. "You can clear it up in the morning!"

At this point David started to edge his way down the stairs so he could get a better listen to what was happening. He did not like what he had heard so far and was starting to get a bit worried. Norman had lost his temper plenty of times before now, but it had been when they had received a large bill or when he had not been able to get work. However, he had never been destructive towards anything.

David thought it would be a good idea just to make his presence unaware to the two of them in the kitchen so he tried to make as little noise as possible. He just sat on the stairs nervously rubbing his head with a concerned look upon his face. Amongst all of the commotion he could just about hear Marilyn talking in a soft voice.

"Are you coming to bed?"

"Huh!" Norman did not sound impressed. "What, with you?"

Marilyn sounded unpleasantly surprised.

"What does that mean?"

"You know. I saw you."

"What did you see, Norm'?"

"You and..." There was a pause for thought. "That arsehole, Brian!"

Marilyn gasped. The shock of the comment had left her standing absolutely dumfounded and frozen still to the spot. She was not sure what to say in her defence, but she tried to make an effort anyway.

"What has Brian got to do with anything?" She asked in a surprised tone of voice. "There's nothing wrong with him."

"What, do you think I'm stupid?" Norman shouted his accusation. "I fucking saw you! Smiling at him with those 'screw me' eyes."

"I did not." Marilyn replied with a hurt manner. "I really didn't Norm'."

"Lying bitch!"

"We're just good friends. He's your friend as well."

"He's a wanker!"

At that point the sound of cutlery hitting the floor came from within the kitchen. The sudden high-pitched noise made David jump and he shuffled nervously on the stairs. Nevertheless, he kept on listening with the same worried expression upon his face.

Marilyn's voice sounded soothing, yet still very frightened.

"All right Norm'. Calm down!"

"You better not even fucking look at him again!" Norman bellowed an order. "Not fucking once!"

"But he means no harm." Marilyn pleaded. "Surely I can talk to him?"

"Don't you argue with me!"

Now there came a different noise. It was not as loud as the cutlery being thrown across the floor, but it fell harder on David's ears. The slap was followed closely by a scream of agony.

Silence rang throughout the house for one long eerie moment. It was almost as if time had stopped and everyone had frozen physically and mentally. No one stirred until a lone crying coming from within the kitchen broke the cold quietness.

"You deserved that." Norman growled. "Now get out of my sight!"

"Norman, I want to talk." Marilyn's words were stuttered by uncontrollable sobs. "I haven't done anything..."

Before she could finish her sentence another slap sounded out, then another and then another. David shuddered after every thud and every scream. He covered his ears to try to block out the heart piercing wails, but it was no good. The hideous yelps that his mother was making were just too loud and high pitched for him to keep them out of his head.

Norman carried on shouting as his clenched fists rained down upon his new fiancé.

"Whore! Slut! Tart!"

"No, Norman. No!" The replies were ignored. "Please!"

David's eyes soon started to turn red and his own tears started to flow. He shook with fright as the sound of his mother being beaten ripped into his soul. In an attempt to hide from the anguish he tucked his head into his arms and then whispered his own plea.

"Please, please stop!"

But the sounds did not go away.

It was no good. Something had to be done. David stood up and ran down the stairs into the kitchen. As he got to the doorway tears were flowing down his cheeks and he shouted as loud as he could.

"Leave her alone!"

At first, the sudden arrival and holler of David made Norman jump, but he soon gained control of himself and turned around to face the young boy. The look upon his face was one of a vicious fury, but it was grimly eclipsed by Marilyn's expression of fear and shock. Her face was badly cut and bruised, but her harrowing look of utter fright stood out amongst her wounds.

Norman took a step forward towards David and spoke in a fierce and temperamental manner.

"Get the fuck out!"

The sound of malice in the big man's voice made David freeze into a statue like state. He could not move, let alone say anything, and this was his undoing. Unfortunately, he had not done as Norman had told him to.

The initial blow was to the right eye and the second was to the young boy's stomach. David keeled over and fell against the kitchen cupboard. At first, he was stunned, but then he realised that his attacker had not finished. Although he could see what was about to happen there was nothing he could do to stop it.

Norman made a grab for David's collar with one hand and his hair with the other. Lifting him up off of the ground with ease, he dragged him into the hall and turned him to face the cupboard door under the stairs.

David tried to beg.

"Please! Please! I'm sorry! I won't do it again!" His fear made him apologise even though he had not done anything wrong. "I didn't mean it!"

Norman ignored the pleas for mercy and carried on with the punishment. He held David's hair at the back of his head and sharply banged his forehead against the cupboard door. Just to make sure that the boy had learnt his lesson he did it another half a dozen times. As the big man battered his future stepson he bellowed out his orders.

"You do as you're fucking told! Don't just ignore me! When I tell you to do something, you do it!"

All this was watched by the tear filled eyes of Marilyn without her uttering a word. As she witnessed the beating of her son her facial expression was empty of concern. She was just glad it was not her who was getting beaten. Besides, she thought it was about time that David learnt to do as he told.

There was a cold silence throughout the entire house. Every room was like an empty crypt, still and sullen. It seemed as if all the noise from the night before had used up all of the sound that there was. There were people there somewhere, but they just had nothing to say.

David winced as he rubbed his badly bruised head. He sat on his bed, pale faced and withdrawn. Thoughts of the terror he had endured the night before raced around his head even though he was trying his best to clear them from his mind. The hurt that he was feeling was like nothing that he had ever experienced before, but it was not just the bruises that caused the pain. There was a mental agony that cut so deep that he wondered if it would make a wound that could never be healed.

It had taken David quite a few hours to finally fall asleep during the night. He had spent most of the time lying on his bed staring at the ceiling whilst crying profusely. The thought of why Norman would want to hurt his mother and him like that was something that he could not understand. They had done nothing to him that could cause him to be so angry. Yet his wrath was so full of temper it seemed as though he had amassed a thousand reasons which were all worthy enough for him to have reason enough to act in such an awful way. If there were answers there somewhere they were very well hidden.

David had woken up with the same thoughts as he had fallen asleep with. All he felt now was numb and tired. He had only slept for about five hours and had woken up with his mind jammed full of the memories from the night before. It was not quite clear to him what had made him wake up so early, but he thought he might have dreamt about the night's events as well.

David had now spent a good hour sitting on his bed thinking about what had happened. They were not pleasant thoughts that he was having, but he had given up trying to keep them out of his head. In the end he decided that he ought to just get on with the day and have breakfast.

As David stood up he caught a glimpse of himself in the small mirror which he kept on his bedside table. At first he turned away not wanting to see, but the urge to look at his wounds soon became too strong. Steadily reaching his arm out, he wrapped his fingers tightly around the frame of the mirror and slowly lifted it up in front of his face.

All David could do at first was stare into the mirror with an expression of utter shock. He could not believe what he saw. There were purple bruises all around his pale face and a large cut above his right eye. When he spoke he just told himself something that he already knew.

"I didn't deserve that."

David closed his eyes and wept.

Norman wrapped his towel round his waist and checked his hair in the bathroom mirror. He soon found a few hairs that were out of place so he pulled his comb out from behind his ear and started to flatten them down. As he did so he noticed that he had bruises on his knuckles, but he chose to ignore them. After having one last look at himself and raising his eyebrows in a suave, yet vain, manner he decided to make his way to back to his bedroom.

Norman paced across the landing idly tapping his comb across his cheek making a hollow sound come out of his mouth. As he passed David's bedroom he heard a murmur come from inside. The door was open so he took a step back to take a look inside. All he saw was his future stepson holding a mirror out in front of him with tears streaming down his badly bruised face.

There were no feelings of remorse or regret and there were certainly no apologies. Norman just raised his eyebrows and casually tucked his comb behind his ear. As he walked into his bedroom he slammed the door behind him and muttered an obscenity to himself.

"Little wanker!"

Marilyn pulled the saucepan of soup off of the gas stove and dipped a wooden spoon into it. As she pulled the spoon out and tasted the soup she winced as it rubbed against her bruised mouth. The rest of her face also had several cuts upon it and her left eye was badly closed up.

When Marilyn had woken up she had asked Norman why he had beaten her and her son. In reply he had given her some feeble excuses and had basically said that she and David had deserved it. He, of course, knew that they had not and so did she, but whether it was through fear of getting hurt again or fear of losing her fiancé altogether she had forgiven him.

"You were flirting at him." Norman had accused her. "And that little bastard shouldn't have got involved in our business."

"I suppose you're right." Marilyn replied. "He should keep out of things that don't concern him."

David had not heard any of this conversation and it was probably just as well. His first thoughts were that his mother would stick up for the both of them to make sure that it would never happen again. He had come to the conclusion that she was either going to get Norman to leave the house or make him stand up and apologise to the both of them. This was, of course, wishful thinking and he could not have been more wrong.

As Marilyn poured the soup into a bowl she became aware of someone standing in the doorway of the kitchen. She looked up and smiled in an attempt to make it look as though she was content with everything, but when she saw that it was her son her face soon became stern. When she sat down at the table she licked her cut lip and prepared herself for what was going to be quite a painful meal.

33

David forced a half smile, but could not hold it for long. Slowly shuffling into the kitchen he pulled out a chair at the table and sat himself down. At first he found it hard to find anything to say even though he had been thinking about what he was going to say in this conversation all morning. Nevertheless, after trying to bring the right words into his mind he plucked up the courage to say what he wanted.

"What are you going to do, Mum?" He asked timidly.

"What do you mean?" Came the reply.

"Well, about Norman?" As David saw his mother take in a deep, exasperated breath he lowered his gaze. "You are going to do something, aren't you?"

"No. Why?" Marilyn took a sip of her soup with a curled up lip. "There's nothing that needs to be done."

"But he beat me up." A surprised look crossed David's face. "He beat *you* up."

"That's none of your business!" A snarl crossed her face. "Anyway, nothing was wrong until you got involved."

David tried to interrupt.

"But..."

"In future you're to keep out of Norman's and my business!" Marilyn became angered and started to raise her voice. "Then maybe you won't need to be punished!"

David sat staring at his mother as she carried on falteringly sipping her soup. He was shocked to realise that she thought that Norman had done the right thing. As he solemnly sat there slowly shaking his head in disbelief Marilyn repeated her demand.

"Just keep out of it in future!"

David sat in kitchen for a long while as he tried to fathom out what was going on. When he finally gave up trying to understand any of his mother's or Norman's actions he got up and started to leave. As he reached the door he turned around to have one more look at his mother, almost as if he might still find some answers, but all he saw was a lone tear fall from her eye and make a small splash in her soup. That said it all.

The assembly hall was slowly vacated in a mournful fashion by the pupils and teachers alike. Some walked with their heads bowed in respect, whilst others muttered a few words amongst themselves about what they had just heard. It was the most quiet morning assembly the school had ever had.

All of the pupils and teachers of the school had been called together to hear of the death of one of the music teachers. The headmaster had stood on the stage and announced that Mr Bishop had died in his sleep and that everyone must pray for his wife and family. Every head in the assembly hall had been solemnly bowed when the prayer had been read out.

In addition to the announcement of the loss of Mr Bishop the headmaster had also told the school of his new replacement who had hurriedly been called in. At the front of the assembly hall sitting in the middle of the line of teachers was a small man in his mid-fifties. It was he who was pointed out to be Mr Scott, the new music teacher.

David had been sitting three rows from the front of the assembly of pupils and had been looking at the expressions on the faces of the teachers. They appeared to be quite numb by the announcement, but at the same time they did not seem as though they were that surprised by the news. Mr Bishop had spent most of his time coughing and wiping his forehead in a feverish manner. There were times when it was hard to make out what he was saying when he used to splutter his words out and cover his mouth with his handkerchief. It seemed as though the man was permanently ill and it was a wonder that he had carried on living for as long as he had.

As David shuffled his way through amongst the other pupils to his next lesson he wondered what Mr Scott was going to be like. He was now going to his art class, but his lesson after that was going to be with the new music teacher. If there was one certainty, it was a pretty safe bet that he was going to be easier to comprehend than Mr Bishop was.

As the school bell sounded out to signify the end of the lesson David breathed out a sigh of relief. Out of all of the subjects he did at school he considered art to be the most boring and pointless of all of them. He had no intentions of becoming an artist when he left school and he could not think of a single moment in the future when he would need to draw something. It was with a great deal of pleasure that he got up and left the classroom.

David spent most of his break times at school reading in the library, but today he decided to find himself a bench on the edge of the school yard as it was such a sunny day. This was a risky thing to do as it made him an easy target for bullies. There were teachers about who were keeping an eye on the pupils, but they could not see everything.

As David sat down on one of the benches on the edge of the yard he looked over his shoulder and saw one of Martin Dent's gang looking round the corner of the gymnasium. He knew that the boy had been told to wait there so as to be a lookout. It was quite obvious what was going on and he could just make out a few puffs of smoke coming out from behind the wall and drift across the schoolyard.

Over by the tennis courts David could see two pupils exchanging harsh words and pushing each other about. One of them suddenly punched the other one in the face and a small scuffle broke out. It was over within seconds and by the state of the two of them afterwards there was no clear winner. Both of the boys friends who had been standing around watching the incident seemed to have enjoyed the whole spectacle immensely and were now trying to talk them into fighting some more.

On the far end of the schoolyard David had noticed that some older pupils had taken a young boy's tennis ball and were refusing to give it back to him. Whenever the hapless boy tried to take it back off of one of the bigger lads they would throw it to one another before he could get it. They seemed to find the whole charade extremely amusing and were having a good laugh at the young boy's expense. There was even more laughter when the boy gave up trying to get his ball back and walked off trying to hold back tears.

After spending half of his break watching what was going on all around the schoolyard David stood up to go to his next lesson. As he walked off he slowly shook his head and said his usual exclamation when he was shocked by something he saw or experienced.

"What is wrong with this world?"

David had decided to go to his next lesson early in the hope that he might meet the new music teacher in advance. When he reached the classroom he noticed that the door was already wide open. This was unusual, as Mr Bishop had always kept it locked due to the expensive musical instruments that were kept there. As he got to the doorway he looked inside and saw Mr Scott sitting at his desk reading some of the pupil's exercise books.

David did not want to startle the teacher so he got his attention by speaking in a quiet tone of voice.

"Excuse me, Sir! May I come in and wait, please?"

Mr Scott turned around and looked over the top of his glasses with a broad smile. He had neatly combed grey hair, with a kind looking face and seemed to have an air of cheerfulness all about him. As he stood up, he showed that he was no more than five-and-a-half foot tall and had quite a stubby frame.

Mr Scott had been teaching for a number of years now and was regrettably at the twilight of his career. No doubt, when he finally did retire he would miss his job, but at the same time he knew that he was well due the rest. His chosen profession had become quite arduous over the years and was very different to when he had started. Drugs, knives and parents with bad attitudes were additions to schooling that he found most unwelcome.

Teaching was not as enjoyable now as it had been when Mr Scott had first started, but he had kept his cheerful approach to the job which he had begun with all those years ago. He had been generally liked by the pupils at his old school, but had also earned himself a reputation for being a little bit too soft. This, however, was something he knew, but did not really mind.

When Mr Scott spoke it was in a jolly and pleasant manner.

"Ah, my first pupil. Of course you may come in."

"Thank you, Sir."

"You could do me a favour actually. I've been looking at some of the pupils work and there are a few that are actually quite good, but this one I have here is different." Mr Scott opened out a book that he had in his hand and started to read from it. "Mozart made it quite plain to all of his dislike for the flute and the harp, yet at that time in history the French courts found both instruments to be most appealing."

David shyly bowed his head whilst the smiling teacher started to walk around the classroom reading the book aloud.

"As was the custom of the time composers were commissioned to write their music by the rich in order to make a living. The Duke of Guines, who was at one time the French Ambassador for London, approached Mozart to write a concerto for him and his daughter. Of course, the duke played the flute and his daughter played the harp, a fact that probably would not have pleased the young composer. However, Mozart agreed to write the concerto and completed one of his most beautiful and compelling pieces of music he had ever written. It is almost as if the concerto is a monument to the magnificent talent of a composer who, although only died at a young age, consistently wrote music to the highest of standards even when it was for instruments he did not like."

As Mr Scott closed the book he looked at the name on the front cover and spoke in a wistful manner.

"Who is David Cain?"

"I am, Sir." The reply was said in a subdued and shy tone.

Mr Scott now appeared to be quite embarrassed, but carried pressing for more information anyway.

"I see." He half smiled. "The reason why I ask is because the project was to write about any musical artist of your choice. Most of the pupils wrote about pop music, but you wrote about the work of Mozart. Why?"

David shrugged his shoulders as quietly answered.

"I just found him to be more interesting."

"*I* find him to be interesting. That's why I enjoyed reading your work so much. I've got to admit it, I actually learnt something from it myself and that's something that has rarely happened to me in my teaching career." He smiled broadly. "Very well done, David."

At that moment the rest of the pupils started to shuffle into the classroom with their usual lack of enthusiasm. This signified the beginning of the lesson so Mr Scott walked over to the front of the room whilst David still stood anchored next to the teacher's desk with a proud smile and a tinge of embarrassment. He liked his new music teacher already.

The rest of the music lesson was a rare pleasure for David. He had found it to be informative and enjoyable at the same time. Most of the other teachers who had taught him either seemed to have a dislike for the way he consistently answered their questions correctly or bored him with information he already knew. This one, however, was different.

Mr Scott seemed to enjoy teaching David and did not seem to mind when he put his hand up to ask him anything. Some of the teachers would tell him to be quiet and not to pester them. It even got to the point where he would not put his hand up anymore for fear of being told off.

When the school bell sounded to end the lesson David reluctantly started to put his books and pens away in his bag. Although music was not one of his favourite subjects he still found it to be more interesting than most. For once he actually found that he was enjoying a lesson and was not waiting for it to end. As he stood up to leave Mr Scott stopped him and spoke in a hopeful tone of voice.

"Excuse me, David! Do you mind if we have a chat?"

"Yes, Sir!" David replied politely. "Of course."

"I just want to ask you a few things." Mr Scott walked over and sat on a desk at the front of the class. "How did you get to learn so much about Mozart?"

"I read about him at the library, Sir." David grabbed a chair and sat down. "I go there quite a lot."

"Really?" Mr Scott paused for thought. "So, can you tell me what his final opera was?"

"The Magic Flute." The answer was spoken quickly and confidently.

"Do you know anything about any other composers?"

"Yes. A bit."

"When did Beethoven die?"

"Eighteen-twenty-seven."

"Who wrote Peer Gynt?"

"Grieg."

"The tenor and baritone who perform the duet in act one of Bizet's opera the 'Pearl Fishers', what do they sing about?"

"The priestess who is praying on the cliff top."

Mr Scott smiled and David did likewise. The both of them spent the next half an hour talking about music and anything else they could think of. Their conversation eventually only came to an end because they had forgotten to go lunch and had become quite hungry.

As David walked down the corridor he wore a contented smile upon his face. He was already thinking about his next lesson with Mr Scott and was thoroughly looking forward to it. Maths, English and science may have been his favourite subjects, but music was certainly going to be the most enjoyable.

David had at last found someone who would talk to him without a sneer or a single derogatory comment, and that felt really good.

"A suicide bomber struck at a joint allied army base in eastern Afghanistan today, killing three soldiers and one civilian."

A middle-aged newsreader read the bulletin with a blank expression etched into his face. It seemed as if it was the hundredth time he had read the same news article, but in a way it was. The only change in the story this time was that it was a different place on a different date. Just another report of suffering in the world did little to provoke a reaction from the newscaster, as it did those who were now watching it in their homes.

The electric fire made a low buzzing noise and sent a warm glow across the living room. Marilyn was sitting next to Norman on the settee with her arm wrapped around him, whilst David was sitting on the rug in front of the television set. It was early in the evening after everyone had just eaten their dinner and they were now feeling quite restful.

Marilyn rarely watched the news and tried not to pay that much attention to current affairs. Most of the time she preferred to be ignorant to what was going on around her and just believe anything that anyone told her, such as taking Norman's word for everything. However, this particular news article that she was watching right now had struck her quite dumfounded. In an attempt to throw some light on the subject she pursued her usual means for an explanation.

"Why do they keep killing our soldiers, Norman?"

"Because they don't like us." The answer was followed by a lethargic wave of the hand. "No one likes us because we're better than everyone else."

"Yeah! We never do anything to them." Marilyn shook her head. "I don't know why they don't leave us alone."

David looked across the room at his mother and Norman with a frown upon his face. Although he knew better than to say anything against the big man's word he thought that on this occasion it would do no harm. He spoke in a *matter-of-fact* manner as he made his point

"We are in the wrong."

"What?" Norman said.

"We are in the wrong. The reason why our country is out there is to steal their oil and other natural resources. We even bomb their infrastructure and then charge them money to rebuild it." David turned to face the television. "That's the reason why they kill our soldiers."

Marilyn was now even more confused and it showed in her tone of voice.

"I don't understand. I mean, we wouldn't do that."

"We've been doing it for centuries." David was quick to correct his mother. "The British Colonial Empire was built on the backs of other countries."

Norman was just as perplexed by David's answer and could not help stuttering whilst trying to get his words out.

"What the fuck are you on about?"

"Why do you think this small country we live in is so rich?" David raised an eyebrow. "Do either of you know?"

"Yeah, because we're better than everyone else." Norman's sat up straight in a proud gesture. "That's why people don't like us."

Marilyn eagerly agreed with her fiancé.

"Yeah, everyone knows that."

David turned himself around to face his mother and Norman in order to stress his point.

"I'm sure there are lots of people watching soaps, quiz shows and talent contests on television who believe that also, but it's simply not the case." This was said with a cynical raise of the eyebrow. "Britain has violently ruled over countries across the world for centuries, and it's always been for the same reasons. We steal their natural resources. There was even a time when we used to steal their people as slaves. All the way through history, we have always been involved with most of the troubles all over the world, including Northern Ireland, Israel, India, and South Africa. It's no different now either. We bombed Iraq and Libya to steal their oil and occupied Afghanistan just to build a pipeline through it. We send our planes in to bomb anything that provides electricity, water and whatever else provides essential utilities for the indigenous people and then multinational companies move in to rebuild the damage that we've caused."

"Yeah, but it's made us richer." A typical selfish remark from Norman. "So fuck them!"

Marilyn was eager to agree.

"It's a dog eat dog world."

David continued with his lesson.

"It hasn't made us rich." He waved his hand at the dilapidated living room they were sitting in. "The only people who benefit from it are the ultra rich people who own the international banks and multi-national companies that profit from it. In the process, millions of people have died for that greed, and not just those living in the foreign lands that we pillage. Our troops are sent out there to give their lives for this greed. But no one cares. What is more important to people in this country is who's having an affair in the latest soaps, who's going to win some dancing competition and which washed up celebrity is having a drug problem. People think that real life is something that happens to characters in a television programme, whereas they think their own real lives are fiction."

Norman turned to Marilyn and spoke to her in a whisper.

"Who taught him all this?"

"Not me." Came the reply.

David then put an ending on his summarisation.

"And that's why they kill our soldiers."

Norman was not about to be corrected in such an overwhelming fashion.

"Yeah, well I don't give a fuck about any of that." He sat forward, gritted his teeth and clenched his fists. "I support our troops and so should you."

"I agree with what you're saying, but if they weren't out there…"

David looked at the temperamental expression on Norman's face and realised that now would be a good time to stop the discussion. He knew that at times like this the big man would resort to his usual philosophy of solving a problem with anger, so he decided that it would be best to let the subject drop. There had been many a time when he had seen what this man was capable of when he lost his temper and, more to the point, he had felt what he could do with his fists. After taking a moment to think about it, he came to the conclusion that it would be safer to just turn around, carry on watching the television and be quiet.

When David had received the first beating off of Norman for interfering with his argument with Marilyn it had not been the last. Between then and now he had been punished on a number of occasions for what were all minor offences. Every time had been as distasteful as the first.

One morning when David was getting the milk in off of the doorstep he had dropped a bottle and smashed it on the hall floor. He had cleaned it up, but when Norman had found out about it he hit him across the face with the buckle of his belt and threw him outside without any breakfast. Making the slightest mistake around the home could be a very costly thing to do.

There had also been a time when Norman had come in drunk and had a large cut on his upper lip as a result of a fight that he had been in at the pub. When Marilyn had tried to nurse it better for him he accused her of trying to make it worse and beat her with a large heavy boot. David had been sitting in the living room watching television at the time and had realised that it would not be safe for him to be downstairs at that particular moment, so he tried to make his way up to bedroom unnoticed. Unfortunately, he was caught and punished for staying up way past his bedtime even though it was only eight o'clock. He had also received a beating around the head with the heavy boot.

David knew that his mother and he did not deserve the beatings that they got, but he also knew that there was nothing that he could do about it. He just tried his best to make sure that any incidents between Norman and him were kept as few and far between as possible. Sometimes, however, he simply had no chance to avoid it. The large man was very good at finding the smallest of excuses to administer a punishment.

With this in mind, David decided that it would be best just to let the discussion on foreign conflicts to come to an end and just stayed watching the television set without saying another word. Although he had more to say on the matter, this was one of the few times that he had crossed Norman and had got away with it without getting at least a slap round the head. He was more than grateful for this piece of good fortune and was content to have his views unheard. This was a satisfactory conclusion to the matter.

Prayers

There are people who will murder another person because their mind is psychologically damaged, some will do it to protect themselves or a member of their family, but some people will kill another human being for greed, religion or simply for their own pleasure. The world is a sick place in which every day reports in newspapers and on television inform us of murders and killings all around the world.

Of course, most people have never taken another person's life and probably never will. It takes a great lack of feeling to do something as terrible as kill someone, whether you know them or not. However, when we read of a person who has been murdered or we see on the television the dead body of an innocent child, we feel a sense of disgust and sorrow. This is because we feel sorry for the person who is dead and for the families who they have left behind.

So, what do we do about it?

Unfortunately, we do as little as nothing.

We may vote for politicians who say that they support world peace and are going to crack down on crime, and we also pay taxes to provide a police force to combat the activities of criminals, but other than that we do nothing.

What are we supposed to do?

Of course, it is obvious that there is nothing we can do to stop the wars and murders all around the entire world.

But why?

Because we are only human. It is impossible to affect the ways of every person alive so that they stop killing their fellow humans.

Does that make us a good race, because we cannot help the way we are?

Well it does not make it right. We just do not like to think that humans are a race of beings that cannot stop themselves from killing one another for no other reason than our own imperfections.

For instance, every person who pays taxes gives their money towards their country's army. There is no particular individual who has any choice of what the taxed proportion taken from their wages is spent on. Their money could contribute towards a bullet, a bomb or even a simple knife. In truth, no one knows exactly where his or her own money goes.

Each weapon that is bought by a government is designed to take a person's life in the most effective way possible. Therefore, anyone whose country has ever gone to war is partly responsible for a death of someone somewhere in the world. That includes every taxpayer from a sixteen year old girl who has just started her first day at work to a retiring sixty-five year old man who is on his very last day.

Either everyone has just got used to that fact that they pay money for other people to be killed or they are so oblivious to what their taxes are spent on that they just do not realise it.

Maybe, in a sick and depraved sought of way, we have got to the point where we now consider it to be acceptable?

Of course, our freedom was bought with the lives of some very brave people during wars against tyrannical regimes like Nazism. We must respect their courage for that. However, someone in Germany paid towards the weapon that killed them. And that someone probably has exactly the same views as us.

I suppose the most logical idea would be to stop paying taxes towards our armies and their weapons. We would all be better off and that someone, somewhere, in the world would live for another day.

But, of course, every person in every country will ask of themselves: "How can we defend ourselves against other countries if we haven't got an army?"

It seems as if it's not just our problem. The real argument is not whether our country should have weapons of mass destruction, but if the world should. Everyone everywhere is wasting their money on preparing for wars with people who they do not even know.

That is ridiculous!

Something has got to be done. But how?

No country will ever suddenly disarm itself for the sake of peace. Everyone would have to do it at the same time.

But who is ever going to make everyone do that?

We would need a miracle. We would need a god.

It is so depressing how savage and limited we actually are. If we travelled to another galaxy and looked upon a planet where the inhabitants killed one another with weapons of mass destruction and had feelings of hate for anything they did not know or understand we would turn away and leave them to it. We would consider them to be depraved and evil.

Unfortunately, we are the inhabitants of that planet. We are just too naive or ashamed to admit it.

What is wrong with this world?

When David was bored he would often hold debates with himself within his mind. Whilst he was walking through the dark miserable streets delivering his morning paper round he was having one such silent discussion with himself. He could not understand how people in a country or of a religion could go to war with each other for what they would call 'the right reasons'. He thought that what they would fight over was always something so minor or so easy to logically solve that it was always both of the sides who were in the wrong.

David had read about every war that had taken place over the last century and had come up with a logical solution for every one of them. He thought that the Second World War should have been solved by the Germans not invading Poland to start it off and he also decided that the Israelis and the Palestinians should not fight against each other and all just live together in peace.

Of course, David was not stupid. He knew that his solutions were obvious to most people and had simply come to the conclusion that wars were fought not because one side was wrong and the other side had to put them right, but it was due to the fact that the human race was imperfect. This self-titled *intelligent* race had been on the planet for thousands of years and still had not been able to live in peace and, unfortunately, it probably never would. Therefore, he had come to the realisation that there were only two ways that the world could ever become a peaceful place. These were for either the human race to become extinct, like the dinosaurs, or for it to evolve into a better more intelligent life form like the physical and mental adaptation from when it was a primate species. Unfortunately, the first of the two solutions seemed to be the one most likely to happen.

David had now reached a point in his life when he had accepted that he was different to everyone else. He knew that he was gifted with a much higher intelligence and he had also been aware for a long time now that his appearance was abnormal as well. However, he could not understand why people would look down on him for it. He considered being clever to be a good thing and as for looking different to everyone else, it hardly thought that was a crime against humanity.

As David wandered up the garden path of a house on his round he pulled out a newspaper from his bag and went to slip it into the letterbox. Just as he went to push it all the way through he noticed an article on the front page. It was about a five-year-old girl who had gone missing and had last been seen getting into a car with a man. A picture of the girl on the front page showed her wearing a bright blue dress with a proud smile upon her innocent face. Little did she know then what kind of world she had been living in.

For a long moment David just frowned at the somewhat morbid picture of the girl and then pushed the newspaper all the way through the letterbox. Seeing the article seemed to confirm the conclusions that he had just reached whilst he had been debating the history and future of the human race. The past was horrifying, so was the present and it did not look as if things were going to get any better either.

David was quite aware that he was a human being as well, but he was sure he was not capable of the things that he would read in the newspapers. He sometimes wondered if he was so different to everyone else that he was almost a separate origin of mammal. Only he was not a member of a small minority, but instead the only member of a minority.

Although the thoughts inside David's head were quite depressing they kept him going in the cold winter mornings whilst he was out on his paper round. Christmas was coming, so for the last couple of months he had started delivering newspapers so that he could save up to buy some presents. He was looking forward to the festive season this year, not because he was going to receive gifts himself, but because he was going to give them out for the first time ever.

Normally David would get just one gift for Christmas off of his mother, but he would never have anything to give to her in return. This always made him feel selfish, so he decided that this year was going to be different. He took up the paper round and put away his money every week so that he would have a good amount to spend on presents when he went shopping.

David was not only going to buy his mother a gift, but he was also going to get his new stepfather a present as well. Marilyn and Norman had been married for about half a year and for a while after the marriage they were like a couple of young lovers who had just met for the first time. Sure enough though the excitement had soon worn off and things had got back to normal. Arguments, beatings and relentless fear inevitably followed.

Norman had quickly settled back into his old ways and had kept on finding the smallest reasons to harm the people closest to him. Marilyn had soon found the excuses to support his actions and consistently put on a brave, but battered face. David also tried his best to pretend that things were not so bad by getting on with his life as best he could. Although he would regularly go to school with bruises and come home with some extra ones as well he was beginning to realise that things were not ever going to get any better.

David was unintentionally starting to accept his way of life. As he walked from house to house delivering the newspapers he could not help but notice the decorations in each of the front windows. They added a pleasant aura of festive spirit to each home and a sense of warmth and happiness. There was no such thing at his house, just the odd empty whisky bottle or an extra letter or two on the front doormat to remind the more observant person that Christmas was on its way.

As David strolled along the street he wondered what other peoples festive seasons were going to be like. Although he was looking forward to Christmas he was sure that there should be a lot more to it than just receiving a present in the morning from his mother which would then be followed by her leaving him to open it while she went around a friend's house for the rest of the day. He was quite adamant that not everyone spent the day like he did, alone and bored.

David posted the last newspaper in the house at the end of the street and patted his large orange bag to make sure that it was empty. As he looked up the road at the decorations in some of the houses he wondered to himself what his Christmas was going to be like. He hoped that maybe this year it would be just a little bit special and everyone would make a bit more of an effort to be happy now that his mother was married to Norman. It did not seem too much to ask for.

As if they had appeared out of thin air overnight a selection of festively wrapped parcels had suddenly colourfully graced the corner of the living room. David had put them there three days before Christmas so as to cheerfully show off his effort towards the holiday proceedings. He was looking forward to when his mother and stepfather asked him what they were so he could proudly announce them to be the gifts that he was going to be giving out this year.

David had neatly spread out the parcels in a random, but deliberate fashion, so as to make it look as if they had been left there by accident. He thought that if there was such a person called Santa Claus then this was how he would have delivered his gifts. For the first time in his life he was actually looking forward to Christmas like other children did.

For most of the day, David had been sitting up in his room reading a book on human biology in a desperate attempt to relieve the boredom of the Christmas holidays. Although he learnt more reading to himself at home rather than in lessons at school he found that he missed his conversations with Mr Scott and there was always the problem of not being able to use the school library. As he idly turned over the page he heard the latch unlock on the front door.

Norman walked into the hallway and with a total lack of awareness let the front door close in Marilyn's face. As he pulled his coat off he turned to face his wife and spoke in an irritable manner.

"Come on, hurry up!" He breathed out an agitated huff of displeasure. "You're letting the cold in."

"OK, Norman!" Marilyn looked up at her husband with an apologetic expression upon her face and hurried into the house. "Sorry about that!"

Norman made his way into the living room and switched on the electric fire. He had spent most of the day going around shops so that Marilyn could choose herself a new dress for Christmas and he had soon become tired of being on his feet. As he let himself collapse down onto the settee he decided that he could do with a hot drink. The order was called out in the usual expectant way.

"Get us a cup of..."

Norman had started to call out his command to his wife for a hot beverage when he had noticed the parcels in the corner of the room. He had stopped halfway through his sentence and now sat gawping at the small mound of presents. Marilyn had heard him start to call out his request, but had obviously not managed to hear the rest of it, so she called out from the kitchen for more clarity.

"What was that?"

Norman stood up and started to make his way over to the corner where the neatly wrapped gifts were on display. He then bent down over them so as to take a closer look. As he did so he finished his sentence.

"Tea! Get us a cup of tea, will you?"

"OK, Norman!" Marilyn's voice sounded tired and falsely contented. "I'll do it now."

As Norman picked up one of the parcels he noticed that something was written on the side of it. He quietly read it out to himself at a gradual pace.

"To my stepfather Norman. Love from David."

Norman frowned and put it back with the others as he shuffled his hand amongst them to find another one. As he picked up one that was adorned with pink wrapping paper he turned it around to see what was written on it. This time, however, he did not speak out aloud when he read it out.

To the best Mum ever. Love from David.

Norman put the parcel back down where he had found it and then slowly stood up. At first he just stared at them all for one long moment and then ever so gradually his face twisted into a sneer. He was not at all impressed. This was clearly an attempt by his stepson to get more money spent on *his* presents and there was no way he was going to fall for that.

After months of saving his money for delivering the paper round David had accumulated quite a large sum of cash. He had not taken long to choose what he was going to buy his mother and stepfather and was quite please with the presents he had got them. For Marilyn he had got a bottle of expensive perfume and mirror for her handbag. As for Norman, he had got him a portable stereo player and an Elvis CD that he could listen to whilst he was working.

David had taken a great deal of pride neatly wrapping up the presents and was thoroughly delighted with what he had done for them. He was sure that they would be grateful for the presents that he had got them as he had overheard them talking about what they wanted for Christmas weeks before. Although he normally found the actual day to be a bit boring, he would at least know they would be happy.

"Look all this shit?"

"He put it there, Norman."

"Well I just tripped over the fucking pile of crap!"

"Careful you may break something!"

"I'll break something all right!"

"Don't do that Norman! Not at Christmas!"

"Shouldn't be here anyway!"

It was two o'clock on Christmas morning and David had been fast asleep when he had been woken up by the noise coming from downstairs. He had instantly recognised it to be an argument and his adrenaline was already keeping him from falling back to sleep. As he listened out he could hear the concentration in Norman's voice whilst he was stamping on the presents in the living room. It was now common knowledge that going downstairs to try to stop it would be a futile and dangerous thing to do, so he just laid in the dark staring at the ceiling waiting for it to stop.

When the shouting and banging had been replaced by silence, David closed his eyes to get back to sleep. It would not be worth going downstairs to assess the damage yet, so he decided to wait until the morning. He should not have really expected his Christmas day to be that much fun anyway.

Bits of wrapping paper and packaging were sprawled across the floor of the living room. Next to an armchair was Norman's portable stereo half wrapped and half smashed. There was shattered glass on the rug in front of the fireplace and a strong smell of perfume coming from the remains of one of Marilyn's presents.

As David slowly walked across the living room, he could not help crushing bits of debris under his feet. When he reached the corner he bent down and moved some wrapping paper off of one of the less damaged gifts. He then slipped it into his coat pocket and took a moment to look around at the mess. Normally he would have cleaned it up, but as it was Christmas morning he simply did not feel like it.

The front door closed behind David and he pulled his key out of the lock. As he walked through the streets he saw children riding their new bikes and running around to their friends and families houses to show off their new presents. They all looked blissfully cheerful and did not seem to have a care in the world. He had no feelings of jealousy, but instead just longed for his own happiness.

When David reached the park he found that it was empty. Normally it would be full of children playing and people going for walks, but today everyone seemed to have decided to stay away. As he sat down on a bench in the middle of the park he pulled the present which he had taken from his house out of his pocket. The wrapping paper had been ripped, but there was still some writing on it that could just be read.

To David. From...

The rest of the writing was missing, but David did not need to read it to know whom it was from. He had managed to have some money left after buying Marilyn and Norman their presents so he had decided to buy himself a gift for Christmas. When he had taken the remainder of the wrapping paper off the present he put it in a bin next to the bench.

David looked at his gift and tried his best to smile. With his remaining money he had bought himself a book entitled 'The Dragon of the Lost Castle'. Although he never read fiction other than at school he had decided to make an exception on this occasion.

For the remainder of the day, David sat in the park contentedly reading his Christmas present, lonely, cold, but out of harm's way.

"He's a right bastard." Explained the young boy. "Complete and utter."

"He gave Robinson the cane last year just for swearing. And that was just two days after they made it legal to use the bloody thing again." His friend added. "I can't believe they legalised caning just because the Prime Minister is an ex-teacher."

The first boy had a glum look upon his face as he spoke.

"Our first day back at school and we go and get Cutter the Nutter for RE." He shook his head. "I don't bloody believe it."

"You think that's bad? I've got him for maths this afternoon as well." The second boy ran his palm down his face in an exasperated manner. "What a start to the new year."

The two boys were complaining about their ill luck whilst shuffling their way up the stairs to their first lesson of the new term. They were both wearing new school uniforms, and although they looked smart, they both appeared to be rather gloomy. As they talked about their misfortune they did not realise that someone was listening into their conversation.

Walking behind the two boys, trying his best to hear what they were saying was David. He had heard about Mr Cutter and his short fused temper and had decided a long time ago that he did not want to cross his path. Unfortunately, he had also been given the misfortune of having him as his teacher for the first lesson of the new school term.

As the two boys came to the top of the stairs they turned into a long corridor which was bustling with children. It looked clean just like the rest of the school did after the summer holidays and it smelt fresh too. Halfway down there was a queue of pupils lining up outside one of the classrooms. This was where the two boys in front of David were heading for their lesson. As they joined the back of the queue their conversation started up again.

"If he catches you talking he gives you two hundred lines, if you don't do all of your homework you get a detention and..." The first boy paused and looked around before he completed his sentence. "If you say anything against his poxy bible he'll cane the hell out of you."

"Yeah! Look what happened to Tony Dell." The second boy agreed in a depressed manner then moved closer to whisper the rest of what he had to say. "Mind you, he's going to hate Cain asking him questions all the bloody time."

They both grinned and nodded their heads at the same time. David did not hear the last part of their conversation.

After a spate of teachers being beaten extremely badly and one getting stabbed to death by parents at schools the government had brought in new legislation to curb the public's approach to interacting with school staff. It had now become illegal to enter a school without prior invitation, any foul language or violence against a teacher was also outlawed, and the cane had been brought back in to *undo bad parenting*. Anyone who broke any of the new laws would be fined extremely heavily or, in extreme cases, jailed. Although some considered the new laws to be somewhat draconian, they did certainly cut back on the assaults on teachers.

From somewhere in the front of the queue the warning to the rest of the pupils was sounded.

"Cutter's coming!"

At the other end of the corridor from which David had entered pupils started to part leaving an opening so that a tall man could make his way through without any hindrance. It was Mr Cutter. He walked straight-backed with the posture of a sergeant major. His face was stern and his eyes stared straight ahead at the pupils waiting outside of his classroom. A cold silence had swept over the whole corridor, as was the norm.

As David looked around at the rest of the pupils he saw fear on all of their faces. He was shocked to see that everyone seemed to be scared of him. This was not what he thought to be acceptable from a person who was merely there just to educate them all.

Mr Cutter reached the queue outside the classroom and pulled out the key to unlock the door. The pupils who were surrounding the entrance quickly shuffled out of the way so as not to cause any inconvenience to him. As the tall man opened the door he gave out his orders.

"Now, I want you all to enter the classroom in single file and find a seat." His voice was deep and full of authority. "And I don't want any talking from any of you!"

The pupils did exactly as they were told without a noise being made other than the shuffling of their feet and the rustle of clothes. As David waited for his part of the queue to start moving he stared at Mr Cutter who was keeping a watchful eye over the class. He was a tall neat man who wore a shirt, tie and blazer, but this did little to set a nice impression. His face was a different story all together.

The years of Mr Cutter unleashing wild tempers upon the pupils of the school were etched into the features upon his face. His eyes were dark and permanently glowering, his mouth was rigidly tight-lipped and his cheeks were a fierce red that seemed to match his fiery hot temper. Everything about the man said that he was a strict disciplinarian.

When Mr Cutter taught his classes he would hold a very large and heavy bible aloft in his left hand as if he were giving a sermon. He would refer to it as the 'Good Book' and would read passages from it as if to confirm the truth in what he was teaching. It was these sort of erratic teaching habits and his wild tempers which had earned him the nickname 'Cutter the Nutter' from the school's pupils. He was, of course, unaware of this.

As David went to make his way into the classroom he stopped in the doorway and looked up at the stern faced teacher who was sliding his key back into his pocket. In an attempt to make a polite gesture he smiled at the tall man in order to greet him, but all he got in return was a well-practised scowl and another order.

"Hurry up!"

David raised his eyebrows in a shock manner and hurried into the classroom to find a seat. He was starting to wonder if the rumours about Mr Cutter were true. There were a number of stories about him having a blazing temper which he lost on a regular basis, but he had always thought that what he had heard was exaggerated.

After half an hour of the lesson, David had decided that Mr Cutter was actually a very good teacher. He explained everything clearly and precisely and had the full attention of the class at all times. Although he seemed to be rather melodramatic in his teaching methods he was actually better than most of the other teachers of the school.

Mr Cutter was teaching the story of how Jesus was resurrected after the crucifixion. He had meticulously told the pupils how God's only son was put on the cross, died and then had come back to life. As he stood in front of the class he asked his first question of the lesson.

"How did the people react when they found out that Jesus had been resurrected?"

Mr Cutter's dark eyes then scoured the classroom to see if anyone had an answer. About seven pupils had put their hands up and he looked among them to decide who should answer. When he finally made up his mind he pointed his finger at a girl by the name of Mary Welsh who was sitting near the front of the class.

"Yes, what's the answer?" His face was quite stern.

The reply was spoken in a quiet and unsure tone of voice.

"They didn't believe it at first, Sir."

"That's right. Not even his closest followers believed that he could come back from the dead." He wistfully gazed around the classroom in a manner that said that he was quite overwhelmed by the glory of what he was teaching. "Even though they saw him standing before them they still did not believe it was him. Does anyone think they know why that was?"

This time Mr Cutter pointed at David who was also still sitting with his hand up.

"Yes, you! What's your name?"

"David Cain, Sir."

"What's the answer?"

The reply was this time spoken in a confident manner.

"Because he had a completely different body and face, Sir."

"What are you talking about?" Mr Cutter frowned. "They didn't believe it was Jesus because of their amazement of the miracle."

"But in the bible, Sir, it says that Jesus had a completely different body and face."

There were now murmurs around the classroom. Some of the pupils started to make quiet remarks under their breaths.

"I never knew that."

"No one's ever told me that before."

"It wasn't him then."

Mr Cutter now realised that his pupils were starting to falter in their beliefs in what he was teaching them and he was not pleased about it to say the least.

"What are you trying to do, Cain?" He raised his bible in his left hand and pointed at it with his right. "Are you trying to tell everyone that Jesus did not resurrect from the dead? Do you want everyone here to not believe the words of the Good Book?"

David sat for a short while contemplating what to say next and then spoke his reply.

"I didn't mean to do that, Sir." He nervously tried to justify himself. "I was just saying that the disciples didn't believe it was Jesus because he looked nothing like him. It's understandable really. It does seem a bit unbelievable."

The pupils in the class gasped, Mr Cutter's eyes opened wide and David just looked around at everyone's faces wondering what he had said that was so shocking.

"Stand up, Cain!" The fuming teacher's words were spoken through clenched teeth. "Stand up right now!"

Every head in the class was now turned in David's direction as he nervously got to his feet. He inquisitively looked around at the expressions on the other pupils' faces in the hope that he might have been able to find an answer to what he had done wrong. There were, however, no clues to be found to tell of the nature of his misdeeds.

Mr Cutter slowly paced across the classroom with his bible at his side and with his eyes firmly fixed upon David. He seemed to glide across the floor in slow motion, as if in an attempt to prolong the wait of not knowing what was going to happen. As he reached the young boy's desk he grasped the bible in both of his hands.

"Do you know what it is called when someone speaks against the word of the Lord Almighty?" His face was red with rage and the words were laced with anger. "There is a single word for it."

David almost spoke too quietly to be heard.

"Blaspheme."

Mr Cutter repeated the answer in a low crackling voice.

"Blaspheme."

There was a moment of silence within the classroom and everyone sat deadly still. All of the pupils held their breaths, including David. Then the storm erupted.

"Get out of my classroom Cain, you heathen! You can spend the rest of the lesson thinking about what you have just said!" Mr Cutter shouted out his demands and held his bible out in front of him. "No one teaches the Good Book in this classroom except me! No one!"

David froze at first, and then as the order sank in he started to make his way towards the door. As he did so he did not see the rest of the pupils in the classroom cringe. He also failed to notice what they were looking at.

Mr Cutter had stepped aside, leaving a clear passage to the door and had lifted his bible up against his chest. Keeping one hand hidden behind the book he rigidly straightened his fingers into an arrow like shape. As soon as the time was right, he forced his fingers deep into David's lower back in a quick and vicious strike.

The whole class winced as a pain filled yelp sounded out across the room. This was then followed by a chorus of sickened murmurs amongst the pupils as they grimaced at what they saw. There were some of them who had also been on the end of such a blow before now.

David turned around and for a short moment stared at Mr Cutter with a look of utter hurt upon his face. Suddenly realising that he might be in for another blow he quickly turned around and made his way towards the door.

The pupils in the classroom watched the proceedings with pale faces. Although they had seen such outbursts many times before each one was as frightening as the last. They all just sat quietly, without moving a muscle so as not to draw attention to themselves.

When David got outside the classroom he closed the door behind him and rubbed his back to try to soothe the pain. He had heard that Mr Cutter was strict, but to punish someone when they had not actually done anything wrong seemed to be way over the top. All he had done was just to answer the question. He was sure that there was nothing morally wrong about that.

David had to wait out in the corridor for the remainder of the lesson and spent the time trying to think of what he could do to get himself out of the trouble in which he had unwittingly got himself into. He had come to the conclusion that he would probably be better off if he did not say anything in his defence as Mr Cutter might just let him off any further punishments as he had already missed half of the lesson. With this in mind he decided to wait patiently for the division bell to ring for the first break of the day.

When the end of the lesson finally did come, the rest of the pupils shuffled their way out of the classroom. David looked at their faces all in turn. They seemed to be looking at him with pity and an air of morbid concern. This made him come to the uncomfortable realisation that his punishment was not yet actually over with.

Mr Cutter's voice called out from inside the classroom.

"Cain, get in here now!" It sounded as though he was still as angry as half an hour before. "And hurry up!"

David waited for the last of the pupils to leave the classroom and then slowly paced his way in. Mr Cutter was unlocking a cupboard in the corner of the room and had his back to him. He did not even turn around to give out his next order.

"Close the door!"

David did as he was told and then walked towards the teacher's desk at the front of the classroom. As he looked around at the empty chairs and clear desks he realised that he was the only pupil there after the lesson had finished. This was something that he was quite sure that he was not envied for. He then heard the door close to the cupboard in the corner of the room and felt the heavy breathing teacher walk up to stand beside him.

Mr Cutter's voice was harsh and steady.

"Face me!"

David had been wondering if he should collect his books and pens off of his desk, but he now thought that it would be best just to turn around and do as he was told. His face then turned from one of concern to a twisted look of horror. It was not, however, the scowling teacher that his gaze was fixed upon, but the long straight cane that he was tightly clutching in his right hand.

Mr Cutter spoke in a menacing tone of voice.

"Put both of your hands out, palms facing up!"

"But I only..."

The plea was interrupted by a bellowed command.

"Do it!"

David slowly lifted his hands out in front of him and winced at what was inevitably just about to happen. Questions of why and how he had got into this situation had deserted his mind and were now replaced by feelings of utter fear and a numbing shock. This was such a dreadful moment that he wondered if he was having some kind of twisted nightmare.

A sneer crossed Mr Cutter's face as he spoke.

"Do you think you have the right to turn people away from the Good Book?"

David just stared at the teacher with a look of fright etched into the features of his face. He was too scared to say anything. Not that he could have found an acceptable reply to such an unanswerable question as he had just been asked.

As Mr Cutter continued with his reprimand he tapped his bible with the cane.

"No one in this classroom questions the word of God." He slowly shook his head. "Especially you!"

The temperamental teacher then leaned forward and put the bible into David's right hand, forcing the terrified boy to grasp hold of it. The weight was far too over-powering and he lowered his arm almost straight away. He had only just managed to stop the book from falling on the floor, but there was no way that he could have stopped what followed afterwards.

The cane was brought down with a loud crack onto David's left hand. He yelped as he felt the pain burn right through his skin and up his arm. There was such a feeling of physical and mental torture that he could barely hear what Mr Cutter was now saying.

"Every time you lower this book with your right hand I'll cane the left one." The fuming teacher sounded quite determined in what he was saying. "You will hold the word of the Lord Almighty in high regard or I will punish you for every time that you don't."

David tried to bring the bible up to the level it was first at, but it was just far too heavy. Another blow from the cane slashed across his palm and then another. He screamed in agony, but it did nothing to stop the punishment.

As Mr Cutter's temper got more and more out of control he continually whipped his cane across the already reddened palm. It was not long before the amount of blows amounted to over half a dozen as each one added to the already excruciating pain. Every time the flailing man struck out, he shouted out a number of words in no particular or understandable order.

"Blaspheme! Impudent! Liar!"

By now David's hand in which he was holding the bible was hanging limply by his side. His other was red raw and was shaking like a leaf. As tears flowed from his eyes he howled out for mercy.

"Please! Please!" He then shouted out one more plea with what seemed to be his last breath. "For God's sake!"

It was at this point that Mr Cutter stopped his wild punishment and spoke through clenched teeth.

"This *is* for God's sake!" He spasmodically shook his head. "And you will hear his word!"

"I will! I will!" David begged. "I promise I will!"

There was now one more final order.

"Now get out of my classroom!"

Mr Cutter pointed the cane at the door and grabbed the bible out of David's hand. His eyes were still enraged with fury whilst he breathed loudly through his nose. Which of the two was feeling the most emotions right now was not quite obvious. One felt pure anger, whilst the other knew nothing but torment.

David quickly walked over to his desk and shoved his books and pens into his bag. The pain in his hand was excruciating, but his main concern was to get out of harm's way. He was crying uncontrollably and wiped his eyes with the sleeve of his shirt. As he left the classroom he closed the door behind him and murmured some muffled words to himself.

"What was that for?" He sobbed. "Why me?"

As David walked through the corridor he carried on crying to himself and covered his tear filled eyes with his arm. Other pupils glimpsed at him as he passed them, but they all looked away just as quickly. He was unaware of their lack of concern, but right now that would not have bothered him anyway.

David finally made his way into a toilet and started to run his hand under the cold water of a tap. His palm had several red slashes across it and it was already starting to badly bruise. As he wiped the tears from his cheeks he looked at himself in the mirror over the sink. He could not help but shake his head in a dejected manner as he stared at his sorry looking reflection. Although his eyes were normally an icy blue colour they were now blood shot and constantly weeping.

Life was so unfair. When David was at home his stepfather regularly beat him, when he was on the schoolyard he was bullied by the other pupils and now it seemed he was not even safe within the four walls of the classroom. With all of these depressing thoughts he unashamedly allowed himself to carry on crying.

The pupils in the music class intently listened as Mr Scott told them of the different types of sections within an orchestra. Although he knew the pale looking boy at the front of the class had learnt all of this along time ago he still had to explain it for the good of the others in the room. The fact that he had taught it a hundred times before did not bother him, but he was sure his top pupil was starting to grow bored.

Almost like a saving grace, the division bell rang out around the school. The pupils in the room immediately started to pack their things away and headed for the door. As they did so, David stood up and made his way to the front of the class. Sitting down on the stool in front of the piano, he smiled at his teacher ready to start their usual conversation.

Ever since Mr Scott had taken over the music class he had always stayed behind after the lesson to have a friendly chat with David. They got on very well together and seemed to share the same interests. Their topics varied to everything from politics to art and history to science. Both of them enjoyed each other's company immensely.

Mr Scott began the discussion.

"Did you see the program on television last night about the Roman archaeological findings in Kent?"

"Yes! Interesting wasn't it?" David answered with a smile. "Just imagine all that gold being under you own feet."

"It was quite surprising to see those spear heads in such good condition."

"I wonder why they didn't erode."

"Maybe they were in..."

Mr Scott then stopped halfway through his sentence and started to stare at David with a frown upon his face. It was not a look of anger, but of displeasure. He had been standing up whilst he was talking, but had now come over to sit on a desk at the front of the class. For some not so apparent reason it seemed as though he was unhappy about what he was going to say.

"David, I've been noticing something about you recently which has got me rather concerned." The small man bowed his head in a morose manner. "You always seem to come to school with bumps and bruises. In fact you have one right now on the top of your head."

At that Mr Scott looked up and pointed his finger at a purple bruise on David's forehead. Both of them immediately seemed to become embarrassed by the situation and they averted their gazes from each other's eyes. There was now an uneasy silence between the two of them and they just sat unmoving whilst not quite knowing how to resolve the awkward situation.

David had made a weak attempt in the morning to comb his hair over the purple coloured bump on his head to hide his shame. He had been punished the night before with a belt buckle by his stepfather for not washing up his glass after having a drink of milk. As it was not unusual for him to have bruises he normally tried his best to cover them up by wearing extra clothes that he did not really need to. There had been a number of occasions when he had worn scarves or long sleeved jumpers so that he could cover the blemishes on his battered body, but whenever he had a mark on his face there was simply nothing he could do to hide it.

David had never been asked a question before like the one he had just been asked and he was not sure how to answer it. He could not help but feel a sense of guilt and embarrassment about it. When he finally did speak he had to clear a lump in the back of his throat first.

"I did it playing rugby."

"Is that really how it happened?"

"Yes!" There was a pause. "That's really how it happened."

At this point of the conversation Mr Scott realised that David did not really want to talk about the subject so he decided to change the topic. He was sure that he had been lied to and he could not hide his frown of displeasure. Nevertheless, he did not want to make any accusations and put his friend in such an unpleasant situation. His response was as diplomatic as it possibly could be.

"I suppose rugby is a rough game." He raised his eyebrows. "I never liked sports myself when I was at school. I always preferred the more academic subjects."

As Mr Scott made an obvious attempt to change the subject of conversation David bowed his head with shame. He had never lied before in his life, yet the first person who he had ever told an untruth to was his one and only friend. It was now even hard for him to lift his head and show his face.

David had experienced a lot of sad feelings before in his life, but never like this. He thought that he had gone through every distressing emotion possible, but it seemed as if life had a habit of always throwing something bad at him when he least expected it. So many miserable things had happened to him in his life now that he was almost getting used to it.

Mr Scott spent the rest of the break trying his hardest to keep the conversation going whilst David replied in short subdued answers. For the first time ever the two of them were pleased to hear the division bell ring for the next lesson. As they went their separate ways they both had feelings of regret and sadness.

Mr Scott wished he had never asked the question in the first place and David wished that he had never lied when he had answered. The only good thing to come from this was that at least the two of them would never make the same mistake again. One would not pry, whilst the other would not lie.

It seemed the only way that David was ever going to learn about life was by his own painful experiences. This may have been a harsh way to live, but he really did not have any choice. There was no one about to teach him otherwise.

As Mr Scott watched the pupils from his next lesson come into the classroom he could not help but think of the look he had seen on David's face. For some time now he had been suspecting that his young friend had been leading an abused home life, but after seeing the hurt in his eyes he was now absolutely sure of it. Something would have to be done.

David walked slowly through the corridor to his next lesson with his hands in his pockets and his head sadly bowed. He wished he had not lied to his friend, but he could think of no other way of keeping his stepfather's vicious beatings a secret. The reason why he could not tell anyone about it was not just because he was scared of Norman finding out that he had told on him, but because he was ashamed and embarrassed about living a loveless life of unhappiness, and that hurt more than anything else.

"Were they ashamed when they had committed abomination? Nay, they were not at all ashamed, neither could they blush. Jeremiah, chapter six, passage fifteen."

The vicar stood aloft in the pulpit looking out over the congregation. As he read passages from the bible and quoted their references he reverently held his arms out at his sides.

"Hear, O earth! Behold, I will bring evil upon this people, even the fruit of their thoughts, because they have not hearkened unto my words, nor to my law, but rejected it. Jeremiah, chapter six, passage nineteen."

Halfway through the service a lone figure got up out of a pew and started walking towards the door at the side of the church. When he cranked open the lock to leave, a few people turned their heads to see what the noise was. As the young man opened the door he took one last look at the vicar who was now turning the pages of his bible to find another chapter to read from. Shaking his head, David walked out of the church and closed the door behind him.

The vicar had spent most of the service telling the story of 'Noah and the ark' and was now reading passages from the bible. Whilst this had been going on the congregation had sat intently listening with only the occasional cough or shuffle of clothes to accompany the reverent man's teachings. When he had called for a hymn they all stood up from their seats at the same time and when he read a prayer they all got down upon their knees in unison.

David had seen and heard enough. He had come to church for the first time in his life in the search for answers, but what he found instead was something that he had sadly expected. Ever since he had received his first caning from Mr Cutter he had wanted to learn more about God. The hot-tempered teacher had told him in no uncertain terms that *he* was evil in the eyes of the Lord, so he had come to church to find out exactly what that meant.

After just twenty minutes of the service, David had come to the conclusion that if there was a God it did not matter if this deity did think that he was an evil person. He had never intentionally hurt anyone and he had never committed a crime. So, as far as speaking against the word of the bible, blaspheme, that was just not a sin.

The vicar had told the congregation that Noah had been told to build an ark to house his family and two of every species because the rest of his people were going to drown. This seemed a bit harsh considering that all life on Earth was meant to have been created by God, yet he was now killing it because he considered it to be evil.

"The Lord works in mysterious ways." The vicar had said.

David thought this was more than mysterious considering that this so called 'all powerful God' was now looking down upon *his* Earth that had been constantly ravaged in one place or another with wars, famine and hunger for the last ten thousand years. He wondered that if there was a god then surely he would sooner be nice to the people of his world rather than just *mysterious*.

When David had said to Mr Cutter that Jesus had come back to life with a different face and body he had been told that he was evil and that it was a sin to say such a thing. However, it seemed a very minor sin compared to killing thousands of people by way of drowning, starvation or pestilence. Even if he himself could work miracles he did not think that he could bring himself to do anything as terrible as that.

So, after David's first visit to a church he had come to the conclusion that if God did look upon him as an evil person then the fellow had an impudent audacity for what he had done himself over the years. Most people would probably have thought this to be a very simplistic view of religion, but to him it was obvious logic. As he made his way home he felt comforted by the fact the he alone did not think of himself as an evil person and to him that was all that mattered.

As Mr Scott walked through the doorway and into the classroom the noise lowered down to a minimum. The pupils who were still standing up shuffled their way to their seats and faced the front of the class ready for the lesson to begin. When they had finally settled down, all of their attentions immediately focused on who was standing at the front of the class, but it was not their teacher who had taken their interest.

Next to Mr Scott was a young girl who no one recognised and was obviously a newcomer to the school. She was tall with straight jet-black hair and had dark auburn coloured skin. Although all of the eyes in the classroom were now fixed upon her she did not seem to be shy or embarrassed by being at the centre of attention.

Mr Scott smiled as he introduced the new addition to his music class in his usual jovial manner.

"Now, I seem to have already got your attention so I'd like to introduce you all to Sally Moore. She has moved all the way over to here from Seattle in the United States of America and I'm sure we will all make her feel welcome." He turned to her and waved his hand towards the class. "Could you find a seat please Miss Moore?"

Sally and her parents had moved over from America just two weeks ago and had bought quite a large detached house in the expensive part of Starrow town. Her mother and father were both career minded people and worked long hours in their jobs. This had meant that their daughter had spent a lot of time left on her own whilst they were pursuing their professions and as a result she had become quite an independent young lady who had learnt from a young age to make her own decisions. There was not a depletion of love in the household due to the lack of family interaction, but instead they more than made up for it when they were together. Evenings, weekends and vacations were taken advantage of to the full and there was never any absence of affection in their moments of togetherness.

Sally's confidence in herself was more than reflected by the way in which she looked. Her whole posture was upright and self-assured. She stood with her chin held high and her gaze to the fore. This was the sort of young lady who people would know from the first moment that they saw her that they would have to treat her with a full and unwavering respect, simply because everything about her said that that was what she demanded.

Even Sally's clothes suited her proud demeanour. Her finely cut school blazer clutched at her slender frame and she wore a purple tie loosely wrapped around the collar of her blouse presenting her with a lady-like appearance. She wore a large black shoulder bag and clutched a long musical instrument case under her arm that in return gave her an air of professionalism. It was quite apparent that she had taken a fairly prolonged amount of time to apply her subtle, but alluring make-up and she had styled her shiny long black hair to the point of making it plainly obvious that she simply knew that she was utterly worth the effort. When it came to knowing her own value, her appraisal was never short of being spot on. Priceless.

As Sally started to walk towards the class some of the boys eagerly watched her in the hope that she might come and sit at a desk near them. She had even caught the attention of Martin Dent who on numerous occasions in the past had voiced his opinion of liking girls as being sissy. Every eye in the room was fixed upon her, except one.

David was quite oblivious to what was happening and was not even aware that Mr Scott had introduced a new pupil to the class. He had brought a new book about composers over the weekend and had been reading it whilst he was waiting for the lesson to begin. When he realised that the rest of the pupils had gone quiet he closed his book and faced the front of the room whilst being quite happy just to dwell in his own idle thoughts.

As Sally went to find a desk she noticed an empty chair near the front of the class next to a young boy who seemed to be the only person in the room who was not gawping at her. She decided that he appeared to look like a normal enough individual, so she elected to sit next to him. After putting her bag on the back of the chair and her case on the desk she sat down and faced the front of the classroom.

The rest of the pupils saw what had happened, Mr Scott had noticed too and now, at last, David had realised as well. At first his only reaction was for his brow to inquisitively furrow and then ever so slowly he turned his head to his right. Much to his amazement, sitting in the chair next to him was a girl who he had never seen before in his life. All he could do was stare.

It did not take long for Sally to sense that the young boy who was sitting at the desk next to her was intensely looking in her direction. She was not sure what to do, so in an attempt to be polite she turned to her left and smiled at him.

At first, David slightly raised his eyebrows in a surprised manner, but then after gaining some self-control he shyly smiled back. He did not consider it to be a bad thing, but he did wonder why the girl had not sat at one of the other desks. For the three-and-a-quarter years he had been at secondary school he had never had anyone choose to sit next to him.

After nervously greeting each other the two of them then turned to face the front of the class. Sally was sure that the boy who she was sitting next to had at first appeared to be surprised about her sitting next to him, but she was pleased to see that he had eventually returned her smile. She wondered if it was because he was just as shy as she was, only maybe he could not hide as well she could.

Mr Scott was aware that David was not very popular with the rest of the pupils at the school and he was quite sure that it had something to do with his difference in appearance. He was actually pleased to see that Sally had chosen to sit next to him, not just for the shy boy's sake, but for hers as well. Having no friends and no one to talk to at a big school in a foreign land was a lonely situation to be in and right now both of them would probably be grateful for the company.

As Mr Scott looked across the class he announced the day's lesson in a cheerful manner.

"Today I want you all to split up into groups of twos, threes and fours."

This resulted in the classroom instantly being filled with the muffled murmurs of pupils choosing who would be in each other's groups. After waiting for the noise to die down Mr Scott patiently carried on with what he was saying.

"When you've sorted out who you are going to be with I want each of you to get a musical instrument from the store cupboard." His smile became broader. "I then want each group to go to the assembly hall and compose a piece of music or a song. You will then all perform your work in front of the rest of the class."

The muttering immediately started again, only this time some of it was comprehendible.

"I don't know how to write music!"

"You aint going to get me singing!"

Mr Scott was not surprised by the reactions from the pupils. The less talented musicians often greeted this particular assignment with shyness and embarrassment. He actually considered them to be the lucky ones, as they would only have to sit through this particular lesson just the once. On a number of occasions in the past he had endured countless so called efforts at music, of which some could only be described as a mindless assembly of broken notes.

To get the lesson moving on Mr Scott unlocked the music cupboard and then turned to face the class as he spoke.

56

"Could you come and choose your instruments in an orderly fashion and then make your way to the assembly hall, please!"

Mr Scott was wise enough to send the pupils somewhere else to practice just so he would not have to listen to several groups obliterating the airwaves all at one time. Although he loved listening to music what he often heard in such lessons as these was far from melodious. It would be bad enough at the end of the lesson when he had to judge their completed work, but to have to endure it whilst they were falteringly preparing it would be unbearable.

As the pupils started choosing their instruments Mr Scott noticed that David and Sally had remained seated. He realised that the two of them were obviously going to find it hard to get partners so he decided that he should be of assistance. As he walked over towards them they both glanced up at him with bewildered looks upon their faces, but with little delay he went about acquainting them with each other.

"Sally, I'd like to introduce you to David." He nodded at both of them in turn. "Seeing that you are both sitting here by yourselves, I'm sure you won't mind partnering each other for the lesson."

At that, the two of them then turned to each other and smiled, only this time it was not a forced gesture. They were both just happy to have found someone to partner. Mr Scott could see the looks of relief upon their faces and subtly hid a smile behind his hand as he cheerfully spoke.

"David, Sally tells me she plays the flute." He pointed with his other hand at the case on her desk. "What instrument are you going to play?"

The music cupboard now appeared to be quite bare other than a symbol, a triangle and a broken drumstick. After looking around the classroom for something more practical David fixed his eyes upon what was standing in the corner. As he spoke, he motioned towards it with his hand.

"Do you mind if I use the piano, Sir?"

"Well, if you like." Mr Scott replied with an inquisitive look upon his face. "I didn't realise you played."

"I don't." David shrugged his shoulders. "But it's better than half a drumstick."

"That's true." Mr Scott nodded his head and then looked at his watch. "Well, as you two are going to be here, I'm going to see someone in the staff room about a cup of tea. I'll be gone for a while. I'm sure I can leave you two here together."

David and Sally both answered in an assured manner.

"Yes sir!"

"Sure!" A crisp American accent.

At that, Mr Scott turned around and wandered off into the corridor, following close behind the rest of the pupils who were making their way to the assembly hall.

Sally had now pulled her flute out of its case and was lovingly rubbing it down with a velvet cloth. After cleaning it of any unwanted blemishes she, much to David's interest, started to practise by going up and down the scales. His intrigue was quite evident as he spoke in an awed manner.

"How did you get to learn that?"

Sally stopped playing and turned to David.

"I've had lessons. It's not too hard. You get better if you practice." She spoke in an encouraging manner. "You should learn to play an instrument. It's quite enjoyable really."

"I should imagine it is." David looked at the piano. "I suppose could start now."

"There's no time like the present." Sally urged. "I know what the notes are on a piano. I can show you, if you like?"

"Really?" David immediately stood up and started to make his way across the classroom. "Could you show me what you were doing just then please?"

Sally got up out of her seat and followed David over to the piano. When she got there she pressed the key middle 'C' and started to explain.

"This is the note middle 'C'." At that Sally put her flute to her mouth and played the same note. "And now this is the key of 'C'." She then played the key of 'C' on the piano and then on her flute. David watched intently at what she was doing and nodded his head in an understanding manner. She then played the key of 'E' on the piano.

"This is 'E'." This she also played on her flute and then looked at David to see if he understood. "Do you see how it works?"

"Yes. The black keys are sharps or flats."

"That's right. You have a go."

David sat on the stool in front of the piano whilst Sally stood watching over him. First he played the key of 'C' and then 'E'. It had not taken him long to work it all out and he confirmed his comprehension as he put his calculations to the test.

"If those are the keys of 'C' and 'E'." He kept looking at the keyboard whilst he was talking. "This must, therefore, be 'A'."

At that David played the key of 'A' perfectly.

"And this must be 'B' minor." Again it was played without error. "The rest of the keys must be just as obtainable in the same way."

Sally stood watching over the piano with a look of astonishment across her face as she remarked upon what she was observing.

"You catch on fast."

David turned around and looked up at her with a retiring expression as he tried to explain himself.

"Well, you started me off."

Sally smiled and bowed her head in a shy manner.

"I think we should start composing?" She asked a rhetorically.

"I think you're right." Came the reply.

As the two of them got down to work they both experimented with ideas on their respective instruments. At first David played with just one hand, but after a while he realised that by using his left hand as well it gave the music depth, so he started to use both.

Sally played some tunes on her flute that she had taught herself before and when David played at the same time on the piano it sounded quite melodious. After a while they had managed to put together a short tune and were quite happy with what they had composed. Now all they had to do was wait for the rest of the class to get back and then perform it.

Mr Scott walked into the room with the rest of the pupils following close behind carrying their instruments. As he stood at the front of the class he waited patiently for everyone to settle down. He was not sure who was dreading this most, him or them.

The expressions on the faces of some of the pupils seemed quite nervous about performing their pieces of music in front of the rest of the class. There were a few groups who appeared to be still trying to put together their work at the last moment. A feeling of dreaded anticipation could be felt throughout the whole room.

Mr Scott took a deep breath and then called for the first group to come up to the front of the class to perform their effort at composing.

"Could I have Martin Dent's group, please." He thought it would be wise to get the worst over with as soon as possible. "If you could come to the front of the class?"

Martin looked up and sneered.

"Aw! Jesus Christ, Mr Scott! Why do I have to go first?"

"So you can set the standard, Martin." A sarcastic reply. "I'm sure your talent will shine through."

"Oh! I suppose you're right."

Mr Scott allowed himself a slight smile.

As Martin and his group tromped their way up to the front of the room they all wore miserable and embarrassed expressions upon their faces. Between them one had a maraca, one had a tambourine and the other had a guitar with just five strings. The rest of the pupils could sense that they were not going to be in for a musical treat.

Martin stood at the front of the classroom holding the guitar with a forced look of exaggerated confidence upon his face. Steve Harding held his maraca with both hands, while Barry Barnet clutched his tambourine out in front of himself with a clenched fist ready to hit it. None of them actually liked music, but they had decided to take the subject as an option because they considered it to be a *doss*. Had they have known that they were going to have to participate in a lesson like this they probably would have played truant.

Martin looked across the classroom and sheepishly announced the name of their effort.

"Our song is called 'Death on the Fields'."

This was greeted with a round of disapproving mutters from the class and a muffled grunt from Mr Scott. At this, he nodded his head in a self assured manner and smiled proudly.

The piece began with Martin stamping his foot on the floor three times in an attempt to signify the start to his fellow musicians; however, the other two were oblivious to his intentions. In a sudden outburst of ferocity, he started strumming his five string guitar, without a hint of melody and with no accompaniment whatsoever. After a short while he realised that he was performing a solo, so he took no time in instructing the other two to join in.

"Come on, for Christ sake!"

At this Steve violently started shaking his maraca with both hands, whilst Barry repeatedly punched his tambourine. There was not a hint of consistency in their timing and the rest of the class was visibly wincing at the racket that was being made. Even Mr Scott had now slapped himself on the forehead and had slumped down in his chair in an exasperated manner. It was not, however, the mind numbing din that grabbed the most attention, but the lyrics of the song. Martin shouted them out just loud enough for the words to be heard over the noise of the instruments.

"Get them in the fields! Get them in the fields! Load your guns! Load your guns! Round them up! Round them up! Drop your bombs! Drop your bombs! And when they're all there, kill everyone of the fu..."

He was now interrupted not a moment too soon.

"Thank-you, Martin!" Mr Scott wiped his brow with his handkerchief and let out an exasperated sigh. "I think that will be enough."

Martin tried to plea for some artistic licence.

"What? But that was the best part."

"I'm sure it was, but we don't have that much time." Mr Scott replied diplomatically. "If you could sit down, please!"

The three unlikely musicians put their instruments back into the cupboard and shuffled their way back to their seats. There was now a stunned silence throughout the room as the rest of the class just sat unmoving, wondering what exactly that they had just been subjected to. After what they had just heard the lull in noise was a welcome rest.

59

The music lesson was now coming to an end and the only two people to have not performed their piece were David and Sally. A couple of the efforts had not been too bad, but the others had left a lot to be desired. Mr Scott could not hide the relief in his voice as he called for the final group.

"And last of all could David and Sally come up to the front of the class and perform their piece please?"

At that, the two of them sheepishly made their way over to the piano and got ready to perform. Most of the class sat with their heads in their hands or with their gaze going to another part of the room. By this time the pupils seemed to be just as pleased as their teacher was that the music lesson was coming to an end. They had all had their eardrums savaged by what was mostly a relentless crashing and banging of relatively good conditioned instruments.

Mr Scott looked at his watch and politely prompted the two hopeful musicians.

"You haven't much time."

The two of them sat with their instruments at the ready and then their piece began. David started with a slow tempo, using just his left hand on the piano keyboard to produce a succession of low notes. It was at a quiet and subtle pulse and its mellifluous splendour filled the classroom with a restful sway.

Mr Scott had been fiddling with his tie, but had now had his attention taken over by the smooth music. Some of the pupils in the class had also turned their minds to what they were now hearing. Early signs showed that this just might not be yet another torturous racket for them to endure.

David now introduced his right hand, first with a long high note and then stepping down the scale blending the piece into a satisfying melody.

Even more of the pupils in the class had now sat up and were looking in wonder as David effortlessly danced his fingers across the piano keyboard. It was as if they were forced to give their attention as the tuneful waves of notes washed over the classroom and mentally soaked them. As Mr Scott watched his young pupil captivate the class he sat back in his chair and smiled to himself in a relaxing posture.

The music then stopped, but only for a short moment. It was a brief pause so as to introduce Sally's flute. She started with a long unwavering note that reached out and ensnared the attention of everyone in the classroom. As she too then glided down the scale, David reintroduced the imposing solemnity of the piano and blended the tune into a melodious harmony.

As the two of them performed their piece the whole class was held under the enchanting spell of the sweet sounding tune. All eyes were fixed upon them as they played their instruments with an effortless perfection. Even Martin Dent and his friends were blissfully captivated by the delicate sound of the duet.

Whilst David was playing the piano he could not help but divide his concentration and listen to Sally's flute. He thought it sounded like the soft voice of an angel singing out from the heavens. A smile crossed his face as he too enjoyed the dulcet beauty of the precious moment.

When their piece finally came to an end Sally finished on a long note which became more and quieter, until it faded out into an obscure silence. David completed the ending on the piano with a few low notes at a slow tempo until he also finished in the same manner as his partner.

A deep lull then swept over the class as all the pupils just stared towards the front of the room. Mr Scott was sitting with a peaceful look upon his face which then turned to a frown when he realised the piece was over. David and Sally just looked at each other and smiled. When they turned to see the class's reaction all they saw was a room full of faces gawping in their direction.

The silence lingered on for a while, but was eventually broken by the distant ringing of the division bell signifying the beginning of the lunch break. This was immediately followed by the dinning noise of chairs scraping across the floor as the pupils stood up to leave. David and Sally just remained seated with contented expressions upon their faces, whilst Mr Scott walked over to the piano and proudly smiled at the both of them. He spoke his praise in an applauding manner.

"Well done! That was extremely good." He looked at Sally and smiled. "You're quite a good flautist."

"Thank you, Sir." She replied shyly. "I try to practice as much as possible."

Mr Scott turned to David.

"That was not bad for your first visit to a piano."

"I did have some help, Sir." David gestured towards Sally.

"I showed him the key of 'C'." She raised her eyebrows. "The rest he picked up himself."

David bowed his head in a flush of embarrassment.

At that, Mr Scott turned to leave with a grin on his face and bid farewell to the both of them.

"I'll see you two later."

"Bye, Sir!" They replied in unison.

There was now a static silence as the two of them suddenly realised that they were now alone in the classroom together. At first they were too shy to look at one another, but they could both feel the same attraction and could not help but impulsively turn their heads to face each other. As soon as their eyes met their expressions lit up into bashful smiles and their delight became quite evident.

As David looked at Sally he felt an emotion of which he had never experienced before. What he could see in Sally was something that he had never seen in another girl at the school. They either all just ignored him or joined in with the ritual hurling of cruel remarks in his direction. She seemed to have an aura of affection and tenderness in the way in which she spoke to him. The glowing warmth from her smile sent a wave of strength flowing throughout his body, and yet at the same time it made him feel pleasantly weak.

As Sally looked at David she lightly bit her lip. He seemed to be nervous like a shy child, but whenever he spoke his words were strong and deliberate. She was sure that she could see a sense of fear in his eyes as if he was scared of something, but if he was, he was trying his best not to let it show. There seemed to be some kind of inner strength that oozed out of him, but at the same time there was something ominously fragile deep within that mystifying mind.

It was up to Sally to finally break the silence.

"I see there's a fish and chip shop over the road from the school." She started to put her flute into its case so as to make it look as if she were making idle conversation. "What's it like?"

I hope he asks me to go to lunch with him.

"It's OK." David replied in an over sure manner to hide his nerves. "I get my lunch from there every day."

I wonder if she will go to lunch with me?

"Good. I'm quite hungry."

Ask me! Ask me!

"Well..." A timid pause. "Would you like to come over there with me?"

Please say yes!

61

"Yes! I'd love to." Sally tried to hide her happiness, but she failed miserably. "Thank you!"

I thought he'd never ask.

She said yes. I don't believe it. Wow!

David got his bag from on top of his desk and waited for Sally at the door. As she put her flute case under her arm she turned to him with an inquisitive look upon her face and spoke in a like manner.

"Do you really have chips every day, David?"

"Well, no. Not every day." He shrugged his shoulders. "Too much cholesterol is bad for you."

In fact, David rarely went to the fish and chip shop, but he did not think that either of them would be bothered over such a small fact. Their whole conversation had really just been a play of words, but neither of them would have wanted it any other way. As they left the classroom they both allowed themselves an abashed smile at their attempts to hide their feelings.

David and Sally had soon become good friends and had spent the rest of the week together. Every break they had at school they arranged to meet each other either in the library or on the schoolyard. They had found out that they lived just a matter of streets away from each other so they even sat next to each other on the school bus. From the very moment that they had first met they were completely inseparable.

Sally had found out that David liked reading about near enough every subject there was apart from religion. He seemed to be a happy person who always looked towards the brighter side of life. Whenever they talked about anything that was less than a cheerful topic he would always change the subject to something more pleasant.

It had not taken long for David to realise that Sally was a strong headed young lady. She was very sure in her views, but she was not single minded in her thoughts. Although she had a petite and slender frame, she also had an innermost strength of character.

The two of them found each other invitingly attractive on an intellectually and physically alluring basis. David had never had these sorts of thoughts about a girl before and it was a whole new unexplored feeling. Up until now he had only felt a mild happiness about his friendship with Mr Scott and as for the other side of his life that just brought emotions of sorrow, fear and hurt. He was unsure of what he was experiencing, but he knew that he was enjoying it.

Sally had had a lot of friends at her previous school in America and was sorry to have parted with them. Nevertheless, she was quite a charismatic girl and she knew it would not be long before she met new companions. However, of all the other friends that she had ever had she had never met someone quite like David. The way he looked, the way he acted and the way he talked were all things that made it hard for her to get him out of her mind.

On the last school day of the week on the bus home David and Sally had had a conversation which had lead to them arranging to meet each other in the park the next day. The two of them had made sure that they had finished all of their homework the night before so they could spend the whole day together. They had practically been with each other for the whole week, so they might as well have kept it going for over the weekend as well.

As David was putting on his coat in the hallway he could sense that Norman was looking intensely at him from the top of the stairs. He had learnt by now to ignore his stepfather as much as possible just to keep out of harm's way, so he did not react to the attention that he was getting. However, the weight of the heavy stare was starting to burden him and it was not long before the silence was broken by a question followed by a profanity.

"Where are you going?"

David looked up at him just before turning the handle on the front door.

"To the park."

"Why?" Norman sneered. "It's not even sunny."

"I just want some fresh air." David shrugged his shoulders and lowered his gaze in an uncomfortable manner.

Norman started to make his way down the stairs and came to stand in front of his stepson.

"There's nothing wrong with the air in this house." He folded his arms. "What's so special about a cold park?"

David knew that Norman was just being awkward and wanted to cause trouble, so he did his best not to say anything which would provoke him. He just stood in front of his stepfather with a slight frown and with his eyes averted away from temperamental man's gaze. It was now just a matter of waiting and hoping for the situation to pass off as peacefully as possible.

Norman poked David in the ribs to make sure he had his attention.

"It sounds like to me that you think your mother and me aint good enough company for you. Maybe we bore that head of yours." He paused for a moment and then produced a sneering smirk. "Go on, piss off you little runt!"

"Thank you!"

David had tried his best to sound grateful and even forced a brief smile in return. As he opened the front door and started to walk out of the house he felt Norman's palm hit him on the back of the head. His stepfather laughed in a playful manner, but he was the only one wearing a smile.

A thick blanket of clouds hid the sun, but it was a sunny day inside David's heart. He sat on a park bench whilst waiting expectantly for Sally to turn up. His excitement was almost too erratic to keep under control and he consistently shifted about on the seat in a fidgeting manner.

As Sally walked out from behind a war memorial in the middle of the park, David eagerly stood up and started to smile broadly. She waved at him as soon as she saw him standing by the bench and also failed miserably at trying to contain her excitement. Deep down, of course, they both knew how the other felt.

Sally called out the first greeting as she approached.

"Hi, David!"

"Hi, Sally!" An eager the reply.

"Have you been waiting long?"

"No. I've only just got here." David started to walk towards Sally. "You didn't spend too long trying to find me did you?"

"No!"

There was now a pause in the conversation as the two of them stood in front of each other with sparkling eyes and bright smiles. They almost appeared to be content with just looking at each other without saying a word. Not that they needed to say anything. Their faces said it all.

Sally then looked over her shoulder towards the sunset and squinted. As she turned back to David she moved closer to him.

"Shall we walk?" She moved closer still. "It's a big park. We might as well make the most of it."

"OK!"

It was then when David felt Sally's hand slide into his. At first he was surprised and it showed as his jaw dropped open. But as he felt her soft skin press against his palm he experienced a satisfyingly warm rush of blood flow up his arm and throughout his body. His expression then turned to one of a satisfying pleasure.

David did not feel shy when he was with Sally, but he was not sure how to act when they were so close together. He sometimes had urges to touch and hold her, but there was a part of him that kept his feelings in check. It was probably because he was not sure if she felt the same way about him.

As David and Sally slowly walked through the park they listened intently to each other's pleasant conversation. It did not matter how long they talked for, the other would never get bored of just hearing the other's voice. They found each other to be interesting, amusing and affectionate.

Whilst they walked, David wondered if Sally had been having the same sleepless nights as he had had over the last few days. It was tiring, but at the same time it created a warm feeling of contentment. With his life full of sadness and strife there suddenly seemed to be a light at the end of a very long dark tunnel.

There was now a break in the conversation and Sally started to wonder if David had been thinking about her as much as she had been about him. Whether it was when she was in class at school or when she was at home she could not stop thinking about him. It was happening so constantly that it almost hurt. However, she had heard that pain was meant to be very close to pleasure and she could not imagine that it could possibly get any closer to what she had been feeling.

It was while they were walking amongst the trees by a pond when the expression on David's face changed into one of horror. Standing by a park bench about fifty yards in front of them was Martin Dent and his gang. The peaceful moment appeared as though it was about to come to an abrupt end.

David straight away started thinking about how he could get past Martin without being noticed. However, the real problem was trying to manage it without Sally realising what was going on. It was not going to be easy. The last thing he wanted was for her to know that he spent the whole of his life constantly being bullied.

As David looked at Sally she glanced up at him with a warm smile. He would hate it if she were to get involved while Martin was beating him up. She seemed to be quite a wilfully strong girl and would probably try to stick up for him. If she were to get hurt because of him he would never be able to forgive himself.

It was at that point that David looked up to see that the situation had now got worse. Standing in the distance staring at him wearing a sardonic smile upon his face and with his fists clenched was Martin. His expression was one of a threatening menace.

After thinking about the situation as quickly as possible, David decided that it would be best if he was to just say that he had to go home. He did not want to go, but it was the only way of keeping Sally out of harm's way. All of his concern was now concentrated on her safety, so much so that he had almost forgotten about his own welfare.

David turned to Sally with a vexed frown and spoke in a strained manner.

"I'm sorry, but..." He paused. "I've got to go."

"Why?" The reply was short and spoken in a hurt tone of voice.

"I've got to do something at home." David hurried his speech as the two of them got closer to Martin's gang. "I'm really sorry, but I have to leave right now."

Sally looked at David with a sad and concerned expression upon her face. She could sense that there was something wrong, but she could not work out what it was. Although she did not want him to leave, she could not help but feel in the back of her mind that it was somehow for the better.

David shook his head in a morose manner as he saw the look of sorrow appear on Sally's face. He felt bad about lying to her and he almost wanted to let her know why he was really going. However, the embarrassment of telling her that he was actually weak and was constantly victimised made him decide to keep her from knowing the truth.

David's plan was to run past Martin Dent and his gang so that they would follow him. His main concern was to make sure that he led them away from Sally. Whether they caught up with him or not was another problem all together. He just wanted to make sure that he was not to be seen getting a beating off of them.

Just before David left he turned to Sally and said his farewell in a wounded manner.

"I'm so sorry!" He let go of her hand. "Good-bye, Sally!"

At that, he made a run for it.

The chase was soon on as Martin Dent and his gang saw their victim make for his escape. As David weaved his way throughout the trees he looked over his shoulder to see that his pursuers were making good ground on him. He was sure that he had brought them far enough away from Sally and he now felt quite relieved that she would not be involved, even though it was quite likely that he was about to get a beating.

Unfortunately for David, Sally had watched him as he raced off into the trees. She was hoping that he would at least turn back to face her and wave whilst he was on his way, but he had instead just kept on running. It was while she was watching him that she saw Martin Dent's gang charging after him shouting out obscenities and threats. With a concerned inquisitiveness, she had decided to follow them to see what was going on.

David was running as fast as he could, but the gang of thugs were constantly getting closer to him. At one point he found himself running across a football pitch whilst a match was being played. A number of the players instantly started to shout out profane remarks at him to get off of the pitch. His pursuers followed his exact route, only when they were sworn at by the footballers they replied with equally foul mouthed remarks.

David could now hear the footsteps of his attackers closing in on him. It was not long before one of them had taken a swing at his legs with a boot, sending him scrawling across the muddy ground. He soon found that he was being kicked from every angle and in every part of his body.

Normally, when David was getting beaten up all that went through his mind was fear and a hoping for it to stop. However, on this occasion he was just thinking about his gladness that Sally was not there to witness it. He would not have liked his fall from grace to be seen by the one person who clearly had a great degree of respect for him.

When the gang had finally decided they had done enough they pulled away and started to walk off. However, just before turning to leave Martin stood over David and made one last threat.

"This park is mine." He sneered. "So you stay out of it!"

David tried to stand up, but could not help wobbling and almost fell back down again. When he did finally manage to get his balance he looked at Martin with a curious expression upon his face. For some reason he was not as scared of the menacing skinhead as he usually was and with this in mind he decided to do a silly thing. In a studious tone of voice he answered back.

"Why *do* you bully me, Martin?"

David knew that he would be punished further for putting forward such a question, but he did not care. That inner strength he had been feeling since spending time with Sally flowed through his veins and gave him a sense of self worth that he had never felt before. It was almost as if it were a barrier of protection around his body.

Martin was not pleased with what he had just been asked and his verbal, then physical reply was not at all surprising.

"Fuck off!"

The punch landed right on David's nose sending him crashing back to the ground. As he sat there a small trickle of blood ran from his nose and he dazedly shook his head. He should have expected such a response and in an ironic sort of way he almost felt as though he had deserved what he had just got.

Martin just took a moment to look at David whilst the battered boy sat on the ground before him. He was rather perplexed at why such a weakling had just deliberately provoked him and had virtually asked to be hit. With a confused expression upon his face he made a parting gesture to the rest of his gang and turned to leave.

David did not get up off of the ground straight away. Instead he just sat there nursing his wounds. He took a moment to wipe the blood from his nose with the back of his hand and rubbed his ribs with the other. It was at this point a handkerchief fell from above onto his lap. He instantaneously looked up to see who had dropped it and, much to his horror, he saw Sally standing over him with streams of tears running from her eyes. With a broken tone of voice, she spoke to him in a pleading manner.

"Why didn't you tell me?"

David's expression had now turned to one of anguish and sorrow. It hurt like hell to see Sally crying and what was worse was that it was because of him. As he answered her question he shook his head.

"I'm so sorry. I just..." He paused and momentarily closed his eyes. "I just didn't want you to get involved."

Sally bent down and softly grasped hold of one of David's hands. She then lifted it up so as to help him off of the ground. As he got to his feet he looked into her eyes and frowned. She just moved closer and spoke in a soft manner whilst still keeping hold of his hand.

"I want you to promise me something."

David nodded his head in reply, but Sally was not satisfied and prompted him for a verbal answer.

"Are you going to promise me?"

"Yes." David nodded his head as he wiped the blood from his nose with the handkerchief. "I'll promise whatever you ask for."

Sally lowered her gaze.

"Next time you ever have to go through anything like that I want to be there right by your side." She now looked back into his eyes. "I don't care if you're being hurt, insulted or whatever people like that do to you. I just want to be there standing right next to you to help you through it, because that's what partners are for."

David stared into Sally's eyes with a look of awe. The strength that she had was breathtaking. She was standing in front of him telling him that she was willing to equally take any pain that he might go through. No one had ever given him anything as remotely valuable as the loyalty that she was offering him right now.

Sally then finished her plea in her crisp American accent.

"And if I should get hurt, then that's my own fault." She put her hand on her chest. "So you promise me right now that you will never leave my side like that again."

David gulped. He would have cried with happiness if he had not thought that it would make him look weak. His answer was what Sally had expected.

"I promise I will never leave your side like that again." He took a deep breath. "But I will never let you get hurt while you are by my side. I'll protect you with my every last bit of strength."

Sally smiled and then moved even closer towards David. Her expression was one of desire and expectancy. As she made yet another request she looked at his lips.

66

"Now kiss me, you fool!" Her expression now begged him to do as she wished. "Just damn well kiss me!"

David's breath had left him at the very instant that he heard Sally's request. He was not, however, so shocked that he could not do as he had been told. Slowly closing his eyes he leant his head down and softly kissed her lips for one long arousing moment.

David felt a flush of excitement flow through his body. Her lips felt as soft as the smoothest silk and tasted as sweet anything he had ever experienced. He wished the moment would never end and he was sure Sally was feeling the same way.

As they carried on kissing David had forgotten about the blood stained handkerchief in his hand and he let it fall lightly to the ground. After all of the violence and commotion that there had been there was now a just a still silence throughout the park. The only two things that were not motionless were the vivaciously beating hearts of the two young lovers.

On the outskirts of the park a gang of young boys were scuffling their way home. As they walked their leader spoke in a proud and boisterous manner.

"It's always a good laugh beating the crap out of Cain."

One of his friends agreed.

"Yeah, I bet he's in agony right now."

In the middle of the park there were two lovers loving.

The blows were hard, the pain was agonising and the blood flowed. David lay on the floor, holding his bruised ribs with one hand and wiping his cut lip with the back of the other. As he tried to get up he started to feel dizzy, so he steadied himself and waited for the numbness to pass. After a while, the disorientation faded and he managed to straighten himself up.

It was David's first day back at school after the Christmas holidays and he had already been ruffed up. Whenever he had received a beating up until now he would only feel the pain of the blows and the humiliation of the embarrassment. However, now that he had met Sally there was a new suffering to be concerned with. She hated it when she saw him with cuts and bruises and to see her distressed made him feel even worse.

Sally and David had now been very close for a number of months and were still as inseparable as ever. They spent their days at school together as well as their weekends. The only reason why they ever parted ways was to go home to bed or because they had separate lessons at school. Luckily, the beating he had just had was one of those times when she was not around.

David had come to the conclusion that whenever he had been bullied it would be best not to tell Sally. This was not so much as to hide his embarrassment, but so as not to upset her. He found that he seemed to have more concern for her well being than his own.

As David leant against the wall of the corridor nursing his wounds he watched the perpetrators of his beating making their way up the corridor boasting about their triumph. They were all in the same year as him and the five of them were either bigger or the same size as him. They offered little excuse for what they had done, but one of them had shouted out hurtful insults whilst the beating had been taking place.

"You ugly, big headed, wanker!" The callous remarks had been just as painful as the blows.

As David pushed himself off of the wall he dusted himself down and checked his clothes for rips. He then felt a drop of blood fall from his lip and looked down just in time to see it splash against the floor. Realising that his face was probably in quite a state, he decided that he ought to get to a toilet so as to clean himself up. Fortunately, there was one close by, although he had a strong feeling that the bullies had not chosen this place for the beating just for his convenience.

As soon as David got to the toilet he looked at himself in the mirror. It was not unusual for him see his face in such a battered state and he sighed as he saw a bruise on his right eye already starting to swell. This would almost certainly mean that Sally would find out about what had happened.

Whilst he was cleaning his wounds with a piece of toilet paper he began to think about what had happened when he was receiving the beating. At one point he remembered being held against the wall by one of the bullies so that the rest of them could hit him. He had tried to struggle free from the hold, but found that he did not have the strength to escape. It was this that had started to make him wonder about his physical state.

David rolled up the sleeve on his right arm and tried to flex his biceps. There was not much muscle to be seen and he frowned at the sight of his weak frame. As he looked back at his face in the reflection of the mirror he spoke to himself in a quiet but resolved manner.

"I need to be stronger." He nodded his head as if to agree with himself. "Then I can get away from them. They won't be able to hurt me if I'm not there."

David straight away began to think about how he was going to start making himself a stronger and fitter person. He knew that it would take some time to get into a reasonably muscular state, but he had already decided that it was going to be well worth it. As he left the toilet with his cut lip and swollen eye he wore a satisfied smile and had a head full of determined thoughts of how things were now going to be.

Mr Scott looked up at the clock on the wall behind him and then turned back to face the class.

"All right you budding young musicians, tidy up your things and when the bell rings I want you all out of my sight!"

As Mr Scott smirked at the pupils some of them acknowledged his humorous request by grinning back at the kind hearted teacher. The division bell then sounded out and the classroom was filled with the noise of chairs being scraped across the floor. Whilst the room was starting to clear David stayed seated while Sally got up out of her chair. She looked down at him and smiled.

"I'll see you tomorrow then!" As she walked off she affectionately waved her fingers at him and called out one last farewell. "Bye!"

"Bye!" He replied in a jovial manner.

Sally slung her school bag over her shoulder and shuffled her way out of the classroom with the rest of the pupils. She would have normally stayed with David after school, but on this occasion she was going to meet her mother to go shopping in town. It was a trip that they had planned a while back as the two of them had decided to treat themselves to a new dress each.

David got up and walked across the room to sit down at the stool in front of the piano. It had come to be quite a regular occurrence for him to stay behind after school to practise playing music. He had now reached quite a good standard and had learnt to play a number of tunes. Mr Scott would also stay behind some nights just to listen to him practice and would say for a joke that his pupil was his prodigy; although it was obvious to them both who was really the better pianist.

"Mind if I stay and listen?" Mr Scott came and sat at a chair next to the piano. "I've got fifteen minutes."

"Of course!" David replied amicably. "I've learnt a new piece of music actually."

"Really? What's that?"

"Beethoven's 'Moonlight Sonata'." David stretched his fingers on the back of his hands. "It's a nice piece, isn't it?"

Mr Scott nodded his head in agreement, but wore a puzzled expression as he carried on the conversation.

"When did you learn that?"

"Last night in the town library." David turned to face the piano and rested his fingers lightly upon the keyboard. "I read one of the manuscript books from the music section."

Mr Scott just smiled and sat back in his chair. He would rarely come across a time when his young friend would not surprise him with his seemingly limitless intellect. What he had yearned to do with music for all his life this boy could do with the minimal amount of effort in the least amount of time.

For as long as Mr Scott could remember he had wanted to be able to read music and then go off and play it without a sheet of manuscript paper in sight. Yet David had learnt to be able to do just that in only a matter of months of playing the piano and what made it more enviable was that he had taught himself. His teacher could not help but feel a certain amount of jealousy, but at the same time he felt the deepest of admiration.

David looked down at the dusty piano keyboard where several of the keys had lost their ivory and took in a deep breath. Then the music flowed. Every note was timed to perfection and was played with an unconsummated ease. As his fingers swept across the keyboard he turned around to face his teacher to talk. The notes, however, did not falter and still kept on flowing with the same unwavering precision.

"I read Beethoven's 'Pathétique Sonata' as well." The expression upon his face showed little concentration in what he was doing with his hands. "I'll try to play that as well afterwards."

Still David kept on idly talking whilst producing the smooth sounding music which washed across the classroom.

"I'm not sure who I prefer actually, Mozart or Beethoven. They're both as good as each other, I think?" He answered his own question. "I suppose I haven't got a preference."

Mr Scott watched with a mystified look upon his face. He wondered if David actually realised that there were times when he could be mistaken for being a show-off. However, he knew this young man and he was not the type to ever intentionally do anything to frustrate or annoy someone else. It was just the way he did things. Everything seemed to be so *bloody* easy.

As Mr Scott leaned forward on his chair he spoke in an inquisitive tone of voice.

"David, what do you plan on doing when you leave school?"

At first David's expression was thoughtful and then he answered.

"Carry on learning." Was all he said.

"University?"

"Yes, I suppose so." David shrugged his shoulders. "I want to learn as much as possible."

"You would enjoy it there." Mr Scott nodded his head in a positive manner. "I did when I was there."

It was then when David stopped playing the piano halfway through a bar. He turned his whole body around to face his teacher and bowed his head in a shy manner. When he spoke he sounded unsure and inferior.

"To tell you the truth, I want to learn more for a reason..." He paused and looked up. "I want to make a difference. I know it sounds stupid, but I want to do things to help other people."

"That isn't stupid." Mr Scott smiled in admiration. "Why shouldn't you want to make things better for others?"

David spoke shyly.

"Well, it's a bit unlikely, isn't it?" He shrugged his shoulders. "I don't just want to be a doctor, a scientist or a politician. I want to be all three and more."

Mr Scott shook his head and looked straight at David. He had always thought a lot of this young man, but now he knew just how special he really was. Most schoolboys of his age would never have said such a thing as he just had and not only did have the nerve to say it, but he would also have the courage to go through with what he had said.

Mr Scott spoke in awe.

"David, don't underestimate yourself! You see, you should never let anyone tell you what to do." His expression became thoughtful. "Make it so it's *you* who decides; because if there's anyone who can achieve exactly what they want in life, it's you!"

David looked at his teacher for a short moment and then lowered his gaze. He was not sure whether he should feel flattered or embarrassed after hearing such a compliment. However, after taking a while to think about what Mr Scott had said he came to a revealing conclusion. If he did not do what he wanted to do he would simply be wasting his talents, and that could only be a loss to himself and anyone else who might have benefited from them.

Turning around to face the piano David carried on playing Beethoven's 'Moonlight Sonata' from exactly the point that he had stopped. Mr Scott just smiled and nodded his head in a contented manner.

"Forty-eight! Forty-nine! Fifty!"

David dropped to the floor and started to breathe heavily in an exhausted manner. He had been doing exercises all evening and had only just finished by completing his last set of fifty press-ups. As he got up onto his knees he took a glass of orange juice off of his bedside cabinet and had a large, well deserved gulp.

Ever since David had taken up exercising he had managed to fit in about three evening sessions a week. He was already starting to feel the difference in how healthy he felt and it was not just because of the training. Over the last few months he had also changed his eating habits by concentrating on all of the right food groups to build up his muscles and give him energy.

Not only was David now starting to win at the sporting events in his physical education class at school, but his appearance was a lot different as well. He had suddenly found that he was getting bulges where he had never had them before. All of his clothes used to fit him quite well, but now they were starting to become a bit too tight in various areas. It was a good thing that he still had his paper-round, just so he could afford to buy new clothes for himself.

David had, of course, not just relied on brawn to develop his physique. On a number of occasions he had gone to the town library and had read books on nutrition, human physiology and physical training. With his will to accomplish in what he was doing combined with his new knowledge of the workings of human biology his exercising had come on in leaps and bounds.

It was, however, not just David who was starting to notice the difference in his appearance. Sally was more than happy with his tightly muscled physique and his sturdy frame. She had suddenly found herself thinking things about him that she had never thought of any man before and she made no attempt at trying to dispel her daring thoughts.

As David walked out of his room to go to the bathroom he heard some talking coming from downstairs. At first he heard a number of swearwords and immediately thought that there might be another argument going on. Just to find out whether he should now keep out of the way he leant over the landing banister and listened to what was going on.

"That wanker thinks he's a hard nut!" Norman's usual low brow conversation. "I could kick him shitless without even thinking about it!"

There was no reply to the comment and David now realised that Norman was on the telephone to one of his friends. As the conversation carried on there were yet more profane ridden, thug like boasts.

"I'll tell you what, when we next see him, Phil, we'll sort him out! That'll teach him to spill his beer on you!" There was a pause. "It don't matter if it was an accident. The twat shouldn't have done it!"

All David could do was shake his head in a saddened manner. He could not understand why Norman felt as though he had to use his size and powerful physique just to hurt other people who did not deserve it. That was something he would never do himself, no matter how strong he became. As he walked off into the bathroom he muttered a quiet remark in soliloquy.

"You should try helping someone for once!" He breathed out an exasperated sigh. "You never know, you might like it!"

The smell of the brand new suit filled the bedroom with a pleasing aroma. It was hanging proudly on a coat hanger on the edge of the wardrobe and still had the price label attached to one of the sleeves. One-hundred-and-ninety pounds was a lot of money for a fifteen-year-old boy to spend on a piece of clothing, but to David it was well worth the amount he had paid. It had taken months of saving, but second to having Sally it was his most valued possession.

Up until now, he had spent most of his newspaper round money on taking Sally out and getting her gifts. She had on a number of occasions told him that he should not just treat her to things, but to instead get himself something that he would like. Therefore, after months of saving he had now bought himself the very classy suit.

As David walked into his bedroom he slipped on a well-ironed white shirt and a flung a tie around his neck. His hair was neatly combed and his black shoes had been painstakingly polished. He then turned around to look at his new suit with a proud expression upon his face. The broad smile that he wore said it all.

When David got to the foot of the stairs he stopped to look at himself in the mirror. He had removed the label from the sleeve of the jacket and was now putting it on for the first time. It fit perfectly and capped his whole demeanour of with a touch of style.

As David left the house, he closed the front door behind him and nodded his head in a self-satisfied manner.

Sally's parents had gone away for the weekend and they were leaving her at home on her own. They had asked if she had wanted to go along with them, but she had declined and said that she would rather stay at home with David. Therefore, both couples had decided to take advantage of their privacy and make a special couple of days out of it.

David and Sally had arranged to do several things, including go to dinner on the Friday night, get the bus down to the beach on the Saturday, and finally, go to see a film at the cinema on the Sunday. The two of them had been looking forward to their weekend together for weeks now and they had both got more and more excited as the time drew nearer. Although they spent most of their time together anyway, this was somehow going to be extra special.

Sally was also now preparing herself for her night out with David at a local restaurant. She slid her new red dress over her slender frame and took a moment to study herself in a long mirror. The tight fit of the garment sensually hugged the curves of her body and almost seemed like another layer of skin. Her shapely physique and the rich design of the dress complimented each other in an arousing manner.

As Sally checked her face in the mirror she sucked in her lips to make sure that her lipstick was evenly spread out. With a modest amount of make-up upon her face and her long black flowing hair she looked quite an alluring young lady. Her boyfriend would be as proud of her tonight as she would be of him.

Sally's parents had already left for their weekend away and had wished her good luck with her time with David. Mike and Melanie had been married for about eighteen years and had only the one daughter. They had put a great amount of effort and love in bringing her up and she was undoubtedly their pride and joy. Their whole family life was blissful and happy.

Mike and Melanie were pleased that Sally had found such a nice young man to go out with. They both always gave the time to converse with David whenever he came round their house and they did not seem to mind their daughter being with someone who was *different*. That alone he considered a welcome blessing.

David sometimes wondered if everyone's parents were like Sally's or there were more like his own. He knew his home life was not normal, but he did not think that he was the only child who had ever been beaten by a parent. However, he had a good idea that he was probably one of the worst off out of all of them. Norman was a big man and enjoyed beating the hell out of him whenever he felt like it.

Whilst David was waiting by the bus stop he looked expectantly up the road towards Sally's house. Whenever anyone walked around the corner at the far end of the path he checked enthusiastically to see if it was his date. He did not mind the waiting. It seemed to be all part of the excitement.

After a short while, Sally finally paced around the corner. David instantly turned to face her as an aroused expression crossed his face. It had been well worth the wait. She wore a burgundy-coloured coat over her red dress and she looked just as stimulating as she always made him feel. The animated look that she wore upon her face showed just how excited she was as well.

When Sally reached David she moved up close to him and put her hands on his chest. In a smooth and careful movement he responded by putting his hands upon her soft red cheeks. Just before they kissed, she sensually ran her tongue across her top lip in provocative gesture and then their mouths came together. As they kissed the blood in their veins flowed throughout their bodies creating a warm and satisfying sensation.

When the two lovers pulled away they still held each other in their tender clutches. David's eyes scoured Sally's curvaceous body in a penetratingly desirable fashion. He could not help but remark upon her graceful appearance.

"You look so adorable." He softly ran his hands down her body stopping only at the firmness of her thighs. "You really do."

It was now Sally's turn to return the compliment. As she looked at David's sturdy chest muscles protruding from his open jacket she lightly bit her lip in a manner which revealed her burning desires and temptations. She spoke in a soft and soothing voice.

"My sweet darling..." She painfully, but excitingly dug her nails into the firm muscles of his chest. "You look deliciously hot."

They kissed again.

The candlelight reflected off of David's pale face and made his light blue eyes sparkle like fine cut crystals. Sally looked across the table at him with a longing and wishful expression upon her delicate features. As the gaze of their eyes met their yearning for each other became an emotion stronger than they had ever known.

They had booked the table at the restaurant a week before and had managed to get a romantically lit table in the corner. The food was expensive, but they had saved up more than enough money just to make the night a special one. However, that was not all they had saved for.

David reached into his trouser pocket and pulled out a small velvet covered black box. As he smiled across the table he lightly grasped hold of Sally's hand. She put down her knife and at first gazed at him with a look of wonder, and then she too started to smile.

David spoke in a calm and quiet tone of voice.

"This is for you." He pushed the small box across the table into her open hand. "With all my love."

Sally took in a deep breath and shook her head.

"I hope you haven't spent too much."

"Don't lie!"

The reply was spoken in a joking manner. They both laughed.

As Sally opened the box the first thing she saw was a sparkle and straight away she knew she had been spoilt. When she realised what it was she looked up at David and gasped. Standing proudly in the centre of the box was a gold ring with a ruby set upon the top.

David knew that red was Sally's favourite colour and the ring would be the jewel on an already beautiful crown. At first, she just sat staring at the ruby in awe of its splendour, but then after getting hold of her senses she reached across the table and handed it to her lover.

"Please, put it on for me." She put her right hand out with her fingers evenly spread out. "It's only right that you put it on my finger."

David took the ring from her and slowly slid it onto the index finger of her right hand. The fit was perfect and the ruby stood out like a glistening dewdrop upon a sun soaked lawn. Sally looked up at her lover and after a slight pause, due being lost for words, she spoke with a voice full of appreciation.

"Oh thank-you, David." She slowly shook her head with delight. "It's so beautiful."

David smiled in return and then carried on eating his dinner. It was at that point when Sally reached her hand into her coat pocket which was hanging over the back of the chair. She then looked across the table at him with a cheerful smile and spoke in a soft tone of voice.

"David!" He looked up. "You didn't think I would leave you out, did you?"

Sally passed a box the size of a fist across the table towards David. He looked up at her with a surprised expression upon his face and almost dropped his cutlery onto his plate as he lowered it down. As he picked up the box he paused before opening it and eyed her with a scrutinising gaze as he questioned her.

"I hope *you* haven't spent too much." He frowned at her. "I mean it!"

Sally just leaned across the table and raised her eyebrows in a playfully stubborn manner as she spoke.

"Well, it's tough shit if I have!"

Again they laughed.

As David opened the box it revealed a gold coloured watch perched aloft in the centre. It was now his turn to gasp at what he saw. He could not help but look up at Sally with a shocked expression upon his face.

"I can't believe it." He took it out of the box. "It's perfect."

David strapped the watch around his left wrist and put it up to the candlelight to get a better look at it. The expression upon his face was one of pleasure and enchantment. He had never received such a beautiful gift in all of his life and his overwhelmed gratitude was quite evident in his tone of voice.

"I don't know what to say to you?"

"You've already said all you need to." Sally raised her hand to show off her ring. "As usual you haven't put a word wrong, David."

For the rest of the dinner the two of them carried on talking about whatever came to mind only to be occasionally interrupted by one of them taking a proud look at their new gift. The whole evening was the most romantic moment the two of them had ever shared. They almost wished that the night would never end.

Somewhere in the world there was hatred, anger and violence, but all these two knew this evening was the strongest emotion of them all. Love.

A distant streetlight shone through the window of the bedroom producing a hazy yellow glow throughout. It was dark, but not too dark to see. There was just enough light so that those who were in the room could view all that was necessary.

David sat on the bed with just the outline of his naked body visible in front of the window. The light reflected off of the curves of his muscles and his sides expanded and decreased in size with every breath. He waited patiently for his loved one.

74

When the bedroom door opened the landing light shone through into the room. As Sally stood in the doorway the outlines of her curvaceous naked body was all that could be seen. She then closed the door behind her and walked up to the foot of the bed. Outstretching her arms, she pushed David back onto the bed so that he lay out flat. Leaning across the bed and over his naked flesh, she slowly rested her body upon his.

They made passionate love.

There were no clouds, just a blue sky that was adorned with a magnificent golden sun. Its hot beating rays washed over all who bathed upon the stony beach below. As a cool sea breeze blew over the people on the shore it cooled them down just enough to make the heat of the sun a bearable bliss.

David lay on a rug spread out on the beach while Sally paddled in the sea. He watched her with wanton eyes and was oblivious of the children who were running past with kites momentarily blocking his vision. Seeing her smiling contentedly as she washed her legs with the water warmed his heart in a way that only she could do to him.

Sally was wearing a white two piece bikini that complimented her auburn coloured skin and showed off the elegant curves of her body. As the sun reflected off of the water it gave off a sparkling backdrop which seemed to frame her against the horizon. The whole scene produced a picture of beauty and graciousness.

When Sally realised that David was watching her she smiled at him and gave him a slight wave. He responded by making a beckoning motion with his finger to get her to come over to him. Walking slowly across the sand she came to kneel by her lover's side.

Sally did not have to say anything and neither did David. The looks upon their faces said it all. Their relationship had got well past the stage of friendly hugs and quick kisses on the lips. Their thoughts for each other now included ones of passion, eroticism and desire.

The expressions on David and Sally's faces said just one thing.

"I want you!"

And there was no way that either of them was going to refuse.

The two of them had never known such feelings of lust as they felt when they looked into each other's eyes. Before now they had held back their emotions in a painful assertion of self-control. However, now they found no reason to withhold their yearning for sexual fulfilment. Whenever they felt a desire to show their love for each other it was invariably done in a physical and emotional way.

The rest of David and Sally's weekend went the same way as it had started. Walks in the park, visits to the cinema and evenings staring at the stars in wonder. These were *always* followed by nights of passion and lovemaking.

David had never known days like these. Up until now all his life had ever known was sorrow and violence. It had taken years of waiting, but the good times had at last come. Being alive was beautiful.

Sally had never had the bad times that David had had, but she too was having the best days of her life. Every morning she woke up thinking about the day ahead and when she went to bed she craved for the few hours that she was about to have. Sleep just interrupted the pleasure of being alive.

Norman picked the morning newspaper up off of the front door mat and started to walk up the stairs with it held out in front of him. On the front page was a sketch of a suspected double rapist of two schoolgirls. However, the headline did not seem to disturb him and he turned straight to the back page to read the sport.

When Norman reached the top of the stairs he looked down at his string vest and noticed a food stain which had been left from his breakfast. It was a blob of red tomato ketchup that had fallen from his sausage. At first he tried to rub it off with the newspaper, but when he realised that the stain was well set in he mouthed a profanity.

"For fuck sake!" He breathed an exasperated sigh.

David was sitting in his room reading at his desk and as soon as he heard Norman swear he instantly looked up. Whenever his stepfather was in a bad mood he would always shout out profane remarks regardless of where he was and whom he was with. This proved to be a good advanced warning to keep out of his way.

The door to David's bedroom was wide open so he thought that it would be a good idea if he was to shut it so as not to attract himself to Norman's attention. He, therefore, turned around on his chair and pushed the door with his fingertips. Something, however, was blocking the doorway and had prevented it from closing.

David muttered a remark of displeasure.

"Oh no!" He frowned and turned away from the door. "Here we go!"

Norman strolled into the room and looked around with an angry expression upon his face. As he saw David sitting at his desk he folded and tucked his newspaper into his back pocket. He was just about to reprimand his stepson for pushing the door into his face and deliberately trying to break his nose when he noticed something.

David was sitting with just a pair of jeans on and no shirt. Norman had never seen or noticed his stepson's muscular physique before and was quite surprised by his appearance. However, he immediately considered this to be an attempt to oust him from his position of 'man of the house' and that was just not acceptable.

Norman poked David on the shoulder blade.

"Oi! What's all this sitting around the house trying to show off your weedy body?" He folded his arms. "You've got something to prove, have you?"

David looked up at him and raised his eyebrows.

"I'll put a shirt on." He grabbed a white T-shirt off of his bed and slipped it over himself. "Sorry!"

Norman sneered and took a step back to get a better look at his stepson. As he did so he huffed and shook his head with displeasure. He now went about making sure that it was quite clear who was the boss.

"So you reckon you've got muscles?" He breathed in and stuck out his chest. "You'll never be as big as me."

David looked at his stepfather with an unimpressed expression upon his face. Norman's chest was quite big, but his stomach still hung below it like a sack of potatoes. The years of drinking and eating unhealthy food had taken their toll. However, he diplomatically, if sardonically agreed with his stepfather just to try to diffuse the situation.

"Yes! I suppose you're right." He slowly nodded his head. "I don't think that I'll ever get like that."

"Too bloody right and I'll prove it as well." Norman sat on the bed and put his right elbow on the desk. "Come on! We'll have an arm wrestle to see who's the strongest."

David sighed and lulled his head back in an act of exasperation. All he wanted to do was to get on with his studying. The last thing he wanted was to be harassed by Norman and his forever-hungry ego.

"Do I have to?" He pleaded. "I need to study."

"Why?" Norman's face grew stern and his right hand clenched into a fist. "Are you a poof or something?"

David now realised that he was not going to get out of this situation without joining in with his stepfather's low brow game. He, therefore, reluctantly turned around on his chair to face Norman and put his elbow on the desk. As he waited for the game to begin he tried his best to appear enthusiastic just to please the foul tempered man.

Norman grabbed hold of David's hand and shuffled his body into position. As he finally readied himself he called out the rules of the competition.

"All right, countdown from three to one and it's the first one to get the others knuckles on the desk." He stared into his stepson's eyes with an aggressive look upon his face. "Are you ready, wimp?"

David's expression had now changed into one of concentration and he just nodded his head without uttering a word. Although he did not care much for physical sports he felt that on this occasion he might just earn some respect from Norman if he put up a reasonable amount of competition. He had decided that if he was forced into participating in his stepfather's game he might as well try to win.

Norman started the countdown to begin.

"Three...two..." The contest began. "One!"

David was caught unaware at first and only just managed to stop his stepfather putting his knuckles to the desk. He was sure that the rules were to start when the countdown had reached one, but it seemed as if they had miraculously changed. However, he was somehow not so surprised that Norman had taken to cheating. Fairness was not one of his more favourable traits.

As the contest progressed David started to realise that his stepfather was starting to tire. He had already pushed their arms up to a vertically level position and he had hardly felt any strain. In fact, he was starting to think that the whole competition was going to be a lot easier than he had originally expected.

Norman's face was increasingly turning more and more red as he frantically tried to battle against his stepson's surprising show of strength. He was now starting to mutter obscenities as he felt his stamina dwindle away into an agonising state of feebleness. Had he have realised that he might just lose the competition he would never have made the challenge.

David had now come to the conclusion that it was just a matter of time before victory was his. He could feel his stepfather becoming weaker with every second that passed. All he had to do now was to decide when to end the contest.

As Norman made a last ditch effort to try to put his stepson's knuckles on the desk he let out a bellowing profanity.

"Fuck!"

There could not have been a better moment for David to finish the competition. He looked at the strain on Norman's face and realised that he was exerting his last bit of strength. Victory was imminent.

With an almighty thud David sent his stepfather's knuckles crashing down against the desk. The win had come as quick as the blink of the eyelid and was astoundingly decisive. Such was the force of the sudden exertion of strength that it left bright red marks across Norman's knuckles.

David let go of his stepfather's hand and rubbed his own arm to soothe his muscles. As he stood up he looked over the wreck of his defeated opponent with an expression of satisfaction upon his face. His content, however, was to be short lived.

At first Norman's head was bowed, but then he looked up at David with a face red with rage. The feelings of humiliation at being so easily beaten had soon transformed into seething emotions of anger and fury, and as always these could only be directed at his stepson through a channel of mindless violence.

Norman stood up with his back straight and his fists clenched tightly at his sides. His face twisted into a sneer as he glowered at David. As he spoke his voice crackled with rage.

"What's your fucking problem?" He pointed a rigid finger at his stepson. "Are you trying to break my fucking arm?"

David took a step back as he realised that his victory had obviously not produced the desired effect. He had hoped that he might have impressed his stepfather with his show of muscle, but this certainly had not been the case. Defeat had obviously been a sour pill, too shameful to swallow for the big man. This was a person who held strength to be a high attribute of someone's characteristics.

David tried to apologise.

"Sorry, I just..." He paused for thought and shrugged his shoulders. "Tried to win."

This was obviously not going to be enough to calm Norman of his anger. His feelings of disgrace at being beaten with such ease were inconsolable. He had no choice but to punish his stepson with a show of violence so full of wrath that such an occurrence would never happen again.

Norman decided that his first punch was going to be aimed straight for David's nose so as to break it across his face and blind him with his own tears. His right fist was straight away flung through the air with unerring accuracy towards his target. It, nevertheless, did not land where he had expected.

David stood with his left hand in front of his own face with Norman's fist clasped tightly in his palm. The force of the blow had not been enough to go past the barrier of defence and was now trapped in an iron like grip. Stopping the attempt at having his nose smashed across his face had been as easy as winning the arm wrestling contest itself.

Norman's mouth dropped open in shock as he realised his first attack had been thwarted. When he tried to pull his fist away he found that it was stuck fast and had now become a useless weapon in his assault. The ease at how his stepson had stopped the blow had been bewildering. He now had no choice but to use his left fist.

David knew what was coming next and put his other hand up in front of his right eye ready for the attack. He caught the punch with the same lack of effort as the first. With his face unblemished and his stepfather's offensive nullified he stood staring at his aggressor with a look upon his face which was void of expression.

David did not feel victorious or relieved that he had not been hurt. He knew what was to be expected now and for some reason it did not seem to bother him. His point had been proved.

Norman glared at his stepson and spoke his demand in a low rumbling voice that was full of fury.

"Let go now, you fucking freak!"

David waited for a while before releasing his stepfather's fists just to show that he still had the strength to hold them if he had wanted to. He really did not mind how painfully he was hurt now as he had shown that he was no longer the weak pushover that he once was. It was now obvious that if he wanted to he could have defended himself with the utmost of ease against one of Norman's onslaughts and for him just knowing that was satisfying enough.

As soon as the fists were freed the blows rained down. Some landed on the face, some on the body, but all were delivered with a vehement rage. This, however, did not lead to the usual unbearable agony followed by a condemning humiliation. There was now something else instead. Within the depths of David's mind came an overwhelming conviction not to go through anymore physical or mental pain. A burning desire flowed through his veins and filled his consciousness with a vigorous determination that literally forbade him to suffer at the hands of another person ever again. He simply chose not to be a victim.

As the powerful punches each landed in turn upon David's body and head he found himself being calm and unstirred by what was happening to him. For the first time in his life the feeling of pain was not something that was unbearable, but it instead filled him with an unconsummated strength. He was not going to let anyone hurt him anymore, simply because he could not see the point in letting it happen. Pain was merely a sensation that he chose not to feel. He switched it off.

Revelling in his own feelings of content and fulfilment he just stared straight into Norman's eyes and endured it all without producing a single tear. Occasionally his head would be punched and his line of vision would momentarily be averted, but it would only be for a split second and he would always just revert back to looking deep into the enraged attacker's gaze. At one point, his stepfather even thought he saw a slight smile appear on his victim's face.

There was no victory to be won by Norman in this battle, but instead only a crushing defeat would be sustained due to him knowing that there was no way that he could possibly win. An unassailable enemy will always triumph simply due to the fact that they just cannot be beaten. His downfall had at last come merely because of the infallibility of his opponent.

Over the coming weeks David's life began to change considerably. He had found himself in a number of violent situations and had dealt with them all in the same manner as he had with the incident with Norman. If he could thwart an attack he would and if there were no escape he would simply just endure it. And he did all of this with the utmost of ease.

None of the boys who bullied David could match his physical strength. He would just effortlessly block their punches and keep pushing them away until they gave up on their egotistic stint of terrorisation. If they were particularly intent on harming him he would run into the nearest classroom and hold the door handle steadfastly until they again tired of trying to out-power him. It was not long before he realised that the average endurance of a school bully was extremely low.

All this happened on the usual regular basis, but it still never led to David retaliating against his tormentors in the like physical manner of which they tried to harm him. Never did it cross his mind to punch, kick or even shout a profane remark back at one of his aggressors. This was simply not in his nature. The plain truth of the matter was that he considered such actions to be nothing short of illogical.

Of all of David's victories the two most notable that had been gained were against the cane happy teacher, Mr Cutter, and the school's most infamous bully, Martin Dent. He had defeated both of them in the same passive manner and with an equal amount of ease. Although he knew that the war had not been won and that it would not be long before he would once again be at the end of one of their assaults, he did know that he had at least left mental wounds within each of their consciousness' that would take some time to heal.

David's triumph over Mr Cutter had come during a break time whilst on his way to his next lesson. He had been walking through the corridors of the mathematics block when he had heard some pain filled yelps coming from within the temperamental teacher's classroom. With his usual inquisitiveness he had looked inside to see what was happening. It was at that point when he had found a young boy receiving a vicious caning for what was probably a minor fracturing of the school rules.

With his new found resolve, David had walked into the classroom and interrupted the violent proceedings by suggesting in an impassive, but sarcastic manner that the flailing teacher should try not to get so agitated, as it was probably not doing his blood pressure any good whatsoever. Mr Cutter had immediately raised his level of fury and dismissed the pupil who he had been punishing so that he could turn his attention to his new prey. Although self-afflicting, this grim conclusion had, of course, been the desired outcome of the plan.

It was not long before Mr Cutter's bible was tightly grasped in David's right palm as the hawk eyed teacher eagerly watched and waited for the weight of the book to take its toll upon the young man's muscles and be lowered to an unacceptable level. This, however, did not happen. Without a single quiver of the hand or even a straining blush of a cheek the arm just stayed unmoving and steady as a rock.

After about a minute Mr Cutter realised that he was simply not going to have the pleasure of seeing the young man break before him. He, therefore, went about punishing him anyway. With a barrage of strikes he brought the cane whipping down upon the left palm leaving long red gashes across the flesh. The onslaught was relentless, but it got him utterly nowhere.

David just stood there still stalwartly holding the bible in his palm whilst keeping his left hand that was receiving the whipping just as steady. There was no pain and definitely no tears. All he knew was the same unwavering strength and willpower to not be beaten. With his mind as calm as a still lake and the features on his face as unmoving as that of a mountain, he just let the moment pass with a blissful ease. And just to top it off he even turned his hand over at one point just to look at his watch to see what the time was so as to give the obvious impression that he was simply getting quite bored with it all.

As for David's victory over Martin Dent, it had come about with the same amount of undemanding nonchalance. It had started with the members of the bully's gang shouting the usual profane remarks at him through the corridors of the school. That then resulted in the inevitable attempt by him at trying to flee their impending beating. With his new found fitness he had soon escaped from all of his exhausted pursuers apart from their leader by running up and down the flights of stairs in the three-storey block.

When David was sure that only Martin Dent was now chasing him he stopped in a communal area of the school and had just waited for the arrival of his aggressor. He had chosen to end the pursuit here as part of a well planned scheme and mindfully looked around at his surroundings to assess how he was going to complete his machinations. There were a number of benches which had pupils sitting on them and the walls were lined with coat hooks, as he was previously well aware of.

As Martin ran into the area he immediately centred on his target and gleefully eyed him up. The surrounding students straight away realised what was happening and started to clear a space between the two opposing pupils. David, however, just stayed where he was in an unworried and confident posture. This would be an eventful and groundbreaking confrontation.

Martin slowly made his way over towards his victim with an aggressive and relishing expression upon his face. David just smiled. Then it began.

A fist was aimed straight for the eye, but was easily evaded with a quick step to the side. Martin found himself lurching straight past his target and falling over a bench. David spun round and grabbed hold of the bully's waist and lifted him up on to his shoulder. Then with the a minimal amount of effort he hooked the back of his assailant's thick trouser belt onto one of the coat hooks on the wall leaving him firmly attached to the wall.

As David stepped back to admire his work he just peacefully gazed at the flailing and bellowing wretch that was incapacitated before him. After ascertaining that he had without a doubt gained yet another unreserved and non-violent victory he turned around and wandered off to enjoy the rest of his day, leaving behind him the now extremely embarrassed and humiliated, hardest bully in the school. This was almost getting too easy.

These were not the only melees that David had found himself in over the last few weeks. There had been occasions when he had just received a blow to the face whilst simply minding his own business on the school yard and another incident when Martin Dent had got his revenge by waiting around a corner and pouncing on him in a sudden and vicious attack. Both of the fracases had, nevertheless, been dealt with in the same calm and calculated way and he had just coolly controlled his mind so that he had not felt the pain. It was obvious that he had not done anything to deserve these beatings, but the way he saw it was that if it did not hurt it did not matter.

So, David had now got to the stage where he could composedly focus his consciousness so acutely that no matter how much physical and mental damage he sustained it simply would not distress him in anyway. The coldness of the cruel remarks, the sensation of having his flesh pounded upon and the gut wrenching unfairness of it all were merely dispelled from his mind and sent to away to a distant place where they simply could not harm him. He was, in essence, impossible to hurt. At least, that is how it seemed.

The recent events had taken their toll upon David's outward physique and although what he had endured of late had been a lot less detrimental than usual he still had enough marks on his body as a testament to what he had been going through. It was not always possible to block or dodge every punch and he was currently adorned with a colourful bruise upon his left cheek and had also once again sustained a large collection of red raw slashes across his left palm. He was, however, proud of himself for doing the things that he had done and he felt as if he had handled everything as well as he could have.

As David looked at himself in the mirror he thought of how he used to wear extra clothing to hide his wounds from Sally. She would always notice them anyway, but he would try to keep her from seeing them regardless. He used to hate the embarrassment of telling her about the beatings he got, but this time he felt different about it.

David wanted to tell Sally what had happened when he had taken a caning to save the young boy from being punished and how he had rendered Martin Dent immobile on the coat hook. He wanted to share with her his good feelings and sense of achievement in what he had done. His only problem was that she would probably not see the situation in the same way that he did.

Sally was due to call round to his house at any moment and he was not sure if he was looking forward to seeing her or not. He loved being in her company, but there were times when he could not bear to face her. She would be cross at him for letting himself be bullied, and that was never an emotion that he liked. However, his feelings of passion for her were always too strong to even consider not actually spending time with the girl he loved.

It was while David was waiting in his bedroom when he heard shouting coming from downstairs. The first voice he could hear call out was Norman's unmistakable bellowing. There were the usual four letter words added for good measure.

"Fuck it! I'm in a bloody hurry here. Get the fuck out my way!" There was no attempt to hide his feelings. "You haven't even made my lunch, you piss ugly tart! Christ woman, what do you do all day?"

"Sorry Norm'!" The usual apologetic reply.

"So what the fucking hell am I going to eat?" There was a pause for an answer, but the reply did not come. "Well, I've had enough of this bollocks! You deserve this!"

The unmistakable sound of fists against flesh echoed throughout the house. It appeared as though the first punch must have hit Marilyn straight in the mouth as the noise of it making contact was followed by a muffled scream. After that all that could be heard was the thudding of the repeated blows and subdued yelps of agony.

David just stood staring at himself in the mirror with a blank expression upon his face. He knew that if he went downstairs to try to stop what was going on he would not be able to prevent his mother from being beaten eventually. Norman would just simply hurt him and then her.

David loved his mother, but at the time he knew that she did not feel the same way about him. He realised that there was little she could do about being abused by her husband, but she always seemed to think it was acceptable for her son to get hurt. This did not mean that he thought it was right when Norman beat her, but he found it hard to feel sorry for her.

David decided just to wait for the violence to stop before he went downstairs to see what had happened. He was expecting to see blood on the walls and floor as well as on his mother's face. It did not matter how many times he saw such a sight it would always make him feel disgusted.

It was while David could hear Marilyn running about the house trying to escape from Norman when he heard the worst noise yet. It was not the sound of a striking blow, or the pain stricken scream of his mother, but something much worse. Amidst all the noise of the commotion going on in the house he heard the ring of the doorbell.

Sally had arrived.

"Oh no!" David muttered to himself in an exasperated manner.

A bitter wind whistled through the air continuously rustling the leaves on the trees. The constant noise of the elements outside in the street made hearing a strain, but Sally could still hear the shouting and screaming coming from inside David's house. She wondered if it would not be such a good idea to go in there right now. There were noises coming from inside that sounded quite disturbing, but to actually be there and see it happening was not something she felt that she would want to witness.

Sally stood at the front door waiting for it to open. She had already pressed the doorbell and was beginning to regret it already. From inside she heard David's stepfather shout out a profanity.

"Who the fucking hell's that?"

This was followed by another voice that came from nearer to the front door.

"It's all right! I've got it!"

At that, the front door opened to reveal David standing in the hallway with a worried expression upon his face. As he looked at Sally standing on the doorstep he lowered his gaze in an ashamed manner and reluctantly stood aside to let her in. When she walked into the house it was hard to tell which of the two was feeling the most discomfort as they stood opposite each other with the noise of the fight going on in the background.

As David closed the front door Sally looked up at him and raised her eyebrows in an uncomfortable manner. He shrugged his shoulders in return, but he could not think of anything to say to ease the situation. It seemed it would have to be up to her to break the uneasy silence.

"What's all that about?" She asked shyly.

"Nothing." David frowned and shook his head as he spoke. "It's always about nothing. It just happens."

Norman now stomped out of the living room where he had left his wife after beating her up and barged passed the two of them in the hallway without uttering a word. As he walked into the kitchen he slammed the door behind him and shouted out another profane remark for all to hear.

"I suppose I've got to make my own fucking lunch!"

David sighed and moved closer towards Sally. She was standing with her arms folded and was looking at the doorway to the living room in a concerned manner. As he spoke to her his voice was soft and gentle.

"I better go and see how my mother is. It won't be a very nice sight. You can go and wait upstairs in my bedroom if you like." He looked through the doorway to where his mother was. "I'll understand if you don't want to be a part of this."

Sally lightly took hold of David's hands and moved slowly across to be in front of his gaze. Although she did not want to see what state his mother was in after what had obviously

82

happened to her she felt as though she could not let her lover deal with it alone. She tried to force a comforting smile as she spoke.

"David, I want to be with you." Her eyes looked deep into his. "I know this is difficult for you and that's why I want to be there to help you."

"Thank-you!" The reply was short, but by the way it was said revealed just how much he really did want for her to be there by his side. "You are my light."

"And you're mine also."

David lightly kissed Sally on the lips then turned to go into the living room. As they walked in through the doorway they could hear Marilyn crying to herself and muttering incomprehensible murmurs. She was sitting in a corner with her face in her hands and her hair draped over her forehead.

"Mum!" David tried to get her attention.

"What?" The reply was accompanied by sobs.

"Do you need any help?"

"No! Go away!"

"Are you sure?" He persisted.

At that Marilyn lifted her head from her hands and pulled her hair away from her forehead. The room was dimly lit, but there was enough light to be able to see her face. It was not a pretty sight.

As Sally saw the state that Marilyn had been left in, she put her hands to her mouth and gasped with shock. She blinked repeatedly and tears started to well in her eyes as she gazed upon the broken woman who was shamelessly sitting on the floor before her. David leaned across and whispered into his girlfriend's ear.

"Welcome to the everyday life of my home!" He spoke in a tone of voice that suggested that such sights within these four walls were quite commonplace. "This, unfortunately, is the norm."

Marilyn's nose had been broken across her face and she had a tooth missing at the front. She had a swollen black eye and there was a trail of blood running down her face from a cut on her forehead. She sat on the floor with her whole body shaking as she looked at the two of them through tear filled eyes.

David was just about to help his mother up off of the floor when Marilyn suddenly reeled back away from him. At first he thought it was something he had done, but then he realised why she had done it. Norman barged past him and bellowed at his wife.

"I've decided that I'm not going to make my own lunch." He pointed at Marilyn. "You fucking are!"

Norman then turned around to face the two who were looking on with revulsion at what was happening. David just lowered his eyes away from his stepfather's gaze. He knew not to get involved with him when he was in this kind of mood. Sally, however, had an unrelenting strength of character that was far too strong to do something as inexcusable as to bow to this wretch of a man. She just intently stared at him with a sneer upon her face and slowly shook her head to show her disgust at him. In a moment of defiance she silently mouthed a single word to him in a manner of which he could lip read.

"Wanker!"

Norman just smiled a sickly grin at Sally to show his pleasure at what he had done. He then made his way into the kitchen to wait for his lunch. As he walked off he made yet another threat to his wife.

"And for Christ's sake, hurry up woman or you'll get some more!"

Marilyn had no intention of getting beaten again so she staggered to her feet and went to do as she was told. When she walked past David and Sally on her way to the kitchen she turned her face away from them in an attempt to cover up her embarrassment. Soon she

83

would be lovingly cooking a meal for the person who had just kicked the living hell out of her and she was far from proud of it.

Sally turned around to David and looked at him with a sorry expression upon her face. She knew that what had just occurred was commonplace in his life, but she was sure he just tried to put on a brave face to hide his emotions. She was not sure whether to admire his resilience or pity him.

The amount of times David had been in the midst of the most terrible of violent conflicts had forcibly numbed him and made him irrepressible to all kinds of suffering. However, he had still managed to keep his warmth, caring and loving nature. Whilst all about him was mayhem and madness he managed to stay calm and rational.

It was these strengths of character that Sally found the most attractive about David. She almost felt envious that he could be so in control of his emotions. He felt no anger, no hatred and never had any feelings of resentment towards others.

Sally also found David's muscular physique attractive as well as his blue crystal like eyes. However, she was also aware that his appearance was different to everyone else's. She knew that the other children at school taunted him about the size of his head, but she ignored the cruel remarks just like he did.

Sally had telephoned David earlier on in the day to ask him if he wanted to go for a walk in the park. It was a bit of a cold day, but he had eagerly agreed to it anyway. Besides, the park was nice this time of year with the sun reflecting off of the golden brown trees and the rustling sound underfoot of fallen leaves as they walked. Today was a good day for loving.

In an attempt to try to clean up the mess that Norman had made, David and Sally had started to pick a few things up off the floor. There were stains of blood on the carpet that needed to be wiped away and small shards of china from a shattered ornament of which neither would be easily removed. It was not long before it became quite apparent that they were going to have to spend far longer on the cleaning up than they wished and the truth was that they simply had much better things to do, such as cuddle each other on a park bench.

Sally was kneeling down picking up bits of an ornament when David bent down beside her to speak.

"Come on! Let's go to the park?" He lightly grasped her hand to help her up. "We'll be here all day otherwise."

Sally nodded her head in agreement and let David help her up. She then put the bits of broken ornament on the coffee table and dusted herself down. For a short moment she looked at him with a slight frown of embarrassment, and then she spoke.

"I don't mean to be impolite, but..." She paused. "The sooner we get out of here the better."

"I understand." David raised his eyebrows. "You should try living in this hell hole!"

At that, the two of them took one last uninterested glance at the mess around them and then hurried out of the house to go to the park. As they walked up the street David looked back over his shoulder in the direction of his home. He wondered what was going on in there right now, but then after considering it for a short while he realised that he did not really care.

Starrow Town Park was nearly empty apart from a few people walking their dogs, a couple on an afternoon stroll and a lone jogger. The wind blew quite heavily across the open spaces, but the sun was shining brightly and just about made the weather bearable. It was a day for the strong hearted and for those who wanted to be alone with their thoughts.

As Sally and David walked arm in arm they laughed at a joke they were sharing together. She playfully pushed him away, then instantly pulled him back into her arms in a romantic gesture. They both stopped to kiss.

When they started walking again Sally decided to bring up the subject of David's mother.

"Does your mum get beaten up a lot by your stepfather?" She asked.

"Yes! I suppose so. More than most wives do by their husbands anyway." He frowned as he spoke. "He probably does it just as much as he hits me."

"What does she do about it? In America women sue men for that sort of thing." The tone of Sally's voice suggested that she was certain of what she was saying. "I mean, if she doesn't do that, she must at least say something to him about it?"

"No!" David shook his head. "She doesn't say anything."

"Why? She can't be that scared..." A slight pause. "Can she?"

David turned to Sally and looked at her with a convincing expression upon his face.

"You saw the state of her. She only has to say one word that displeases him and that's what she gets." He raised his eyebrows and spoke in a wistful manner. "Come to think of it, most of the time it happens for no reason whatsoever."

"That's terrible."

"What's terrible is that I've learnt to live with it." David shook his head in disgust. "How can someone get used to a life of violence?"

"It won't last forever." Sally rested her head on his shoulder in a comforting gesture. "You'll be alright someday."

For a while the two of them carried on walking without saying anything. Their thoughts were reflecting on the conversation they had just been having. Then David spoke in an inquisitive tone of voice.

"Have either of your parents ever said that they love you?" It was a question that came out of the blue, but there was obviously a deep reason for why he had asked it.

"Yes! Why?"

Sally replied with a question even though she knew what the answer was going to be. She had realised a long time ago that David's mother was estranged from him. However, she had never heard his views on it and she guessed now that she was about to.

"My mother doesn't even talk to me unless I talk to her first. She doesn't have that much time for me really. She occasionally cooks my food for me and she does my washing every now and again, but other than that she just tries her best to ignore me." He shrugged his shoulders in an attempt to appear as if he did not care. "It could be a lot worse though, she might have just got rid of me when I was born."

Sally shook her head in exasperation.

"It could be a lot *better* as well." Her voice became agitated. "Has she always been like it?"

"Do you want the truth?" The reply was returned in the form of a warning disguised as a question.

"Yes! I suppose so."

The pain of the subject started to show on David's face as he tried to explain.

"When I was young she didn't even go out of the house with me. She was so ashamed about my appearance; she thought other people would look at her as if she were some kind freak herself..."

He was interrupted.

"You're not a freak, David!"

"Thanks!"

The reassurance was warmly received. Any kind of affection would be gratefully received right now. After a deep breath, David carried on with what he was saying.

"There were times when I couldn't tell if she was trying to compliment or criticise me."

"How do you mean?" Sally looked confused.

"Well, there was a time when I was in a supermarket with her and a baby was crying in one of the isles. I asked her if I ever used to do the same thing." David shook his head in a confused manner. "And what she said was something that I could never quite understand."

"What was that?"

"She said that I never used to cry when I had a wet nappy. Instead I just used to try and take it off myself. I'll always remember her exact words..." His expression became befuddled. "She said 'You always had to be different!'"

Sally affectionately rubbed her hand on David's back to comfort him. She did not like to hear him talk about the hurtful things that happened to him in his life, but she could tell that he wanted to get them off of his chest. However, the remark he made next took her completely by surprise.

"I learnt at an early age that because of the way I look my mother has never loved me." David looked up into the sky as if to search for the answers he craved for. "But I could never understand why she *hated* me for it."

Sally was at first shocked by what she had heard. She had unintentionally stopped in her tracks and let her hand slip off of his back. However, when she realised that her affection was badly needed she lunged forward and embraced her lover with both arms. Then, in a sweet act of tenderness she told David of her feelings for him.

"Maybe your mother doesn't love you, but I promise you something..." She looked deep in to his eyes. "I'll always make up for what you're missing out on."

It felt as if time had stopped to preserve the moment of harmony. They both held each other tightly and let their body heat warm the others flesh. Somehow life seemed to have frozen still, but in their union of devotion there was an ever-flowing fountain of pleasure. The next kiss seemed to last for eternity, but it still did not feel like it was long enough. Love can sometimes be endless.

Since the two of them had been in the park David had been looking for the right moment to tell Sally about his last few weeks. He had wanted to explain to her about how and why he had obtained his latest injuries, but up until now he had not found the appropriate occasion. It was only when he felt the warmth of her touch as she hugged him closely that he realised that anytime would be suitable to inform her of everything, simply because deep down he knew she cared about him as much as he did about her.

The two of them were standing near a large oak tree with a park bench next to it. In a gesture with his hand, David ushered Sally to come and sit with him. As they both sat down he turned to her and put his hand on her thigh in a comforting manner.

David then went about telling Sally all about how he pinned Martin Dent up onto the wall in the communal area and then just walked away. He also told her how he deliberately got himself caned by Mr Cutter just so he could get the young pupil out of trouble. As he explained all about what else had happened to him he also expressed how proud he was of himself and that he felt a great deal of achievement in what he had done.

Sally listened intently to everything that David had to say without uttering a word herself. She sat with such a blank expression upon her face that the only reason why he knew that she was giving him her attention was because she was staring straight into his eyes. When he had finished all that he had to say he waited for her reaction.

For a long moment Sally just sat facing David with the same emotionless expression upon her face. By the way she was looking at him he thought that she was not going to say anything. However, just as he was about to ask her what was wrong she spoke in an exasperated tone of voice.

"For fuck sake, David..." She breathed out a long sigh. "You've done some damn weird things in your time, but this beats them all."

David lowered his gaze with embarrassment and took in a deep breath. He knew that Sally would not be pleased with what he had done, but the reaction he had just got had taken him completely by surprise. His intentions were to at least make her understand that he thought that he had done the right thing, but this did not seem to be the case.

Sally tried to get more information about what had happened.

"So did you know the boy who was getting caned?" Her voice sounded annoyed and frustrated.

"No. I've never even seen him before." The reply was spoken in a subdued manner.

"So why take a caning for him?" Sally sat back on the bench and folded her arms in disgust. "He wouldn't have done it for you."

David tried to reason with her.

"I know he wouldn't, but..." He paused for thought. "He was getting badly hurt."

"That's irrelevant!" Sally turned back to face David. "That's still no reason for you to suffer instead of him."

"He was only young!" He attempted to appeal to the more compassionate side of her nature.

Sally frowned at David and put her hands on her thighs in a resolute stance.

"So how do you explain not hitting that mental arsehole, Dent when you had the chance?" She prompted for a quick answer to the question. "Well?"

"I couldn't do something like that. He couldn't even defend himself stuck on that hook." David instantly knew that this reply was not going to win her over.

"It's not as if you owe him any favours." Sally raised her voice. "What's he ever done for you other than bully you for no reason?"

"He might have appreciated me not hitting him. It might have shown him what it's like to be in a position of defencelessness and made him realise how bad it feels."

"Like hell!" She frowned intensely at him. "You know that's not what he'd think. Don't try to fool me, David Cain." Sally clasped her fist in front of herself. "You should have stuffed the fucking hook right up his arse!"

David chuckled at the unexpected remark. He was not used to Sally speaking in such a manner or being in this kind of temper. However, he knew it was because she was concerned for him and he almost found it quite titillating. When she saw that he was smiling at what she had said she scolded him for it.

"It isn't funny David!" She turned to face away from him. "Just shut up!"

At that moment, Sally saw the funny side of what she had said and started to laugh as well. Both of them then had a good chuckle at the situation and the tension of the stormy conversation started to die down. David then made another attempt at trying to explain himself.

"I know it doesn't seem right to deliberately get hurt for someone else. But if you had of seen the look of utter fear on that boy's face when he was getting caned you would have wanted to do something to stop it as well." He leant across the bench and put his arm around Sally's shoulder. "And you know that when Mr Cutter wants to hurt someone that's *all* he wants to do. He's actually mentally unstable."

"It must have really hurt you though." She looked at him with a saddened and concerned expression upon her face. "I hate to think of you going through any kind of pain."

David carried on explaining himself.

"As for Martin Dent, how can someone like him learn about pity, humanity and concern for other people's feelings if no one shows him what those things mean?"

Sally just nodded her head in return. She knew that deep down what he was saying was right. It was just so hard for her to accept such acts of unfeeling violence against the person who she loved.

David stood up and then slowly walked over to the large oak tree next to the bench. He leant his shoulder against the trunk and stared out across the park. As he spoke he remained standing with his back to Sally.

"There are people dying in this world because their country doesn't have enough money to spend on medical equipment and the drugs they needs to stay alive." He slowly shook his head and frowned. "Yet those same countries spend billions of pounds a year on weapons and armies just to kill other people."

David turned around to momentarily face Sally with a look of deep torment in his light blue eyes. His expression was solemn and he held his head low in a morose manner. As he carried on talking he walked over to stand in front of the bench.

"There are terrible wars going on all the time around the world just because of religion, greed or any number of other pointless reasons. People are dying of diseases, hunger and all kinds of illnesses simply because there's not enough done to get the cures they need to survive." He lowered himself down and squatted down in front of her. "How can I just go on living my life as if everything is alright when I know such things are going on all around me? All I want to do is make the world a better place. And more importantly, I know I'm capable of doing it."

Sally had sat with her eyes lowered throughout the time David had been talking, but now she found herself looking directly into his gaze. She knew what he was saying was true, even if she did not like to accept it. As she spoke she leant forward and tried her best not to look displeased.

"I know the world's not perfect..." She paused and took in a deep breath. "But why does it have to be you on this righteous crusade, like some kind of messiah? Why should you suffer? Why should you have to go through pain for others?"

"There is no reason why I *have* to do it..." David lightly took hold of her hands. "But I want to. I could become a doctor and create cures for diseases. Maybe I could become a scientist who can find the chemical formula for an ecologically clean fuel. Or even a politician who helps everyone. I know what I'm capable of. There's so much I want to do and so much I can do."

Sally nodded her head in understanding and softy rubbed the back of his hands. However, there was still something else that she wanted to say.

"I'm really proud of you David, and I know you could achieve all of what you set out to do." She then asked a rhetorical question. "But do you know what happened to the last person who tried to help the whole of humanity?"

"What?" David's brow furrowed inquisitively.

"They put him in front of all the people who he tried to help..." Sally raised her eyebrows to show that she was sure of what she was saying. "And they crucified him."

David just nodded his head and then after a brief moment to think about what he was going to say he gave his reply.

"Yes, the bible says that Jesus could work all kinds of wondrous miracles. He could heal the sick with the touch of the hand and he could feed five thousand people with just a couple of baskets of food, and still they persecuted him and then took his life." He leant forward and moved his face within inches of Sally's. "But *he* didn't have a beautiful, brilliant woman by his side; especially one like mine."

They were exactly the right words, said in exactly the right way, at exactly the right time. The only obvious outcome was for them both to kiss and show how they felt about each other. And that was precisely what they did.

88

That day, the two of them left just one reminder of them ever being there in the park. Sally had got the sharp penknife that she kept attached to her key ring out of her handbag and had carved some simple words into the large oak tree next to the bench on which they had been sitting. To any passerby it would have seemed like the vandalism of some immature youngsters, but to the two of them it meant so much more. The inscription simply read exactly how they felt.

David
4
Sally

Nothing else needed to be said.

An elaborate melody swept across the classroom as the pianist's hands moved gracefully across the piano keyboard. When the tune came to a stop it was instantly replaced with a round of praise from an onlooker who was clearly more than impressed.

"Excellent! Brilliant! Magnificent!"

Mr Scott sat back in his chair and applauded his pupil. He had been reading the manuscript note for note while the young man had performed the piece of music for the exam. As the fervent teacher commented on what he had just heard he could not help but smile broadly.

"Your timing was perfect, you played with passion..." He paused for thought and then nodded his head in a satisfied manner. "And it was a very good tune as well."

"Thank-you Mr Scott!" David turned around on the stool in front of the piano to face his teacher. "I wrote the piece last weekend. I've entitled it 'The Fall of Man'"

The other examining music teacher who was sitting in the classroom seemed less impressed by the performance. Mrs Hoggett sat with her arms folded and wore a bland expression upon her face. She was in her mid fifties and wore a colourful flowery dress. However, her bright appearance was no indication of her nature. Among pupils and other teachers alike she was considered to be rather a dull and cheerless person.

As Mrs Hoggett spoke she slipped her glasses down onto the end of her nose and looked over the top of them in a blasé manner.

"It is possible to be *too* complicated." She breathed out a long sigh. "A person can only take so many notes in one go."

Mr Scott looked at Mrs Hoggett with a confused look upon his face. He considered what he had just witnessed to be the best example of musical talent he had heard from any pupil he had ever taught. As he got up off of his chair he leant across and spoke quietly to her so that David could not hear.

"Emily! That was the best piano solo for an exam entry that either of us have ever had the pleasure of listening to in both of our careers." He showed her the manuscript paper. "Have you ever known any pupil write music as good as this? Look at the composition! There's not even a single mistake."

"He needs practice." Mrs Hoggett got up off of her chair and slung her handbag over her shoulder. "We all need practice."

David could have sworn that many great composers had written much more complicated pieces of music than what he had. His piano sonata only lasted for seven minutes and he considered it to be quite melodious. He could not understand how Mrs Hoggett could have got so bored so quickly.

Mr Scott came over to sit in front of the piano next to David. He smiled at his pupil in a gesture to show that *he* at least was impressed by the young man's effort. As Mrs Hoggett walked past them to leave the room she spoke in a tone of voice that was void of expression.

"I'll let you know of my markings." She put her copy of the manuscript on top of the piano. "Goodbye!"

At that, she left.

"It looks like I've failed my music A-level." David bowed his head in a morose manner. "Mrs Hoggett didn't appear to be very impressed, did she?"

"Well, don't give up hope yet!" Mr Scott smiled at his pupil in an attempt to cheer him up. "You've still got a good chance."

David knew the kind-hearted teacher was only trying to buck up his morale. Mrs Hoggett had made it quite clear that she was going to give him a low mark and he therefore would fail the exam. As he spoke, he idly tapped a few of the keys on the piano in a tuneful order.

"I'll be lucky if I get *fifteen* GCSE's at this rate!" He hit a low note on the keyboard. "I probably won't get anymore A-levels either. I haven't got a chance."

Mr Scott looked at him in an inquisitive manner.

"How many GCSE's and A-levels have you got?"

"Nine and three."

"That isn't bad! You are only fifteen." Mr Scott shrugged his shoulders. "Most other pupils of your age haven't even taken an exam yet."

"I do work hard though, Sir!" David pleaded. "I should've taken most of my A-levels a long time ago, especially maths."

"So why didn't you?"

"Mr Cutter said I wasn't ready. He thinks I haven't grasped trigonometry yet."

"I didn't know he took you for maths." Mr Scott sounded mildly surprised. "I thought you said you were taught by Mrs Blake?"

"I used to be." David frowned. "But at the beginning of the year Mr Cutter took over."

Mr Scott nodded his head and spoke in an understanding manner.

"Yes, of course. He teaches maths as well as religious education." He smiled at David. "Mr Cutter's a good teacher, isn't he?"

"I suppose so." The reply was subdued.

"You don't seem too convinced?"

David was not sure how to express his feelings about Mr Cutter. His own opinion of the teacher was that he was a status abusing, foul tempered and psychologically impaired man. However, he could not tell this to Mr Scott, so he decided to just moderate his descriptive views.

"Well, he's a bit strict." He was oblivious to the fact that he was now rubbing his palms together. "And he does tend to use his cane more than the other teachers do."

Mr Scott was aware that Mr Cutter was a stringent teacher by the way he authoritatively spoke about his pupils in the staff room. However, he and the other teachers knew little about the way that he administered his punishments with such ferocity. The temperamental man kept information like that a tight secret from the other members of the school staff.

Although Mr Scott was getting to the end of his teaching career he was still just as aware of what was going on as he was when he had first started. He could sense that David was not telling him all that he knew about his experiences with Mr Cutter, but he also realised that the young pupil clearly did not want to talk about it. However, he did have a strong feeling that the subject should not be left alone.

Mr Scott decided to indirectly ask David why he had such views about Mr Cutter.

"What makes you think he uses his cane too much?" He spoke about it as if it was a frivolous matter. "I should imagine he's always had a good enough reason to use it on someone."

The conversation was now starting to make David feel uneasy and the depressive features upon his face showed just how much so. He was desperately trying to think of what to say without revealing to Mr Scott the truth about how many times he had received the cane off of Mr Cutter. After considering what to say he found that he had no choice other than to bend the truth.

"I've seen Mr Cutter on a couple of occasions cane boys for simply just saying their own views on religion. I mean..." He sighed and bowed his head. "You don't *have* to believe in God."

"That's true." Mr Scott stood up and leant on the top of the piano. "But I'm sure he's never caned anyone just for that."

"Well, maybe not." The answer was spoken in a sullen voice.

Mr Scott frowned and thoughtfully rubbed his chin. He was beginning to think that maybe there was a lot more to this than he had first realised. It was not like him to get involved with other people's business, but he felt that this just might be an occasion when it was warranted.

"Have you ever seen Mr Cutter cane any pupils?" As he spoke he leant over the piano in an attentive manner.

David looked up at Mr Scott and stared into his eyes for a long moment before answering. He felt his blood rush through his veins as his nerves tingled all over his body. When he did reply to the question he uttered his words with a nervous stutter.

"Yes! Many times."

Of course, this was untrue, but David felt that he had to tell Mr Scott the truth about Mr Cutter even if it was in the form of a lie. He had only seen the ill tempered teacher cane a small number of other pupils before, but of the majority of the punishments he had witnessed he had been on the end of them himself. Whether anything could be done to stop it was another matter, but he felt that at least someone should know about it.

Although David felt quite guilty about not being honest with Mr Scott he had a feeling that his teacher was more aware of the truth of the situation than he was letting on. It seemed an unusual way of putting over his view, but it was the only way that he could think of. He knew that his teacher was quite wise to the world and was fairly sure that he understood the true meaning of what he had just said.

For a short while the two of them remained silent so that they could ponder upon their thoughts about the conversation they had just had. Mr Scott had a rare expression of concern on his normally cheerful face, while David sat at the piano gazing at the floor of the classroom. There was an uncomfortable stillness that was crying out to be broken, and it was the always prepared and conscientious teacher who broke the silence with an idle piece of small talk.

"So, how many more exams have you got before Christmas?" He asked.

"Three A-levels and a GCSE."

The two of them then drifted off into their usual form of conversation as if nothing had ever happened. Of course, neither of them had forgotten what had been said, but that was best left at the back of their minds for now. There was plenty of time to consider *that* subject at a later date.

"How could someone do such a disgusting thing to their wife?" There was sadness and anger mixed together in the tone of the voice. "What's wrong with these people that they can do such a grotesque thing to a member of their own family?"

Mike asked the question, but he did not really expect an answer from his wife or his daughter. Melanie and Sally just sat staring at the television set with glum faces. The six o'clock news was again bringing stories of hideous depravity into the living rooms of the common people.

The female newsreader was young and attractive, but not even her own good looks could bring any pleasantness to the report she was reading. She tried her best to appear unmoved by what she was saying, but such news would make anyone wince no matter how prepared they were and her distaste was quite evident. She had just announced the murder of a wife by her husband and had probably caused thousands of households around the country to be stricken with depression.

"Julie Hinchcliff was only twenty-four years old and was due to have her twenty-fifth birthday in eight days time. She never made it that far. Her headless corpse was found..."

As the television set was turned off a cold blanket of silence enshrouded the room. No one spoke and no one moved. It was as if they were paying a moment of grim respect to the life of the young woman who had been slain. Of course, none of them knew her, but at that moment in time it felt like the right thing to do.

Sally's parents were a middle aged friendly couple who had time to spare for anyone they met. They had emigrated over from America when her father had been offered a computer programming teaching post for the software company that he worked for. Although the distance of the move seemed to be a lot for just a job opportunity they were not leaving much behind in the way of family. Both of them had been single children in their upbringings so they had brought the most important part of their family with them in the way of their daughter.

Mike was of a medium build and wore a pair of round thin rimmed glasses that seemed to enhance his already intelligent appearance. Melanie looked quite similar to her daughter with her dark coloured skin and jet black hair, but she was a bit shorter and also wore spectacles. They were the perfect family with everything going for them and very few worries in the world.

It was after about five minutes of silence that Sally interrupted the lull that had been had created.

"Does violence in the home happen much?" The question was aimed at both of her parents.

"More than it should do." Mike replied.

Melanie looked at her daughter with a perplexed expression upon her face.

"Why do you ask that?" She asked.

Sally was about to answer when her father beat her to it.

"I know why." Mike looked across the living room towards his daughter and nodded his head. "I think your mother and I both know why."

Melanie instantly looked at her husband and raised her eyebrows in a forewarning manner. In return, Mike coolly patted her on the knee to assure her of his intentions. He then turned to his daughter and took in a deep breath to prepare himself for what he was about to say.

Sally had now sensed that something was coming up that she was not going to like. She had seen the nervous expressions on both of the faces or her parents and was now wondering just how bad this was going to be. As she sat up in her chair she braced herself for whatever might be coming.

Mike stood up and slowly made his way across the room to stand in front of the fireplace. He then took a moment to gather his thoughts to make sure his words came out exactly the right way. As he spoke he uneasily rubbed his hand on his forehead.

"Your mother and I have noticed something about David since you've been seeing him." He shrugged his shoulders. "I know you probably don't want to talk about it, but I think something's got to be said."

Sally sighed and nodded her head in an understanding manner. She knew what her father was talking about and he was right when he had said that she did not want to talk about it. For a moment, she closed her eyes in an attempt to shut out the pain that she was feeling, but, of course, it did not work.

Mike carried on speaking in a slow and uncomfortable voice.

"Whenever he comes around here he seems to be covered in cuts and bruises." He waved his hand in a restless manner. "At first your mother and I thought he might have just

93

picked up the occasional knock here and there like any other young lad of his age, but then we noticed that whenever one healed another appeared."

Sally lightly bit her lip and bowed her head so that her hair draped over her forehead. A feeling of sickness instantly swept over her as visions of David's wounds crowded into her mind. As she looked through the gaps in her hair across the room at her father she spoke in a distressed tone of voice.

"It happens all the time, Dad. His stepfather whips him with his belt, punches him around and even does the same to his mother. The bullies at school don't leave him alone and what's worse is that even one of the school teachers treats him badly." As she explained the full details of David's troubled life she raised her head and revealed streams of tears running down her cheeks. "The other day he told me that his mother has never loved him. All he's ever known is hate, anger and violence. It's so unfair. So, so unfair!"

Mike now realised that he had hit upon a subject that had obviously been a big concern to Sally for quite some time. It was not like any other problem his daughter might have had, as it did not directly involve her, and this would make it harder to deal with. As he spoke he slowly paced around the room.

"Why didn't you tell us before? You know we're always there for you." He stopped moving so he could take a good look at his daughter. "There are ways of dealing with things like this. There are people who can sort it out."

Sally wiped the tears from her eyes and shook her head.

"He asked me not to tell anyone. Please, you mustn't tell anyone!" She paused to try and gain control of her emotions. "If his stepfather finds out he'll hurt him even more."

Mike raised his hands in a bewildered manner.

"We can't just ignore it."

"I know, but..." Sally sniffed and folded her arms across her stomach. "I just don't want him to go through anymore bad times. He simply doesn't deserve it"

Mike looked towards Melanie and raised his eyebrows in a perturbed manner. He could understand why Sally was so concerned with David's safety, but they could not just let what was happening to him carry on the way it was. There was no way he could come up with an instant solution to the problem, but he thought that he could at least say some words to try to make his daughter feel at ease.

"We obviously don't want David to be hurt anymore than he already has. So, therefore, we won't say anything to anyone, but..." Before finishing his sentence he slowly walked across the room and rested his hand on his daughter's shoulder in an attempt to reassure her. "We will try our best to do something about it in the long run"

Sally tried to force a smile in return to make it look as if her father's words were appreciated. However, the simple truth was that nothing could be said to make her feel better and it soon showed. She lowered her head into her hands and shamelessly sobbed in front of both of her parents.

Mike and Melanie now realised that Sally needed to be comforted, so they both slowly moved over to her and sat on each side of her armchair. As they affectionately wrapped their arms around her they spoke soft and reassuring words to her.

"It's alright. I promise everything will be alright." Melanie whispered.

"Just don't worry about it! We're right here for you." Mike said quietly.

The both of them simply went about giving Sally the one thing that no parent had ever given David. Love.

Mr Cutter sat at his desk staring out across the classroom with a scowl etched into the features of his face. He studied each of the pupils in turn waiting for one of them to stop working or talk to a friend so that he could have the pleasure of issuing a reprimand. When he was satisfied that he had them all under his control his gaze went to a young man at the front of the room.

David was sitting with his head bowed and with his mind's full attention set upon his maths work. He was unaware that Mr Cutter was glaring at him, but if he had have known he would not have been at all surprised. On a number of occasions in the past he had looked up to see the temperamental teacher staring in his direction whilst wearing a glowering expression.

It used to make David feel uneasy when he noticed Mr Cutter watching him with his cold unfeeling eyes, but now he just ignored it. Like most things in his life he had just become used to it and had done his best to get on with whatever he was doing at the time regardless of the unwanted attention that he was receiving. However, he did sometimes wonder what went through the volatile teacher's mind while he was looking at him.

God created man in his own image. Unlike David Cain! He sits there in my classroom with all those blasphemous thoughts in his head. And those eyes! They see no light, just the darkness of evil.

The demon is within him. It needs to be dispelled just as Jesus cured the demonic boy when his father brought him before him.

And how appropriate that his name is Cain. Does he plan to kill, like Cain murdered his brother Abel?

There is no knowing what vile and depraved deeds this boy is capable of. He must have the evil wrenched from his body and soul.

The eccentric thoughts that would pass through Mr Cutter's mind were brought about by the strain of teaching for over twenty years and the loss of his wife to cancer just over a decade ago. When he had started in his profession he was an even-tempered and mildly religious man, but due to suddenly finding himself alone and the constant stress of his job, his mental condition had slowly degenerated into a state of an antisocial personality disorder. His behaviour had become quite impulsive and he dealt with every problem with the use of anger.

Mr Cutter had no other immediate relatives or friends to support him. The only people who he ever came into contact with were the other teachers of the school, the pupils who he taught and the congregation of his local church. All he had in his life was the one thing that he could always rely upon. Religion.

God, Jesus and the Holy Spirit were all whom Mr Cutter needed to turn to. They were always there, always listening and they always answered all of his questions before he had even asked them. This was no miracle and it did not even require a prayer.

The Bible. Every parable, miracle and verse of the 'Good Book' guided Mr Cutter on his way through life. Wherever he went it was always with him either clasped tightly in his hand or in his old brown leather case. Just as someone turns to their family or to a friend for help and advice he would find the answers that he looked for within the pages of his book.

Mr Cutter did not consider himself to be an evil man. He just punished the sinful. If a pupil misbehaved in his class whilst he was teaching he would not consider himself as being too harsh when he caned them for it. In fact, he thought of himself as being a righteous man carrying out the work of God.

Mr Cutter would never feel guilty when he sent a young boy away from his classroom crying because he had viciously caned him. Instead he would wait for the reprimanded pupil's next lesson with him and then watch him intently to see how he would react to the punishment. The boy would feverishly complete his work without even looking up from his books. This, the erratic teacher, would proudly consider to be because he had banished the evil from him.

Obviously, the reason why the boy would be so well behaved was because of his utter fear of being caned again. Mr Cutter was, of course, completely unaware of this due to being blinded by his own reverence in what he thought he had succeeded in doing. He would actually be so self assured by what he had done that he would go to church on the next Sunday and pray to God to thank him for helping him spread the good of Christianity.

No one knew of Mr Cutter's psychological disorder. Most of the other teachers at the school thought he was just a strict teacher who was also a little bit weird. The pupils simply feared him. As for the vicar and congregation of the church he went to every Sunday, they just thought of him as a lonely man who preferred his own company.

It was whilst Mr Cutter was having his erratic thoughts about David that his consciousness was interrupted by the ringing of the school bell. The pupils in the class instantly looked up at him to await his permission to go to their lunch break. As soon as he was sure that none of them had started to pack up their belongings too early he announced the end of the lesson.

"Very well! You may go to lunch!" He sat back in his chair and pointed to his desk. "Make sure you hand your books in before you leave!"

As the pupils made their way out of the classroom a pile of books started to build up on Mr Cutter's desk. At first he did not notice that an untidy mess was being made until David put his book on top. The short fused teacher straight away let his discontent be known.

"Cain, don't just shove your book anywhere on my desk!" He stood up and pointed to the pile. "Tidy that mess up now!"

"Yes, Sir!"

David replied unenthusiastically and started to arrange the books on the desk into a neat pile. He realised that he was being victimised, but he did as he was told nevertheless. As he tried to gather up all of the books the other pupils still kept on adding theirs to the pile making the mess more and more untidy.

Mr Cutter was not pleased that his desk was getting into such a state and made his feelings clear.

"Hurry up, Cain!" He ordered in an irritable tone of voice. "Don't try my patience."

Soon the rest of the pupils had gone leaving just the two of them behind. When David had finally put all of the books in a neat pile he went to make his way out of the classroom. However, before he could get to the door Mr Cutter stopped him and gave out another order.

"Not so fast, Cain!" He slapped his hand on his desk to make sure that he was getting the pupil's full attention. "I want you to clean the white-board before you go!"

As David heard the demand his shoulders slumped in an exasperated manner. He desperately wanted to go and meet Sally for lunch, but he knew better than to question the easily provoked teacher. Turning around slowly, he put his school bag on a nearby desk and picked up the cloth to clean the white-board.

Mr Cutter watched the proceedings very carefully to make sure the job was done properly. His hawk like eyes checked every bit of the white-board for any remaining dry ink marks. When David had finished the task he did not pick up his bag to leave the classroom, instead he just waited for the inevitable next order. And, of course, it came.

"Now make sure that all of the chairs are neatly put behind the desks!" Mr Cutter pointed his finger at David. "And don't scrape any of the legs on the floor. I don't want to hear any unnecessary racket."

Again the orders were carried out to each word exactly. David carefully lifted each chair up off of the floor and put it directly behind its desk as quietly as possible. When he had finished he waited at the front of the classroom for the next demand. He did not even look in the direction of his teacher and just stood there with his head bowed in a depressed manner.

Mr Cutter looked around the classroom desperately trying to find some other menial task for David to do. It was only after a prolonged period of time that he realised that there was nothing else that needed to be done. In an irritated tone of voice he ended the charade.

"I suppose that will *have* to do." He nonchalantly waved his hand towards the door. "You can go away now!"

David felt quite upset by the way he had been treated and shook his head in a peeved manner. It was obvious that Mr Cutter did not like him, but he did not know why. He could not understand why the irrational teacher would give him things to do after a lesson when he would have thought that he would have wanted to get rid of him as quickly as possible if he hated him as much as he thought that he did.

David had just reached the doorway on his way out when he stopped and turned around to face the room. Mr Cutter was now sitting down at his desk and was pulling a newspaper out of his leather case. He was unaware that he still had company until he heard a voice.

"Why do you dislike me *so* much?" David asked in an inquisitive tone. "What have I ever done to you?"

The reply to the question was spoken with malice.

"What?"

"I don't understand. For some reason you seem to resent me." There was a pause. "Why?"

"Don't you dare question me, Cain!" Mr Cutter stood up and threw his newspaper onto his desk. "I don't have to answer to you. It's about time you learnt some manners."

Although David knew that he had just got himself into trouble he still wanted his question to be answered.

"I'm sorry, Sir! I didn't mean any disrespect by what I said." He half raised his hands in a submissive manner. "I just wanted to know..."

Mr Cutter interrupted him.

"Don't you listen? I said you weren't to question me!" He walked across the room and pointed his finger within millimetres of David's face. "You're bad mannered and you don't do as you're told."

Still there was a need for answers.

"I know you're just about to punish me for being what you consider to be insolent and for whatever other reasons you can think of." David took in an exasperated deep breath. "But do you think you could at least tell me why you dislike me after you've done it?"

"Right, that's it!"

Sally glanced at her watch as she quickly made her way through the corridors. She had arranged with David to meet him in the front entrance of the school, but she had decided to go directly to his last lesson instead. As she passed the flow of the other pupils on their way to lunch she eagerly looked among them for her lover.

It had not taken Sally long to reach the corridor which lead to Mr Cutter's mathematics class, but she had made herself slightly out of breath due to her haste. There were now only a few pupils wandering around and she was beginning to think that she may have somehow missed David whilst making her way there. For a while she just stood there looking around in a bemused manner whilst considering what to do next. It was then when she heard a raised voice coming from inside one of the rooms.

"Put your hand out!" The tone was low and laced with anger. "You will learn to do as you're told!"

Sally instantly recognised that the voice belonged to Mr Cutter, and as usual he did not seem to be in a good mood. It appeared as if yet another pupil was in for a vicious caning at the hands of the vile tempered teacher. Such sounds coming from inside his classroom were not uncommon.

However, on this occasion Sally had a nagging feeling that she was not going to like what was going on inside the classroom. In an attempt to cure her curiosity she slowly made her way over to the open door to take a look in. As she poked her head around the corner she gasped at what she saw.

David stood with his arms hanging limply by his sides with a weary look upon his face. Standing in front of him with a cane clasped tightly in his hand was Mr Cutter, red faced and enraged. The whole scene was as depraved and sickening as any Sally had ever seen. After their conversation in the park she could not believe that her loved one could have ever have deservedly got into such a situation.

Mr Cutter repeated his demand.

"Put your hand out, Cain!"

Before doing as he was told David made one last request in a pleading manner.

"Very well, but afterwards could you please tell me why you feel *so* much hatred towards me!"

He then put his hand out ready to be caned.

"Quiet boy!" Mr Cutter raised his arm. "You just take what you deserve and learn from it!"

At that, the cane came slashing down. This was immediately followed by an anguished shout from the entrance of the class.

"No!"

Sally called out in desperation as she darted into the room. As David looked around to see who had called out his eyes instantly widened. Up until now his face had been quite expressionless, but now it was one of deep concern. It was bad enough him being punished for such a frivolous reason, but having it done in such a belittling manner in front of the person who he loved was more degrading than he could imagine.

Mr Cutter turned to the intruder and bellowed out a command.

"Get out of my classroom, girl!"

Sally just stood staring at the both of them with a distressed look upon her face. Normally she would have done as the teacher had said, but on this occasion the welfare of her lover was at the forefront of her concern. She knew that she would get into trouble for interfering with Mr Cutter's business, but she just simply had to find out what was going on.

"What's happening?" She asked David. "Why are you being caned?"

Mr Cutter answered for him.

"For disobedience!" He pointed his finger at Sally. "And you'll be punished as well if you don't get out of this classroom right now!"

At that, Mr Cutter turned to face David to carry on with the punishment. Again the cane came slicing down producing a hideous crack as the bamboo struck the flesh. The sound it made was almost as repelling as the pain.

Sally could still not bring herself to leave her loved one in such a situation. She again tried to find out what was going on. Only this time she turned her attention to Mr Cutter.

"What has he done wrong?" Her voice was distraught and erratic. "Why are you hurting him?"

This time David turned to speak to Sally in a pleading manner.

"Please leave!" He looked at her with saddened eyes. "You shouldn't be here."

The whole situation was now getting out of hand and it was starting to make Mr Cutter even more infuriated. Yet again he turned around to face Sally and stared at her with his scowling fierce eyes. This time he spoke his demands quietly, but his words were still full of viciousness.

"Get out now!" He gritted his teeth. "And don't come back!"

David looked at Sally and nodded his head to show that he agreed with what Mr Cutter was saying even though it was for a different reason. He did not want her to get hurt as well. There was no telling what depths this ill-tempered teacher would stoop to.

Sally now realised that the reason why David did not want her there to witness his punishment was because of his shame, so she turned to leave. She knew that he would feel embarrassed by being caned in front of her, so the least she could do for him was not be there. However, something inside her kept telling her that she could not just simply walk off and leave her lover to be hurt in such a callous way.

Mr Cutter bent his cane with both hands and then raised it above his head in a ready position. David just stood motionless staring into the cruel teacher's eyes. He would not cry or show any signs that he was in pain simply as a defiant act of stubborn pride. Instead, he would do as he always did and just hold his head up high with all of his dignity intact.

The cane came down upon David's hand sending a shudder shooting straight up his arm. He did not flinch, nor did he make a noise to reveal his suffering. With every bit of his mind concentrated on cancelling out the pain from his consciousness he just stood firm with his pride aloft.

Mr Cutter was almost like a wild animal as he brought the cane down time after time in quick succession. Red marks instantly appeared on David's palm as each of the blows struck against his flesh. The whole scene resembled some kind of medieval torture.

Sally was now standing in the corridor leaning up against the wall next to the door of Mr Cutter's classroom. Although she tried not to listen she could still hear the whipping noise of the cane every time it struck its target. The grim sound it made hurt her just as much as it would have if had it have been her who was receiving the punishment.

It was not long before a single tear started to flow from Sally's right eye. The sickening thoughts of what was going on inside the classroom made her cringe with desperation. She could not bear being away from her lover when he was enduring such pain. There was simply too much hurt for her to endure.

Neither Mr Cutter nor David saw it coming. It was almost as if it had materialised out of thin air. The speed and the sheer accuracy of it were as surprising as the fact that it had actually happened.

Sally aimed her slap for Mr Cutter's right cheek and that was exactly where it hit, with full power and with a shocking degree of sting. It instantly left a red handprint on the side of his face as if it were a reminder of what had happened. Neither of the two in the room had seen her enter, but they were now very aware of her presence.

It took some time before Mr Cutter could come to his senses and restore his balance. When he did he shook his head in a dazed manner and then his expression turned to one of absolute fury. He was just about to say his piece when he was suddenly interrupted by Sally who was now standing in between David and him.

"Just leave him alone!" Her face was twisted into a threatening sneer. "You fucking arsehole!"

For a short moment Mr Cutter looked stunned. Not only had he been struck, but now he was even being insulted. However, as usual his temper took over and he went about reprimanding his new antagonist.

"You are in serious trouble." He bellowed the next order. "Girl, put your hand out, right now!"

It was only now that Sally had been shouted at that she realised the magnitude of what she had done. All of a sudden she had found herself in the most serious of trouble that she had ever been involved in her life. As a surge of fright flooded over her she gave into the furious teacher's demands. She raised her hand ready to be caned.

Mr Cutter raised his arm and took aim at Sally's palm. The cane floated motionlessly above his head for a long moment as he took time to eye up his target for the utmost accuracy. Then, when he was sure of a direct hit, he brought it crashing down onto the middle of the hand.

However, it was not Sally's palm that was struck. David stood with the cane clasped tightly in his hand staring straight into Mr Cutter's eyes. His face was expressionless as he spoke, but his voice was full of resolve.

"You are not going to hurt her!" He slowly shook his head. "You are never going to hurt *her*!"

Before Mr Cutter could even contemplate what was happening he found that the cane had been snatched from his grasp. David now stood holding it with both hands in front of the shocked teacher's face whilst still staring deep into his eyes. Then with the utmost of ease he snapped the cane in two and in a defiant manner he threw the pieces across the room.

Sally was now too frightened to even move. Both she and David had gone too far and the whole situation had become way out of control. She was now surely going to be in deep trouble and she was not looking forward to paying the consequences for it.

David felt no such fear. His only concern now was making sure that Sally remained unharmed by the sadistic teacher. In the back of his mind he knew that he was going to be in serious trouble, but there was nothing new about that.

Mr Cutter looked at the pieces of his broken cane on the floor and then back to David. The expression upon his face was one of shock and disbelief. Up until now every pupil who he had ever caned had never done anything but taken their punishment and learnt from it. In an attempt to gain some self-respect he did his best to try to show that he still had some authority.

"You two go and see the head of year now!"

It was a weak display of power, but Mr Cutter was desperate to get back some of the dignity that he had so obviously lost. The look upon his face was not one of temper anymore, but one of shock and defeat. He had never been so humbled by a pupil before in the whole of his teaching career. There was still a rush of anger flowing through his veins, but the feeling of humiliation diminished it.

David turned around to look at Sally and immediately noticed the frightened expression upon her face. She was not used to such situations and the whole confrontation had obviously been too much for her to cope with. He knew that he was probably going to bear the brunt of the punishment, but she was still his main concern. Realising that she needed some comforting he put his arm around her shoulder in an attempt to ease her worries. As they started to make their way to the head of year's office he whispered some soothing words into her ear.

"It's all right my darling." He leant his head against hers. "I'll make sure you don't get into too much trouble."

Sally replied in a nervous manner.

"What about you?"

"Never mind about me." David half smiled. "They can't hurt me."

The head of the year was a tall well built man and he used his size with great effect when reprimanding a pupil. Mr Ketteridge had been at the school for thirty years and had picked up all of the useful techniques when dealing with a wayward troublemaker. He would deliberately stand close to the boy who he was telling off and use his large frame to tower over them in a cowering manner. On this occasion, however, it was simply not working.

David stood up straight in front of Mr Ketteridge staring straight into his eyes with a blank expression upon his face. It was plainly obvious that he was not bothered about being in trouble and his lack of concern was starting to agitate the head of year. The normally calm and calculated man was becoming quite enraged and it showed in the way that he repeatedly blinked whilst he was trying to exercise his authority.

It seemed as though David was the only person in the office who was not distressed by the state of affairs. Mr Cutter was, of course, utterly infuriated by it all and was standing in the corner of the office with his brow deeply furrowed. As for Sally, she just stood with her head bowed in a nervous and submissive manner.

Mr Ketteridge asked the usual obvious questions.

"So, what have you both got to say for yourselves?" He looked at David and Sally in turn. "I trust there's a reason for your inexcusable behaviour?"

Mr Cutter answered for them.

"There's no excuse for such an outrage!" He raised his voice. "It's the most disgusting display of..."

David interrupted him.

"I take full responsibility for everything that has happened." His voice was low and calm. "It was entirely all my fault."

Mr Cutter was only too pleased to agree.

"It certainly was entirely all your fault, Cain." He folded his arms and nodded his head in an erratic manner. "There's no question of that."

David looked over in Sally's direction and noticed that she was watching him with an uneasy expression upon her face. He knew that she would not want him to take the full blame, but he could not let her be caned in the same way as he was expecting to be himself. There was no doubt that the two of them were going to be punished, but he wanted to make sure that it was him who took the majority of what was coming to them.

Mr Ketteridge frowned inquisitively at David as he spoke.

"So this was all your doing?"

"Yes, Sir!" The reply was apathetically muttered in an expressionless tone of voice. "It was all me."

Mr Cutter was quite content that David was taking the full blame and he intended to make the most of it. He would be more than pleased to see the demonic boy take the best part of the punishment for what had happened. His only regret was that it was not going to be him who was going to administer the caning.

David carried on with confessing to the entirety of the incident.

"I was rude to Mr Cutter, I was disobedient and I snapped his cane." He shrugged his shoulders in a nonchalant manner. "I did it all."

At that, Mr Ketteridge walked over to his desk and opened the top draw. He then pulled out a cane and put it on the top of the desk for all to see. As he turned round to face David he pointed his finger at him.

"You're in serious trouble young man." He nodded his head as if to confirm his own words. "Very, very serious trouble."

Mr Cutter stepped forward.

"I suggest a two week suspension for the both of them." He pointed at David and sneered. "And a good caning for him at the very least."

After a short amount of deliberation, Mr Ketteridge approved the suggested punishments and then carried them out without any delay.

Sally stood shivering in the cold air outside the school gates whilst watching David approach from the front entrance. As he walked towards her he unconsciously rubbed the red marks on his hand from where he had been caned by Mr Ketteridge. He did not seem too distressed by the pain, but that was because having his palm beaten with a piece of flexible bamboo had happened so much to him that he had got used to it.

When David reached Sally he stopped within feet of her and took a moment to study her face so as to assess how she was feeling. He knew that she was foreign to such violent encounters as the one that they had just experienced and it showed in her worried expression. Although he had taken the larger part of the punishment he still found himself to be more concerned for her welfare than his own.

David was just about to take Sally's hand so as to walk her home when, almost as if to plead for him to comfort her, a single tear trickled from her eye. As soon as he saw it run down her cheek he immediately stepped forward and affectionately embraced her. Although he had just been caned for the second time in half an hour he felt more pain now whilst his lover was crying on his shoulder than in any other moment of the day.

It was while David was consoling Sally that he saw an all too familiar face in the front entrance of the school staring straight back at him. Mr Cutter looked at the two pupils outside the school gates with his mind producing his usual hate filled thoughts. His expression was still glowering and his eyes burned with rage as he watched the display of loving affection.

Mr Cutter realised that David was now staring back at him so he turned away and walked off. As he made his way to his next lesson he muttered some remarks of disapproval.

"That damned boy is evil!" He breathed out a temperamental sigh. "Utterly evil!"

As David watched Mr Cutter walk off he slowly shook his head in a resentful manner. He had been at the brunt of the wicked man's temper on a number of occasions, but he had never felt like this. Being caned himself was one thing, but Sally being upset was an entirely different matter all together. There was no way he would accept that.

With half of the week's suspension completed Sally and David were starting to wish that they would never have to go back to school again. They had spent every day together and had thoroughly enjoyed doing whatever they wanted without anyone telling them what to do. It almost made them being punished worthwhile.

Mike was at work and Melanie was out shopping, leaving the house empty, so David and Sally had made good use of their privacy. Making love at half past two in the afternoon was a lot more satisfying than reading Shakespeare's 'Hamlet' in an English literature class. They may not have been learning anything, but they simply did not care.

As David sat on the bed he picked up a packet of condoms and shook it to see if there were any left. When he did not hear a rattle he smiled to himself and then threw the empty packet into the bin in the corner of the room. Over the last few days contraception had become quite an expensive accessory to life, but he cheerfully considered it to be money well spent.

When Sally got out of the shower she picked up a towel and wrapped it around her body. As she walked into the bedroom she shook her wet hair over David's half-naked body in a playful gesture. He immediately arched his back and laughed at his own comeuppance. However, he soon got his own back when he pulled her towel away from her body.

Sally smiled and raised her eyebrows.

"You don't even give us time to rest, do you?" She sat down next to him and lightly ran her nails down the muscles of his back. "You're insatiable."

David laughed and lay back on the bed.

"Well we could try to cure that insatiable appetite of mine, but unfortunately we've run out of condoms."

"Already?"

"I'm afraid so!"

Sally took the towel off of David and started to dry herself. As she did so she became aware that the eager eyes of her lover were closely watching her. In an attempt to entice him further she deliberately slowed down her movements into an erotic pace.

David's eyes fervently opened wide, but as he leant forward he quietly whispered into Sally's ear in a reluctant manner.

"We can't without condoms."

"Look in the top draw of the cabinet!" The reply was spoken in a sensual tone of voice. "Where I keep my underwear."

David leant over the bed and pulled open the top draw of the cabinet. When he saw what was lying on top of the pile of underwear he slowly nodded his head in an excited manner. Just as he picked up the full packet of condoms, Sally's towel flew through the air and completely covered his head. All he heard was a playful laugh and then the bed creak as she sensually lay back upon it.

"Mum! Dad! Would you like tea or coffee?"

"Two coffees please, Sally." Mike replied. "We'll be down in a minute."

Melanie looked at her husband from across the bedroom and smiled at him in a contented manner. As she walked up to him she put her arms around his waist and kissed him on the cheek. Mike just looked around at her and raised his eyebrows as he spoke.

"I wish I was as calm as you."

Melanie leant back to get a better look at his face and replied to the statement in an inquisitive manner.

"What do you mean?"

"Well, today's the day." Mike shrugged his shoulders. "How do you think she'll take it?"

Melanie spoke in an assured tone of voice.

"She'll be all right." She nodded her head. "We've done the right thing."

"I know." Mike leant his cheek against the top his wife's head. "I know we have."

The two of them kissed and then left the room.

Sally was sitting in the dining room waiting for her parents to come down from their bedroom. She had prepared their breakfasts for them and had even put the morning newspapers on the table ready for them to read. It was not a job that she had been asked to do, but it was something that she enjoyed doing and it had become a regular occurrence every Sunday.

Whilst Sally was getting some plates out of a cupboard she noticed some opened letters on the work top. As she picked one of them up and read the envelope, a curious expression crossed her face. On the front of it was a company logo with picture of a house and the words 'Castle Estate Agents'.

Although the letter was addressed to Sally's father she took it out anyway and began to read the contents. After a while she managed to get the gist of it, and when she did her expression turned from one of perplexity to one of shock. It was only when she heard someone approaching that she slid it back into its envelope and deceivingly put it back amongst the other correspondence. In an attempt to appear as if nothing had happened she started to spread out the plates on the kitchen table ready to put the food on.

As Melanie walked into the room she smiled and looked at the table.

"What have we got, Sally?"

"Heated croissants and grapefruit."

Mike stood in the doorway and stretched his arms out as he yawned.

"I think I'll have the croissants today." He took in a deep breath through his nose. "They smell nice."

103

Mike and Melanie sat down at the table and started to help themselves to the food. Sally had already put some grapefruit on her plate and was generously sprinkling sugar on it. There was a long moment of silence as they all got stuck into their breakfasts and sifted through the morning papers.

When Melanie had finished her croissant she turned to her husband and tapped him on the back of the hand. As Mike looked up at her she raised her eyebrows to let him know that it was time. He nodded his head in return and put his newspaper back on the table. After taking a moment to study his daughter he spoke to her in a calm tone of voice.

"Sally, we've got something to tell you."

"What's that?"

"Well, it will probably affect you more than it will us." Mike put his right elbow on the table and rested his chin upon his hand. "Due to certain circumstances we have decided to..."

As Sally ran out of the house she did not even look back. Mike and Melanie both stood at the front window watching their daughter as she made her way up the garden path. They had never seen her act in such a way.

"Who the fuck's that?" Norman's mouthed the obscenity to no one in particular. "They've only got to ring the doorbell once. We're not deaf."

"I'll get it."

David got up out of an armchair and made his way into the hall. He also wondered who could be repeatedly ringing the doorbell on a Sunday morning. As he opened the front door he was surprised to see Sally standing on the step with an apprehensive look upon her face. After taking a moment to clear her throat she spoke in an anxious tone of voice.

"Hello David!"

"Hi Sally! I wasn't expecting to see you until midday."

Sally lightly grabbed hold of David's hands and pulled him towards her. He could see that she had something heavy on her mind, but he did not know what it was. She took in a deep breath and looked straight into his eyes as she spoke.

"I've got something that I need to tell you." She lightly bit her lip with anticipation. "And it's really important."

"Really? What?"

"I can't tell you here." Sally glanced over David's shoulder into the house and then looked back at him. "Get your coat! We'll go for a walk in the park and I'll tell you when we get to our usual spot."

Just as David went to get his long winter coat, Norman bellowed out another foul-mouthed remark.

"It's getting bloody cold in here." He added an extra insult. "Close the door, you arsehole!"

"Sorry!" David called out and then whispered his next comment to Sally. "Norman's in even more of a bad mood right now. He's working night shifts."

After closing the front door, David put on his coat and looked around at Sally with a perplexed expression upon his face. She was standing with her hands clasped together and her head bowed. Whatever it was that she was going to tell him in the park it was obviously something quite momentous.

Whilst David and Sally were walking arm in arm towards the park he looked at her with a mystified expression upon his face. He did not know whether to be worried or excited about what she was about to tell him. In truth he had no idea what to expect. In all of the

104

time that he had known her he had never seen her so candid and so obviously contemplative about something.

David did not want to wait to find out what was going on and went about trying to prematurely get some answers.

"What have you got to tell me Sally?"

"I'll tell you when we reach the bench in the park." She squeezed him tightly around the waist with her arm and quietly spoke her next remark. "It's all right! Everything's all right!"

It was a twenty-minute walk to the park and the two of them had to pass through a number of streets to get there. When they finally got near the entrance, Sally started to lead David across the road by his hand. As they walked she turned to speak to him in a reassuring tone of voice.

"Don't look so worried!" She slowly shook her head. "I said everything would be..."

The car hit Sally at approximately forty miles per hour. She did not have a chance to see it, let alone avoid it. Everything just happened far too quickly.

David had been holding Sally's hand when it had suddenly been whipped from his grasp. In one moment he was looking into her eyes and in the next all he could see was a blank space. He suddenly found himself standing alone on the edge of the road with his now empty hand held out and his gaze fixed upon nothing.

The driver of the car had simply not seen Sally walk into the road. A combination of not concentrating on what he was doing and the fact that he was speeding lead to him not even getting enough time to brake, let alone swerve out of the way. In just that split second many lives would change forever.

After the car had hit Sally it spun out of control and careered onto the other side of the road. With a loud bang it went straight into a tree and came to a sudden halt. The front end of it was completely mangled up with the blood-splattered body of the driver now lying motionless on the bonnet.

It only took a short moment of time for David to come to his senses, but it felt like a lot longer. As soon as he became aware of what had happened the expression upon his face turned into one of utter shock. He instantly turned his head to look up the street in search for Sally. And then he found her.

A lonely figure lay in a heap in the middle of the road twisted and unmoving. Her long black hair was spread out across the tarmac and her arms and legs were bent into awkward positions. Blood seeped from her ears and various other wounds upon her body making ever widening puddles upon the ground.

At first, David sprinted towards Sally, but when he got closer to her he gradually slowed down to a stop. For a moment he just stood looking over her with an expression of utter horror upon his face. As his pale blue eyes scoured her crushed and wretched body he put his hands upon his head and muttered an exclamation.

"Oh no!"

David slowly lowered himself down to kneel next to Sally and then put his hand to her neck to feel for her pulse. For a long moment he closed his eyes so as to concentrate on what he could sense on the tips of his fingers. As he slowly removed his hand he let out a deep-exasperated breath. He then made a quiet and imploring plea.

"Come on, Sally!" He bowed his head. "Please, hang in there!"

A crowd had now started to form in the street as people came over to view the carnage. Some offered David words of consolation and advice whereas others just turned the heads away from the sickening sight of bloodshed. It was a wonder why some of the people were even there by the way they looked so obviously disgusted by what they saw, but for some depraved reason they all just seemed to want to keep on viewing another person's misery.

Whilst David was waiting for an ambulance to arrive he stayed by Sally's side with her hand grasped in his and with his head lowly bowed. For the first time since he could remember he did not feel ashamed to cry in front of his lover. Even with all of the people gathered around he felt no disgrace as tears welled in his eyes and rolled down his cheeks.

There was a morbid silence throughout the corridor of the casualty ward as David, Mike and Melanie sat waiting for news of Sally's condition. They had been in the hospital for a number of hours and the length of time they had spent in anticipation of being informed of the extent of her injuries had only increased their anxiety. It almost seemed as though the waiting was as painful as the remorse.

The only news that the doctors had given so far was that Sally had an excessive amount of bleeding under the skull and would have to be operated on immediately. She also had a number of broken bones and several deep cuts that would need to be worked on. None of the doctors had said it literally, but the whole situation was not looking at all promising, and the three waiting in the corridor knew it.

Every now and again shouts could be heard coming from inside the operating theatre and each time it sent shivers down David's spine. Sally had been in surgery for over six hours and with each minute that passed the more agonising the wait became. It was like a mental torture. The not knowing, the hoping and utter fear of having nothing left to live for.

Melanie had been crying for most of the time that they had been waiting in the corridor. Mike sat with his arm wrapped around her and occasionally wiped her eyes with an already damp handkerchief. The two of them did not look at each other. They just stared into empty spaces with only their thoughts of hope to keep them from losing their minds.

The three of them in the corridor had been waiting for so long that at first none of them had even noticed the surgeon walk out of the operating theatre and stand in front of them. It was only when he spoke that he got their attention.

"I have some news." His voice was subdued and quiet. "We've finished operating."

Mike and Melanie immediately both stood up and started to question him.

"Is she all right?"

"What's happened?"

As David also got up the surgeon now found that he was surrounded by three very worried looking faces. Although he was middle aged and had years of experienced he still did not look at ease for what he was about to say. He spoke slowly and clearly so that he would not have to repeat himself.

"Sally is going to live."

This was immediately followed by sighs of relief. The surgeon carried on with his summary.

"However, the car hit her very hard and..." He paused for a short moment. "It looks as if her wounds could well be permanent."

Mike tried to extract some more information.

"Will she be able to walk? Has she lost any limbs?" He put his hands out in an erratic manner. "What do you mean?"

The surgeon frowned as he spoke.

"We've put her on life support and she's in a stable condition. She received an extremely hard blow to the head and has suffered a subdural haematoma. That basically means that she had a large amount of blood on her brain that we've had to surgically remove. However, when we carried out a PET scan we came across an abnormal lack of brain activity." He took in a deep breath and slowly shook his head. "I'm afraid the damage is so bad that she's fallen into a vegetative state. It's very unlikely that she'll ever recover from it."

Melanie barely managed to get her sentence out due to her shock.

"What are the chances?"

The surgeon looked at her with a saddened expression.

"Virtually zero."

For a long moment there was a cold silence. No one spoke a word or moved a muscle. However, after managing to gain enough self-control Mike asked another question.

"How long will she be on life support for?"

The surgeon shrugged his shoulders.

"Days, weeks, we simply can't tell."

Mike closed his eyes for a short moment and then looked at the surgeon straight in the eyes.

"Is she in pain?" It showed on his face how much it hurt him to ask the question. "I need to know this."

"She's in a coma and shouldn't be able to feel a thing." The surgeon lowered his gaze. "But if she awakes there's no telling how much she pain might be in."

David had heard enough. He had not spoken a word throughout hearing the surgeon's diagnosis and had just listened to everyone else. Even if he had have wanted to say something at a moment like this he would have found it hard to get the right words out anyway.

Ever since Sally had gone into the operating theatre all David had wanted was to be by her side. Of course, he had not been allowed to be in there and had just had to be content with staying in the corridor. However, now that the operation had finished and there seemed to be no one about he saw his chance to be with her. Although he knew that no one was allowed to see her yet, he found the temptation far too strong.

As David stood at the doors of the operating theatre he looked in through the window. He saw Sally lying on a bed surrounded by several medical apparatus and with a number of tubes hanging off of her. At first the hideous sight of his lover's broken body made him wince, but he still could not take his eyes off of her.

David looked up and down the corridor to make sure that there were not any nurses or doctors about who might stop him from going into the operating theatre. When he was satisfied that the coast was clear he slipped in through the doors and quietly made his way towards Sally. As he came to stand next to her he noticed the full extent of her injuries and could not help but voice his heartache.

"My poor Sally. How could this happen to you?" He took in a deep breath and then slowly raised his head in a determined manner. "I swear this is not how it is meant to be. I just won't let it happen. I refuse to accept this."

Sally lay with her head slanted to one side and her hands bent in towards her body in an enfeebled posture. She had a breathing tube going into her windpipe and there were several stitched up wounds on her body where she had broken bones. The side of her head had been shaven and revealed a long cut where the surgeons had operated on her skull.

Sally's horrific appearance forced David to close his eyes and shut the scene out of his mind. He had seen his own face battered and bruised on a number of occasions and he had seen his own mother in a similar condition, but this was the most sickening sight he had ever witnessed. As he bowed his head he spoke some conclusive words as if to offer a remedy.

"I will bring you back Sally. I don't care how long it takes and I don't care what I have to do." He closed his eyes and let out a long breath. "Nothing will stop me."

No one spoke a word as the three dull looking figures in the car sat staring out at the twilight lit streets whilst on their way home. There was a cold mournful aura that enshrouded everyone and right now that was the way that they wanted it. It was obvious what each of them was thinking about, but none of them wanted to voice their opinions.

David sat on the back seat of the car with a distant look in his eyes and his face void of expression. A soft shower of rain lightly sprayed against the windows of the car as he gazed out at the dark outlines of the houses as they slowly passed them by. There was a sombre stillness in the surrounding streets that seemed somehow akin to his drained thoughts of hopelessness.

When the car reached David's house he did not even realise where he was. He just kept staring out of the window into a seemingly empty space. It was only when Melanie spoke to him that he turned his attention to the outside world.

"You're home David!"

He just nodded his head and went to pull the handle of the car door. It was then when Mike turned around to look at him with a pained expression upon his face.

"There's something you should know before you go." He glanced at Melanie then back again. "Sally is in a very bad way."

David just looked at him with his same empty and impassive appearance. Melanie was now resting her head in her hands in a self-effacing manner. As Mike spoke it was obvious that he did not want to say what he was about to.

"She has very bad damage to her head and there's no telling how long she'll be in the coma for. Even if she does come out of it she'll probably always be in a vegetative state." He rubbed the side of his head in a pensive manner. "The doctor says she might also be in a lot of pain if she awakes."

David knew all of this and could not understand why Mike was repeating it all. The last thing that he wanted was to be reminded of Sally's tragic condition. As he spoke he looked out of the window at nothing in particular.

"We don't know that for sure." His face remained stony and expressionless. "She might recover."

"I really hope that's true David." Mike sighed. "I really do!"

A whimper came from Melanie's direction and she started to shake as she cried. The whole atmosphere of the car had now become unbearable and they all just wanted to get home. Mike now wanted to end the conversation as quickly as possible so as to get on his way.

"I'm sorry to say this David." He shook his head with sheer grief. "It looks like Sally is never going to be completely alright after what has happened. I know this is a horrible thing to say, but her life is virtually already over."

David did not want to hear anymore and had already started to get out of the car. He did not know if Mike had finished what he was saying, but the fact that he was now listening to someone talk about the end of his lover's life was an insufferable torture. In the depths of his heart and mind he knew what he had just heard was true, but he simply did not want to hear such sickening facts.

For all of the time that David had known Sally he had never realised that he actually had something to lose. He had almost taken her for granted and now just as everything was going right in his life he had suddenly ended up with absolutely nothing. To be put up to a level of happiness that was so high and then to be dropped to a depth of sorrow so low was a torment too painful to endure.

David now found himself standing on the edge of the pavement with his head bowed in a desolate manner as Mike and Melanie drove off up the street. The wind blew his coat across his body and streams of rain ran down his face. As the setting sun carved an opening in the clouds it created an almost sinister red glow across the street.

All David could think of was seeing Sally's battered and feeble body lying in the operating theatre. The sight of tubes sticking out of various parts of her body and the grotesque wounds that had been stitched up by the doctors were as terrible as anything he had ever seen. And then to hear Mike's words as he had got out of the car seemed to torture him even further.

"Her life is virtually already over!"

As the visions of Sally's humbled and wretched frame lying on the hospital bed passed through David's consciousness he now started to feel an uncontrollable sensation of tumultuous grief wash over his body. His mind became overwrought with emotion as anguish flooded through his veins. Although the outside air was cold and bitter he suddenly broke out in a chilling sweat.

David turned around and looked at his home with a harrowed expression upon his face. With the dim twilight of dusk only just managing to illuminate the outline of the depressing looking house the whole sombre picture seemed to reflect all that he had left in the world. His future held little for him but a dull colourless life with nothing to look forward to other than a bleak and loveless existence.

With all the grim images passing through David's mind he suddenly felt a compulsive urge just to run away from it all. In a rush of energy he turned from his house and started to run up the street without any sense of direction or plan of destination. He had never done anything so pointless or erratic in his life, but on a day when nothing seemed to make sense it almost felt as if it was most normal thing that had happened so far.

As David sprinted along the pavement rain lashed against his face and mingled in with the tears that flowed from his eyes. A strong wind blew at him full on and as his coat fluttered around him it acted like a sail repeatedly knocking him off balance. The sight of him stumbling up the street without any guidance or purpose seemed to depict the delirious state in which his mind was in.

David had soon reached a narrow footpath that ran through the side streets and lead out towards the outskirts of the town. He found himself knocking into garden fences and brick walls as he staggered his way along in a frenzied and futile attempt to flee from his life. It did not matter how fast he tried to run he could not escape from the torturing grief that was laying siege to his mind.

After splashing through numerous puddles and running full on into the wind, David's clothes had soon become drenched with rain. An icy chill clutched at his body, but due to his emotional state he did not even notice his discomfort. It seemed as though there was nothing right now that could warrant a single thought of self-concern from his overwrought mind.

It had not taken long for David to reach the open spaces of the countryside on the outskirts of the town. The houses and garden fences of the streets had now been left behind and replaced by the woodland and fields of farmland. Even the sombre everyday sounds of the town were now distant murmurs drowned out by the rustling of the wind through the trees.

Whereas before, David had been running on hard concrete paths, he now found himself treading through thick mud. On a number of occasions he had lost his footing and only just managed to keep himself upright by using his hands to stop his fall. He had soon become splattered with mud and now looked quite unkempt in his appearance.

Unlike the buildings in the streets the vast open spaces of the countryside offered no protection from the now worsening weather. Heavy gales blew the rain across the fields relentlessly flattening the crops. Trees dangerously swayed in the wind forcing flocks of birds to take to the air forming dark cloud like shapes in the sky. Nothing was exempt from the increasingly aggressive onslaught of the elements.

David had now tired into just a staggering jog as he made his way along a muddy track. His aimless trek was now becoming increasingly rigorous and he suddenly found his way blocked by a rusty old metal gate. As he clambered over it he unceremoniously tumbled to the ground on the other side. Wearily picking himself up out of the mud he looked up to see a large cornfield in front of him. It resembled a rough sea as the wind swept across it in wave like gusts.

Even though David was now almost too tired to even stand up he kept on moving towards his non-existent destination. His soaking hair draped over his brow and his mud stained coat flapped about his body. As he trudged through the corn in the field it dragged against his legs and slowed him down to a clumsy walk. It was not long before his muscles could take no more of the self imposed mental and physical punishment and he fell to his knees in an exasperated act of submission.

Still the wind blew the rain mercilessly against David's face as he knelt in the middle of the field shattered and defeated. He tried in vain to keep his head held up high, but even that was now a strain. His arms hung limply at his sides as he swayed about on his knees in an enervated manner.

Slowly lifting his head in one last show of strength, David exhaustedly looked up to the sky as if to seek a divine answer to his woes. As he scoured the heavens for inspiration all he saw was a swirling mass of dark and ominous looking clouds. The grim sight above him almost seemed like a sinister omen foretelling him of the emptiness of his future. He now finally knew that he had nothing left to live for. Lowering his head down in a humbled manner he at last accepted his downfall.

David's life was over.

The flimsy curtains fluttered in the wind and lightly brushed against David's arms as he stood looking out of the open window. His bedroom was lit by the moon's subtle blue glow and it illuminated his face giving it a deathly pale looking colour. As he gazed out across the dark and gloomy streets a single pearl like tear rolled down his cheek and glistened in the light.

Memories of Sally's broken body relentlessly tortured David's mind and with every thought of her his grief stricken state worsened. He found it to be astonishing that so much sadness could be brought to him by the one and only person who he had ever truly loved. She had been his life, his hope and his only reason for wanting to live in such a cruel world.

Sally had educated David in a subject which no book or teacher could ever do. She had taught him the meaning of true love. When they were together what happened in the world about them, the hate, the violence, the cruelty, none of it mattered. To them, their devotion for each other was all that existed.

Sally was now lying motionless in a hospital bed barely hanging onto her life. Where thoughts of happiness and well being had passed through her once intelligent and active mind were now just subconscious dreams. The only consolation was that she probably did not know of the depressing condition that she was in.

It was the first time that David had ever cried about something other than the harm that had been done to him and he found this pain to be even worse. No kick, punch or cruel remark had ever hurt like this did. The suffering was simply unbearable.

With tear filled eyes, David looked at the clock on his bedside table. His vision was blurred, but he managed to make out that the time was just past two o'clock in the morning. Now that he knew how late it was he suddenly realised how tired his aching muscles were. He had not had any sleep for quite some time and his lack of rest was starting to take its toll.

As David sat down on his bed it creaked like an old barn door. That same noise before had been a sound that he would yearn for every night, but now it only made him feel sadder than ever. His bed creaked a lot when the both of them were on it.

Whilst David was undressing he continuously kept wiping the tears from his cheeks. His eyes seemed like bottomless wells as rivers of salty tears flowed down his face and onto his lips. He wondered that even if he did get to sleep that it still would not subdue his thoughts of grief even if it did cure his tiredness.

After forlornly sitting on his bed for a prolonged period of time David at last succumb to his weak state and lay down. He could not even be bothered to get under the sheets, even though the room had now become uncomfortably cold and bitter. Just before he closed his eyes to go to sleep, he quietly let out one last weary exclamation.

"What is wrong with this world?"

A flock of birds fluttered from the trees forming a dark cloud like shape in the sky. A thin band of light from the small table lamp illuminated the pages of the book. Several of the keys on the dusty old piano had lost their ivory.

As David slowly lost consciousness, his mind started to create random and irrelevant thoughts. The tears on his cheeks had dried up and he at last had a restful look upon his face. Only the sound of the curtains fluttering in the wind and the ticking of the bedside clock could be heard whilst he lay motionless upon his bed.

Finally, a deep sleep.
Silence. Alive. Alone.

The dull grey landscape was flat for as far as the eye could see. A still and sullen sky rested upon it like an exact reflection on a still lake. There was an eerie calm all around which seemed akin to the emptiness of the vast barren land.

David stood with his eyes wide open and with his hair fluttering in a slight wind. As he looked down at himself he noticed that he was wearing his school uniform. He did not remember putting it on, but could not remember taking it off either.

The ground David was standing on was hard and grey like the school playground, but it looked smooth instead of rough. As for the sky, it was a lighter grey, but it was clear and the air was easy to breathe. All that could be seen on the horizon was where the ground and the sky were separated by each other.

David's brow furrowed as he looked around at his surroundings. He did not know where he was. All around him was a vast blank landscape. A grey void stretching out towards a never-ending emptiness, yet it somehow felt familiar.

David tried to recall his short-term memory to try to work out how he had got there. He wondered if he had walked or taken the school bus. He looked around for the other pupils, but no one else was there. As usual he was alone without anyone seeming to be aware of his existence.

It was these thoughts that made David suddenly understand where he was; a place null of colour, substance or being. There was no love here, no happiness and no future whatsoever. All that was here was his thoughts.

David was surrounded by a grey emptiness and he knew only one place where there was such desolation. It was the world where he lived. In fact, it was more than that. It was his life. There was nothing worth being there for, no one to love, just one person alone in a land barren of emotion.

Only now, David's loneliness did not feel uncomfortable. His solitude felt wanted. There was no one there to hate him or shout at him and there was no pain.

A wry smile crossed David's face as he looked around at the bland landscape of his world. He was free and he liked it. No one wanted him and he wanted no one. For once he could do what he wanted without anyone sneering at him or telling him to do as they told him to.

David felt as if he could do anything. As he took in a deep breath, a surge of positive energy flowed through his veins. Even though no one was there to hear it, he shouted out as if to prove to himself that he could do anything that he pleased.

"I'm free!" He closed his eyes and leant his head back. "At last, I'm free!"

It was at that point when David suddenly felt a rise in the temperature of the air. The change was so slight that he wondered if it had happened at all. Quickly moving his head about to look out across the landscape he noticed that it had somewhat changed colour. There seemed to be a hint of red in the sky and on the ground.

Now there was movement. In the distance, there seemed to be some flickering on the horizon. Far away, David could see what appeared to be small flashes in between the sky and the ground. As he looked around to see if there were any other changes in the landscape he became aware that the whole colour was rapidly beginning to change into a burning red.

David now noticed that the ground was not smooth anymore and that it was breaking up into a rough gravel. The sky was also changing as swirling masses of red clouds started to form above him. He was also now certain of the change of temperature as the air around him started to provide a comfortable warmth.

It was now obvious that the whole landscape was erratically transforming and with it David's life. He could not understand why, but it made him feel good. Something sensational was happening and for some reason he had a feeling that it was for the better.

The flickering that David had seen far away on the horizon had now moved close enough for him to be able to make out what it was. He was surrounded by fire and it was getting a lot closer. It was almost as if he was in some kind of magical land as all about him was rapidly beginning to transform in a wondrous manner. As the flames gradually moved closer and grew taller they seemed to reach for the sky and grab at the clouds. This in return was greeted by streaks of lightning that came down accompanied by crashes of deafening thunder.

David's world had now become an unstable and dangerous place. The ground had changed into a black gravel that was slowly being eaten up by ferocious flames. Up above him in the sky were masses of swirling clouds that were constantly being split by blinding flashes of lightning. If there was such a place as a personal hell, this was it.

The flames had now come so close to David that he was standing in the only place in the land which was untouched by fire. However, it would not be for long. Soon there would be nowhere left that was safe.

It was at that point when a familiar voice called out from behind David. Each of the words was mouthed with a spiteful loathing.

"Cain, what the fuck are you doing here?"

A feeling of anger instantly swept over David as he wondered who was questioning him. This was *his* world. He did not have to answer other people's questions. In a slow movement he turned around to see who it was.

Standing in front of David, with his fists clenched and a snarling look upon his face was Martin Dent. For some reason he was dressed in his full school uniform and was not with any of his gang. He seemed to be in the most violent of tempers and was breathing heavily through his gritted his teeth.

David would normally feel a sense of unease at seeing this sight, but not now. As he looked at the threatening figure in front of him he was calm and composed. He felt nothing but pride and he stood tall with an unstirred look upon his face.

Martin's expression was distorted with rage as he shouted out his intentions.

"I'm going to smash your face in, Cain!"

David did not reply. He just stood his ground, not scared, not moving and with the red glow of the sky and surrounding flames reflecting off of his pale face. Pride flowed through his veins, producing an overwhelming sensation of self worth.

Suddenly, there was another voice that shouted out at David with as much fury as the first.

"Cain, this is the last time you test my authority!"

This time it came from over his left shoulder. As he turned to see who it was he saw Mr Cutter standing with his cane in one hand and his heavy bible in the other. The temperamental teacher seemed to be fuming with anger as he spoke with an uncontrollable rage.

"I'm going to cane you for every time you lower this book, Cain!"

David again just looked at him with the same uncaring expression upon his face. He was not worried by these futile threats. They wasted their time. His fear had been replaced with pride and he simply felt as if nothing could harm him ever again.

"You spilt a whole bottle of fucking milk! Jesus boy, you're going to pay for this one!"

David knew straight away who was shouting at him now and he instantly turned around to face him. Norman was drunk and enraged as he stood with his belt half wrapped around his fist with the buckle hanging limply over the side. As he swayed backwards and forwards he made one of his drunkenly slurred threats.

"I'm going to make you ache for a week!"

Still David just stood there unmoving with a fearless expression upon his face. He was capable of taking any beating off of any of them and that was something that he had proved on numerous occasions before now. It did not matter where on his body they hit him or what they struck him with he would never let them see pain or anguish in his eyes. Instead all they would sense from him would be an overwhelming amount of dignity and self-respect fashioned by his unwavering resolve not to be a victim.

David's attention had now been taken away from the three antagonists and to the landscape beyond them. As he looked at the surrounding fire and lightning he realised that it was getting increasingly closer to him and it did not look like it was going to stop. It now seemed inevitable that he would be engulfed in flames and would die a slow and painful death where he stood. He certainly had nothing to fear now from the weak threats of those who were trying to torment him. His own demise amidst the scorching fire was imminent and as a result of this those before him who thought they were so significant to his life simply did not matter anymore.

David watched in wonder at the surrounding landscape as bolts of lightning split the sky in an awesome show of power whilst flames from the ground seemed to leap up into the air to greet their presence. At the same time thunder erupted all around in a deafening chorus of explosions. The immense power of the land was completely overawing.

David just ironically smiled. He knew that he was going to die in the searing flames, but at least he would have the pleasure of seeing the three people who had brought him all of his misery and suffering perish first. Their deaths would be a fitting show to be put before him in his last moments alive.

The fire moved nearer, the lightning struck closer and the thunder grew louder.

David braced himself. He stood up straight with his hands by his sides and with a proud look upon his face. A sense of excited anticipation crossed over him as he eagerly yearned to see the painful deaths of his foes even though he was about to die himself. The last sight he would ever see would be a welcome one.

A soul-piercing scream suddenly sounded out to David's left and he instantly turned around to see whom it had come from. There before him was the sight of Martin falling to his knees as the flames mercilessly engulfed him. His clothes instantly disintegrated and his skin started to boil. Soon his flesh was gone and just a charred corpse remained in a kneeling position with its hands held out in a pleading manner.

Now there were more screams. Mr Cutter and Norman were both wrapped in flames and were clearly in unbearable agony. They both tried to struggle, but their futile panic would not put a stop to the impending snuffing out of their lives.

David watched the slow and painful deaths with a wry smile upon his face. Even though his own life was soon to be ended, he was still enjoying his final moments alive.

Mr Cutter held his bible up to the heavens as if in a last prayer for mercy, but it caught into flames along with his cane. Norman's belt melted around his hand and his head drooped forward as the last bit of life ebbed away from his scorched body. The screams then came to an abrupt end.

All that surrounded David now were the three charred corpses of his enemies and the raging fire that was engulfing them. They had all died on their knees in various final postures depicting their own pleas for leniency, but it had obviously not come. Their deaths had been painful and had come without mercy.

David looked at them all in turn. He thought of how fitting it was that they should all have died whilst begging for clemency, the same thing that he had pleaded for on a number of occasions when they had beaten him. His last moments alive had been extremely satisfying and it had made him feel as if his own death was going to be a worthy sacrifice.

As the flames moved within inches of David's body he closed his eyes and smiled. A restful expression crossed over his face as he embraced himself for the pain. With one last thought his mind went back to what he was leaving behind. No more belt buckles around the face, no more kicks to the ribs and no more canes across the palms. He was at last free from the hell that he called life.

David waited patiently for the searing heat of the relentless flames. Time somehow seemed to pass more slowly as he prepared himself for the inevitable pain. It would not be long now.

Still nothing happened. David almost felt agitated at being made to wait and his impatience urged him to find out why he was not in the process of being burnt alive. As he slowly opened his eyes he looked down at himself to see why he had not yet even been scolded. He had expected to see that the fire had not reached him yet, but it had.

An expression of awe crossed David's pale face as he looked at the incredible sight. The flames lashed against his skin and entwined around his body, but they did not burn him. He was still alive.

David stood amongst the fire with his flesh unscathed and his face full of wonder. The flames leapt into the air as if to celebrate their conqueror. Lightning crashed all around him making the features upon his face radiate into a brilliant glow. Almighty cracks of thunder repeatedly shook the land almost as if it were a fanfare saluting his glory.

David stood defiantly amongst the flames that had taken the lives of his enemies and had left their charred bodies lying at his feet. Whilst he had watched the grotesque looks of agony upon their faces and had heard their diminishing screams of pain he had felt the utmost pleasure, but for him to have lived through what had slain them had given him an immense feeling of satisfaction. As he stood exultantly looking over their lifeless corpses he finally realised what it was like to be the true victor.

This was David's life. He was the ruler of his world. There was no other king. Only one GOD could hold dominion. No one would dare oppose him now. And for those who did, death would surely come to them and, prior to it, the utmost pain.

David stood tall and almighty as the flames caressed his body in a show of affection to the new ruler of the world. In reply he sanctimoniously raised his arms up above him as if to grasp at the sky. Lightning immediately came down from the heavens and struck his fingertips so as to greet the solitary king of the land. Thunder then sounded all around almost like an adoring and blessed hymn to praise the one and only supreme god of the realm. This was true power.

As David opened his eyes and leant his head back he let out a victorious yell. Suddenly, just to show that there could be only one true ruler of the world that he had created, he gave out a demonstration of exceptional power. He forced the searing flames around him to leap high up into the air and break up the clouds. Lightning crashed against the ground sending explosions of gravel scattering all around. Then, in a final show of strength, his crystal blue eyes lit up into blinding brilliant white flashes and sent beams of light stretching out across the land.

David Cain ruled his world and all who entered it. Hail the messiah, the king, the god. And be warned all those who dare to oppose him. For his wrath is as unforgiving, as his power is indomitable.

David Cain, the GOD.

"Hurry up!" Marilyn called out in an impatient tone of voice. "I want to talk to you."

David appeared at the top of the stairs wearing just his underwear. He nonchalantly combed back his hair with his fingers and looked at his mother in an uncaring manner. Marilyn was glaring up at him from the hallway with an irritated look upon her face. She had a number of full bags and cases around her on the floor and was obviously in a hurry to get somewhere. When she noticed his lack of haste she went about reprimanding him.

"I said 'hurry up!' I haven't got all day." She put her hands on her hips in an attempt to show her annoyance. "Get down here and listen to me!"

David stood for a moment at the top of the stairs and then slowly started to make his way down. As he walked he studied his mother with an expressionless look upon his face. She had her arm in a sling and was adorned with a collection of cuts and bruises to the face. He did not have to think for too long to work out how she had got those.

When David got to the bottom of the stairs Marilyn started to speak in an agitated tone of voice.

"Your stepfather got drunk before going to work last night. I don't suppose I have to tell you how I got these." She pointed to the marks on her face and then to her arm. "Well, it's the last time he's going do it to me."

Marilyn lifted her chin in a resolute manner to show that she meant what she was saying. David just kept staring at her with the same stony expression upon his face and with a distinct lack of interest. She carried on with her speech even though she was not getting a very attentive reaction.

"I'm leaving. I'm even getting out of here before the bastard gets back from work. I can't live with his bloody tempers anymore. And..." A tear started to trickle from her eye so she took a moment to gain control of her emotions. "I'm going by myself."

David remained unmoving and composed. Marilyn had expected a show of surprise, but it had not come. Nevertheless, she carried on explaining what she was planning to do.

"I've found somewhere else to live where he can't find me." She looked at her son with an uncaring expression upon her face. "You'll have to sort yourself out. You're sixteen now. That's old enough to deal with your own problems."

Marilyn had given no consideration to what David was going to do with himself, but that was because she simply did not care. All that mattered to her was that everything would be alright for herself and that she was out of harm's way. She was not bothered about leaving her son alone with Norman, but she tried to justify her actions anyway.

"I know you're my son, but I can't take it anymore. I just can't live like this." She shook with agitation. "He fractured three of my ribs last night, he broke my arm and just look at my bloody face! The doctor said I would need treatment and..."

David shouted at the top of his voice with a vehement rage.

"Shut up, you pathetic fool!" A vicious scowl crossed his face as he pointed a rigid finger at her. "I don't want to hear about your pain. It means nothing to me."

"But David..." Marilyn stammered out her words. "What's got into you?"

"Life. That's what has got into me. And I've learnt by it." David opened the front door for her to leave and stared at her with fiery ice like eyes. "If you're going to leave, just get the hell out!"

A startled look crossed Marilyn's face as she felt the coldness of her son's words. She had expected him to beg her not to leave or at least ask if he could go with her. Instead he made it clearly obvious that he would rather be rid of her.

Feeling a sense of inferiority, Marilyn nervously picked up her cases and started to uneasily shuffle out of the front door. David just stood watching over her with the same

116

enraged expression upon his face. As she got outside the house she turned to him and spoke in an apprehensive tone of voice.

"I suppose this is good-bye then?"

David's reply was as abrasive as it was bitter.

"Get out of my sight! I don't ever want to see you again."

Marilyn was shocked at the way her son could so willingly part from her. She had never loved David, but she had always thought that he had cared about her. However, he now seemed to be so keen to rid her from his life that it was obvious that he did not have any feelings for her whatsoever. The way he so relentlessly shunned her was quite hurtful.

As Marilyn turned away and started to walk down the garden path she heard the front door pitilessly close behind her. Although she now had a new future ahead of her and the wreckage of her past safely behind her she could not help but feel a sense of failure. She had always had aspirations of having a happy family life, but now it seemed as if her wishes were never going to come true.

First there was a click, then a fizzing noise as the dusty old television set started to warm up. As the picture and sound started to emerge David took a few steps back to gain a better view of the screen. He stood motionless staring at the television with a bitter expression etched into his pale face. His light blue eyes were akin to the coldness as his thoughts.

A sharp chill in the mid winter air made the small sparsely decorated living room feel bitter and uninviting. Most of the pictures on the walls had been taken away leaving the outlines of their frames as reminders of their once being there. The ornaments that had lined the windowsills and cabinets were also gone along with everything else Marilyn owned. Only the television set was left due to it being too heavy to carry.

The introduction music of the early morning news was just coming to an end and the solemn faced newscaster started to read out the headlines. A grey studio set behind the middle aged man seemed to reflect the mood of the news that he was just about to read.

"Israel again saw the face of terrorism yesterday when a car bomb was detonated outside an army recruitment office in the centre of Tel Aviv. Four people were killed and eleven injured. This brings the total deaths to twenty-three in the last two weeks..."

The newscaster was replaced by footage of people running through debris covered streets in utter panic. They almost seemed to be unaware of the dead and injured people lying at their feet. David slowly shook his head in disgust. He had seen many such images before, but they still repulsed him.

Again the newscaster returned to the screen just as glum faced as before. The news he was reading seemed to dictate the expression he wore upon his face.

"Also, the Police are continuing to look for the rapist and murderer of the eighty-six year old pensioner, Margaret Everett, who died of thirty-seven knife wounds to the body after she had been brutally raped..."

After this headline a still picture belonging to the family of the murdered woman was shown with her sitting with her two young grandchildren who had had their faces blacked out to protect their identities.

David still stood in the centre of the room staring at the screen with a menacing scowl etched into features of his face.

When the newscaster returned he could not hide an ever so slight shake of his head to reveal his own abhorrence at what he was reading.

"And reports have now come in that a seventh man has been arrested in connection with the Harking Town paedophile sex ring..."

117

As David's face twisted into a sneering snarl his eyes burned white hot with rage. His blood almost seemed to boil as it rushed through his veins. He then spoke with a voice that came out of the depths of his hatred.

"What the *hell* is wrong with this world?"

David's muscles tightened all over his body as the anger took a grip of his senses. He had never felt such a surge of emotional energy. His breathing had now become heavy and his fists were clenched so firmly that his nails were digging deep into his palms. As he spoke, his words were uttered with an intense rage.

"It's unbelievable to think I came from this. The whole world is sick with a disease." His brow furrowed into a fierce scowl. "Well, it needs a cure. And I am that cure."

It was at that point when the front door opened and a familiar voice called out in a just as recognisable brusque manner.

"Marilyn, I want something to eat!" Norman threw his tool bag onto the hallway floor. "You know I've been working nights, so hurry up! I'm so bloody hungry I could die."

As David looked over his shoulder his face twisted into an insidious smile as he whispered to himself in a sly tone of voice.

"Die? All in good time my loving stepfather." He repeated himself. "All in good time."

Norman's face became perplexed as he gazed around the bare looking house. He had noticed that something was not right straight away, but could not quite work out what it was. As he walked through into the kitchen he found a note on the dining table with his name written on it.

"What the fuck's this?" He muttered to himself.

Norman picked up the note and sat down to read it to himself. The further he got through it the more the expression changed upon his face. His look of bewilderment was slowly being replaced by one of anger.

Dear Norman

By the time you read this I'll be gone. I can't live with your tempers and violence anymore. I wish it all could have gone better and that we both had have ended up happy. Please don't try to find me.

Marilyn   X X X

David had followed Norman into the kitchen and was now leaning up against a wall in a blasé manner. This was something that he wanted to see. As he watched his stepfather read the note left by Marilyn a subtle grin crossed his face as he waited for the inevitable eruption of violence.

"That fucking bitch!" Norman threw the note onto the table. "You wait until I bloody find her. I'll knock her black and fucking blue."

David started to slowly walk across the kitchen floor towards his stepfather, but with his smile now concealed behind a fake look of concern. His tone of voice was just as feigned.

"She left about fifteen minutes ago. You just missed her."

Norman looked at his watch and then back to David.

"I bet that fucking tart is seeing someone else." He nodded his head as if to agree with himself. "If she is, I'll kill the bastard and her."

David just raised his eyebrows and did not say a word. It was quite obvious to him that Marilyn had run away simply because she did not want to be beaten anymore. That was a view, however, that Norman did not share. The blatantly arrogant man saw no reason why she would want to leave him other than her own reasons of selfishness. These were typical views of someone so self-centred.

Norman had now pulled his comb out of his back pocket and was erratically waving it in David's face as he started to question his stepson in an accusative tone of voice.

"Did you know she was going to do this?"

"No. It is as much of a surprise to me as it clearly is to you." David shrugged his shoulders. "I came downstairs just to find her walking out the door."

Norman shook his head in disgust and carried on with his inquest.

"Did she tell you where she was going?"

"No."

"If you're lying to me I'll kick the shit out of you!"

David casually put his hands behind his back and raised his eyebrows. He stood before his infuriated stepfather in a cool and calm posture. For someone who had just lost his mother and was clearly in danger of getting a beating he seemed quite laid back. As he spoke his voice was as relaxed as his appearance.

"I didn't ask where she was going, because I thought it was quite obvious."

Norman took a moment to think about it, but after only a short amount of time he gave up the idea of using his brain and searched for the answer to the question elsewhere.

"Where is she then?"

"She'll be at her sister's, Geraldine."

At this, Norman started to nod his head as he slowly realised that this actually was the obvious place where Marilyn would go to. Her sister was always the one who she turned to when she was in need. However, something crossed his mind that did not seem quite right. He turned to David with a scrutinising look upon his face and spoke in a distrusting tone of voice.

"Why are you being so helpful?" Norman pointed his comb right into his stepson's face. "And why are you still here?"

"Because my *dear* stepfather..." David smiled at him in a sardonic manner. "I'm going to kill you!"

Norman was not quick enough to thwart the vicious attack. David grabbed the comb out of his stepfather's hand and immediately shoved it deep down into the large man's throat. There was a grotesque scraping noise as the teeth of the comb scraped against his tonsils.

Norman instantly fell back against the dining table and tried to put his fingers into his mouth to pull out the obstructing object from his windpipe. Seeing that his victim was attempting to alleviate himself from his punishment, David went about making sure that there was no mercy. He straightaway rammed his fist right into the choking man's mouth sending him stumbling across the kitchen. As he watched his stepfather's enfeebled frame struggling to stay upright he spoke in a calm, yet resolute tone of voice.

"When I first met you all I wanted was for you to make my mother happy. Instead you battered her." David shook his head in disbelief. "And what made it worse was that you always thought that you had a good excuse for doing it. Well, you had no right. No right whatsoever."

The scene was quite sickening as Norman repeatedly coughed up blood and fell around the kitchen in a bewildered manner. He did, however, still have some of his strength left in him. In an attempt to stop the retribution he limply swung a fist out at his aggressor.

As soon as David saw Norman lift up his arm he took a step back and watched as the blow sailed wildly past his face. This was clearly all that his stepfather could muster up in his defence and it confirmed that the contest was now over. The whole one-sided scenario was similar to other beatings that had taken place in the same house.

119

Norman was now so dazed that he did not even notice that David had walked out of the kitchen. He was so unaware of what was happening that he could not even take advantage of the break in the violence and pull the comb out from his mouth. Instead, he just leant up against the working top choking up phlegm and blood. If he had have seen his assailant leave him he might have thought it was an act of mercy, however, that appeared not to be the case.

David walked straight back into the kitchen clutching a ball hammer that he had got out of Norman's tool bag. It was only small, but the head was a menacing bullet shape. As he approached his stepfather he spoke in a quiet and calm tone of voice.

"All I wanted was a happy life. Everyone deserves to live in peace. Every child should be given a chance in life. I wouldn't have minded if you had of just left me alone to go about things my own way." He lifted the hammer above his head. "But you didn't. For some utterly sick reason you abused me."

The first blow came crashing across the side of Norman's nose sending a splatter of blood onto a cabinet. David straight away took aim for the second and then sent it smashing into the side of his stepfather's chin instantly forcing his jaw out of line. Both strikes of the hammer made a grim cracking noise as the bones shattered with a brittle ease.

Norman was now covered in blood and had fallen to the floor into an unceremonious heap. Nevertheless, he still somehow managed to be semiconscious and almost seemed to be aware of what was going on. In a feeble attempt at trying to escape he slowly crawled towards the back door and lifted his hand up to reach the handle. David immediately realised what his stepfather was trying to do and went about scotching any hopes of him absconding.

"You haven't got a chance." He shook his head as he watched the weak attempt at survival. "Just like you never gave me a chance."

David then forced the hammer down onto Norman's hand squashing it against the door handle. There was a hideous crushing sound as the bones instantly splintered under the force of the blow. Blood spurted up his arm and a downward squirt immediately formed a puddle on the floor. Even the windowpane in the door had shattered due to the power of the impact.

Norman was now aware of the fact that his defeat was imminent. In an attempt to see if there was any chance of mercy he sluggishly looked up at his victor. In one last hope of hanging onto his life he exhaustedly raised his hand in a submissive manner, but as he looked into David's eyes he instantly realised that his plea for compassion would never come. He lowered his arm and then his head.

The wait for the final vicious frenzy of violence was not long in coming. A dozen blows of the hammer were unleashed down onto the top of Norman's head as David just let go of all of his fury. Every now and again the nose of the blood soaked tool got caught in the skull and he had to use both of his hands to free it from where it was caught within the split bone. Each strike had sent a splatter of blood across the kitchen floor and up the walls making the scene look like one of a slaughterhouse. After about thirty seconds the job was finished.

When David was absolutely sure that there was no life left in his stepfather he took a step back to assess his work. He stood tall whilst at his feet lay the body of his enemy. Norman was defeated, humbled and dead. There could have been only one sentence passed for the crimes he had committed.

Execution.

There were pools of blood in the bottom of the bath that had not been washed away from when David had showered. Whist he calmly dried himself with a large towel he gazed at his misted reflection in the bathroom mirror. He felt composed and at ease as he prepared himself for his day at school. It was almost as if it had been just another normal morning and that he had not just seen his mother for the last time and murdered his stepfather.

Although David had felt a burning anger flow through his veins throughout the ordeal he had still remained clear-headed and in control. Even when committing his first murder he still used the fullness of his intelligence so as to be aware of any unforeseen contingencies. He had made sure that Norman would not have a chance of escaping and that his mother was not in the house to witness it.

David had no intention of getting away with murdering his stepfather and was not bothered about paying the consequences. However, he still had a lot more work to do before handing himself in to the police. Taking Norman's life was not just revenge. This was the primary step of his overall plan.

The first thing that had entered David's mind when he had woken up in the morning was the dream he had had from the night before. He had laid on his bed thinking about his enemies burning to death in the scorching fires and what it had all meant to him. It was a feeling of pure exultation to see them perish so painfully and to have lived through it all himself. Fantasy, however, had now become reality and that felt even better.

When David had taken Norman's life he had experienced emotions of which he had never encountered before in his life. He had felt the sweet taste of revenge, a sensational rush of savagery and an overwhelming feeling of power. The satisfaction was so strong that he wondered why he had never done such a thing before.

David Cain was now a very different person from whom he used to be.

"Did you hear about what happened to Sally Moore?"

"No. What?"

"She got run over yesterday, near the park." The boy fervently nodded his head in a gesture to show that he was telling the truth. "She's half dead."

"Bloody hell!" The other boy was momentarily shocked by what he had heard, but as the news sunk in a smile crossed his face. "I bet it was well gory. Great!"

There was a bout of laughter as the two schoolboys waiting at the bus stop took a moment to enjoy their morbid conversation. Neither of them seemed to have any remorse about the subject and were quite happy just to talk about it in a jovial manner. The first boy then carried on with his description of events.

"My little brother was there. He didn't see it happen, but he saw the ambulance come and take her away." He then leant forward as he added the last part of his report. "But he also said that David Cain was with her when she actually got hit by the car."

"Bloody hell!" The second boy raised his eyebrows. "He was going out with her, wasn't he?"

"Yeah!"

At that, the first boy saw David approaching the bus stop from the other side of the road and pointed his arrival out to his friend.

"Jesus! Here comes Cain now."

The second boy looked around over his shoulder and then back again.

"Shall I say something to him?" He grinned at the prospect of his cruel game. "You know, something about cars."

"Yeah! Go on!" The reply was said in an enthusiastic manner. "That'd be a right laugh."

It was just a matter of time before David reached the two boys waiting at the bus stop. They both watched him approach with eager expressions upon their faces. As he drew nearer the second boy turned around ready to make his heartless remark.

David walked across the road in a nonchalant manner almost as if he had not just murdered his stepfather. As he approached the bus stop there were two boys staring at him with wry smiles upon their faces. One seemed to be just about to say something to him and appeared to be quite excited about it. However, the remark was never made. A fist was rammed into the boy's face knocking him straight down onto the pavement.

As David had approached the bus stop he had seen the way the two boys were looking at him and had guessed that one of them was going to make a callous remark to him. It was just a matter of working out which one it was going to be. As soon as he had seen one of them open his mouth he knew who was going to be the antagonist. He, therefore, simply applied the punishment before the crime had been committed.

The boy who had been punched was now dazedly sitting on the pavement with a badly bleeding nose. He had had no idea that he was going to be attacked and was not really sure that it had happened either. His friend just stood in a shocked manner gawping at David as he casually carried on walking past them. Today was a bad day to pick on the school weakling.

Martin Dent was standing in a corridor in an annoyingly blasé manner whilst Mrs Line, the geography teacher, was giving him a telling off. He was on his way to his first lesson of the week and had already been pulled up for swearing. As the lecture on discipline took place he just stayed gazing in the opposite direction and ignored whatever was being said. This, of course, infuriated the already fuming teacher even more and she started to raise her voice in an attempt to get some respect.

"Don't just stand there and pretend you can't hear me, Dent! Pay attention to me when I'm talking to you!" She moved her head around into his line of vision. "Now I've had enough of your swearing and bad attitude, and it's going to stop right now!"

Mrs Line was only a small woman, but she was known amongst the pupils of the school for being a strict disciplinarian. This, however, did not bother Martin. He had received many a telling of at the hands of much harsher teachers than her and it showed in his actions just how little he was bothered by it all. Nevertheless, he still tried to talk his way out of the trouble that he had got himself into.

"But I didn't swear." He shrugged his shoulders. "All I said was that 'geography is a boring load of old bollocks!'"

This was immediately followed by Mrs Line handing out yet another reprimand.

"I know what you said and I told you not to use words like that. I don't care if you don't think it's swearing or not. Don't to use that word again! So make that the last time!" She waved her finger at him. "Now, for deliberately disobeying me you can do two hundred lines each saying 'I must not...'"

A third party suddenly interrupted Mrs Line.

"Dent, I want to see you on the school yard outside the gym at morning break. So, make sure you're there!"

Martin turned around to see David staring at him with a scowling expression etched into his face. At first he was shocked to see his favourite bullying target speak to him in such a demanding way. Then, as he came to his senses, he returned to being his usual self and mouthed his reply through clenched teeth.

"Yeah! You want some, do you?"

David repeated his order.

"Just make sure you're there!"

The part of the schoolyard outside the gym was a well-known place amongst the pupils for fights to take place. Nevertheless, Martin wanted to make completely sure of what David's intentions were.

"Why? You want a fucking fight, do ya?"

"Of course I do." David pointed his finger right into Martin's face and spoke in a viciously self-assured manner. "You're going pay! This time, you're going to pay!"

Whilst all this had gone on, Mrs Line had suddenly found herself being ignored and sworn in front of again. She was not pleased about this at all and went about getting their attention.

"Now you two listen to me! I'm not going to have you two speak like that in front of..."

David interrupted Mrs Line again. Only this time his remarks were aimed at her.

"I don't want to listen to you. You ignorance bores me." He then turned to Martin before going on his way. "Just make sure you're there!"

Mrs Line was totally taken aback by the way she had just been spoken to. In all of her years of teaching she had never had any pupil speak to her in such a way that had just occurred. It took a while for her to come to her senses and when she did, she shouted out an order at David who was now walking away from her.

"Cain, come back here now!"

Mrs Line, of course, got no reaction to her demand. David just ignored her and kept on walking. She was in such a state of shock that all she could do was stand there gawping at him as he made his way along the corridor. His outright refusal to even acknowledge her made her feel powerless and insignificant.

It seemed as if no one had any power over David anymore. He did what he wanted, when he wanted and how he wanted. After years of abuse and being told what to do he had at last set himself free from the rules set by other people.

David was the master of his own destiny.

The mathematics lesson seemed to have passed quite quickly. The division bell had just sounded to announce the morning break and as usual the pupils were now waiting for Mr Cutter's permission to let them get on their way. When he had carefully scoured the classroom to make sure that no one had tried to leave prematurely he gave his consent for them to depart.

"Go on then, off you go!" He lowered his gaze back down to a book he was reading. "And leave quietly without making a fuss!"

The pupils all got out of their chairs at the same time and started to put their belongings away into their school bags. As they made their way out of the classroom none of them made a noise in case they provoked the temperamental teacher. It did not take long for the room to empty leaving just Mr Cutter reading at his desk and a lone figure sitting at the back.

David sat with his head slightly bowed gazing across the room. His icy light blue eyes were radiating a chilling glow as they studied his intended victim. The thoughts that were passing through his mind seemed to be as cold as his stare.

Mr Cutter was not aware that he was being watched, let alone that he had company. He carried on reading the book in front of him unaware of what he was about to encounter. It was only when he heard the faint sound of breathing at the back of the classroom that he finally looked up. Within an instant he was demanding answers for this invasion of privacy.

"Cain, what are you doing here?" He closed his book. "I told everyone to go."

For a long moment, David just stayed staring at the irritated teacher with the same bitter expression upon his face. The cold silence that enshrouded the classroom seemed to be akin to the iciness of his gaze. When he finally did decide to answer Mr Cutter's question he stood up and spoke in a calm tone of voice.

"I have a few questions I would like to ask you." He started to slowly walk across the classroom. "I would like to know some things about your god."

A twisted scowl crossed Mr Cutter's face as he spoke.

"What do you want to know about God for?"

"I want to understand."

"What does someone like you want to know about God for?"

David came to stand right in front of Mr Cutter's desk and looked down upon him as he asked his questions.

"In the second world war six million Jews were systematically murdered by the Nazi's simply because of their religion." There was now a vexed expression upon his face as he suddenly started to become angered. "Where was God was when all this happened?"

Mr Cutter's face immediately went red with rage at being asked such an insolent question. As he went to reprimand the disrespectful pupil he leant forward and spoke with a twisted snarl.

"This is your first day back at school after your suspension, Cain." He paused and took in a deep breath. "And I'll make it's your last for a month if you try my patience again."

In return, David just became more temperamental and raised his voice.

"And the children starving in the third world, where are the miracles for them? There are diseases killing thousands a day. Where is their divine intervention? All through history people have been slaughtered across the world because of religion, greed or a number of other pointless reasons." He started to wave his hand about in an erratic manner as he listed just some of places of humanities crimes. "War after war, after war. How has God helped all the people who have suffered?"

Mr Cutter was now standing up and was glowering at David with a vicious look etched into his face. As he started to speak he shook his head with rage.

"How dare you ask me such questions, Cain!" He banged his hand upon his desk. "I will punish you severely for this."

David was not going to be intimidated by the irate teacher and as he still pressed for answers he raised his voice even further.

"Just answer the question! There's suffering all over this world, people starving, being murdered, so while it's all happening..." He picked up Mr Cutter's bible off of his desk and lifted up into his line of vision. "Where's God?"

David did not give enough time for the question to be answered. He swung the heavy bible around onto the side of Mr Cutter's head, instantly knocking him off balance. The bemused teacher wobbled about for a long moment with his arms hanging limply by his sides. When he eventually did regain some of his senses he spoke in a subdued and quiet voice.

"You won't get away with this."

The reply was blunt and simplistic.

"I don't want to get away with it."

At that, David thrust his foot into Mr Cutter's midriff. The wincing teacher immediately emptied his lungs of air as he keeled over and fell to his knees. As he knelt on the floor he looked up at his attacker in a state of utter shock.

David just stood staring at his victim with a wistful look upon his face as he spoke.

"You see, the idea of religion is good. The concept of people gathering together in a church to be happy and live in peace should be a good thing, but for humanity that's just too much of a hard thing to accomplish. You have to go around causing harm to others in the name of your gods." His voice became louder and the tone scornful as he mimicked a typical human. "'He deserves to die because he's Jewish. I can't live in the same country as him because he's a Catholic. My daughter can't marry him because he's a Muslim. She must not learn because she is a woman.' How can people be so pathetically stupid? And you say *I'm* evil in the eyes of God."

Mr Cutter just knelt on the floor staring at David in a stunned manner. The pain in his midriff was unbearable and he tried to take in as many deep breaths as possible. Although he was humbly kneeling on the floor at the feet of one of his pupils his pride was actually not at the forefront of his mind. Self-preservation was the first of his concerns.

David had now decided that he had made his point to Mr Cutter and that it was now time to end what he had started. He reached his hand into his inside coat pocket and pulled out a kitchen knife which he had taken from his home. As he lifted it into his line of vision he ran his finger along the blade to check its sharpness. A drop of blood instantly appeared as it cut through his skin and he nodded to himself in a malicious manner.

Mr Cutter was now slowly getting to his feet and was swaying in a shaken manner. In his weak state he had to use the desk to pull himself up off the floor. He could now see that he had somehow ended up in a very unsafe state of affairs and that he would have to escape to avoid any further harm. Without turning to see if his aggressor was looking he tried to make a run for safety.

David was not going to be so easily deprived of his victory. In a moment of quick thinking he saw Mr Cutter's hand on the desk and rammed the knife straight through the middle of it. There was a pained yell as the panicked teacher tried to run away, but was instantly yanked back by his impaled hand. The blade had stuck deep into the desk and had held him fast. He could not help but collapse onto the floor and just lay there in a state of utter shock.

David watched as Mr Cutter hung helplessly by his mangled hand. There was blood pouring all the way down the petrified teacher's arm into a puddle on the floor. The sight was quite sickening, but not enough to warrant an offering of mercy.

Lowering himself down to Mr Cutter's eye level, David started to speak in an enraged, but steady tone of voice.

"You see, this world needs a god, but not the out-dated hypocritical one's that have been created by your inferior minds. The bible tells of its god as having punished the city of Sodom, yet on another page it says that he is all forgiving." He huffed in an exasperated manner. "Well, if your god can't even live by his own teachings, then what good is he to anyone?"

Mr Cutter looked at David with a pained, but resolute stare as he replied.

"The Lord is all powerful and he shall provide. He always looks over me." He nodded his head as if to agree with himself. "God is by my side."

David smiled wryly and spoke in a scornful manner.

"Not today he isn't. The Lord almighty has been ousted by a new deity. Your life is mine now. And what I giveth with one hand and taketh away with the other." He slowly stood up straight and raised his arms out by his sides in a mockingly divine posture. "I am *your* God."

At that, David callously yanked the knife from Mr Cutter's hand. There was another cry of agony as the wretched teacher withered under the unbearable pain. As his arm flopped down by his side it left a bloodied palm print upon the desk.

David did not even give Mr Cutter any time to recover from the shock of having the knife pulled from his hand. He grabbed hold of the tormented teacher's hair and pushed his head back against the top of the desk. As he lifted the knife up above his head he spoke in a resolute tone of voice.

"You didn't have to cane me like you did. I never deserved what I got off of you. You could see how much pain I was in when you looked into my eyes, but still you kept on hurting me regardless. Well, I just want to look into your eyes as I tell you this..." He paused. "I am now going to kill you."

For a moment, Mr Cutter's eyes opened wide as he acknowledged what had just been said to him, but then the punishment began. David slowly ran the knife across the stunned man's throat leaving a long deep cut in his neck. As the blood flowed he ran the blade back again, and again, and again. A number of slashes appeared across the traumatised teacher's neck as blood poured from his jugular vein. It was only when a dozen incisions had been made that the onslaught finally stopped.

David did not need the knife anymore, so he recklessly threw it across the room. Although he had not done it on purpose, the blade ironically stuck into the word 'sin' on a religious poster on the wall. He now stepped back to gleefully watch as his victim sat against the desk shaking erratically. Mr Cutter's eyes seemed to grow ever more distant as his life slowly ebbed away from him. It did not take long for him to completely stop moving leaving just a corpse lying on the floor in a pool of blood.

Again the punishment for the crime of victimising David Cain was death. He had been the judge, jury and executioner. However, the trial had not finished yet. There was still one more to be put in the dock.

"Dent's going to kick his head in."
"It won't last two seconds."
"Should be good though."

The usual schoolyard conversations were going on as the pupils flocked to see the arranged fight between Martin Dent and David Cain. Most of them considered it to be a gross mismatch, but the lack of contest did not bother them. As long as there was going to be some blood and violence they were simply not bothered who won.

There was now quite a large crowd of pupils gathering on the schoolyard outside the gym. Martin was standing in the middle of them boasting to the members of his gang about what he intended to do to David. As he spoke they all listened to him intently.

"I'll put him on the deck first." He clenched his fist and made a swiping motion. "Then I'll kick his ribs in."

Steve Harding leant forward and grinned in a sly manner as he gave a piece of advice.

"Poke your fingers in his eyes!" He nodded his head as if to agree with himself. "So he can't see you and hit back."

Martin's face twisted into an unimpressed scowl and he immediately went about correcting his friend's misguided views.

"He aint going to hit me anyway, you prat!" He shook his head with disgust. "I'm going to knock him shitless before he gets the chance to even think about it."

Steve lowered his gaze in a shameful manner.

"Yeah! Sorry, Martin!"

Terry Barnet then added some cautious words into the conversation.

"You want to watch it though, Martin!" He nervously shrugged his shoulders. "Didn't the headmaster say he'd suspend you if you ever got in another fight?"

Martin lifted up his hands in an exasperated manner.

"So what am I meant to do?" He added an element of scorn into his tone of voice. "I suppose I should say 'Sorry Cain! I don't want to fight you. You can *have* me any day.'"

At that, the rest of the boys laughed at Terry in a mocking manner and playfully started to push him around. They only stopped when Martin got their attention with one last prediction.

"I'll tell you what though, Cain is going to get well done. I mean, I'm really going to hurt him." He wiped his sleeve across his mouth and thoughtfully gazed across the schoolyard. "I'm going to put the freak in hospital."

A lone person's footsteps echoed through the cold empty corridor. The sound of each stride was evenly spaced apart and appeared to be unhurried. As the solitary figure came to stand by the door which lead out onto the school yard a drop of blood dripped from a part of his body and splashed onto the shiny surface of the floor.

David stood in the middle of the corridor unmoving and with an expressionless look upon his face. His long winter coat was covered in blood, but it did not show up all that well due to it being dark in colour. He had buttoned it up to hide the stains on his white shirt, but he could do nothing to conceal his right hand that was drenched in the thick scarlet fluid.

As David opened the door the sound of the schoolyard immediately flooded into the corridor. He waited for a moment to make sure that he was completely mentally and physically ready for what he was about to do. When he was satisfied that he was fully prepared he stepped outside to complete the beginning of his future.

Still David walked at an even pace. There was a composed air about him and the expression upon his face reflected his calmness. His pulse stayed at a regular rate and he was in complete control of his mind. Nothing could stop him now.

"He's coming!"

The announcement sounded out from somewhere in the crowd. There was now a highly spirited mob of about a hundred and fifty pupils on the schoolyard all gathered around to see the spectacle. As soon as they saw David coming they instantly parted to let him through. They all wore hungered expressions upon their faces and there was an aura of excitement throughout.

Martin was standing in the middle of the crowd with his sleeves rolled up and with a twisted sneer upon his face. He slowly started to walk towards his opponent with the eager members of his gang following close behind him. The whole sight looked quite intimidating as they approached David and started to surround him. Fear, however, was not among this young man's inventory of emotions.

The large gathering had now attracted the attention of other pupils around the school yard and it had not taken them long to swarm around to take a look at what was going on. There were excited murmurs as the atmosphere started to build up and everyone waited expectantly for the entertainment to begin. As the two opponents stood opposite each other there was a quiet lull in the noise in anticipation for the storm to erupt.

David stood for a moment with his head bowed and with his arms by his sides. As he slowly looked up he revealed an expression upon his face which no other living person had ever seen on him before. His cold features seemed to be fashioned of stone and eyes burned like white-hot flames. In truth, it was the face of a killer. Fierce, ruthless and sadistic.

The crowd had expected to see David wearing an expression of fear, but quite the opposite appeared to be the case. There were now quite a few surprised faces among the pupils as they realised that he actually was there with the intention to fight. It was, however, what happened next that really shocked them. He took off his coat and revealed his heavily bloodstained shirt.

All the eager expressions upon the faces of the crowd had now turned into looks of horror. They were not sure whether it was David's blood or someone else's, but either way somebody had been badly cut. Some of the pupils standing at the front even started to nervously shuffle their way to the back just as a precaution.

Martin's expression had also changed to one of shock, but as he got a hold of himself he managed to revert back to his original scowl and sent out a bellowed battle cry.

"Cain!" He took a few steps forward and pointed his finger at David. "You're fucking dead!"

This immediately put the thrill of the fight back into the gathering of onlookers who in return started cheering for the contest to begin. Martin's heartbeat instantly reacted to the noise of the crowd and he felt a rush of adrenaline flow though him. He had already thought of what he was going to do. A right hook to the face and then a knee to the groin. Now it was time to put his plan into action.

The first punch was swung straight for the left eye, but was easily blocked. A knee was thrust towards the groin, but a step back averted the blow. In reply a fist was shoved into the mouth and immediately split the lip. Martin stumbled back and David raised his eyebrows in a sardonic manner.

Surprised gasps came from all around the crowd as they saw the favourite clearly lose the first bout. From some sections of the spectators there were even cheers. This, however, just strengthened Martin's resolve and increased his temper. As he ran towards David with his fist clenched he shouted out a foul mouthed exclamation.

"Wanker!"

Martin threw a succession of punches at his opponent, all aiming for the head. David, however, did not try to block them this time. Instead, he just lunged back in return.

Blow after blow landed on each of them as they did their best to harm each other in any way that they could. Cuts instantly appeared on their faces and blood started to flow, but still the savagery carried on. The way they were going at each other it looked like they were both going to end up losers.

As each blow landed on David he still managed to keep his mind on what he was doing. A punch would hit him in the face, but he would still be able to keep his concentration and think about where he was going to hit his opponent next. For every fist in the mouth he received he gave back a strike to the nose in return. It was a deadly combination of intelligence and violence.

Martin's temper kept him going as he flailed his fists about in an almost random manner. The only thing that went through his mind was the sheer will to smash the hell out of his opponent. He did not think of the victory celebrations afterwards or the consequences that he would inevitably have to pay when he was put before the headmaster. All he wanted to see at the end of it all was David lying on the floor battered, bleeding and unconscious.

The fight seemed as if it was going to last all the way through to the end of the morning break. Most of the other violent disputes on the schoolyard would only last for about thirty seconds, but this was one they all would remember for a long time. It was almost too brutal.

David had taken many beatings in his life at the hands of a number of people. The way he took each punch without even faltering was almost as if he had been toughened up for it. He could, of course, feel the pain, but he just ignored it.

Martin had never been beaten up by any of the other pupils in his life. All he had ever done was punch and kick without ever getting even a slap back. Every time he got hit he could feel the pain of the blow and it was now starting to get to him.

Whilst all this was going on the pupils who were gathered around were shouting and screaming to urge the both of them on. They had never seen such a good show that had also lasted so long. It seemed as if there would never be a winner, but then a hammer blow was struck.

David launched a left fist aiming right for his opponent's chin and connected perfectly. Martin fell back onto the crowd of onlookers and only just managed to keep on his feet. His mind was still alert and he remained just as enraged as when the fight had broken out, but the pain he was feeling was now unbearable. He had a broken nose, a deep cut above his right eye and a selection of other abrasions and bruises.

Martin now knew he had lost. He could not endure another onslaught of blows as he had just gone through. What was even worse was that his opponent seemed to be unhurt by the punishment he had received.

David stood with a badly swollen left eye and a big split across his mouth. He appeared to be in quite bad condition what with his already blood stained clothes and the state his face was in. However, he still had a look about him as if he had no concern for his own welfare and that his only consideration was that of victory.

Martin had only one option left. It was his last resort, but defeat was something he was not willing to accept. He reached into his back pocket and pulled out a flick knife. As he pressed the button on the side the blade menacingly sprung up through the handle and was immediately greeted by a chorus of gasps from those who were looking on.

The crowd of pupils gathered around had now seen enough. They did not want to be a part of something like this. It had all gone too far and was becoming quite frightening. Some of them even started to run away just for the sake of their own safety.

David, however, still remained calm and unmoved. His opponent seemed to have suddenly gained the upper hand, but that was no cause for alarm. He took a moment to study the knife carefully and then spoke in a steady tone of voice.

"Have you got the guts to use it?"

Martin tried to feign confidence.

"You bet I fucking have!"

David now felt that it was time that the fight was ended. He had put his point across to Martin and all the pupils who had gathered around. No one would ever disrespect him now. It was time to finish it *all*.

"Very well, I'll make it easy for you." At that, he ripped open his shirt to reveal the centre of his bare chest. "Put it in my heart!"

David stood in a completely defenceless posture and seemed to have no fear of dying. As he glared at Martin straight in the eye he had a look upon his face which seemed as if his own death was what he wanted. After all, the end of his life would also practically mean the end of his archenemy's life, considering the rest of it would be spent behind bars for his murder.

The whole situation had now come to a standoff of nerves. David's chest expanded with every breath he took and was still stained with Mr Cutter's blood. As he looked deep into Martin's eyes he realised that the invitation to kill him was not going to be refused. All he had to do now was wait.

It had not taken David long during the day to accomplish what he had set out to do. No one would ever speak of him now as just the 'weird looking disfigured boy'. They would all know his name and would talk about him for years to come. He would essentially be immortal.

The pressure was now on Martin. He stood with the flick knife tightly clasped in his hand, with the blade pointing towards David. He glanced around nervously at the remainder of the surrounding pupils who were all in return looking at him with horrified expressions upon their faces. There seemed to be only one person on the schoolyard who was not feeling any fear and he was the one whose life was in danger.

Martin looked into David's fearless eyes and then lowered his gaze down to the unwavering young man's bare chest. A thousand thoughts swirled about in his mind as to why he should stab him and another thousand of why he should not. It all seemed so easy, yet so hard. Just plunge the knife in between the ribs, but face the consequences afterwards.

There were now only about twenty pupils who were still standing around David and Martin. The rest had run off into the school building or were watching from a safe distance. Nearly every face on the yard was a picture of horror. It was at that point when Steve Harding decided to give his friend some advice.

"Do it Martin!" He spoke in a forceful, yet sly manner. "Go on!"

David just kept on staring into his aggressor's eyes. He did not move, nor did he speak a word. Soon it would all be over.

Martin tightened his grasp on the knife. As he prepared himself he took in a deep breath and nervously winced. He took aim at the bare flesh and then he did it.

They both simultaneously jolted as Martin made contact with David. The knife travelled straight for the centre of the chest and right for the heart. Now they both just stood face to face and unmoving.

Time stopped as the whole school yard froze. Every pupil's face was aghast with terror as they stood helplessly looking on. Just as it seemed as if no one was ever going to move, David's mouth slowly started to open. As he spoke his voice was quiet and at ease.

"I'm not stupid."

The knife hovered just millimetres away from David's chest and was going nowhere. His left hand had hold of Martin's wrist and his right had a firm grasp on the elbow. In one quick movement he twisted the arm, put it over his knee and pushed down either side. There was a hideously low sounding crunch as the bones decrepitly crumbled.

Martin screamed with agony as the pain ripped through his arm. He instantly dropped the knife and feebly fell to his knees. As he looked at his arm he saw the broken bones poking through the flesh and blood pouring from the wound. Seeing the state he was in made him go into shock and he started to yell out in a hysterical and incomprehensible manner.

David now knew that it was just a matter of time before a teacher arrived, so he acted swiftly and efficiently. He grabbed hold of Martin's chin with one hand and the back of his head with the other. Just as he was about to carry out the final execution he made one last statement.

"I bet you wish we were friends now?"

At that, David pulled Martin's chin round to the back of the head with a vicious twist instantly breaking the neck. The now flaccid body of the so-called school bully just limply fell to the floor and landed in a contorted and dilapidated posture. As he lay there in a heap his lifeless eyes remained wide open and his mouth seemed to be yelling out in a terminal silent scream.

There were frightened screams from watching girls and yells of disgust from the boys. Some of the pupils even started to vomit, whereas others just fled in panic. The whole scene was quite horrific for every person there, apart from one.

David stood for a moment to admire his final deed of the day. As he looked at Martin's still and twisted body he nodded his head in a satisfied manner. It had been as easy as the other two.

David now started to walk across the schoolyard. As he slowly paced his way along, the pupils who had been watching immediately scattered out of his path so as not to provoke him. He just ignored them all and calmly made his way over to a bench. When he sat down he comfortably rested his hands upon his lap and waited for the police to arrive.

It had not taken long for some teachers to appear on the schoolyard and start asking questions. When they saw Martin's lifeless body and the knife laying next to him on the ground they quickly began sending the pupils into the building. None of them approached David. They realised that it would probably not be such a safe thing to do. Instead they just left him sitting alone on the bench.

130

For all the lives that David had taken during the course of the day he felt no remorse at all. There was something, however, that he did not notice, and if he had he probably would have put it down to a piece of dirt in his eye anyway. A symbolic lone tear rolled down his bruised cheek and fell to the ground.

It was almost as if there was still some of the old David Cain left inside him who knew it simply should never have of been this way. Once there was a time when he could never have brought himself to even consider hurting another person, but now those days were long gone. The future would now only hold thoughts of hate, emotions of anger and acts of violence.

As Mr Scott walked into the office he apologised in a jovial manner.

"Sorry I'm late! B3 hadn't finished deafening me with their music recitals."

This was greeted with a smile from the headmaster and a beckoning motion to sit down. Mr Longman was a tubby man with thick rimmed glasses and always wore a pair of colourfully bright braces. His whole appearance was relaxed, but at the same time he would also be strict enough with the pupils of the school in order to gain their respect. As he turned to the other two people who were sitting in his office he spoke in an inquisitive tone of voice.

"So, how long have you been planning all of this?"

"We've been arranging it for some months now." Mike replied. "We made sure that it was all possible with David's mother before we went ahead with it and we've been keeping in contact with Mr Scott in regard to his school work."

Sally's parents were obviously still hurting from the news of their daughter's accident from the day before. They had not got much sleep during the night and their withdrawn complexions showed just how mentally exhausted they were. However, there was a matter that they had to see to today which they had been planning to resolve for quite some time. Although they were still very depressed, they, nevertheless, felt that they ought to come to the school to see the headmaster and sort it out.

Mr Longman was not exactly clear of what they were intending to do and went about trying to find out.

"Why do you want to do this?" He rubbed his chin and sat back in his chair. "Is this what he wants?"

Mike slowly nodded his head in a forlorn manner as he spoke.

"Yes, he'll want it. David is repeatedly abused by his stepfather and often comes round to our house with a number of cuts and bruises. When I spoke to his mother about it she just said that he deserved it and that she couldn't wait to get rid of him." He breathed out an exasperated sigh. "I know for a fact that he doesn't deserve the beatings that he gets."

Melanie nervously rubbed her hand on her husband's thigh and spoke in a gloomy tone of voice.

"It's obvious that David's mother doesn't love him. I don't think she ever has."

The headmaster raised his eyebrow and leant his elbows upon his desk.

"So why doesn't David know about what you intend to do?"

Mike reluctantly answered.

"Sally..." He uneasily paused for a moment and then started his sentence again. "Sally was going to tell him yesterday at the park, but because of the accident I don't think she had the chance to."

This was greeted by the four people in the office with a period of sullen silence. Everyone felt the same uneasiness due to the weight of the subject and the lull was brought about by a mutual respect for Sally's welfare. The headmaster finally broke the moment of gloom as he turned to Mr Scott to speak.

131

"And what about his education?" His expression was one of forewarning. "This sudden change at such a late stage of his school years could badly affect him."

"I don't think it will." Mr Scott shook his head and half smiled in a proud manner. "David has now earned enough GCSE's and A-levels to get into any college or university in the country. I can't see that changing schools is going to ruin any of his career prospects, especially as he's going to King William's Private School."

"Maybe, but how are the school fees going to be paid?" The headmaster spoke cautiously. "They'll be expensive."

Mike answered for Mr Scott.

"We have enough money to pay for it. Besides, we think that David's worth it." He looked at his wife and forced a smile. "It's what Sally wanted. She was so delighted when we told her of our plans. The look on her face was just..."

Melanie interrupted him.

"She was even more pleased when we told her that we were going to foster David and that he was going to come to live with us. We've even found ourselves a bigger house on the outside of town, just so we can fit him in." She lowered her head and spoke in a serene manner. "She said it was like 'a beautiful dream come true.'"

The headmaster slowly nodded his head and spoke in a conclusive tone of voice.

"So, now we've got to find David so that we can tell him that you're going to foster him and put him in a private school." He raised his eyebrows and smiled. "It should be quite a pleasant surprise for him."

Mr Scott wore a satisfied smile as he fervently agreed with Mr Longman.

"It will be. He'll have the future that he deserves." He turned to Sally's parents. "He always said he wanted to be a doctor, a scientist and a politician. The thing is; he really did mean all three."

Melanie added to the list of accomplishments.

"And he'll have a family who cares for him."

It was left up to Mike to make the final summary.

"I can only think that the world will somehow be a much better place now that David can have the education and home life that is befitting such a fine young man." He spoke in a wistful tone of voice. "I just look forward to seeing the person who he eventually becomes."

At that, the door of the headmaster's office suddenly swung open momentarily startling everyone in the room. Standing in the doorway was an out of breath young girl with tears flowing from her eyes. She seemed to want to say something, but by the frantic look upon her face she appeared to be finding it quite difficult to steady herself. However, when she finally did manage to get her words out they were nervously stuttered.

"Sir! Sir! Something terrible has happened." She wiped her eyes with the back of her hand. "It's David Cain. He's done something absolutely..."

The schoolyard was virtually empty other than a small group of teachers gathered around a corpse on the ground and a solitary boy sitting on a bench some distance away from them. There was a subtle rustling noise as a soft wind blew through the trees producing a relaxing stillness all around. It seemed so ironic that an atmosphere so tranquil should replace such a violent storm of anger.

David sat with a restful look upon his face. He now knew that he had to pay the consequences for what he had done, but that was something that he had quite deliberately planned. As he waited for the police to arrive a number of impassioned thoughts passed through his mind.

They wanted a god. They wanted something to believe in. Well, they better believe in me, because what I've got planned for them is a godlike miracle.

Humanity is about to lose its accolade of being the master race. I will bring a wrath unto them that will perish them all. There will be no mercy for any of them.

My time has at last come, and so has theirs.

David wanted to be and would have been a pioneering doctor, an innovating scientist and a respected politician. He could have done so many things for the better of humanity. Instead, society fashioned a ruthless killer out of someone who would have made everyone's future so much better than it would have been.

There was once a bright spark of hope in what David might have become, but now there was just a burning flame of despair. His immense intelligence could have been put towards helping every living person, but now it would only make plans to bring about their demise. He was once a happy and kind young man, but now his mind would only house thoughts of hatred and torment.

In just one morning, David Cain had mercilessly taken three lives. One was just a boy, one was a holy man of education and one was his stepfather. At just sixteen years old he had become an unforgiving and calculated mass murderer. However, what was really inauspicious was that he had only just begun.

A strong wind blew the heavy rain against the windscreen of the taxi as it pulled up at the edge of the curb. As the driver pressed the button on the meter he took a quick look at himself in the rear-view mirror and casually combed his hair with his fingers. Without even looking at his customer he called out the fare for the journey.

"Seven-eighty, mate!" This was followed by a large carefree sniff.

The passenger pulled his wallet out of his back pocket and then handed the taxi driver a ten pound note.

"Thank you! Keep the change!" He felt the money sharply leave his hand.

As the passenger leant across the back seat to pick up his briefcase he knocked his spectacles off of the end of his nose onto his lap. Slowly shaking his head in an exasperated manner he muttered an exclamation.

"Damn!" He picked up the glasses and quickly wiped them clean with the sleeve of his suit jacket.

Edward Beauchamp was a duty barrister at the crown courts in the city of Southfield. He was in his mid thirties and was of a skinny build. His appearance was more of that of an accountant what with his round spectacles and pin striped suit.

For all of the years that Edward had been in the law profession he had always enjoyed it enough to have never wanted to change to a different occupation. However, what he was going to have to endure today was tempting him to consider otherwise.

It had been on the television and in all of the newspapers. In a small town called Starrow a horrific triple murder had taken place. One man had been found dead at his home and two more people had been killed at the local comprehensive school. Therefore, unfortunately for Edward, he had been called upon to represent the accused of the crimes. David Cain.

At his opening hearing he had not even requested a barrister and had just pleaded guilty without a hint of regret. Before that, he had confessed to the police to the entirety of all of the murders and had not even tried to escape from the scene of the killings at the school. He had done everything seemingly without a care in the world about what he had done. All that was left for him to do now was to hear his sentence. At least that was what Edward was hoping for.

The public had already voiced their disgust at the seemingly senseless murders and several members of Parliament had also condemned David's actions as being utterly evil. Every newspaper had printed the story of the 'Starrow School Slaughterer' on the front pages for a number of days after the killings had taken place. There was even expected to be a big turnout in the public gallery, just so people could see the face of the teenage mass killer and witness his prosecution as it happened. It was almost as if some of the people who were turning up were doing it just to make sure for that he did not receive a too lighter sentence.

It had, therefore, been much to Edward's displeasure that he had been requested by David to represent him. His own feelings about the case were just as full of disgust as the public, only he was not allowed to make his views known like they were. As he looked out of the taxi at the pouring rain he muttered to himself in a distressed manner.

"What a day! It just about sums it all up." He paused before getting out and slowly shook his head. "Here goes!"

As Edward opened the door and put his leg out onto the pavement he immediately stepped into a deep puddle. The water splashed straight up his trouser leg and instantly sent a chill throughout his body. Today was not his day.

"There's Beauchamp!"

The declaration was sounded out from the group of newspaper reporters and television crews near the entrance to the courthouse. They all straight away ran over to the taxi and surrounded Edward as he stepped out into the pouring rain. He suddenly found himself having to answer a dozen questions all at once, even though at that particular moment in time he was more distracted by his soaked leg. As he shook his trousers with his hand he made an attempt to try to get some calm out of the situation.

"One at a time, please!" He raised his index finger and frowned irritably. "I can't hear you if you all talk at once."

A woman with long blond hair standing next to a television camera put a microphone up to his face and managed to get in the first question.

"Mr Beauchamp, you've only just been appointed by Cain, is he still pleading guilty?"

"Yes he is." There was a hint of satisfaction in his voice. "My client has completely confessed to everything and has not changed his stance on the matter."

"Why did he choose to kill those particular three people?"

"That is something that the court will disclose today." Edward shook his head. "It is not my place to quote my client."

His answer was immediately followed up by another question.

"What outcome are you hoping for?"

"He wants life imprisonment."

"Is he insane?" Now that the woman reporter had got the barrister's sole attention she had several microphones put to her mouth every time she spoke. "Has he been diagnosed as having a mental disorder?"

"The psychiatrists have informed me that he needs to receive counselling." Edward nodded his head. "I concur with that."

"Well, do *you* think he's insane?"

"I don't know. I'm not a psychologist."

"Well, you must have some idea. I mean, you have met him."

"Actually, I haven't." Edward shrugged his shoulders and looked quite bemused. "As you know, he didn't have any legal counsel present at his original plea. The only contact I've had with him so far is through sending and receiving letters."

"What did the letters say?"

"They all just gave me instructions of what he wanted me to do today."

"And what's that?"

"Sustain his plea of guilty to murder and get him locked up in a secured hospital prison."

"Why a secured hospital?"

"Because my client feels that is where he should be."

This was followed by another bout of questions from all of the other reporters.

"Why doesn't he plead guilty to manslaughter through diminished responsibility?"

"Will the case be adjourned?"

"Does he ever want to be set free?"

At the sudden din of raised voices, Edward decided that it would be best to start to shuffle his way through the cramped mass of reporters to get to the courthouse. His efforts were momentarily thwarted until a small group of police officers barged their way through the crowd and started to help him on his way. Whilst he was slowly bustling forward he was still being asked questions by the ever hungry media.

"Did he approach you personally for representation?"

"I was the duty barrister at the time."

"Did you have a choice?"

"Yes, I did."

This was not exactly true. As Edward was only young and inexperienced he had little choice in what cases to take on or disregard. It was then when he heard one of the journalists ask a question that he had been dreading to answer more than any.

"How do you feel about representing one of the most hated people in the country?"

For a moment, Edward stopped and just bowed his head in a desolate manner. He then answered in a diplomatic fashion.

"My client deserves a fair representation regardless of his popularity."

After a lot of pushing and shoving the police finally managed to get Edward into the courthouse and away from all of the journalists. He was quite relieved to have broken free from the interrogations and the bustling about. Some of the questions he had been asked not even he knew the answers to and if he had have known he probably would have felt a lot easier than he already did.

As Edward walked into the large marble walled front entrance of the courthouse a police officer approached him.

"Mr Beauchamp?"

"Yes."

"Your client, Cain, is in a court cell waiting to see you." He guided the way with his hand. "If you would like to follow me?"

Edward's reply was rather unenthusiastic.

"Thank you."

The officer led the nervous barrister through a number of corridors and down a flight of stairs until they came to a block of cells. They soon reached a door which had two policemen posted outside, just to make sure of the suspect's confinement. It seemed to be a lot of security for just a sixteen-year-old, but on the other hand, he was a mass murderer. For him to have gained such an accolade proved that there must be something dangerously volatile about him.

As the policemen saw Edward being led towards them by the officer one of them immediately stepped forward to question them.

"Can I help you?"

The officer with Edward introduced him.

"It's the defendant's barrister, Mr Beauchamp."

At that, the policeman turned around to face the cell and pulled a key out of his pocket. Before he opened the door he knocked on it and called out to the occupants inside.

"The boy's barrister's here."

"All right, let him in!" Came the reply.

Edward stood for a moment and took in a deep breath to try to calm his nerves. As the door of the room started to slowly open he lowered his gaze in a nervous manner. It was only when the police officer behind him spoke to him that he finally realised that they were waiting for him to go in.

"When you're ready."

"Thank-you." There was little gratitude in the reply.

At first, all Edward could see as he slowly paced into the cell was a table next to the centre of the back wall. As he got further in he saw a young looking police officer with spectacles standing in the far corner and then another older one with a big moustache just to the right of him. It was only when he felt a seemingly cold and uncomfortable aura to his left that he finally realised where his client was.

Sitting up straight with his head slightly bowed and with his hands securely handcuffed behind his back was David Cain. He was wearing an all-in-one white custody suit that had been given to him by the police. His time in remand had been spent in the cells of the Southfield police station and not in a prison due to the unusual nature of the case. The abundance of negative press coverage had meant that transporting him around from place to place could provoke a number of unwanted gatherings of angry members of the public.

As David heard Edward walk into the room he raised his head and carefully studied him with his light blue crystal like eyes. For a moment the nervous looking barrister felt an uncomfortable lump in the back of his throat as he cast his eyes upon the mass murderer. However, when he managed to get back his composure he reluctantly introduced himself.

"Hello, Mr Cain." He nervously sat down on the chair at the opposite side of the table. "I'm Edward Beauchamp, your barrister."

David just kept on staring at him with a studious expression upon his face. It seemed as if he was reading into the skinny man's mind as he looked deep beyond his spectacles and into his eyes. As Edward carried on with his introduction his nervousness became quite apparent by the way he stuttered his words.

"I'll be representing you in court today. So if you have any questions don't be afraid to ask me about anything you need to know."

David greeted this with a slight raise of the eyebrows. Edward carried on regardless.

"You refused to have me present when you were interviewed by the police and by the psychologists." He looked at his client in an inquisitive manner. "In fact, this is the first time that you've agreed to see me. Why is that?"

At that David leant forward across the table and spoke in a calm yet firm tone of voice.

"That is none of your concern." He then sat back in his chair again.

Edward could only sit staring at his client with a stunned look upon his face. He had not expected such a cold reply to such a harmless question. When he regained control of his senses he went about asking another question. Only this time he was a bit more wary.

"Now, I've read the reports produced by the psychologists who interviewed you and they've stated that you should go to a secured hospital prison." He shook his head in disagreement. "But I think I can do better than that for you. Considering your age and if you say the right things to the judge, I think I might be able to get you sent to an ordinary medium security prison."

David took in a deep breath and then followed it by announcing his own plans of what he intended the court to do with him.

"I do not want to go to an ordinary prison. I wish to go to a secure hospital prison. I informed you of that in the letters that I sent you." He spoke slowly and precisely to make sure that his words were completely understood. "Therefore, as my barrister, that is exactly what I wish you to do."

Edward had other ideas.

"But things will be so much easier..."

He was interrupted by the now raised voice of his infuriated client.

"Listen to me, you imbecile!" David's words were spoken with a scorching temperament. "I told you that I want to go to a secured hospital prison and that's where I want you to get me sent to. So, if you don't carry out my instructions exactly as I tell you I'll get rid of you and get myself another more capable barrister."

Edward fearfully raised his hands in a submissive manner as he tried to make amends.

"I'll do as you ask." He breathed out a nervous breath. "You don't need to discharge me."

David just shook his head and went back to speaking in a calm and steady manner as if he had never even raised his voice in the first place.

"I have no intention of firing you." He slowly leant forward across the table. "My threat was upon your worthless life."

At that, the older one of the two police officers in the cell stepped forward and reprimanded the defendant.

"Less of that, Cain!" He grasped hold of a baton that was attached to his belt. "Don't make trouble for yourself!"

David just turned to the guard and stared at him for a long moment. His expression was cold and clearly showed that he was unimpressed by the weak threat. When he turned back to his barrister he concluded the interview.

"You have your orders." His face twisted into a forewarning scowl. "Just make sure that you follow them out exactly as I've told you!"

Edward just nodded his head in a yielding manner and answered in a meek tone of voice.

"Alright, I'll try to have you sent to a secured hospital prison." He could not help but ask one last question. "And you're sure that you want life imprisonment?"

David answered by just deepening his scowl to show that his patience was again wearing thin.

Edward closed his eyes almost in an attempt to shut out the trauma of the situation and then spoke with a subdued murmur as he got up out of the chair.

"Very well, I'll do as you ask."

As he quickly made his way towards the door he turned to have one last glimpse at David who was just sitting in the same upright posture with his head bowed as he had been when the nervous barrister had entered the room. This was certainly not like any of other case that Edward had taken on before.

When the cell door slammed shut it was followed by the confining sound of the key as it turned in the lock. Still David just sat unmoving with his head bowed in a contemplative manner. His mind was producing thoughts of what he was expecting to endure during the day and whatever other contingencies that he might encounter.

This should be relatively easy. They never cease to amaze me with their childlike naiveté.

The psychologists' reports will give the evidence on my state of mental health. I've already convinced them to believe that I'm insane. I'll have no problems there.

As for that weak barrister, he will be an easily controlled puppet. He will not fail me. His fear will see to that.

The judge. I haven't had a chance to influence him yet, but no doubt he is just as feeble minded as the others. When he asks me if I have anything to say before he passes sentence I'll just tell him what I intend to do to the human race. He'll then be so outraged that he'll give me the life sentence that I want. The inferior imbecile will probably think that he's punishing me harshly.

They simply won't suspect a thing. None of them will even begin to imagine what lies ahead of them. It's just a matter of time before I bring them all to their knees.

Fools! They're all fools!

David's plans had been worked out a long time ago. He had devised them all in the morning of the killings. For most first time pre-meditated murderers such a calculated degree of thinking would have been too much to cope with before taking their first life. This, however, was not the case for this decisive young man. Quick and impeccably intelligent thought was his greatest asset and he used it to his advantage at every moment of every day.

All of the details of David's plans had been carefully thought out and had the necessary action taken to make sure that they were executed exactly as required. He had even gone to the town library on his way to school just to gain some needed knowledge and this was even after murdering his stepfather first thing in the morning. Throughout that whole day and every day since every contrivance had been calculated and carried out to perfection.

The three main components needed for David's overall plan to work were time, privacy and the education that he would need to enhance his knowledge. Without any one of these attributes his plans would not be successful. It was for these reasons why he was now trying to make sure that he was going to be locked up by himself in a single cell for an indefinite period of time. He would have no one to disturb him, he could take as long as he liked to study and with a manipulative amount of bargaining he would be able to get the books that he would need to learn about the subjects which he would find most beneficial.

Giving up his freedom may have seemed to be a bit of a heavy price to pay for David, but isolation was actually something he wanted. He could have just killed Norman, Mr Cutter and Martin Dent in ways which he would never have even been suspected of their murders. However, that would have meant having to carry on living amongst humans and they were the main reason for why he was going through all of this.

David despised the sickness of society. His plan was to punish the human race for its history of crimes. They were the inventors of evil and the architects of the destruction of nature, and even through all of this they still somehow managed to be the master race of the planet. It just all had to be changed.

So now David found himself just about to be judged for his crimes by this self-titled intelligent race. Whereas they considered him to be a depraved killer of three innocent people, he thought of himself as having rid the flesh of the earth of just three of its billions of diseased cells.

It was while David was sitting in the interview room pondering his plans that he was again interrupted by the older of the two police officers standing in the cell with him.

"Your problem, Cain, is that you've never been taught to have respect for your elders. I would've never have let you get this way if you were my son." He walked over to stand on the opposite side of the table. "I would've taught you how to behave right from the start."

David's reply was spoken without looking up and with little expression in his voice.

"Don't talk to me!"

The older officer had an almost cumbersomely big build and stood quite tall as he stared down at the young defendant. He seemed to have a number of permanent lines upon his face, which were etched into a scowling snarl almost as if he had spent the whole of his life in an irritated mood. As he carried on stating his views he sat down on the chair at the opposite end of the table and started to idly run his fingers across his moustache.

"You see, if I had have been your father or stepfather I would've made sure you learnt manners and respect." He raised his eyebrows and nodded his head in self-agreement. "I would've made sure that you done as you were told."

Again the reply came in just one short sentence.

"You talk foolishly."

"Do you know what I do to my six year old son when he disobeys me?" The officer paused as if to wait for an answer to his question even though he knew he was not going to get one. "I give him a whack. Nothing too hard, but enough to let him know he's done wrong. That's what should've happened to you."

The not so wise remark immediately caught the entirety of David's attention. As he sharply raised his head his face twisted in to look of searing rage. Then, within an instant, almost as if he had not even heard what had been said, his expression changed back to one of complete calmness. This, however, would prove to be a very inauspicious illusion.

The other younger policeman in the room now realised that things were getting a bit out of hand and he nervously adjusted his spectacles as he stood leaning against the far wall.

His build was nothing like his older colleague's. He may have been quite tall, but he had little weight on him that he could call upon for physical power.

David had now had enough of the antagonising police officer and thought that it was time that he dealt out the required punishment. His mind took a fraction of a moment to plot how he was going to apply the penalty and he would not even need to be free from his bondage to do it. It was all a simple matter of physics. Degrees of angles, distances, pivots, weights, applied force and a carefree willingness to viciously smash in the face of another person.

The older officer was now sitting with his arms crossed in front of his chest with a self-assured expression upon his face. There was a moment when he had thought that he had said something that had extremely irritated the prisoner, but within a blink of an eye it seemed not have had such a vexing effect after all. He was then taken abruptly by surprise.

David quickly stood up and powerfully forced the side of his hip onto the edge of the table sending it sliding across the floor and into the startled policeman's chest. The large man immediately toppled back pivoting upon the back legs of his chair and landed heavily against the wall behind him. The objective of the initial blow was not to floor him, but to put his mouth in line with the top of the table. Now it was time for the finishing blow.

Just before David completed the onslaught he repeated his initial demand.

"I said don't talk to me!"

The older officer now knew what was just about to happen, but there was nothing he could do about it. His arms were now flat against the wall behind him from when he had tried to instinctively to break his fall. There was simply not enough time for him to protect himself from what was to come. All he could do was just wince and take his punishment.

Within an instant of finishing his sentence, David again pushed his hip onto the edge of the table sending it crashing deep into the policeman's mouth. Blood spurted across the tabletop in a fan like pattern and there was a low crumbling noise as his teeth got forced down into his throat. As the large man rapidly lost consciousness his arms slumped down by his sides and his eyes slowly rolled up into his eyelids.

The younger officer in the room also had no chance of trying to prevent the attack and much to his despair he now found himself locked in the same room alone with the mass murderer. A wave of trepidation instantly washed over him, but with his training in mind he did his best not to let it show and pulled his baton from his belt. As he looked at the wreck of his colleague he tried to feign an expression of boldness. This proved to be quite difficult as the body of his much larger colleague was just ominously sitting up against the wall with the occasional air bubble seeping out from the side of his mouth.

David was now standing motionless gazing at the young policeman. After he had studied him for a long enough period of time he came to the conclusion that what he saw before him was an extremely poor attempt at trying to appear to have confidence in oneself. With this in mind he started to slowly pace across the room towards the nerve wracked officer. When he came to be within a few feet of the terrified man he just took a moment to stare at him eye to eye.

The young policeman stood with a hopelessly feigned look of bravery upon his face and with his baton held aloft. He could feel a cold and unfeeling aura coming from the impulsive prisoner. It was almost as if he was staring straight into the face of the devil himself. Although the prisoner before him had eyes that seemed to burn white hot it felt as though they had made his own blood freeze solid in his veins.

Even though the young officer had his baton at the ready he still did not feel as though he had the upper hand in the situation. He had already seen his colleague fall foul to one of this young man's unerring onslaughts. All he could do was do his best to make sure he was prepared for whatever was about to happen, but secretly hope for leniency.

David had no intention of killing for fun. He had only ever done it to hand out a deserved punishment to another. Such a weak specimen was no trouble to him. Therefore, in an act of mercy, he just took one step to his right and nudged with his elbow against a red panic button that was mounted upon the wall of the cell. This instantaneously set off a number of high-pitched alarms around the building.

The young officer's shoulders immediately slumped as he thankfully realised that he was not going to receive the same fate as his colleague. All he could do was just stand there and wait for the back up to arrive.

It did not take long for the door to the cell to swing open and for a crowd of police officers to charge in and grapple David to the floor. There was lots of shouting and swearing, especially when they found that one of their colleagues had received a rather unconventional course of dentistry. They instantly started to treat the prisoner with a lot more coercion as they dragged him up off of the floor clutching him by his hair and by the scruff of his neck.

As the young officer stood staring at the fracas all he could do was mutter aloud in an exasperated manner.

"Fuck that!"

The low numbing sound of people murmuring amongst themselves instantly filled the air as the accused was led into the courtroom handcuffed and surrounded by four policemen. Members of the press feverishly started to scribble in their note pads to describe the atmosphere of their surroundings. There was not a gaze in the room that was not centred upon the one person whose retribution they had all come to witness. That, however, was of little concern to him.

David could feel the piercing stares of the people in the courtroom scouring over him. It did not bother him to be at the centre of everyone's attention, even though they all viewed him with expressions of disgust. He had got quite used to being looked upon with loathing eyes at an early age of his life.

Since the day that David had been born he had always found himself shunned by those around him due to his difference in appearance. His head was only fractionally larger than normal, but for some reason there were plenty of members of society who felt offended by his being in their vicinity. They, therefore, went about making sure that he was made fully aware of the fact by both verbal and violent means.

It was the constant physical and mental attacks at the hands of David's aggressors and the sudden demise of Sally that had finally caused him to snap. The culmination of years of wounding remarks about his appearance, mercilessly brutal beatings and the tragic loss of the only one true love he had in the world had been too much for him to take. Unfortunately, the result had been one of a more vehement destructiveness. The wild demon from within had been released and it was the very people who had summoned it who were the first to fall foul to its ruthless wrath.

Society was oblivious to what had driven David to commit three murders in just one day. No one knew of the torturous life that he had led up until the point in which he had changed into a psychopathic killer. He had not told the police or the psychiatrists about the harsh cruelty he had endured whilst growing up. If he had they might have decided to be lenient and not lock him up away from society. Instead, he just made it look as if he had turned insane and had taken the lives of those nearest to him at the time without the slightest of motive.

The day had now come for David to find out if his plans had worked. He would be told at the trial if was to be sent away to a secured hospital prison for the mentally ill or that he had not succeeded in his attempts to fool them. Failure was not an option to be considered.

David had not even thought about what he would do if he had not convinced the necessary people that he was insane. He rarely miscalculated anything and he was not about to make such a costly mistake with something as important as this. Waiting to hear the judge pass his sentence was not a question of whether or not he had failed, but one of how well he had succeeded.

Today was basically just going to be yet another step completed in David's overall plan. The fact that he was just about to be sentenced for the crime of murder was not of any importance to him. There were a number of aims for him today and one was to announce to the world that a day would come when they would all come to fear his name. With these thoughts passing through his mind he allowed himself a slight grin while all around him were faces of disgust and horror.

As the usher instructed everyone to stand for the entrance of the judge the noise in the courtroom died down as quickly as it had started when David had entered. There was a lull of anticipation for what lay ahead. It would not be long before the boy of evil was deservedly punished.

David stood with his head bowed and his gaze going directly to the floor in front of him. As the judge entered the room and sat down at the bench he took a moment to study the defendant. He did this with a furrowed brow whilst breathing heavily through his nose. When he was ready to commence with the hearing he made a waving motion to the clerk of the court. This was followed by the noise of scraping chairs and rustling of clothes as the people in the courtroom all sat down at the same time. Just the accused remained standing.

It took a while for something to happen and when it did the first question of the hearing was directed at David.

"Are you, David Cain, of 66 Amos Street, Starrow Town?"

"Yes!"

David did not look up whilst answering. He did not even know where the voice had come from. For now he would just remain restrained, but very prepared.

The court now went about sorting out the rest of the formal proceedings. A number of psychologists gave their reports of the accused mental health, all of which confirmed his insanity. Edward, David's barrister, told the court that it was for the best interest of society that he was locked up in a secured hospital prison and not able to harm any more innocent people. Everything was going to plan.

After hearing all of the required reports the judge had taken a while to sum up all that he had heard. When he finally got ready to proceed there was an air of anticipation for him to finally announce the punishment for the defendant's crimes. Before giving his sentence he took a moment to study the accused.

The judge was in his mid sixties and looked not a year younger. His wig did little to improve his ageing appearance and the fact that he wore a pair of reading glasses perched upon the end of his nose made him look quite pompous. What with his constant tapping of his fingers upon the bench it was obvious that he was trying to put over an appearance of stature.

This, of course, did little to impress David. Not only was he not looking in the direction of the judge, but such a weak show of power would be quite pointless to him considering he was just about to be put away for murder regardless of the way the man before him went about it. He then heard the question that would bring about the completion of his plan.

The judge spoke in a stern tone of voice and stressed each of his words with a strong sense of disgust.

"David Cain, you have pleaded guilty to the three heinous murders which took place on the ninth of February of this year, of Samuel Cutter, Norman Knight and Martin Dent.

Before I pass sentence upon you is there anything you have to say which you feel will be of any benefit to you?"

"Yes!"

"Very well, say what you will!"

For the first time throughout the hearing David now raised his head. He did not speak straight away. For a long moment he just looked around the courtroom at the people present. They were at first all staring at him, but whenever he looked at any of them in the eye they quickly diverted their gaze away from him.

There had been no pictures of David released to the newspapers or the television companies. This was not because the police did not want it shown, but because his mother did not have any photographs of him at their home. The only descriptions the public had obtained of him so far were his name, age, school and address.

This was the first time members of the public had seen the mass murdering schoolboy and they cowered at what they saw. He even looked *different*. There was something about his eyes that took the breath out of the lungs and made the skin shiver. If this was the face of a person who had callously taken the lives of three people then his cold appearance seemed to match the heartlessness of his crimes.

David now turned his gaze towards the judge. His icy cold stare seemed to look deep into the mind in the search of fear, and fear was what he found.

The ageing man did not expect to feel such an alarming sense of bitterness just by looking at the face of the killer. As the judge's expression twisted into one of horror he felt his mouth go uncomfortably dry. This was no ordinary run-of-the-mill killer.

Whilst keeping his crystal blue eyes fixed upon the startled judge, David spoke in an incensed tone of voice which came from the depths of his rage.

"I am Omega and Alpha, the end and the beginning, the last and the first. You dare to judge me? It is I who will pass sentence upon you all. The human race is about to lay down at the dusk of its existence and I shall stand at the dawn of the new world." He slowly looked across the courtroom with a twisted sneer as if to show his disgust at what he saw. "You call yourselves an intelligent species. You murder each other for enjoyment, greed and because you think your gods want you to. Well, I kill to rid the world of a terminal disease called humanity..."

The judge interrupted him.

"You're human too."

It was such a typically naive remark. The audacity of it enraged David and he felt a burning anger surge through his veins. His voice was now so laced with venom that the intensity of his fury could be felt within the hearts of every person within the courtroom.

"You ignorant fool!" He shook his head at the startled judge. "You dare to associate me with your depraved race? Every day your kind murder, steal and rape. If there was any other creature on this earth that did such vile things you would have them all wiped out."

The police officers standing either side of David now realised that his outburst had gone on for far too long and was getting well out of hand. They both grabbed each of his arms in a futile attempt to try to calm him down, but this did little to stop his verbal retribution. He now went about announcing his own sentence upon humanity.

"You have made enough harmless creatures extinct from this planet for your own meagre benefits. Your way is to kill anything that mildly hinders you or is less intelligent than you. So, therefore, I shall do the same. By my hand humanity will be wiped from the face of the Earth." He took in a deep breath and then spoke his final vow in a voice so full of ferocity that its ruthless words sent shivers down the spines of all whom heard them. "Hear my name! For I am David Cain. Fear my wrath! For I am the one true messiah who shall

143

reap vengeance upon you all. And take heed of my words! For I swear that I will rid the world of the foul disease that is the human race. So it is said, and so it shall be done!"

The people in the courtroom just sat staring at David with horrified expressions upon their gaunt faces. They were enshrouded by a stony silence that seemed to be akin to the statue like state of them all. All that could be felt in the air was a bitter and harrowing fear.

David Cain had spoken and the world had heard.

The news reporter ran her fingers through her long blond hair and looked directly into the lens of the camera. After taking a moment to mentally prepare herself she put her microphone to her mouth.

"Is it running?"

A voice from behind the camera replied.

"Yeah!"

"OK, let's do it!" A slight pause. "David Cain, the Starrow School Slaughterer, was today sentenced to three life terms for the triple murders of his stepfather, a school teacher and a fellow pupil of the school of which he attended. He is to spend his time in custody in Blackmoor Prison, the newest, high security hospital in which the country's most dangerous criminals are held. When the judge asked Cain if he had anything to say before he was sentenced he made a chilling speech about his intention to rid the world of humanity. He spoke about himself as being Omega and Alpha. The exact opposite of which God speaks of himself in 'Revelations' the last book of the Bible, in which the end of the world is foretold. David Cain is without doubt a very ill and dangerous person who simply cannot be considered any longer as being just a schoolboy. The world will certainly be a much safer place now that he is to spend what should be a very long time in prison. This is Kim Walters, reporting for the South East, Six O'clock News, at the Southfield Crown Courts."

She stayed looking into the camera lens for a short while and then lowered her microphone. After a deep sigh she turned to look at the courthouse behind her and muttered to her colleagues in a depleted tone of voice.

"Now let's get the hell out of here!" She looked back at the camera. "This has totally given me the creeps today."

Ashes

There is a spark that lies within the ashes of my weak and feeble past. It is dull now, but from this day onwards it will be fanned by the incompetence of all of mankind. The day shall come when its exiguous glow will flourish into a blazing fire which will burn so fiercely that there will not be a place on Earth where its searing heat will not be felt. And when they look into the brilliant light that the flames will shed it will blind their eyes.

So, feed my fire, fools! Give me knowledge, time and solitude, and I shall in return hand you all your demise.

David sat in the middle of the prison security van with his hands and feet shackled whilst two police officers sat either side of him. The thoughts that were passing through his mind were now not unfamiliar ones. Hatred, violence and anger were frequently brought to the forefront of his consciousness.

As the van came to a stop, the two doors at the back opened to reveal a prison officer standing in a large courtyard. He was a short chubby man with a round face and had a long baton hanging from his belt. In a low and husky voice he spoke in a sardonic then commanding manner.

"Welcome to Blackmoor prison." He pointed a plump finger to the side of the van. "Get out and stand there!"

David stared at him for a short moment of time with an expressionless look upon his face and then started to do as he was told. As he got up he slowly shuffled his way out of the van and came to stop where the prison officer had instructed him to stand. Although he had been spoken to in a blunt and less than polite manner he did not seem to be too bothered by it.

Now that David had finally reached his destination he decided that it would be a good time to examine his new surroundings. As he gazed around at the prison grounds he saw a number of various sized buildings all sealed with iron doors and barred windows. The whole complex was confined within towering razor wire clad walls that seemed to compete with the clouds for the supremacy of the sky. This was a place that was built with the intention of mentally incarcerating a person as well as physically. Just the sight from within the grounds of Blackmoor was enough to make a person feel as if they were to be eternally excluded from the outside world.

The chubby prison officer standing outside the van took a moment to study David by looking up and down his stature. When he thought that he had gained the physical and psychological profile that he required he began to nod his head in a self-assured manner. It was obvious that he naively considered the young man before him to be nothing more than just a worried boy who had at some point in his life made a wrong decision and was now paying the ultimate price for it.

The prison officer spoke his next order.

"Follow me!" As he turned around and started to walk off he voiced another command without even looking behind him. "And keep up!"

David just compliantly followed the brusque instruction without a word and with the chains of his shackles clanking as a walked. He was led across the prison grounds through an open doorway and into a long corridor. As he walked the chubby officer was in front of him whilst another taller one was behind. When he got halfway down the hallway the stout guard turned around and gave another instruction.

"Wait at the line!" He pointed a finger at a band of red paint that stretched across the floor.

David stopped without saying a word or raising an eyebrow. By his outward appearance he seemed to be totally unconcerned by the constant orders. He just idly stood with his hands clasped in front of himself and with his eyes staring straight ahead of him.

The chubby prison officer paced up to the end of the corridor leaving David and the other guard waiting at the red line. When he reached the iron door at the end he pulled a plastic card out of his top pocket and then ran it through a small terminal mounted on the wall which had a numeric keypad positioned next to it. With a single finger he typed in his personal identification number on the keys and then looked up at a close circuit security camera that was attached to the ceiling. After a brief wait the iron door in front of him automatically opened.

Although David was a good fifteen yards away he had closely watched everything that the guard had done. It seemed as though the security at the prison was quite stringent and that nothing was left to chance. For someone to pass through one of these doors they would have to be in possession of a switch card, know the corresponding personal identification number to match it and, most important of all, be a recognised member of the authorised personnel. There would definitely be easier ways to get out of Blackmoor than just walking straight out.

It was not long before David was led into one of the cell blocks of the prison. As he paced through the wing he immediately became the centre of attention of a number of inmates who were standing around. They already seemed to know who he was and they made no attempt to hide their interest. Some glared at him with sneering expressions upon their faces, whereas others just eyed him with an almost scrutinising curiosity.

The chubby prison officer led David halfway through the block until they came to stand outside the open doorway of a cell. It was obvious that this was his destination so he made his way in and stood in the middle of the cramped room. He then heard the large iron door slam shut behind him.

For a moment, David just stood in the cell staring at the small window in the far wall. At first, his face was void of expression, but then it slowly twisted into a wry smile. As he took in a deep breath and closed his eyes he whispered a single word to himself which summed up the pleasure that he felt at his new surroundings.

"Perfect."

The silence within the office was broken by the ring of the telephone that was perched on the corner on the desk. A man with a dark moustache who was sitting close by hurriedly picked it up. As he listened into the receiver he intently leaned forward in his chair and slowly nodded his head. After a short while he put it back down and then looked up at another man who was sitting in the far corner of the room. He spoke just two words to announce the news.

"Cain's arrived."

The man in the corner raised his eyebrows and spoke in a wistful tone of voice.

"I should imagine that he'll be one of the more interesting inmates." A shrug of the shoulders. "From a psychological view point, that is."

The reply to the remark was spoken in a stern tone of voice.

"He's just one more murderer, Richard."

Howard was not very pleased at the show of intrigue in the new inmate. As far as he was concerned every criminal that was locked up in Blackmoor prison was nothing more than a thorn in the side of society. There was not a single one of them that warranted any kind of special consideration that would separate them from any of the other convicts. And that included the 'Starrow School Slaughterer'.

Blackmoor secure hospital had been open for three years now, of which Howard Fenton had been the warden ever since. What with his unforgiving hard nature and the equally relentless regime of the prison it was a very good match. The newest of the country's penal correction facilities had already earned a reputation for it being the most implacable of

146

its kind. This simply made it more fitting that he was also known for being a man who was not to be crossed.

Howard was of medium build and had a greying moustache that he carefully combed on a regular basis. He always wore well-tailored expensive suits which he bought from the city and regularly adorned his shirts with an equally costly silk tie. His whole image suggested that he was a man of success and power, and to bring judgement upon him by his appearance was not such an inaccurate way of analysing him.

When the prison service finished building Blackmoor the first person they had approached to take control of it was Howard. He had been the warden of other secure hospitals for a good fifteen years and the reputation he had earned for his work was highly thought of. When he was offered the post he accepted it straight away due to the fact that it was considered to be the highest possible position in his profession. To head the country's top prison would certainly put him at the pinnacle of his career.

Howard had not got where he was in the service by being sparing with his judgement. He was strict in his ways, but at the same time he was also a very fair man. Every rule of the prison was clearly laid down and allowed each and every inmate to just get on and do their time. However, if anyone was to cross the line of right and wrong then any meagre benefits they had already attained would be stripped off of them straight away as well as earning themselves a very likely chance of being sent to solitary confinement.

It was while Howard was discussing the latest inmate to arrive at Blackmoor with the other man sitting in his office that his stringent personality was made apparent.

"I don't care how old Cain is. I don't care about what reasons he had for doing what he did. And I certainly don't care if he does want to kill off the entire human race like he said in that 'Omega' speech of his. He's still going to get treated like every inmate does here, without exception." He shook his head. "To me, he's just another criminal who needs to be locked well away from society."

The man sitting in the far corner of Howard's office had completely different views towards the inmates in Blackmoor. Richard Lewis was the prison psychiatrist, and he did not just see the collection of wayward individuals as criminals, but instead saw the result of society's wrong doings. To him a man was not born evil, but was made that way by the ways of the world. He simply believed that every immoral act that was carried out by one person was done because someone else had previously committed an equally heinous psychological act upon that person beforehand. Extremes simply bred extremes.

Richard was a tall man in his late twenties with a prematurely balding head. Although his height would have normally made a man of his stature appear to be lanky, his muscular physique made him look quite sturdy. He did not wear a suit like Howard, but instead wore just a shirt, a tie and casual trousers. His whole appearance suggested that he was a very relaxed person, however, he would always spare as much time and dedication as possible into whatever he was dealing with.

Richard's pursuit in a career in psychiatry was more brought about by the passion of studying the enigma that is the human mind rather than the want of a steady job. There was never a definitive answer to any question. If a boy was badly beaten by both of his parents whilst growing up there could be a high probability that he might become a violent mugger, whereas there was also the possibility that another individual of the same upbringing could even become a pacifistic vicar. It was these constant changes in the subject matter that had meant his work was always different from day to day, and with this latest addition to Blackmoor prison had brought an even more appealing case to examine.

After taking a short while to think about what he was about to say, Richard gave his views to Howard in a calm tone of voice.

"I quite agree, David Cain does need to be separated from the outside world, but you must understand my psychological interest in him." He stood up and paced over towards a window that looked out across the prison grounds. "Most sixteen year old boys follow football or are interested in the latest pop music, but not him. He becomes a mass murderer."

Howard reminded Richard of the nature of the person he was talking about.

"He says he wants to wipe out the whole of the human race." As he leant back in his chair he folded his arms in a steadfast manner. "I don't find that interesting. I find it damn sick."

"It is sick. *He's* sick." Richard turned to face Howard and spoke in a thoughtful tone of voice. "But what could possibly make someone so young become so bad? What happened to him? What changed his whole life so dramatically to make him want to take three people's lives?"

Howard shook his head and shrugged his shoulders.

"Well, I don't know. But what I do know is that it's my job to make sure that he does his time and is kept well within the walls of this prison. That's all I'm bothered about." He unfolded his arms and pointed a finger at Richard. "You can ask him what you like. If you find out what the reason was for him doing what he did, then so be it, but we both know it won't change a thing."

Richard bowed his head in a submissive manner and spoke in a quiet tone of voice.

"I know." He dejectedly sighed. "He's not going to be let out for years even if he does change."

"It's the best thing."

"Maybe." Richard slowly nodded his head as he repeated himself. "Maybe."

"Cain, you've got an appointment with..."

Before the prison officer could finish his sentence he was interrupted.

"The psychiatrist." As David got up off of the bed he faced the guard and raised his eyebrows in a nonchalant manner. "I've been expecting his summons."

The prison officer just stood for a moment with a dumfounded expression upon his face. He seemed to be rather perplexed at the way that David had correctly anticipated and completed his sentence for him. Nevertheless, after giving up trying to fathom out what had made him so predictable he turned around and muttered a half hearted order.

"Follow me!"

David unenthusiastically did as he was told and went with the two prison officers who were waiting outside of his cell.

On the way to the psychiatrist's office David was led through a number of corridors which each had the usual security measures which had to be adhered to. Stand at the red line, wait to get clearance to pass through the door and then move on. When he finally reached his destination he was told to wait outside of a room whilst one of the prison officers who he was with went in to announce his arrival. The door was left ajar and he could not help but overhear the conversation coming from within the room.

"Cain's here."

"Does he know what he's been called here for?"

"Well, he might do." The tone of voice sounded vague. "He seemed to know that you wanted to see him without me even telling him."

There was a long pause.

"Could you bring him in, please?"

At that, David was called to enter the office. This he did in a slow carefree manner as if it was only his time that mattered. When he finally did pace through the doorway he came in to stand in front of a desk in the corner of the room. Sitting behind it was a balding man who seemed to be preoccupied with something other than him at that moment in time. The guard who had called him in just walked straight out and then closed the door behind him leaving just the two of them in the office. Although this may have seemed to be a bit of a risk to the safety of the man who occupied the room the camera mounted on the ceiling above him suggested otherwise.

Richard Lewis did not look up straight away, but instead just sat reading an open file in front of him. This was his way of hiding the large amount of intrigue that he had in David. He wanted it to appear as if he had no extra interest in the new inmate and that to him this was just another prisoner who he had to interview. It was out of the question that he should ever show that he enjoyed doing his job and that he actually found all of his cases to be somewhat fascinating.

After Richard thought that he had made David wait for long enough he slowly looked up and gazed at the young man in front of him. Although he had thought on a number of occasions about what this sixteen-year-old mass murderer might look like he was still not sure what to expect. Maybe he would be a skinhead with a permanent sneer, a teenager with long unkempt hair harbouring an anti-parent attitude or a mentally deranged psychopath whom knew no better than to stave in a person's head with a ball hammer? However, the young man who stood before him seemed to be more intent on trying to assess him.

David studied Richard with a scouring and relentless stare. His crystalline light blue eyes seemed to cut right through the mental wall that the psychiatrist had erected about him and deep into his mind. It was if there was not a thought that could be hidden from the incessant delving of the deliberative inmate's penetrating gaze.

Richard could not help bet gulp as he felt the pressure of David's attentive stare. He was not being looked at in the same way as the other prisoners eyed him. Instead it seemed to be as if the almost hypnotic gaze of the young man was mentally devouring him.

It was a struggle, but Richard tried to make some normality of the situation.

"Hello, I'm Richard Lewis, Blackmoor's counsellor. Please, sit down."

David pulled the chair out and lowered himself onto it without saying a word. He did this whilst still staring at Richard with the same glaring gaze. The psychiatrist uneasily carried on with his introduction.

"I'll start by saying it's not compulsory that you talk to me. You can leave at any time or cancel any appointments that we might make in the future. I'm simply here to give you any help and guidance for coping with prison life." He put the palms of his hands flat down on the table in front of him. "I just want to make sure that you know that I'm here to help you. So, is there anything you wish to ask or tell me?"

David did not answer the question, but instead spoke in a cold and almost arrogant manner whilst still keeping a rigid eye on Richard.

"I am quite aware of what you are here for and I know exactly what you want from me." A scowling expression crossed his face. "So why don't you just say what you've really got me here for?"

Richard felt quite surprised by the enmity that was being shown towards him and it made him feel quite insecure. He had been waiting for this moment for a number of weeks since he had heard that the 'Starrow School Slaughterer' was coming to Blackmoor prison. His normal approach was to at first introduce himself and then try to build up a rapport between him and the inmate, but instead the young man before him seemed to think that he was holding back from the real subject matter that he was intending to approach. This was, of course true, but this sixteen-year-old could not possibly know that.

Richard thought that he ought to just carry on with his usual methodology.

"You might encounter a number of problems which I can help you with whilst you are here, such as..."

A temperamental interruption.

"Stop acting like a fool! I can tell that you have a higher intelligence than the rest of them, so why don't you use it." David shook his head. "I don't want your help and I could never have a problem here that I could not solve myself."

Richard still tried to hide his hidden agenda.

"I'm just making sure that you know what I'm here for."

David's reply was spoken in an agitated tone of voice.

"I know exactly what you want to ask me and I will not let you waste hours of my time with your pathetic inconsequential drivel." He straightened his back as he continued. "You want to know why I killed them, what made me suddenly become a murderer and if I really meant it when I said that I wanted to wipe out the entire human race."

Richard was more than surprised to realise that David had quite obviously worked out exactly what the real reasons for the interview were. He had not expected the sixteen-year-old to be so forward with his appraisal of what the whole point of the discussion was. There was nothing left for him to do but to admit his intentions, which he did in a somewhat sheepish manner.

"Very well, you're right. I do want to know why at the age of just sixteen you murdered your stepfather, a school teacher and a pupil." Richard took in a deep breath and then shook his head. "And most of all, I want to know why you could possibly want to eradicate the whole of humanity."

"Well, I am willing to give you such information. I will let you probe whatever parts of my mind that you wish to." David raised his eyebrows. "However, there is also something that you can give me."

"What's that?"

"Books."

"You can get those from the library."

David leaned back in his seat and pressed both of the palms of his hands together in front of his chin in a posture that was almost similar to praying.

"I am fully aware of that, but I doubt that what I want will be in the prison library." He lowered his head, but kept his gaze fixed upon Richard. "You see, what I need are books on such subjects as chemistry, biology and other sciences. I'm sure you agree that the library would not be able to provide such things."

"That's true. But the prison can get them from outside if you earn them by doing various jobs around the prison."

As David spoke a snarling sneer crossed his face.

"I will not clean floors, toilets nor do any other such menial tasks as you would have any of the other fools in here do."

Richard just slowly shook his head in an almost apologetic manner.

"Then I'm afraid you won't be able to have the books that you want."

"What if I offered you something more valuable in return for the books?"

"Like what?"

A penetrating expression crossed David's face as he made his offer.

"I will give you information, if you give me whatever book that I want."

"What sort of information?"

"Psychoanalysis of the inmates. In depth profiles of their personalities, such as what made them become murderers, how they developed their adverse emotions towards other human beings and, basically, why they are who they are."

Richard was slightly taken aback by the rather over exuberant offer and almost felt too embarrassed to answer.

"Well, I don't think that we need help on such matters." The expression upon his face was almost one of pity for the inmate in front of him. "I mean, do you really think that there is anything that you could tell us that we don't already know?"

"I believe I could educate you."

"I'm afraid I can't see that myself."

At that, David stood up and turned towards the door. Just as he grasped the handle he looked over his shoulder at Richard. His tone of voice was settled and quiet, yet at the same time it had an element of resolve.

"Then I shall have to prove myself to you."

David then opened the door and paced into the corridor leaving Richard sitting at the desk with a somewhat perplexed expression upon his face. He was more than mystified by what he had just encountered. Not even all of the years he had spent studying at university could have prepared in any degree for the situation that he had just experienced. Although the psychiatrist was alone he mouthed a single sentence aloud.

"He is a very disturbed person."

There was a hush as Howard sat in his office with his arms folded and with his gaze going out of the window that looked out across the prison grounds. Richard had just told the warden about his first interview with David and the peculiar offer. He was not impressed.

"This Cain sounds more insane than I originally thought. Psychoanalyse the inmates for us." A shake of the head showed his disbelief. "He thinks he's still at school, doesn't he? What a strange suggestion."

"I must confess, I've never experienced anything quite like it before." Richard shrugged his shoulders and then sat down on the chair on the other side of the desk to Howard. "There have been a few occasions when inmates have offered me information about others in exchange for cigarettes, but this..."

"I think he's been watching too many films." The prison warden huffed in an unimpressed manner. "What psychological information can he offer you which you don't already know?"

"Nothing that I can think of."

Howard now turned around to face Richard and then leant his elbows on the desk. A deliberative expression crossed his face as he took a moment to think about the situation. When he had finally constructed his hypothesis he started to nod his head as if to show that he was quite sure of his calculations.

"It's probably an immature attempt at trying to hide his fear. He suddenly finds himself in strange and dangerous surroundings, and is trying to portray himself as something more than he actually is."

"That would be my normal response. Put up some kind of front in an attempt to hide his fears." Richard frowned. "But I just don't think that's it's like that. It was as if he really thought that he could have something valuable to offer me."

"So what are you going to do?"

There was a pause as Richard considered his options. It was not a serious situation that he had to deal with, but it was, nevertheless, rather perplexing. After a short while he stated his conclusion.

"I'll wait." He raised his eyebrows. "It's probably nothing anyway."

And wait he did. Several weeks passed without another word from David. It seemed as though it really had been nothing, until some rather unusual events occurred in Blackmoor secure hospital. Much to the surprise of those involved the newest inmate in the prison showed his true capabilities.

A large black man with a tattooed neck stood at the end of the prison wing and eyed it with a sneering expression upon his face. It was a solemn dour place and the people who resided within it did not appear to be that much more animated. Just before leaving through the open iron door to the side of him he slightly nodded his head and spoke in a low whisper.

"Most hell-like, shit-hole I've ever laid my eyes on."

The prison guard standing behind him muttered a sly remark in return.

"You better just make sure that you never come back here then, Longden!"

"If I do..." The now ex-inmate turned to face the guard. "It won't be to see you, Gov'!"

"The feelings are mutual." Came the reply.

Shane Longden had just served ten years in Blackmoor for the murder of a store detective at a supermarket in Cawling Town. After he had committed the crime most of the people who knew him were very taken aback by what he had done due to him always being considered to be a reasonably placid person. Up until the point of the murder he had only ever been in trouble with the law for crimes of petty theft and a few other misdemeanours. For him to have actually stabbed a man to death, without even a thought about the consequences seemed to be quite out of character.

When the judge had sentenced Shane after he had been found guilty he had given him a stretch of fifteen years, but this had since been reduced. Although he had been involved in the occasional fight in Blackmoor during his ten years his behaviour had been deemed good enough by the parole board for him to be released. He had done just enough to convince them that he had learnt the error of his ways and was now not a threat to the safety of the public. It was a unanimous decision that had given him his freedom.

The parole board was made up of three people, one of which was the prison psychiatrist, Richard. He had given them a psychological profile of Shane Longden and had informed them that although he might have a violent tendency on a low level if provoked he would not, however, be at all likely to ever take a person's life again. His testimony had swayed the committee and they had agreed to release him five years before the end of his actual sentence. Their words offered redemption as well as freedom.

"You've served your time and you've learnt that the crime you committed was not an act that is acceptable in a normal society. You are, therefore, free to go!"

That afternoon, Shane collected from his cell what belongings he considered to be of any value to him and began his walk to freedom. He did not say goodbye to any of the other inmates and just let himself be led by two guards to the gates of the prison. When he finally took his first step outside for ten whole years he spoke just two words to himself.

"At last!"

The end of the Friday evening was now approaching and most of the inmates in the wing were heading back to their cells. In every part of the prison the sound of iron doors closing could be heard. This was, as usual, followed by the occasional muffled shout as the convicts called out from somewhere amongst the corridors until silence enshrouded the entirety of the dingy place. It was not long before just the guards and a few inmates who were late returning to their cells remained in the wings.

The next part of the plan then went into operation.

"I want this delivered."

"What?" The guard turned swiftly on his heel and immediately wore a scowl upon his face. "You heard the call, Cain, get to your cell!"

152

"The psychiatrist instructed me to give this to a guard as soon as it was ready." David held out a folded piece of paper that was crudely sealed with a piece of melted plastic from a cup. Written on the front of it were the words 'Richard Lewis – Psychiatrist'. "He said he wanted it by Monday morning."

"What is it?" The guard replied.

David had already anticipated this question and had already thought of the lie he was going to give.

"He asked me to list the parts of my body that my stepfather used to touch." The words were spoken with a well-feigned expression of discomfort and a quite deliberate amount of stuttering. "I just couldn't say it to his face."

The guard uneasily took the piece of folded paper and slipped it into his top pocket. A look of embarrassment and perturbation crossed his face as he struggled to deal with the situation. His voice was broken and his face went a daunting shade of pale as he tried to keep his gaze diverted from David's.

"I'll put it in his mailbox." A deep swallow separated the nervously muttered sentences. "You better get back to your cell now."

As the guard turned away he did not see the wry smile appear upon the face of the inmate standing behind him.

Richard placed his briefcase next to the filing cabinet in the corner of the office and then slumped himself down onto the chair behind his desk. He wearily rubbed his eyes as he tried his best to summon his mental strength ready for the week ahead. It was not long, however, before he was to be given something that was to bring him about to a completely lucid consciousness.

A hurried sounding knock on the door startled Richard at first, but when he had got a hold of himself he called out.

"Come in!"

The door quickly opened and a prison officer took one step in before giving his message.

"The warden wants to see you." He raised his eyebrows in a sheepish manner. "He said 'right away!'"

Richard just sighed and then sluggishly got to his feet.

Howard was standing in front of his desk with the knuckles of his fists leaning on the leather-covered top. His whole stature suggested that his frame of mind was far from cheerful. It was when a knock on the door of his office broke his concentration that his state of annoyance became completely apparent.

"Yes!"

This was bellowed out without a consideration of who might be outside waiting to see him. After a brief pause the door slowly opened to reveal Richard standing there with an uncomfortable expression upon his face. He almost felt as if he should not speak at all, but thought it might be a good idea to find out what he was there for so as to throw some light on the situation at hand.

"You wanted to see me?"

Howard turned around and put a hand to his forehead in an exasperated manner.

"You will not fucking believe this!" He expelled a deep breath. "Shane Longden has just been arrested for battering to death a barrister with a bloody vodka bottle in Cawling Town."

"He only got out on Friday." Richard put his arms out with the palms of his hands facing upwards in a helpless manner. "He seemed alright. It was the third time he had applied for parole."

"Yeah, well now we know why he wanted to get out. The barrister whose head he split in two was the same one who represented him at his trial. The bastard didn't even try to get away after he had done it. He just stayed there waiting in his office for the police to arrest him." Howard sat back on his desk and lowered his head. "We're going to look like right fucking idiots!"

Richard certainly felt this of himself. He was the one who had convinced the parole board that Shane Longden was fit to be sent back into society. In a depleted tone voice he tried to make some sense of it all.

"He had only ever killed one person and that was just done in the spur of the moment. Even the judge at his trial agreed that it was not premeditated." Richard shook his head in disbelief. "He had no background of violence in his life. A normal upbringing and he had never set foot in a prison before."

Howard's patience was at an end and he wanted to get straight on with the enquiry.

"Well, I want to see all his files! I want lists of his previous crimes, your psychological analysis and any other fucking thing that can throw some light on this!"

Richard nervously replied.

"I'll get them now." At which point he left without any delay.

The middle draw to the cabinet was stuck at first, but it soon opened after an impatient fist was banged against the side of it. After fumbling through the abundance of files inside he pulled out one with the words 'Longden, Shane' written on the top in thick black ink. Richard put it down onto his desk and then closed the draw afterwards. It was at that point that something rather peculiar caught his eye.

"What's that?" He whispered in soliloquy.

In Richard's mailbox tray was a single piece of paper with his name written on it. With an inquisitive look upon his face he picked it up and opened it, breaking a melted plastic seal as he did so. It took him about two minutes to read the entirety of its contents, which was then followed by him this time speaking aloud.

"Jesus Christ!"

Howard looked at the piece of paper at first as if it were nothing more than a shopping receipt. After unfolding it he started to read through what was written inside. The further he got through, the more the expression upon his face changed to being one of utter shock. Even though he knew that Richard had about as much idea as he did about what he had just read he still, nevertheless, tried to get some answers.

"When did he give you this?"

"He didn't. He must have given it to one of the officers to put in my mail tray."

"It's dated for the Friday just gone. How the hell could he have known?"

The confusion was rampant and showed no signs of coming to any subsidence. In a morning that had already brought about a considerable amount of disarray this had only worsened things. On just one piece of paper, David had somehow written of what the future was to hold.

Friday 21ˢᵗ April

Richard Lewis,

By now you would have heard about Shane Longden murdering the barrister who represented him at his trial. His weapon was a whole bottle of vodka and his capture brought about by him simply not leaving the scene of the crime. This must have come as a surprise to you considering that you thought that he was a one off killer when he came to Blackmoor.

You were, of course, very wrong.

David Cain

Howard held up the piece of paper and uttered a fervent order.

"Get him in here, now!"

Richard attentively watched the expression upon David's face as he stood in front of Howard's desk. The young inmate seemed not to be at all phased by the stony glare that he was receiving off of the prison warden and it almost appeared as though he was making the most of the attention. His relaxed attitude became even more so apparent by the way he addressed those in the room in a rather blasé manner.

"So, you got my message?"

Howard did not hold back.

"You're damn right we did." He lifted David's letter off of the desk. "And you better explain all of this right now!"

David replied in a nonchalant manner.

"Which part did you not understand?" His brow inquisitively furrowed in a sarcastic gesture. "I thought I wrote it down in quite a self-explanatory manner."

"You know exactly what I mean, Cain. Don't play games with me or you'll be spending the next month in solitary!" Howard was now obviously screwing up the letter in his fist. "I want to know exactly how you got this information!"

A slight wry smile crossed David's face as he went about explaining his actions.

"To a psychologist it would be called psychoanalysis." He briefly glanced at Richard. "But I call it simple applied logic."

Howard was unimpressed by the answer to his question.

"What are you talking about?"

"By studying Shane Longden from a distance I assessed his habitual behaviour patterns and listened to his conversations with other inmates. With the information that I had collated I then analysed how he had come to develop his current personality and why he displayed abnormal emotional responses to certain incidents. With these taken into consideration I concluded that he was already a multiple murderer by the time that he had got to Blackmoor." David paused. "And, of course, I predicted the fact that he was going to increase his tally when he left."

Richard was sitting at the edge of the room and as he spoke he leant forward on his seat in an inquisitive manner.

"Are you saying that you somehow got all of that information in the letter just by psychoanalysing him or as you put it, by using simple applied logic?"

"That is correct." The reply was short and deliberate.

Howard was not going to be that easily persuaded.

"You can't expect us to believe that, Cain!" He had now put the crumpled letter back down onto his desk and was sitting back in his chair with his arms tightly folded. "Longden or someone else told you all of this."

It was also rather hard for Richard to believe.

"What you are saying does sound a bit unlikely. Are you sure that you just didn't overhear it whilst Longden was talking to one of the other inmates?" He wore a suspecting expression upon his face. "To have known all that you claimed to about Shane Longden by just psychoanalysing him is virtually impossible."

The truth was that deep down Richard was hoping that David was not able to do such a thing. He could not help but feel jealous that someone could actually be capable of knowing such in depth details about a person without even doing extensive psychological research or by directly interviewing the subject. However, this person before him was claiming to be gifted in being able to do such a thing and the fact that he had already half proved it was clawing deep into the psychiatrist's mind.

David was not pleased by the show of ignorance towards his intellect and slowly shook his head with displeasure.

"It appears that even though I correctly predicted what Longden was going to do you still find it hard to comprehend what I am capable of. Maybe if I explain how I came to my conclusions you will begin to understand."

Richard prompted David to prove himself, but was consciously hopeful that the attempt would bring about failure.

"If you can give us proof, go ahead!"

David just slightly nodded his head and went about explaining himself in greater detail.

"Cast your mind back to when Longden murdered the store detective! Ask yourself, why did he do it in broad daylight in front of witnesses? What possibly made him think that he could get away with it? How could a previously non-violent person suddenly kill someone in such a carefree way? It is actually quite simple. He thought that he could get away with murder, because he had got away with it before. The violent nature had already long been there. At some time, not too long before Longden had killed the store detective, somewhere in the town of Cawling there was a murder which has either not yet been solved or has had someone else convicted of it. It is likely that the victim was a woman and that he knew her. The crime would most likely have been committed due to a sudden massive emotional surge of anger and violence."

Howard and Richard sat intently listening to David as he effortlessly reeled off what seemed to be a number of factual details about someone who he simply could not know anything about.

"As for killing the barrister who represented Longden at his trial, this had a very different motive. What you must ask yourselves is; why did he murder someone who had previously tried to help him? For what reason did he use a bottle of vodka? The answer to these questions can be found at the time when he killed the store detective and the trial that followed. Longden had the delusion that the law could not touch him after getting away with his first murder. He thought that he could not possibly be found guilty. Obviously, an inevitable amount of eyewitnesses gave evidence against him and no doubt his own half-prepared testimony would have been taken to pieces by the prosecution. This, therefore, resulted in him being found guilty of murder. So, now as the realisation of his demise settled in he wanted someone else to blame for it. The store detective was already dead and he was never going to find out where all of the witnesses lived. Therefore, just one person remained. Someone easy to find and whose office he could get the whereabouts with ease. The barrister who represented him at his trial. He would be punished for the mistakes that he never made. Longden even found it befitting to kill him with exactly what he had been caught stealing from the supermarket; a bottle of vodka. His view was probably something like; 'why should my life be ruined over a bottle of vodka and he get away with it?' The calculations of a deranged man. And finally, staying at the scene of the crime. There is not much of a life to be had for a murderer in the outside world, but they respect their own in Blackmoor. Here, quite simply, Longden is someone."

At that, David finished with an element of sarcasm.

"I hope this has educated you."

Richard just stayed unmoving with a stunned expression upon his face. He found it rather unbelievable, but the psychoanalysis he had just heard sounded as though it was completely correct. The description of Shane Longden's behavioural patterns and emotional responses seemed to be totally in line with the occurrences of extreme violence in his life.

In a weak attempt at trying to appear as though he was still not entirely convinced, Richard tried to revert back to his original assessment.

"You still could have heard about all of this from either Longden or another inmate. Even if he did kill someone before the store detective you could have been told about that as well." He tried to force a look of resolve and shook his head. "I don't think that this is conclusive enough."

A slight smile turned up one side of David's mouth.

"I can read your mind just as well as I can Longden's." He raised his eyebrows in a self-confident manner. "And I know that you are convinced by what I have just said."

Howard could now see that this inmate before him was starting to get above his station, so he went about putting him back down to the low level that he thought was more appropriate for someone of his standing.

"For all I care everything you have just said could be exactly right, Cain, but it still makes no difference whatsoever. There will be a thorough number investigation into Longden's recent activities as well as his past and in the mean time you will just get on with doing your time!" He waved a finger at the door. "So, you get back to your cell and keep well out of our business! This matter from now on does not concern you. Is that clear?"

"Indeed." Came the reply.

David was now satisfied enough that he had convinced the two of them of his abilities and he could see no harm in their discussion ending now. It was, therefore, a matter of waiting for them to except the offer of him psychoanalysing the inmates in return for the books that he wanted. Just before he went to leave the office he gave one last show of his excessive confidence.

"When you decide to take up my offer I will be quite content to receive a book on advanced chemistry."

David then made his way over to the door and let himself out into the corridor. Richard just sat with a perplexed expression upon his face whilst staring at a blank wall across the room. Howard was still feeling a sense of agitation at having an inmate coming into his office and showing such a lack recognition to their high status within the prison. However, he was also still unsure if what he had just witnessed was for real or not and he wanted to get a few more answers to find out for certain.

"He couldn't know all of that, could he?" He stood up and turned to look out of the window behind his desk. "I know Cain has something in his file about him having a high intelligence, but that means nothing."

It took a while for Richard to wake himself from his state of numbness and when he did he tried to make some sense of what he had just experienced.

"Before now I would've said that there was no way that someone could know that much about a person's past, personality and state of mind without knowing them well enough or at least at one point conducting an in depth conversation with them, but..." He paused to think about what he was about to say. "Everything he said made sense. The first murder of which Longden didn't get caught, the not caring about killing the store detective in front of witnesses and the willingness to come back to Blackmoor. It's all so accurate. It just fits into place perfectly."

"And what if he's right? What do you want to do?"

"You mean, should we give him books and the inmates files so that he can psychoanalyse them?" Richard took in a deep breath and rubbed the palm of his hand on his forehead in a perplexed manner. "Well, if he really is capable of knowing that much about a single person just by studying them from a distance then what he could find out with one of their files could be almost inconceivable."

Howard turned around to face the room and sat back on the windowsill behind him. The expression upon his face was one of thoughtfulness as he lightly bit his lip and considered what was to be done. When he had finally come to a conclusion he looked up at Richard and spoke in a proposing tone of voice.

"You can't do that. It would be illegal to divulge such information." His eyes suspiciously squinted. "You want to let him do it, don't you?"

A purposeful expression crossed Richard's face as he slowly looked up at Howard and vigorously uttered his intentions.

"I want to find out as much about Cain as possible. I want to know about his past, his emotions, his views, why he has become the person that he is and everything else there is to know about him. He is unique. And I think that if we do give him the inmates files as well, even if just to find out how intelligent he really is, then it can only help me even more so with my studies of him." He paused for a brief moment and then summarised his feelings about David. "He is a remarkable piece of subject matter."

Howard picked up the telephone on his desk and just before dialling made clear his decisions of what he was going to have done about it.

"I'll get the police to investigate into Longden's past, get them to find out if anyone was murdered over ten years ago in Cawling Town and then they can interview him about it." He pointed the telephone receiver at Richard. "And if Cain has been right about all of this, you can do with him what you like."

"What? You mean give him the other inmates files and the books that he wants?"

"You can give him his books and excerpts from the inmates files that don't infringe the Data Protection Act, but that's it."

Richard just lowered his gaze and slightly nodded his head. He was half pleased that he was going to be given such an opportunity to divulge into this most fascinating of inmates, yet at the same time he also felt as though the interviews would not just be one-way traffic. Something told him that he would not be the only one gaining information about the other person and that he would be getting analysed just as stringently or even more so.

A month had gone by since David had handed in his profile of Shane Longden and his version of events that had lead up to ex-inmate taking the life of his third victim. Needless to say, he had been exactly right on every account.

Twelve years ago a young girl by the name of Shirley Yale had been raped and murdered in a park in the town of Cawling. She had been a pupil at the same school as Shane Longden a number of years before and had been seen with him around the time that she was killed. The only reason that he was never found out was because a man by the name of Stewart Kiln had been found guilty of the crime along with two other murder-rapes that he had himself actually committed. Although he had admitted to the two slayings he had done and denied the other that he had not, he was, nevertheless, convicted of all three crimes. His modus operandi was similar, but he had premeditated his misdeeds and had done them on the outskirts of Cawling on farmland rather than within the town.

Not too much proof was needed in the end for Shane Longden to be charged for his real first crime due to him quite willingly admitting to it after being questioned for just a short time. It seemed as though he did not really care about hiding his guilt. This just solidified the reason why he stayed at the office of the barrister who he had killed. One more murder and one more life sentence would not make much of a difference to him now.

The results of the investigation had been delivered two days ago to Blackmoor prison, and Howard and Richard had just finished reading them. They were understandably taken aback by the findings, not least due to the fact that they had been given almost exactly the same information about the events a good month earlier by David. Although they had been half expecting it they still found the surreal nature of the situation rather hard to accept.

Richard pensively stared at the report in front of him on his desk as he sat in his office musing over what he had just read. The brown envelope that held the findings lay on a number of files of the inmates that he had gathered together for his consideration. It took a knock on the door to break him away from his state of thoughtful consciousness.

"Come in!" He replied.

A prison officer opened the door and announced the presence of the person who had come to see the psychiatrist.

"Cain's here."

"Could you bring him in please?"

The prison officer turned around and made a beckoning motion with his hand towards the end of the corridor. About ten seconds later David stepped into the office and closed the door behind him. He stood for a moment and then spoke in a smooth tone of voice.

"I should imagine the reason for me being here is that the investigation of Longden has been completed."

"That's correct." Richard raised his eyebrows. "Do I need to tell you the results?"

"That won't be necessary."

"Please, take a seat."

David pulled the chair out in front of the desk and then sat down. There was a momentary silence in the office as Richard lifted the pile of files in front of him and pulled out a book from underneath. He then reached it out and spoke with a slight hint of contentment in his voice.

"I believe this is what you wanted?"

On the front cover of the book were the words 'Advanced Chemistry'. David took it and looked at it for a while before speaking.

"That is what I require."

Richard sat back in his chair in a relaxed posture and wasted no time in starting the interview.

"I suppose we had better get on with it. I would like to start by asking you a few questions about your past, such as your relationship with your stepfather. Is that alright?"

"Yes, it is. You can ask me whatever you like about my life, but..." David leant forward and furrowed his brow. "Don't waste my time with any insignificant talk. If you want me to tell you if it hurt when my stepfather split my lips open with the buckle of his belt and when he broke my ribs with his steel toe capped boots then I will have no problems with telling you that it did. So, I would appreciate it if you get straight to any point that you wish to raise."

Richard was at first slightly shocked by the way that David could show so much lack of emotion towards what should have been a sickening subject for him to recall. It appeared as though he had somehow turned the negative things of his past into just inconsequential topics of which he had no problem with making any discussion out of. His attitude towards what had happened to him seemed to be almost as cold as the acts themselves.

159

With David making his feelings quite clear, Richard began the interview.

"When did you first experience any enmity towards yourself from anyone and why do you think it happened?"

"It was about when I was three. My mother wanted a girl and a normal looking child to call her own." David rubbed the side of his head. "I noticed her sneering at me on a regular basis and she rarely tried to hide any derogatory remarks she made about me to her friends or members of the family."

"And did this bother you?"

"I coped with it."

The discussion went on for quite some time. On a number of occasions Richard was horrified at the stories that David told him about his life leading up to him committing the three murders that had got him sent to Blackmoor. He described beatings at the hands of a number of school pupils all at the same time, relentless whippings with a cane off of one of the teachers and a countless amount of vicious beatings given to him by his mother's husband. It was when they reached the subject of whether he felt good when he made the killings that the course of the interview changed.

David spoke in a tone of voice that was null of emotion.

"I didn't feel good or pleased about any of them. I just did it because it had to be done." He pointed at the inmates' files on the desk. "It's probably just the same as most of them. For instance, when a human steps on an ant they do not sense a feeling of sorrow, because they do not care about how the creature feels. A wolf does not lose sleep over the pain of sheep. When something is in your way, you simply remove it from being there."

"I see. And you say that this is the same as some of the inmates we have here." Richard picked a file out of the pile on the desk. "I have here the documents on a prisoner in 'D' block called Roy Douglas. All the private information has been removed. All that is left are the notes that I have made. He killed his own father with an iron poker taken from the family fireplace. Why do you think that he did that?"

"He hasn't told you that himself, then?" David took the file and opened it. "Have you interviewed him at all?"

"He refused to talk to me."

David sat for about five minutes reading the file on Roy Douglas. He flicked forward through the pages and sometimes back again in order to piece together all of the information. When he had finished he put it back down onto the desk and began to state some of his findings.

"It is written in there that he has a number of tattoos, including two which have the word 'Mum' and one which has a three letter word blackened over. He comes from a redundant coal mining town up north and had never found employment whilst he was in his teens or early twenties prior to committing the murder. Before killing his father he had four previous convictions for assault and one for grievous bodily harm. However, since being inside this prison he has not been in trouble for any act of violence." David paused to think about how he was going to explain his conclusions. "These facts and among others say to me that he committed the crime of murder because his mother and himself had been at the brunt of a number of beatings at the hands of his depressed probably unemployed father. The reason why he has not displayed any signs of violent behaviour since is because he feels that his work has been done. Regular punishment from his father resulted in him being regularly in trouble with the law for crimes of violence. As soon as he killed his father, so too did his own brutal nature die."

David did not wait for a reaction and just carried on with the rest of his assessment.

"But you already knew all of this, didn't you?"

"What makes you think that?"

"Because you've already interviewed him and got all of this information for yourself."

Richard blinked repeatedly as he tried to make some sense of David's accusation.

"How did you come to that conclusion?"

"It says in the file that Roy Douglas runs the prison library in his spare time and serves food in the canteen at every meal time of the day. At his trial he apologised to the court for committing such a depraved act of violence and even suggested that he serve a full life sentence. This does not sound like a person who is unapproachable and wishes to be disassociated with his crime. Roy Douglas told you exactly why he killed his father when you interviewed him. That's why you got me to read it. So you could test me." David raised a finger and slowly wagged it at Richard. "You foolishly waste your time when you still doubt me like this."

"I was only seeing if you..."

An impatient interruption.

"It will be more beneficial to you if you give me a file of which you can gain something from the information that I give you."

Richard's shoulders slumped as he spoke in a sheepish manner.

"Very well." He stood up and walked across the office to some cabinets in the corner. "I have some in here which I want you to look at."

From that point onwards David was only given the files of inmates that Richard had not been able to interview or fathom out. Each one was read through thoroughly with a studious eye and was then given a perfect psychoanalysis of it afterwards. Not only was it done with an unnerving accuracy, but also with an unconsummated ease.

After a number of successful weeks of results Richard had even agreed to hold the meetings in David's cell. The young inmate had requested this because he had said that it took up too much of his time walking through the large prison and passing each of the security check points just to get to the interview room. He had used the temptation of an extra ten minutes per session to entice the psychiatrist into agreeing to it.

This was the beginning of a very valuable deal for the both of them. What they exchanged were only minor services, yet worth so much to the both of them. Information for books, and education for knowledge. It was genius in its simplicity.

There was, however, one question that remained unasked, which of them would gain from it the most?

The word that David was now helping the prison psychiatrist had somehow got out and had soon spread amongst the other inmates. On a number of occasions he had be stopped and questioned about his actions, but each time he had just walked off and ignored whoever was wasting his time. It was only when the inquisitiveness turned to threats that he changed his reaction to it.

"Oi, Cain! I hear Mervin Lock's after you. He says he thinks that it was you who grassed on him for having weed in his cell."

The accusation was not true, but, nevertheless, that careless remark from a fellow inmate had cost Mervin Lock his life. Two minutes after it was made David walked straight into the unsuspecting man's cell and pulled one of his eyeballs out of its socket. The person who had given out the initial information then received the severed organ as a thank-you present and a stark message.

You do not fuck with David Cain.

Over the last two years there had been about half a dozen inmates in Blackmoor prison who had thought that a schoolboy might be easy pickings. There were people who had wanted to make names for themselves, some that wanted to maintain their reputations and some who simply felt like beating up the person who was nearest to them at the time. However, one snapped leg, a fractured skull, two broken arms, five shattered noses, one paralysed back and a countless amount of deep cuts had been the punishment issued for their acts of foolishness.

It took some time, but in the end the inmates finally came to realise that no one was allowed to speak to David, go in his cell or basically have anything to do with him. To the other inmates he was known as being a nutter. Although they were all there for serious crimes, most of which were violence related themselves, they were still fully aware of what this volatile young man was willing to do to a person.

Countless amounts of stories had gone around the prison such as the time when David had broken an inmate's leg and had bent it up so badly that the victim could not even crawl away to get help. On one occasion he had run a shard of glass across the knuckles of a man's hands just for accidentally knocking on his cell door. However, the one beating that had stood out as the biggest warning to them all was when a prison officer had prodded him in the back with his baton in an attempt to hurry him along in the dinner queue in the canteen. Most of the inmates would have just ignored it, some would have sworn at the guard in an attempt to show that they did not take any shit from anyone, but with all the other officers standing around none of them would have retaliated in a physical manner. Nevertheless, on this occasion, for the crime of hindrance a severe punishment was dealt out.

Within an instant, David had grabbed the baton off of the prison officer and had proceeded to beat him around the head with it. Each blow was hard and fast, producing a crunching noise as the bones fractured under the force. There were no screams of pain or cries for mercy simply because the first strike had quite deliberately brought about the guard's unconsciousness. It was a distasteful display of causing as much damage to a person, in the shortest amount of time possible, without giving them the slightest chance to mount any kind of worthy defence.

Of course, it had not taken long for the other guards to circle around and try to stop David from carrying on with what he was doing. Although the odds were stacked against him it still did not prove to be an easy task. As soon as he saw them draw near he turned around to square up to them. Knowing that they were definitely going to use physical force against him he thought he might as well injure as many of them before they got to him.

As soon as the first guard tried to make a move to tackle David he turned around and grabbed a large pot of creamed rice from off of the food counter throwing it in a wide arc at the surrounding officers. There were multiple yells of agony as the steaming hot food scorched into their skin sending them momentarily falling back. For a short while they all just stood staring at the lone man who was glaring back at them with a burning fire in his eyes. They then made another rush at him.

For the first fifteen seconds David held them off by making a number of calculated direct hits with his baton, but in the end their numbers were just far too great for him to overpower them all. With a kick to the stomach, a strike across the face and an arm around the throat he was finally thrown to the floor. In an act of temperamental vengeance the guards carried on kicking and beating their victim so as to teach him a lesson. Unfortunately for them, they should have just first tried to handcuff him and make sure he was fully bound.

David had taken many beatings in his life and pain was a feeling that had long lost its place in his mind. Whilst virtually every part of his body was getting repeatedly battered he sluggishly managed to get to his knees. Seeing a guard standing directly in front of him who was clearly off balance due to trying to dish out a bout of wild kicks he saw his chance to get back at least one more of them.

In a sudden rush of speed and power, David pushed himself up and grappled hold of the guard's waist sending them both hurtling over the food counter knocking a number of pots across the kitchen area in the process. As they landed on the floor on the other side he managed to grab hold of an empty pot and then began to batter the officer's face with the flat bottom of it. Blood splattered all over the floor and the surrounding oven doors as the metal split the flesh with every strike that rained down.

Realising that they had again misjudged their aggressor the rest of the guards stumbled over the counter to wrestle hold of David. This time they thought it would be a good idea to handcuff him straight away so that they would all be a whole lot safer. After a while, five of them managed to grab hold of his arms, legs and neck and started to carry him off to the solitary confinement cells to finish off their punishment beating. And a beating he got.

This, of course, was of little consequence to David. He had put his message across quite clearly. Even as the guards left the solitary cell he made one last remark.

"Thank you." A blood soaked smile. "If you hadn't had done that no one would have known what I am willing to go through."

The rest of the inmates who had been standing around in the canteen had just watched the whole proceedings with looks of shock upon their faces. No one had ever done that to a bunch of screws before. This was not a person who should be crossed.

So with all these stories of brutal violence the population of Blackmoor prison had soon come to realise that David Cain was best left to himself. He bothered no one, if no one bothered him and that was the way that everyone liked it. Whether you were an inmate or a guard, cell number 'A14' was a place that you kept well away from, especially if you valued your safety.

Of course, there were people in the prison who were hardened killers who feared no one, but the thought of what would happen to them if they did lose out to David was enough to make them think twice about crossing him. It was not that they were scared of death, but it was what their lives would be like if they were to be allowed to live. Having to live life of not being able to walk, their face almost unrecognisable to how it was before or having their eyesight as just a distant memory, were all things that did not appeal to even the most mentally unstable or toughest amongst them.

It was these stories about David, which were now being passed onto the new inmate who had arrived in cell A13. Every name of every victim, their reputation prior to being

163

attacked and exactly what had happened to them were all graphically being explained. This was a grizzly introduction to Blackmoor prison.

Jimmy O'Neill was the new resident of cell A13. He had been sentenced to eight years imprisonment for the manslaughter of a man who had accidentally spilt beer down his shirt in a nightclub. It was not his intention to take his life, but when you push a glass into a man's throat, death is rarely a surprising outcome.

Jimmy was an Irish born Protestant who had moved across to the mainland when he had left school. Although he was in his mid twenties, his scrawny adolescent like appearance, bright ginger hair and thick spectacles were actually an accurate reflection upon his puerile personality. He was not really what could be called a hardened criminal, but in just one night, after a bad day at work he had let go of his temper in an act of madness and the worst possible scenario had come about. The moment he saw the blood gush from the other man's neck he knew that he had needlessly taken a life. After being examined by a psychologist it was found that he was suffering from post traumatic stress disorder due to his eight-year-old son dying of cancer just weeks before. It was, therefore, deemed that he would not get any better. So, two months later after being found guilty of manslaughter due to diminished responsibility, he now found himself in Blackmoor prison alongside the likes of mass murderers and violent bank robbers. And if all this was not bad enough, he was now finding out that he had been put in the cell next to the infamous 'Starrow School Slaughterer'.

As Jimmy sat there on his bed next to Paul Burrell, another one off killer like himself, he nervously ran his fingers through his curly ginger hair. He had a reasonably good idea that prison was not exactly going to be a nice place, but he had hardly expected to hear such hideous tales of extreme violence within the first minute of setting foot into his cell. His reaction to the barbaric tales revealed just how nervous he was about the volatile place he was in.

"It sounds as if I better not make a fucking sound in case I disturb him." Jimmy shook his head and adjusted his glasses in an uncomfortable manner. "He'll probably put a frigging knife to my throat just for closing my door too loudly."

Paul shook his head.

"Well, he's not that bad. He normally only does someone who's done something to him first." He shrugged his shoulders. "You just want to make sure you don't do anything to fuck him off."

Paul Burrell had been in Blackmoor for six years now and he had a reasonably good idea what was going on around him. He knew who to watch out for and who to be in with. Due to being on the right side of most of the inmates in the prison he had managed to get himself accepted by just about everyone.

Since Paul had been serving time in Blackmoor his appearance had changed dramatically. He had gained about a dozen tattoos to his arms, chest and neck, even though that was not allowed, and he had also acquired seven earrings and a nose ring. In all, he had changed the way he looked to match the extremity of his surroundings. His nature, nevertheless, was not entirely bad.

Paul had seen Jimmy arrive at his cell so he had come over to talk to him and give him the lowdown on his new surroundings. It had not taken him long to get onto the subject of violence and especially the story of the prison guards getting beaten up in the canteen. Although the incident had happened about four months ago it had again become a popular topic within the prison because David had only just got out of solitary confinement that very day.

As Paul carried on with his explanation of events it became quite obvious that he enjoyed the thrill of describing the violence.

"Yeah, when Cain got hold of Jack Melley he put his arm in a cell door and fucking slammed it shut. The bone shattered first time, but he still kept on ramming the door against it." He sadistically grinned in a wry manner. "That poor fucker Melley didn't stop screaming for a whole bloody hour. You could still hear him when he was in the infirmary."

Jimmy was less impressed.

"By Jesus! That's sick."

"Fucking right!" Paul nodded his head. "Still, as long as it don't happen to me."

By now Jimmy was starting to grow more and more uncomfortable with the topic of discussion so he decided to try to change it.

"I hear they've got a carpentry workshop here. Where's that?"

"It's down the end of the wing, for what it's worth." Paul pointed in the general direction of the workshop with his thumb. "Most of us here aint going to get jobs when we get out anyway. I mean, what's the fucking point in training us?"

Jimmy was not really interested in Paul's views.

"What's the workshop like? Has it got any decent gear?"

"Yeah, I suppose so."

"Do you want to show me where it is?"

"If you like. You aren't allowed in there now, but I can point it out to you across the prison grounds."

"Cheers!"

The two of them then got up off of the bed and made their way out of the cell. As they walked through the prison wing Paul carried on the conversation.

"Why are you so interested in woodwork?"

"I'm a carpenter by trade."

"Really? What sort of stuff can you make?"

"Practically anything."

Paul raised his eyebrows.

"Fucking hell! I could do with a new chair in my cell."

Jimmy's expression turned to one of inquisitiveness.

"So, how much wood are you allowed?"

"I don't know. Some of the others have made stools, racks and other shit like that." Paul raised a finger. "But don't even think about making a club or any kind of weapon. They check everything that leaves that fucking workshop."

The two of them carried on talking as they made their way towards their destination. It was probably not going to be the best friendship either of them would ever have, but it was alright for now. After all, they did at least share one thing in common, a large amount of years ahead of them in a hell like place called Blackmoor prison.

The sheets on the bed were cold at first, but the warmth that they would soon ensure would be most welcome. As David pulled the blanket over his chest he took a moment to gaze at the ceiling of his cell. Its dull colourlessness helped him concentrate on a few thoughts that were currently passing through his mind. When they were finally processed and dealt with he closed his eyes to go to sleep, even though it was only two o'clock in the afternoon. With very few schedules to stick to he could do pretty much what he liked when he liked, and right now he had decided that he might as well get some rest. It was at that moment when he heard a type of sound that he had not experienced for a very long time.

In a sudden and unannounced arrival, an arrangement of delicate notes drifted out across the entire prison wing. The softness of their subtle tone immediately ensnared the mind as well as the heart. It seemed as if an angel had floated down from the heavens and had sung out to those below to lighten the darkness of their lives. In a place of such mental sorrow and pain this was truly a colourful enchantment.

For the first time in years, David could hear the resplendent sound of a flute, only this time it did not bring the pleasure that it had once done. The beauty of its melodious tune seemed to relentlessly search deep into his mind for harmful memories that had long been dismissed. With every note came a clawing at his consciousness to get to his most distant and well-hidden thoughts.

This was real torture. Physical pain goes away or can be controlled, but mental agony is a thorn that cannot be removed or endured. There was really only one outcome.

David started to think of Sally.

Jimmy O'Neill studied his creation with an air of self-admiration. His work of art was as aesthetically pleasing as it was audibly perfect. Carved out of a mediocre type of wood, but with an excessive amount of care, there in his hands was an impeccably formed musical instrument.

Jimmy's first creation forged in the workshop of Blackmoor prison was a beautifully ornate wooden flute. Its long shaft was delicately smooth to the touch and was adorned with spiralling twists carved all the way up the shaft. What with his knowledge of music it even played as exquisitely as it looked.

As a young boy, Jimmy's father had taught him how to play the flute as soon as he was able to talk. He had always enjoyed playing the instrument and had never regretted having to learn. Although he had never been given the choice it was one of those things in life that he had not minded being forced upon him.

Jimmy's father, Jerry O'Neill, had been a member of a band for an order called the 'Orangemen'. They would go on marches every year that would take them through a number of streets in the province of where they lived. Although it was meant to be an enjoyable time of year it was taken very seriously.

Due to his young age at the time Jimmy could not quite understand why the marches were so important to his father and why he would spend most of his time cursing various groups of people when they were taking place. It appeared that some of the inhabitants of the streets through which the Orangemen travelled did not like the parade going past their homes. Sometimes they even tried to stop the event from taking place.

Of course, as Jimmy got older he came to understand what it was all about and he suddenly found himself having to take a side to the argument. This was a choice that was virtually made up for him due to the area in which he lived in. A Protestant with nationalist views living in a unionist area would not go down very well. However, after all the years of violence and terror his real views eventually became apparent. His exact words to his father were spoken in a blasé manner.

"I don't really give a shit!"

Although Jimmy's talent with the flute was bred from a life ruled by religious and political feuds he still had an unequalled love for the instrument. He would liken the haunting sound that it made to that of a zephyr passing through the trees of his country's green land. For a man who had so viciously taken another man's life his impassioned affection for music almost seemed misplaced.

After scrupulously checking every inch of the flute for any unwanted blemishes, Jimmy once more put it to his lips ready to play it again. As he blew across the mouthpiece, another wave of delicate notes flowed out of his cell and into the prison wing. With the beauty of the moment almost overwhelming his senses he did not even consider what he was invoking elsewhere.

David walked out of the doorway of his cell and stood for a moment to look around to determine where the sound of the flute was coming from. It was association period and a number of inmates were standing around, but it appeared as though this interruption to his rest was none of their doing. His pale eyes scoured the prison wing until his gaze finally went to the cell next to his. As he started to walk towards it he pulled a long piece of wire out of his pocket and wrapped both ends around each of his hands so as to make a garrotting instrument. Although his mind was made up to commit a vicious act of violence the expression upon his face was almost vacantly inanimate.

The door to Jimmy's cell had been left slightly ajar and as it was pushed from the outside it quietly swung open on its hinges. David stood at the entrance for short while to eye up his prey and assess the situation. Every contingency was thought of with his usual degree of precision, whilst a counter measure was also calculated in case there was a need for a response if things did not quite go to plan.

Jimmy was sitting on a chair with his back to the doorway and could not see David staring at him. He was quite oblivious to the danger that he was in and carried on playing his flute regardless. Whilst behind him there was a man who was intending on taking his life all he was thinking about was which notes to play next.

As David slowly approached Jimmy he tightly pulled the wire out in front of himself ready to wrap the garrotte around his victim's neck. The kill would be executed in the utmost efficient manner. First the wire would cut deep into the neck slicing through the jugular vein and then the windpipe would be crushed under the extreme force. There would be no chance of survival.

Then David froze. A studious expression suddenly crossed his face as he stared down at his unsuspecting prey. With his initial intentions held at bay by a thought that had just entered his mind he gradually lowered the wire. Turning around to leave the cell he slipped the garrotte back into his pocket and walked off as if he had never even been there.

It was not an act of mercy, and it certainly was not brought about by the prospect of having a guilty conscience. David had simply realised that what he was going to do was not logical. The thought that had entered his mind was as efficient as it was augured in its calculation.

I need him alive.

As David paced into the centre of the prison wing he looked around to see if anyone had been watching him. When he was satisfied that he had not been seen he changed his direction and made his way over to a cell which had its door ajar. After taking one last opportunity to look around he made his way in.

David could see that the inmate who normally occupied the cell he was in was talking to another prisoner on the top floor right now and due to his distance away would not be back for at least forty-five seconds. As he pulled the door behind him so that it was just ajar he took a moment to look around to see if everything that he needed was there. His close inspection determined that he was not to be disappointed.

At first, David pulled the thick grey blanket off of the bed, folded it into a quarter of its size and then draped it over his left forearm. He then walked across the cell to the window in the far wall and gazed at it intently. It had four iron bars vertically imbedded into the concrete with a single pane of glass behind them.

As David held the blanket up to the window it covered the whole of the opening in the wall. He then felt his hand around the iron bars and pushed the cloth against the pane of glass. Clenching his fist about a foot away from the target, he took aim.

The noise of the windowpane being smashed was muffled by the thick blanket and was heard by no one in the prison but David. As he carefully pulled the cloth from his arm he laid it back down onto the bed whilst still managing to keep the shards of glass on it which it had collected. Some of the pieces were large and some were small. After taking a while to sift through them he finally took two fragments which were both about two inches in diameter.

Using one of the shards he had taken David cut a corner out of the blanket the size of a handkerchief. He then wrapped the small piece of cloth around the two fragments of glass that he had collected and slipped it into his pocket. Although he had made a mess he had no intention of clearing it up.

Now that David had finished getting all that he needed he went to leave the cell. As he stepped through the doorway he took a moment to check that no one was in the close proximity. There was nobody about, so he quickly stepped out and closed the door behind him.

By the time that David had got back to his own cell no one had noticed any of his actions. Every deed he had undertaken had been executed exactly as he had planned. There was, however, a loud exclamation made a while later that was heard throughout the whole prison wing.

"Who the fuck's done this?"

The sun shone through the window of David's cell creating a hazy amber glow throughout. Its restful aura seemed to be akin to his relaxed and calm state as he lay flat out upon his bed. However, his mind was not so tranquil. There were too many thoughts passing through his consciousness to allow him to completely rest.

Since hearing the sound of the flute come from the cell next to his David had not stopped being plagued by thoughts of Sally. All the memories he had of the days of his past were like a relentless torture upon his mind, yet at the same time he could not help but think of them with a cherished affection. With every note he had heard came a wave of elated feelings and hurtful emotions.

It was these thoughts that David was having whilst he was waiting for Richard to arrive for his weekly psychological session. He would normally consider the interviews to be a waste of his time, but today was different. This time he planned to gain something extra from it.

For the first time since he was at school David was going to ask someone for a favour. It was only a simple task which he wanted to be done, but, nevertheless, an important one to him. If he could have done it without anyone else's assistance then he would have. Unfortunately, as much as he hated the fact, he actually needed somebody else's help.

As Richard made his way through the prison wing towards David's cell he was unaware of what he was about to encounter. Up until now he had always thought of this particular inmate as being a very strong minded individual who literally had no mental weaknesses. To have actually thought of this rigidly independent person as having to need someone else's help was almost inconceivable.

There had only been one time when David had ever requested something off of Richard and that was when they had made the bargain of psychoanalysis for books. The psychiatrist thought that he was getting the better part of the deal and was blissfully unaware of the importance of what he was handing over. To him he was simply providing something that was being used to do nothing more than to pass the time with.

So with an understandable obliviousness to what was about to occur, Richard paced into David's cell expecting just another psychological session. It was only when he saw the prisoner already sitting down staring at him that he realised that not everything was quite right. At first it made him feel a bit nervous and he even started to consider his own safety. The reputation that this inmate had earned since being in Blackmoor was quite horrific and he had spent quite a large amount of time in solitary confinement paying for it. However, when he saw that the killer was only holding a piece of white card and not a knife or heavy object he started to feel a bit more relaxed.

In an attempt to make light of the situation, Richard made a flippant remark.

"What's this, do you look forward to seeing me so much that you now wait in anticipation for me?"

"Believe me, this is not the highlight of any of my days." The cold response was accompanied by a sneer.

Richard forced a smile.

"Just wondered."

David had sensed the sarcasm in the psychiatrist's voice and it had made him feel quite agitated. Although he would have normally administered a punishment to most people for such a crime he decided to let it pass just this time. After all, dead people do not do favours for live people.

Richard still wore the risky smile as he sat down on the edge of the bed and flicked through the pieces of paper on his clipboard. He had already mentally prepared what he was going to talk to David about on his way to work and was now making sure that all of his notes were in order. As he started he announced what topics the day's session would cover.

"I would like to talk about the school teacher who you killed and what were his reasons for why he used to cane you. I would also like to know what he used to say after he had..."

David interrupted.

"I need you to do something for me."

"Pardon?"

"I would like you to do me a favour." There was a pause. "Please."

"What, exactly?"

David lowered his gaze and took in a deep breath. His uneasiness was quite apparent and he seemed to be making no attempt to hide it. It was almost as if he had forgotten that he was meant to be a ruthless killer. Whatever he wanted done for him was certainly something that was causing him a large amount of mental strain.

David reached out with the piece of folded plain white card in his hand.

"I need you to post this for me."

"What is it?"

"A message to someone I once knew."

Richard took the card and held it out in front of himself. He studied it for a moment and then turned his gaze to David. As he spoke the tone of his voice was tentative and forewarning.

"You know that I have to read this first, don't you?"

"I am aware of that."

Richard raised his eyebrows and carefully unfolded the piece of card. Just before he started to read what was inside he looked up at David with an apologetic expression upon his face. He could not help but make his feelings about the situation clear.

"I'm sorry about this." He slowly shook his head. "I realise that this is obviously personal to you."

David just sat with his eyes fixed up Richard. He clearly did not want anyone to see what was written on the piece of card, but he realised that on this occasion he had no choice. This was obviously a situation that was putting him in a very vulnerable mental state.

As Richard's eyes scanned across the writing on the card the expression upon his face was deliberately emotionless. It was only when he had finished that he turned his gaze to David and slowly nodded his head in a comprehending manner. Although it did not really need to be said he spoke a few words to reassure the tormented man before him.

"I understand." Richard put the piece of card in the inside pocket of his jacket. "I'll make sure that no one else sees it and I'll post it this afternoon."

David slightly nodded his head and then did something that he had not done in a very long time. It was not to make sure that the favour would still be done, but was actually to show his gratitude. He spoke to a human in a respectful manner.

"I'm very grateful for that." David looked straight into Richard's eyes so as to show the sincerity of what he was saying. "Thank-you."

"That's alright!"

"Now, you wanted to know about that school teacher?"

"Ah, yes!"

"He was mentally deranged, probably due to a stressful incident that had taken place at some point in his life, like a death of someone close to him. This, of course, resulted in him being violent and sadistic..."

It was a sudden change of topic and it had been done quite deliberately. David had wanted to get away from the subject of the piece of white card as soon as possible and if it meant having to talk about one of the people who he had hated more than any other then so be it. All that mattered to him right now was for his mind to dispel the agonising ghosts of the past that weakened him so much.

The atmosphere in the kitchen was still and sullen. A lone woman sat at an oak table with her chin resting upon her hands and her elbows perched upon the shiny wood. Her greying dark hair hung lifelessly over her brow as her eyes gazed upon what lay in the centre of the table in front of her. She did not move, nor did she even blink.

It had come that very morning, unannounced and uninvited. Whether it was an act of love or had been the result of a deranged man's insanity the woman at the table simply did not know. There was, however, one thing for certain; it had re-opened a wound that she thought was well healed.

From somewhere in the background the clanking noise of a turning lock could be heard. At first the woman remained frozen in her forlorn state and did not notice it. It was only when a voice called out that she finally responded.

"Hi, I'm home."

Melanie started to blink repeatedly and then raised her head to look around. Although she would have normally been quite aware that it was only her husband coming home after a day at work this occasion was an exception. Something had completely taken over her mind and had left her senses in disarray.

As Mike strolled into the dining room he put his briefcase on the table and then kissed his wife on the cheek. He was obviously unaware of Melanie's discomfort and quite blamelessly opened the fridge to look for a snack. It was only when he turned around to start a conversation that he finally realised that something was amiss. A sorrowful expression immediately crossed his face as he spoke in a concerned tone of voice.

"Are you alright?"

"Not really."

Mike pulled a chair out from the table and then pushed it across the floor next to Melanie. As he sat down he put his hand around her shoulder in a comforting gesture. In a calm manner, he tried to give his wife some well-needed support.

"I know it's hard. My god! It never gets any easier." He put his face into Melanie's line of vision. "But we've got to try to be strong; if not for ourselves, at least for Sally."

"I know that." A muttered reply.

"So come on! Get your chin up!" Mike forced a smile. "We'll give Sally her birthday present now and then I'll cook tonight's dinner."

Melanie slowly lifted her head in a strained manner and looked into her husband's eyes. This was not a usual bout of sadness brought about by her daughter's broken state, but was due to something that had made it all even more distressing. As she spoke, her voice became a whisper making her words almost inaudible.

"You'd better look at that." She pointed to a white piece of folded plain card next to an empty opened envelope in the middle of the table. "It came this morning."

Mike's expression now became one of intrigue as he reached across the table and picked up the white piece of card. As he unfolded it with one hand he turned over the envelope with the other and read the front of it. His voice sounded quite perplexed as he tried to unravel the mystery.

"I don't recognise the handwriting on the envelope."

"Neither do I."

"Who's it from?"

"Just..." A pause. "Please, read it."

Mike's eyes scanned across the writing on the inside of the white piece of card. The further he got through it the more the expression upon his face changed. It was only when he had finished reading it that he finally spoke again.

"Jesus!"

Although the message inside the piece of white card was only short its words had been written with an overwhelming amount of passion.

Sally,

It still hurts whenever I think of you,
but I've never known a pain that feels so good.

Happy birthday my sweet darling.

With my deepest love,

David

XXX

Mike put the piece of white card back on the table and then turned to Melanie.

"Why?"

"I don't know."

"I mean, why after all this time?" Mike raised his eyebrows and sat back in the chair. "He's never contacted us before."

Melanie picked up the envelope and screwed it up, but kept the white piece of card. As she gazed at it she had a pensive look upon her face. Her voice sounded just as thoughtful.

"Maybe something suddenly jogged his memory."

"I don't think so. He would've never of forgotten Sally. It's more likely that he just wanted to get her out of his mind."

"What do you mean?"

"Well, right now he's locked in a cramped dark cell and is surrounded by all sorts of depraved people. He probably has other things to think about."

Melanie disagreed.

"Surely he would want to think about nice things and keep the horrible things out of his mind."

"Not really." Mike shook his head. "Why think about the one thing that you want more than anything else when you know that you can never have it?"

Melanie just sighed. She knew her husband was right, even though she did not like it. The real truth of the matter was that they both still felt for David. They knew that deep down somewhere hidden in the depths of his nature was the kind and caring person who they once knew.

Mike and Melanie had talked about David on a number of occasions since that last day at school. The conversations were mostly based on the regret of what he had become and of what might have been. Whereas the whole world thought of him as being just an evil killer they knew how things really should have been.

Although the views of others were vastly different, Mike and Melanie remembered David as being a polite and intellectual young man who had won the heart of their daughter. Now they were not sure if he had really drifted into insanity as the newspapers would have had everyone believe or if he had just murdered to protect himself. The real truth was that they just did not know. They could not see how it was possible for someone so thoughtful and pleasant to actually turn into such a seemingly mindless killer.

It was with these thoughts in mind that Mike and Melanie started to wonder whether they should put the plain piece of white card with the other birthday cards that Sally had received in the morning. A message from a mass murderer amongst best wishes from relatives seemed as if it might be a bit out of place. This was certainly a peculiar predicament.

Melanie, however, after some thought decided to bring it all to a final conclusion.

"Well, he wrote this letter." She stood up and started to walk out of the kitchen. "And that means only one thing."

"What?"

Just before Melanie reached the doorway to leave she stopped and turned around to face her husband.

"Maybe David is a killer and maybe he's not the person that we once knew..." She lifted up the piece of white card. "But I now know that the part of him that made our daughter the happiest that she's ever been is still very much alive somewhere within him. After all this time, in his heart of hearts, he still loves her more than ever."

Mike slowly nodded his head and raised his eyebrows.

"So, are you going to put it with her other birthday cards?"

"I'm going to put it at the front."

They both smiled contentedly.

That night a white piece of card stood right on the edge of Sally's bedside table proudly looking over her. It was almost as if it were guarding her against any evils that might come her way. Although she had not read it or even looked at it, it still somehow managed to bring a warm and satisfied smile to her face. There was only one person who could ever do that to her.

David. Her lover. Her worshipper. Her guiding light. Some things do last for eternity.

A glimmer of light sparkled off of the edge of the razor producing a glint almost as sharp as the blade itself. The hand that was clenching hold of the weapon appeared to be just as menacing, what with its long healed scars and profane tattoos. This was not a scene that suggested good intentions.

Although the blade of the tool was slightly bent its sharp edge was still very much acute to the touch. The shaft of the handmade tool was made out of three pencils shabbily taped together with the head of a disposable razor fastened to the top. It was a very crude looking weapon, but its level of efficiency would be unquestionable.

Liam Govan stood in the middle of his cell with the palm of his left hand outstretched and his ill-crafted knife grasped tightly in the right. A distorted sneer crossed his scarred face as he closed his eyes and bowed his head. Every breath he took was deep and long as he waited for his mind to reach the point of no return. In a few moments time he would be completely prepared to carry out what he had to do. Cut himself to dispel his fears and then kill someone else to forget the years.

The way Liam was dressed was nothing short of bizarre. He wore a white blouse that was far too tight for the large muscles of his body and he had make-up on his face that had been painted on in a very artless manner. There were also a number of holes in his black leggings and the soles on his pink slippers were coming adrift.

After a childhood of abuse at the hands of his cruel mother, a career in prostitution in his teens and a young adult crime ridden life in and out of prison, Liam had inevitably become a psychopathic killer. All the years of physical and mental torture had produced a man who had learnt to ignore pain and, worse of all, crave for it. Whether it was his agony or someone else's it really just did not matter. Pain was the ultimate sensation.

Liam's mother had become a drug addict after he was born and as she had no partner there was no one else to take the cold turkey out on. Someone had to share the stress and from the age of three and upwards her son was the obvious choice. Punishments included cigarette burns on the arms, fingernails dug deep into the flesh and, the most common of all, a heel of a stiletto shoe around the face.

At the age of fourteen Liam had been thrown out of his home and left to fend for himself. It might have seemed a blessing at the time, but life's harsh realities soon became apparent. The only way to survive was by waiting down at the train station for men in long raincoats. Being alive was full of all different kinds of pain.

Drugs relieved some of the agony, but then created new ones. Theft paid for the craving for a while, but inevitably led to jail. From then onwards he led his life in the company of killers, robbers and rapists. Even an angel surrounded by evil will soon lose its halo. Liam was halfway there anyway and this simply just helped him go all the way.

The first kill was made when it was discovered that he was gay. Someone had witnessed a sexual act through a cell door that was ajar and word had soon got out. It was just a matter of time before someone made the wrong remark.

"Govan, you faggot!"

It had led to a shard of glass being sliced across the man's jugular vein. That in return culminated in the hunger for more. Since then two other men had suffered similar fates at his bloodied hands.

Liam had now earned himself a reputation. Although he regularly wore women's clothes no one would ever say anything about his strange appearance. In fact, today's killing spree was not even an act of revenge.

A telegram had been delivered to his cell in the morning. It was actually the first piece of mail that Liam had received since he had come to Blackmoor, but its arrival was not as surprising as the news that it carried.   As he read it to himself a tear rolled down his cheek, but it was not shed for anyone but himself.

Liam Govan - Your mother died of heart failure at Tillingham Hospital on October 12th...

There was more to the message, but Liam had not bothered to read it. At first, he felt pure exaltation at the news, but that was soon replaced by an overwhelming anger. The one thought that had entered his mind that had finally forced him to turn had been as simple in its complexity as it was extreme in its impetuosity.

The fucking bitch has died and she never even got see what she did to me.

Liam now had to prove that his mother had never really hurt him. Whether it was for himself or anyone else was not really important to him. He just had to let it show that he could take a lot more pain than she had ever tried to give him and that it had been his choice at the time for her not to have to pay for her actions. His mental strength now simply had to be demonstrated.

First Liam raised his outstretched left hand and then the razor. A twisted smile crossed his face as he rested the blade upon the flesh of his palm. He then made the incision.

There was immense agony, but it was ignored. Through an impulsive instinct Liam dug his fingers deep into his palm immediately increasing the size of the gaping wound. Blood oozed all down his wrist until it dripped off of the tip of his elbow and onto the floor.

Now it was time to decide who should die. This was an easy choice. Samuel Mornay had stopped being Liam's sexual partner just over a week ago and he was already screwing someone else. He was just like all those men with their fifty pounds and family saloons who did not care about whom they were with. They loved him one day and ignored him the next. Their affection was never everlasting.

Liam nodded his head as he confirmed to himself who he was going to kill. He even allowed himself a slight crazed laugh at what was about to happen. This was truly going to release him from the grip of all of those years of torture. At least he thought it would.

Samuel Mornay stood leaning against a wall on the ground floor of the west prison wing with his hands tucked into his trouser pockets. His head was turned to his right as he gazed at a young inmate who was in his early twenties and had just arrived at Blackmoor. There was a slight smile on his face as a number of lurid thoughts crossed his mind. He then had his throat slit.

Liam held Samuel up by the collar with his own cut and bloodied hand. The young man frantically shook as the thick red liquid gushed from his jugular vein and down the front of his shirt. It was a pointless act to even struggle. Although his heart was still beating, from the very moment that his neck had been cut he was practically dead already.

When Samuel's body finally went limp Liam let go of him. The now lifeless corpse immediately fell to the floor in a heap. As his head hit the concrete there was a loud splitting noise as his skull cracked under the force.

It did not take long for the other inmates to notice what had happened and there was instantly a large amount of shouting and running around. Some of what was hollered was comprehensible, yet some was not. Enough words, however, could be understood for the prison officers to realise that something was wrong and as a result a security alarm was eventually sounded.

Liam soon found that he had a guard either side of him with their batons at the ready. He had absolutely no intention of surrendering and simply had to decide which one to go for first. It was when he saw the prison psychiatrist walking down the stairs on the other side of the officer to his left that he decided that he would launch his attack on that flank first so he could get to the man beyond the guard. That nosey bastard with his constant delving questions would be a welcome next victim.

Liam was no stranger to physical conflicts and experience told him that the first strike was always the most important one. Although he knew that he would be the first to get hit due to the guard's distinct advantage of having the lengthy baton he would still be assured of at least administering one fatal slash of the blade. It was that fact that would make it worth him being struck.

In a quick and agile movement of the body Liam darted towards the prison officer to his left. With the razor raised above his head it was just a matter of timing the strike. The guard also responded by bringing back his baton and taking aim. Then they clashed.

There was a low sounding crack followed by a high pitched scream as the two of them stuck each other simultaneously. The deep breaking noise came from Liam's collarbone as it was crushed by the guard's baton being forced down upon it. However, the yell of agony did not come from him. Just as he had been stuck he had brought the razor down the side of the prison officer's head half-severing off the left ear.

Liam now had the advantage and he used it to great effect. Quickly adjusting the centre of gravity of his body he swung around on his heel and slashed the razor across the back of the guard's neck instantly sending him flailing to the ground in agony. Blood immediately started to pour from the wound and mingled in with the stream of scarlet fluid that was already pouring from the half severed off ear. The path was now clear to get to the psychiatrist.

There was no time to waste. Liam could hear the other guards in the prison making their way towards him as he fled across the wing towards his next victim. This strike would have to be quick so as to make sure that he had enough time to prepare himself to face the rest of the officers when they reached him. It would be a simple slash to the throat and then the course of time would take the life away from his prey.

Liam took aim with the bloodied razor as he approached the psychiatrist. The neck was completely unprotected and by the way his target was looking around it seemed as though he was not even aware of where the fight was which had caused the alarms to be sounded. This would be an easy kill

It was at that point that Liam suddenly found himself sprawling across the floor. He was only partly aware that he had been hit in the chest by something quite hefty due to the suddenness of the blow. As he lay on the floor he started to look around to see what exactly had happened. Then he saw him.

Joseph McKinnie. Without a doubt, the hardest screw in Blackmoor. Born in Glasgow, bred the highland way and had as much notches on his baton as he did on his right boot. 'Hard bastard' was an understatement.

Joseph was not particularly tall, nor was he very muscular, but he had enough size to tackle just about any wayward inmate. He was quick, accurate, strong and willing to do just about anything to keep a prisoner in line. If ever there had been a reputation that had been well earned, he had deserved his tenfold.

Everything about Joseph said that he was a ferocious character. His hair and beard were a fiery ginger, his cheeks were an equally searing bright red and his dark eyes seemed to burn like pieces of scorched coal. He was rough, ready and bloody well willing.

Of course, most of the other inmates would have cowered at the arrival of Joseph, but with Liam's current state of mentality he was simply not bothered. In the back of his mind he knew that he would probably get just as severely harmed as his assailant, but he did not care. The adrenaline was flowing and as it rushed through his veins he revelled in its overwhelming sensation.

175

In an attempt to show that he had no fears Liam made his intentions quite clear to Joseph.

"I'm going fucking kill you and then rip up that nosey wanker straight after." He pointed a finger at the psychiatrist.

Richard was now aware of what was happening and suddenly found himself being the target of a crazed killer. He realised that Joseph had obviously just thwarted the initial attack by the way the bloodied inmate was getting up off of the floor. Although the prison guard was in between him and his aggressor he still felt as if he was at a distinct disadvantage. There was nothing but cells and locked security doors all around him, so his only means of escape were the stairs that Liam was standing at the foot of.

It was not unusual for Richard to witness violence inside Blackmoor, but this was the first time it had ever been aimed at him. He knew that he was no match for any inmate who wanted to harm him and the idea of even putting up a fight was a wasted thought altogether. The only hope he had of getting out of this predicament was if the prison guard who was protecting him could hold the deranged psychopath at bay until the other guards got there to help. Unfortunately for him it did not look like that was going to happen.

Joseph had decided to give Liam an ultimatum to either get him to make the first move or give himself up now. He knew that the maniacal inmate would not throw down his weapon, but at least it would finish quickly either way. As he shouted his commands the veins in his face protruded from his head.

"Drop the knife, Govan!" He raised his baton. "I know you won't use it on me, so put it down!"

Joseph knew that Liam would have absolutely no qualms about using the blade on him and the last remark was made so as to provoke him into making the first move. If he could taunt the inmate into doing that he could then apply his counter attack plan. Invite the prisoner to take a swing at him, make it look as if he has lost his balance to give a false sense of victory and then quickly move out of the way ready to apply the decisive blow.

Of course, Joseph would be used to seeing inmates lower their weapons at this point, but in this instance that did not seem to be the case. His provocative remark seemed only to refuel the prisoner's desire for violence. Liam appeared to be preparing himself to make the first move.

It all seemed to be a foregone conclusion to Joseph. He had seen it all a number of times before. He was just waiting to make the fake slip and then apply the telling blow with his baton. The passage of time was all that delayed the end of the conflict.

Liam, however, was no fool. He was quite aware of the guard's advantage and was not about to commit himself so easily. In a moment of astute thinking he put both of his hands behind his back so as to hide which one held the blade.

It was quite a straightforward tactic. The prison officer would not know which one to block. Liam would first bring around the empty hand that the guard would have to parry and then the fatal blow would be made with the knife held in the other. Just to make it even harder to assess which one would have hold of the weapon, he would even clasp the blade in his already cut left hand and make his right the initial feigned strike. The whole contrivance was uncomplicated, yet at the same time it would be extremely effective.

Now all that was left to do was for Liam to take full advantage of his underestimated position of having the upper hand. First he would swing his empty right hand around towards the guard's head, therefore, forcing the officer to raise his arm which was holding the baton to block the blow. He would then bring the blade slashing across the wrist deep into the unprotected vein. His victim would suffer before dying.

Liam took aim. He readied himself to enable his attack to be carried out exactly as he had planned. Then he heard a voice to his right.

176

"If you do that, Govan, I'll kill you." Each word was spoken in a calm and steady manner. "I won't do it now, however, but I'll wait until later when you're in your cell."

Whilst Liam and Joseph had been squaring up to each other Richard was quite pleased to have been pushed to the background of their attention. Although this was momentarily comforting he still knew that his safety was drastically in the balance. However, it now seemed as though his chances of getting away unscathed had grown considerably. Even he knew that no one in Blackmoor prison pushed their luck with David Cain.

As Liam turned around to face his new tormentor his expression immediately turned gaunt. He was aware of what this person was capable of and he knew that this would be a completely different matter to deal with. Just as he was about to make a decision of what to do David spoke again.

"I know that you have no fear of dying and that you ignore the pain. Your mind controls it well." He took a step forward. "Death could come slowly or quickly. It would make no difference to you."

At this point, Joseph started to move towards Liam, but suddenly found a hand on his shoulder holding him back. As he looked around to see who it was he saw Richard looking at him shaking his head. The psychiatrist then whispered a plea.

"Not yet!" He looked towards David. "This will end without any more violence."

Joseph did not seem too pleased about the intrusion into his duties and frowned at Richard in return. He was used to solving the prison's problems with his boots or baton. However, he thought that he ought to wait and see what might happen before making a move. After all, there was a point when he had thought that he might have been in a bit of trouble when the psychopathic inmate had decided to hide his hands behind his back.

David continued making his warning.

"I know there would be little point in me hurting you now, therefore, I'll wait."

"You're fucking scared!"

"Not at all. You will suffer more this way."

"You don't know what the fuck you're talking about. I'll have it with you now or anytime." Liam raised the razor in a threatening manner. "I'm not bothered when you come after me, Cain."

"Really? So when you're in your cell, waiting for me to come for you and everywhere is quiet, what will you be listening for?" David raised his eyebrows. "My voice? Will you expect a knock on the door? Maybe you think that someone will announce my arrival for you? You just won't know when I'm coming, will you?"

Liam spoke in an uneasy tone of voice.

"I'll be ready though."

A wry smile slowly crossed David's face.

"I'm sure you will." He slightly nodded his head. "But when you're waiting there, listening for every sound, what will be the one thing that you'll hear amongst all those noises?"

Liam stood there with an apprehensive expression upon his face. There was something not quite right about this. What this person before him was saying was starting to have an uncomfortable effect on him.

By the way David was talking it was almost as if he was discussing the weather. His tone of voice seemed to suggest that he was just making idle conversation. That, however, was certainly not the case.

Although David had asked Liam a question, he answered it himself.

"You'll hear footsteps." He spoke a self-assured manner. "It will almost be as if they're all coming for you. They will be all around you. One after the other, walking up those stairs and along that landing. Not hurried, from no particular direction, but certain in their arrival."

For some reason, which Liam simply could not fathom out, he was starting to feel quite concerned. There was something about what was being said to him that made him feel very nervous. Thoughts that had been kept well at the back of his mind were now coming to the forefront of his consciousness. Years ago he had covered his ears from these same noises and yet somehow they were once again in his head.

David could see that his words were starting to take an effect on Liam, but this was certainly no reason to stop what he was doing.

"And just as they start to get close to the door, they'll pause. Only for two seconds mind you. They'll undoubtedly continue, and when they do the sound will be different. One step will make the same noise as before, whereas the other will be the soft sound of bare foot." He held a clenched fist up in his line of vision. "The shoe will be off and held tightly in the hand."

There was now a large gathering of prison officers surrounding the two inmates as they stood facing each other. The guards would have normally pounced on them both by now, but Richard had managed to keep them at bay for the sake of not causing any more bloodshed. Even though they had already had a colleague brought down they still held back due to a healthy bout of fear, which, of course, was not just brought about by the prisoner with the razor.

David now started to force Liam to concentrate on the noises that only he could hear in his head.

"But you've heard all that many times before, haven't you, Govan? Those same old sounds." His voice almost became a whisper. "Even the wind can sound like footsteps when you're alone in the dark."

Liam's mind was now producing scenes of him as a boy waiting in his bedroom. He sat on the edge of his bed watching the closed door whilst his hands were covering his ears. Tears rolled down his cheeks as he unintentionally bit hard into his bottom lip. Still the door did not open and no one ever came into the room.

There was a look of utter horror upon Liam's face as he stood with his arms hanging limply by his sides. The scenes and thoughts that were passing through his mind were now blending in with reality. All around him there suddenly seemed to be the numbing sound of scraping soles on concrete floors and the stepping of heels on metal stairs. He erratically turned his head in every direction in a weak attempt to seek out where the noises were coming from, but they seemed to be originating from everywhere. His body and mind were both surrounded by the torturous din.

It was now time for David to put on the finishing touches.

"What do you dread the most? The not knowing when they'll reach you? Is it the pause when the shoe is taken off? The turning of the door handle? It will almost be a relief when it does finally reach you and the waiting is over, but this time that just won't happen. All you'll hear is one footstep after the other, over and over again. It will never stop. It will be all that you ever hear. Just like when you used to wait in your bedroom for your mother. You'll simply never know when the footsteps are going to reach you." He stated his conclusion. "Your pain is in the mind, not the body. It always has been and it always will be. It is your torment. It is your hell."

It had now got far too much for Liam to cope with and the enfeebled state of his mind resulted in him losing control of his bodily functions. His eyes erratically blinked and his hands fitfully shook. A puddle of urine started to appear around his feet and welled out across the floor surrounding him. Soon the razor slipped from his grasp and dropped into the amber coloured liquid creating a small splash.

178

Liam had well and truly been broken.

There was silence all around. The prison guards all stood staring at the spectacle in disbelief. How a man who had just so ruthlessly disfigured one man and taken the life of another could suddenly become such a nervous wreck was beyond their comprehension.

Even the inmates who were watching were taken aback by what they had just witnessed. They had been expecting a vicious show of violence, but that had simply not happened. Instead they had seen a show of extremely advanced psychology which they could not even begin to conceive the magnitude of.

There was, however, one person who had at least understood the reasons for what had just occurred even though he was just as amazed as everyone else. He knew that David had set out to mentally break Liam, but how he had done it so thoroughly and quickly was completely unintelligible to him. Richard whispered to himself his own psychological conclusion with a sullen awe.

"This is the most dangerous man alive."

David saw what he had just done as a simple piece of mind manipulation. Richard had given him Liam Govan's prison file a long time ago and he had remembered every detail that was in it. He had found the mental obliteration of the insecure man an easy task that had required little of his intelligence to complete. It was almost laughable how easily the emotions of these human beings could be turned around and used against them for their own destruction.

David had now decided that he had spent long enough wasting his time on this fool and started to head back to his cell. On his way, he walked passed Richard who was still staring at him in a daunted manner. As he did so, the psychiatrist spoke to him in a nervously subdued tone of voice.

"Thank-you!"

At that, David stopped in front of Richard and just stared at him with his ice like eyes. He had a bland expression upon his face and did not utter a word. It almost seemed as though he had found the show of appreciation towards him as being nothing more than patronising. After shaking his head in a contemptuous manner he turned around and continued to make his way back to his cell.

$$4\,Fe + 3\,O_2 \longrightarrow 2\,Fe_2O_3$$
The chemical process that iron goes through when turning into rust.

It was not a piece of information that would ever be useful to David, but if he was going read about such subjects as advanced chemistry he might as well learn every aspect of it. With all of the different branches of science he was studying it would be a waste of his brain's capability to not absorb every bit of information that was put before him. It would be like running a marathon without completing the last two metres.

As David closed the textbook on the desk in front of him he sat up straight in his chair and rested his hands upon his lap. He had not finished reading the book, but he knew that he was about to be interrupted. Any second now Richard would appear at his doorway for his psychoanalysis session.

Although David had allowed it to happen a long time ago he still did not like the fact that he was verbally prodded around. There were times when he felt that he was like a guinea pig having demeaning tests carried out upon it. However, what he gained because of the sessions made it all worth his while.

They gave David the books that he needed to learn from and he gave them the psychological profiles of the inmates that they required. It was a fair exchange. His knowledge for their knowledge.

Richard slowly paced along the corridor flicking his fountain pen through the fingers of one hand whilst clasping his clipboard in the other. Although his appearance seemed to be quite relaxed he was actually rather excited about what lay ahead. He was about to question a person whose intention it was to kill the entire human race. It was every psychiatrist's dream to have such a patient.

Richard had been having regular interviews with David for quite some time now and whenever they talked he seemed to learn more and more every session. Not even his studying at university had prepared him for the events he had encountered. This was a unique case in every sense.

Here was a young man who at the age of just sixteen had butchered his stepfather, a teacher and a fellow pupil from his school all in one day. It appeared to be the backlash of years of violent abuse at the hands of the people who he had killed, but deep in the back of Richard's mind there seemed to be another more pressing reason for it all. Something had triggered the reaction. At one time in this person's life there was an incident that had occurred that had caused him to turn from being a seemingly caring and nice individual into a psychotic murderer.

David had said that he had killed his victims because they had deserved it, but he had also said that he intended to wipe out the entire human race. Richard found it hard to make sense of this because he could not see how all of humanity could have possibly earned the same fate. It was this that was going to be the subject of today's session.

Why does everyone deserve to die?

This sentence was also written at the top of the piece of paper that was attached to Richard's clipboard. As he approached David's cell he slowed his pace down and gradually stepped into the doorway. His attention was immediately drawn towards the man sitting at the desk at the end of the room who was simply doing nothing more than staring at the blank wall in front of him. In a moment of contemplation the enthused psychiatrist put his fountain pen into his shirt pocket and just stood gazing at his patient with an attentive expression upon his face.

It was at that point when David spoke.

"Come in!"

Richard's expression became bemused.

"How did you know that I was here?"

David turned around on his chair to face the psychiatrist.

"You always wear the same aftershave, there is always a silence from the other inmates as you pass through the prison wing, the keys in your pocket rattle and..." He raised a rigid finger to indicate the validity of his point. "You're just as plainly predictable as the rest of them."

A slightly agitated expression crossed Richard's face as he paced into the cell and sat down on the bed to face David. He knew that this man was very talented and intellectually gifted, but, nevertheless, it still made him rather irritated when he was made to look so inferior. It was not so much that the remarks were insulting it was more the fact that there was some truth in it, and that hurt.

David could see that his last remark had ruffled Richard and as a result a wry smile crossed his face. Although he could sometimes see similarities between the psychiatrist and himself he still despised him. Maybe they did both have an overwhelming desire to learn all that they could, but that was not enough reason for him to like the man. The truth was that he hated all that was weak and it was only he who was strong.

Richard decided that it would be best for him to just ignore David's comment and get on with the psychological session. He could not be bothered with any small talk so he got straight to the point. As he spoke he pulled the fountain pen from his top pocket and started to write notes on the top piece of paper on his clipboard.

"I want to start today by asking you a question which I've being leading up to gradually since you've been here." He looked up at David and gazed at him with a studious expression. "Why..."

He was interrupted.

"Why do I want to wipe out the entire human race?"

Richard paused for a moment due to being stunned by the correct anticipation of his question. Yet again he had had his predictability exposed by the perceptiveness of this unforgiving young man. When he finally did manage to gain back his composure he spoke in a tentative manner.

"Yes, I would like to know why you should want to do something so depraved."

"It's not a bad thing."

"How can you say that murdering millions of people isn't a bad thing?" Richard shook his head with distaste. "It's the worst crime possible."

David breathed out an agitated sigh and stood up.

"A crime, you say. You think that murdering millions of human beings would be bad?" He did not face the psychiatrist, but instead just pensively gazed out of the small window in the wall at the end of the cell. "I suppose you think that I'm insane and that there could not possibly be any reason which could even remotely justify such an act."

"So, you have a reason?"

"Of course I do!" David turned around and looked at Richard with a supercilious expression. "But I wonder if I should tell you. You see, I don't think you're ready to hear my reasons for bringing about the extinction of the human race. I really don't think you could cope with the facts."

Richard huffed.

"I think I could manage."

"Are you aware of what it could actually mean to you?"

"I've got some idea."

David shook his head in disagreement.

"That isn't enough. If you want me to tell you why I intend to systematically wipe out the human race you have to be willing to face the facts."

"Which are?"

"The obvious fact that if someone has a reason to kill you, wants to kill you and is able to kill you, then kill you they will." David raised his eyebrows. "Are you ready to hear why your life is so close to ending?"

This was now getting a bit too grim for Richard and he was starting to wonder if there was really more to this subject than he had expected. He could not see how someone else could justify his own death to him, but David did seem to be extremely adamant about what he was saying. Nevertheless, he just had to know the answer to the question and he decided to get it no matter what the costs.

As Richard spoke his voice was full of resolve.

"I can handle what you have to say." He nodded his head is if to assure himself. "Tell me why you intend to wipe out humanity."

"Very well, I will give you what you ask for."

David took in a deep breath. He had never told anyone before about his reasons for what he was planning to do and he wanted to make sure that every point he made was spoken to perfection. After all, he was just about to attempt to justify the entire annihilation of a race.

When David was ready, he began.

"I'm going to explain to you how I feel." He put his hand to his chest. "And how I see my life."

"OK!" Richard nodded his head. "Carry on!"

Every word that left David's mouth was said in a clear and comprehensible manner.

"I want you to imagine yourself as being a Jew. It's the Second World War and you are being led out of a concentration camp that has been your prison for more days than you can remember. Your clothes are ripped and stained with other people's blood as well as your own. The cold winter air is clawing at your skin and biting into your aching muscles, but the pain you are feeling is nowhere near the forefront of your mind. All you know right now is fear, and the mental torture that it brings is worse than any agony you've ever felt before. You're surrounded by Nazi soldiers and they look upon you like you're dirt. They're leading you through some dense woodland of which you can't see through more than thirty yards due to the thickness of the trees. However, after a while you notice that there's a clearing up ahead and you realise that this must be your destination."

Richard's mind was now starting to picture the scenes. The images that were passing through his consciousness seemed to be in black and white, almost as if to reflect upon the grimness of their description. This was not a bad dream, but more akin to a living nightmare.

As David continued creating the scenario with his hypnotic words the thoughts in Richard's mind almost seemed to become reality.

"You feel one of the soldiers prod you in the back with his rifle to hurry you up. Knowing that it would mean your certain death if you do not do as he is instructing you, you quicken your pace towards the direction that you are heading. But it is not enough though. You're still too slow and for this you receive..."

...A hefty kick to the left leg. Richard instantly fell to the floor grasping his aching limb. This immediately resulted with another kick to the lower back for wasting the soldier's time. The pain was unbearable, but it was not bad enough to stop him from getting up off of the ground so as not to earn another blow.

As soon as Richard got to his feet he quickly took a couple of long strides so as to get out of the striking range of the Nazi soldier who had just kicked him. He could feel the muscles in his leg tighten and the throbbing cramp that begun to come about soon forced him to sluggishly limp. Although each step was pure agony he knew he had little choice but to keep on going. There had been many occasions when he had seen people just like him executed for not doing as they were told.

Since Richard had been in the concentration camp he had been made to cut wood, break rocks and many other gruelling tasks. However, in the last few weeks he had started to tire due to a lack of good rest and nutritious food. This had meant that he had collapsed almost half a dozen times because of his weak state. He had been hit for this repeatedly, even though his declining health was being caused by the conditions that they had been forcing him to live in.

Richard had noticed that he was not the only prisoner on this day to have been led off to this unknown place. A man who had a broken his arm and a couple of old men had also been taken away. Whatever task they were being sent to do it certainly was not one which required a great deal of physical agility.

The inquisitiveness of where Richard was being led to was now getting the better of him and as he got closer to the clearing he tried to focus his vision on what was up ahead. In the distance there were a number of Nazi soldiers standing around all holdings guns. What they were there for he simply did not know. There were no other prisoners and he could not see any rocks or wood to be split up. All he could make out was a long mound that was about waste high and seemed to have absolutely no purpose in being there.

As Richard got closer he started to find that he had become the centre of attention of the Nazi soldiers. It immediately made him feel unsafe and a lot more nervous than he already was. All of their gazes seemed to be fixed upon him. Some eyed him with expressions of loathing and disgust, yet some almost appeared to look straight through him as if he were not even there. There was not, however, one amongst them who was not staring straight at him.

Richard was now a matter of yards away from the clearing and he could just make out that the Nazi soldiers were standing around something on the ground. A few more paces revealed that it was a long rectangular pit that had been dug out of the mud. It was on his next step that he realised what it actually was.

As soon as Richard saw the grotesque sight in the middle of the clearing he turned around to face the Nazi soldier behind him and spoke just one word in a desperate tone of voice.

"No!"

Whether it was said as a plea or even a statement of disbelief was not really apparent. There is not much that can be said when you find out that you only have less than a minute to live. This was at the very height of mental anguish.

Right in the middle of the clearing, no more than five yards from Richard, was the grave of more than a hundred Jews. Each body in the macabre pit was unceremoniously slumped in its final resting place without a single degree of respect whatsoever. Men, women and even children, all with their lives callously taken away from them without even receiving the most dignified of burials. The iniquity of death had reached a whole new level of depravity.

Without even realising it Richard had stopped in his tracks and was staring straight at the Nazi soldier behind him. This cost him a forceful blow to the face with a leather-gloved fist. As the knuckles made contact with his nose it instantly broke sending a spurt of blood out onto his mouth and down his chest.

After staggering about for a short moment of time Richard managed to clear his head and regain his balance. He then felt another push in his back and found himself uncontrollably staggering forward towards the mass grave. It was not long before his mind refocused on what was just about to become of him.

Richard could feel the blood freeze in his veins. His muscles painfully tightened all over his body and his throat constricted making it almost impossible for him to breathe. He had never seen a sight like this in his life and worst of all it seemed as if it was going to be the last thing that he would ever see.

The Nazi soldier behind Richard was now leading him along the side of the grave. As he walked the length of the foul smelling pit he grimly gazed upon the bodies that lay below. Each had a single bullet hole to the body or head and had fallen at the place at which they had last been standing. There also seemed to be a gruesome reminder on some of them of the lives that they had been leading before their deaths. Some had long deep cuts on their bodies, whereas others had their jaws, arms and legs hideously broken from previous acts of barbarism. These were ruthless and depraved killings.

Richard soon reached the end of the grave and came to stand at the edge. There were not as many bodies in this part of the pit and this was obviously where he was going to be put. He then heard the order.

"Get in!" The Nazi soldier pointed to the grave with his pistol.

This was it. Death was imminent. Richard's life was about to end.

David stood over Richard staring at him whilst he unravelled the gruesome scenario. Each word helped produce a picture with a grim authenticity. It was almost as if he was creating a separate reality.

183

As David continued with his morbid explanation he started to give suggestions of how Richard could avoid his impending demise.

"How can you possibly avoid your death? Is there any chance that you could live through this? Maybe you could try to flee?"

Richard looked around at the Nazi soldiers who were surrounding him. Each of them was staring back at him and pointing a gun in his direction. If he were going to flee he would have to be very quick.

As Richard tried to plot an escape route the soldier behind him repeated his command.

"Get in!"

If there were ever going to be a time to make a run for it, it would have to be now. Richard could hear that the soldier standing behind him was starting to grow impatient by the tone of his voice and if he did not move away from the edge of the pit now he would surely be pushed. He had no choice. It was a simple case of having to run for his life.

Richard quickly turned and made a dash towards the dense woodland. Although the muscles in his body were weak and aching his mind automatically ignored their pleas for rest. He had never run so fast in his life. It was, however, not quick enough.

The heavy butt of a rifle hit Richard on the forehead immediately sending him crashing to the ground. Another blow followed and was then accompanied by a number of kicks to the body as the other soldiers joined in. This went on for about half a minute, but it felt like hours.

When the beating finally came to a stop, Richard rolled onto his back. His face was badly cut and bruised and he had several broken bones in his body. As he looked up at the soldiers surrounding him he saw one of them cock a machine gun and point it straight at him. The last thing he saw was a split second volley of shots spray out from the gun's barrel.

"There is no escape from their tyranny." David's voice was full of vehemence. "But maybe they will decide not to kill you. You could always try begging for mercy."

Richard stood on the edge of the pit staring at the twisted bodies below. It was a hideous sight and he could not help but turn his head away in abhorrence. Even when he closed his eyes he still found that he was not able to shut out the horror. He could not help it, but a wave of panic suddenly washed over him.

In an act of desperation Richard turned around and faced the Nazi soldier behind him. He then fell to his knees and put his hands out with the palms facing up in a begging posture. As he cried out for mercy his panicked words were almost incomprehensible.

"No! No! Please! I've done nothing to you." Tears flowed from his eyes, blurring his vision, as he bowed his head in a desperate reverence. "Please don't kill me!"

At that, Richard heard the soldier who was standing over him cock his pistol. He immediately raised his head and looked up through his tear filled eyes to see the barrel of the gun aiming straight at his forehead. There was just one shot.

"Their evil knows no mercy. Is there anything else left for you to try?" David raised his eyebrows in a suggestive manner. "How about prayer? Maybe your god can help you now?"

Richard slowly lowered himself down into the pit. The bottom of it was completely covered with bodies and wherever he put his feet he could not help but tread on the corpses. With every step he took towards the middle of the grave he heard the crushing of the deceased fragile bones. If there were ever such sickening sounds that could match the hideousness of this scene these were those.

As Richard stood in the middle of the pit he bowed his head and closed his eyes. If escape was impossible and there was no chance of mercy then maybe his god could save him. There were few words to his prayer, but they were spoken with a despairing intensity.

"Please God, save me! Amen!"

This was then followed by the sound of a pistol being cocked. Richard opened his eyes and looked up at the Nazi soldier who was standing in the edge of the pit. The gun was then pointed at him.

From a distance smoke could be seen coming from the barrel of the pistol and was then closely followed by the sound of a single shot. Richard's body then slumped into its final resting-place. It lay motionless among the other dead bodies with a lone bullet hole to the centre of his forehead. He had become just another victim of a cruel and callous regime of evil. One insignificant dead body amongst many.

David was not finished. There was more to his explanation and it would now come to its conclusion. His passionate tone of voice underlined his feelings about what he was saying.

"You see, I am that victim."

There was now a different person standing in the middle of the grave. He was not like the one before. No fear tortured his mind and no panic took control of his nerves. He just stood in a calm and unmoving posture with his head bowed.

It now seemed as though David was about to go the same way as those who lay beneath his feet. The vile smell of rotting corpses rose up from the mass grave almost as if it was the scent of death creeping up on him. There was soon to be another life lost in this place of degradation.

With every word that David spoke to describe the scenario a graphic picture continually passed through Richard's mind.

"I am surrounded by people who wish to harm me for no reason other than my being different to them."

As David raised his head he looked at the Nazi soldiers who were standing around the grave. Each of them stared back at him with expressions of hate and self-superiority. They seemed to think that they had a right to do what they were doing.

"I have tried to run, but they never let me leave."

David looked around and could see that there was no escape for him. All of the Nazi soldiers were armed with guns and there was no doubt that they each had a willingness to use them. Even if he did make it past them there would be more beyond the woodland that would have just as much desire to harm him.

"I have begged for mercy, but it is never given."

The Nazi soldier who was standing on the edge of the grave was eagerly reloading his gun and was clearly looking forward to what he was just about to do. There would be no point in trying to beg to him for leniency. His executioner even wore a slight smile of anticipation on his face.

"I have even tried looking towards your gods, but there was nothing to be found."

David now looked to the sky almost as if he was seeking a divine intervention to prevent his execution. However, as he gazed heavenwards there seemed to be little more than an empty greyness. There was nothing there that could help him.

"So, I came to realise that there was only one who can save the planet from this sickness called humanity."

The Nazi soldier had now loaded his gun and had just cocked it. As he looked up to get ready to take aim at his target a look of shock crossed his face. Now, standing just inches away from him was David.

"There is only one who has the power to stop them from bringing more harm to the land and all that is living on it."

It did not take long for the Nazi soldier to get over the sensation of astonishment even though he still had no idea how his prisoner could have just suddenly materialised from

185

being in the grave to be standing right in front of him in a sheer instant. He raised his gun right up to David's head and then pulled the trigger. This time, however, there was no shot.

"There is only one who can repair the damage that they have done."

The sides of the mass grave behind David now started to cave in. As the mud slowly covered the carcasses the sight of twisted and broken bodies gradually disappeared. What had once been a scene of a macabre foulness had now just become a nondescript grassy piece of landscape.

"And I am that one."

The Nazi soldier who had been aiming the gun at David now found that he could not breathe. His hands clasped his neck as his throat started to burn with pain. It was not long before his lungs became empty and he fell to his knees. Death then claimed its next victim.

"I will let none of them escape."

The Nazi soldiers surrounding David had at first tried to shoot him, but they too found that their guns did not work. Some of them tried to run when they saw what had happened to their comrade, but as they fled they all simultaneously collapsed to the floor holding their throats. After a short while their bodies were also stripped of life.

"I shall give no mercy."

A handful of the other Nazi soldiers now realised that they were very close to death and they immediately started to beg David for leniency. Some of them fell to their knees, whereas others just started to cry out for pity upon their souls. They all, however, died in the same unforgiving manner as the others whilst hopelessly gasping for air.

"And it will be their turn for their gods to ignore them."

There were only two Nazi soldiers left now and they both clearly realised that they had little chance of survival. One of them clutched a crucifix necklace that hung from his neck and the other put his hands together to pray for his passage to heaven. Seconds later they both fell to the ground dead without any air in their lungs.

"So now the Earth will be able to heal."

The bodies of the Nazi soldiers started to decompose at an extremely fast and unnatural rate. When they had finally turned into just skeletal frames they sunk into the earth and left absolutely no trace of their being there. Humanity had now become extinct.

"And when the land has revitalised itself it will be able to grow once more."

As David started to walk through the trees of the woodland new breeds of plant life sprung up out of the ground and flourished all around him. With every step he took the landscape dramatically changed. He soon came to be standing at the edge of a large valley which he gazed over with a peaceful expression upon his face. A river with clean water flowed through the centre of it, the hills either side of it had all kinds of free uninterrupted wildlife and the sky above was crystal clear.

"So there will now be room for another race to inhabit this land."

A small amount of buildings made out of wood and other extracts from nature rose up from the landscape. Each structure was perched upon stilts so as not to clutter up the ground below. Upon their roofs were windmills providing just enough power for those whom lived within.

"A new untainted race that can survive without being distracted by sloth, which sees no logic in pollution, and does not kill other creatures for its own benefits."

There were no television aerials, no cables and no chimneys. All of the food for this new race was grown in an abundance of fields and orchards that could also feed all the other creatures of the land. This was a world where all life forms lived with an equal respect for each other.

"So why have a race that murders it own, destroys the planet and makes other creatures extinct when it can be replaced by one which is capable of so much more?"

Several beings started to emerge from the valley and paced up towards David. He watched them all with an expression of pride and content. As they got closer they raised their heads and looked up at the one who had created them. Each of them had light blue crystal like eyes, oversize craniums and pale skin. This was a race bred by a genius, raised by a genius and had inevitably become a society of geniuses.

"Just imagine a being that has the intelligence to develop a cure for every disease, not just for its own kind, but for every creature. A society of brilliant minds who can invent a means of living which will not pollute the atmosphere or destroy the landscape. And when they see differences in each other, such as physically or mentally, they simply admire each other for it. This is the utopia that I will create and which will not be stricken by the inequities of the human race. This is the world that I shall live in."

David stood over Richard in a reverent posture. His head was held high and his eyes gazed out as if they could see the future that lay ahead. As he spoke his words they were laced with an unwavering resolve and a might which was almost divine.

"The Earth has been a place of devastation for far too long and it is time for it to be free from the cause of its suffering. It needs someone to release it from its torment, and I am the one who shall lead it out of the darkness and into the light." He closed his eyes and breathed out a satisfied sigh. "I shall bring peace on Earth."

Richard sat with his head bowed and his eyes closed. Every muscle in his body was weak and his mind was exhausted. What he had just heard had not just physically broken him, but had also mentally desolated him.

Richard did not like it, but David had just justified the genocide of the entire human race.

There was an unceremonious thud as the mashed potato landed on the plastic dinner tray. This was greeted with a depressed wince as Jimmy O'Neill looked upon his meagre dinner. It was not so much that the meal was laid out in such a carefree way, but more the fact that the food itself was so bland. Mashed potato, two thin sausages, a handful of mushy peas and a cup of weak tea was not exactly his idea of an appetising meal.

Although Jimmy had been at Blackmoor for quite some time now he still could not quite get used to prison life. The food was terrible, the cells were cold and there seemed to be a fight every other week. He knew that it was not going to be easy, but he never thought that it would be this hard.

As Jimmy looked around the canteen for anyone who probably would not mind him sitting with them he noticed a table at the back that had no one sitting at it. With a sudden desire for solitude he decided that he would prefer to sit by himself today. It would make a nice change for him to be able to eat a meal without someone else's elbows digging into him whilst he was trying to put his food into his mouth.

For the first instance, Jimmy managed to enjoy his food in isolation, but after a while the canteen started to fill up. A few of the inmates came over to sit at the same table as him so he decided that he ought to quickly eat his meal before anyone came and sat on the chair right next to him. Unfortunately for him, he suddenly realised that it was too late.

Jimmy felt the figure of a tall man pull the chair out next to him. It appeared that the person did not have a food tray and was happy just to settle for a solitary apple that he had placed on the table in front of himself. As the inmate sat down he did not say anything and seemed quite content to equally keep himself to himself.

At first Jimmy was quite pleased to find that he was not being interrupted, but then he realised that that was not quite the case. It was after about half a minute when he noticed that the person next to him was staring in his direction. His first reaction was to look around to find out who it was. He then wished that he had never have been so inquisitive.

Sitting next to Jimmy, glaring at him with cold ice like eyes was David Cain, the 'Starrow School Slaughterer'. At first the Irishman immediately turned his gaze away, but it was to no avail. He could still feel the weight of the undeviating stare piercing straight through him like a dagger through flesh.

Jimmy just did not know what to do. For an uncomfortable moment he nervously carried on eating his food as if nothing was happening, but his sudden loss of appetite made each mouthful awkwardly hard to swallow. It was not long before his attempt at acting as if everything was normal had turned into a lost cause. David then spoke to him.

"In half an hour I will go to your cell where you will be waiting for me alone." Each word was said in a clear and precise manner. "Make sure that you do not fail me!"

Jimmy now found himself looking straight back into David's crystal blue like eyes. It was almost as if he had been hypnotised by their pellucid brilliance. In a weak attempt at trying to pull free of the penetrating gaze he tried to bargain for mercy.

"Why me?" He erratically shook his head. "I don't even know you."

David just picked up his apple off of the table and stood up. There was a stern expression upon his face and the muscles in his body seemed to tighten as if ready to expel a sudden amount of energy. As he spoke his final command he stayed staring straight into Jimmy's constantly blinking eyes.

"Make that the last time that you ever question my instructions!"

At that, David just calmly walked off as if he had done nothing more than ask Jimmy for the time of day. It was a chilling display of how this person could be so ruthless one moment and yet so composed the next. This was without doubt someone who was in complete control of his body and mind.

Jimmy sat on the bed in his cell nervously biting his fingernails. Every now and again he would hear a noise outside the door and would instantly look up with a gaunt expression upon his face. His fear had clasped hold of him like an eagle's claw upon its prey.

Thoughts of why he had been chosen continuously passed through Jimmy's mind. He was not aware of how he might have done anything to earn reprisal from David Cain and the more that he thought about it the more frightened he became. The worst part of it all was the not knowing.

Jimmy could only think of two reasons why David would want to harm him. It would either be because he was playing his flute too loud or if someone else had been making up lies about him. Whatever it was, he just wanted to get it all over and done with.

Just as Jimmy thought he was going to lose his mind with despair he felt the door to his cell slowly open. As he sharply looked up he saw David standing in the doorway already staring straight back at him. His fear may have now doubled, but at least the waiting was over.

David pushed the door behind him so that it was covering the doorway as much as possible without actually closing and took two steps into the centre of the cell. He waited for a moment before commencing with what he had to say just to make sure that the anxious man before him was in a calm enough state to hear his words. Then, in a steady and relaxed tone of voice, he spoke.

"You will do the following..."

Six hours after their conversation a man by the name of Jarrod Pike was found lying in his cell with a broken neck and an electrocution burn to one of his hands. It appeared to be an accident, but there were two people in Blackmoor prison who knew different. David and Jimmy were more than aware of the truth and they were not about to tell anyone of the real facts.

Richard shook his head in a perplexed manner as he sat in the middle of the uncomfortably cramped cell. The more he looked at the personal psychiatric files in front of him the more he became confused. He simply could not understand it.

"I don't see how it would affect him in that way." Richard put his hands to his head and closed his eyes. "I mean, this bit about the swastikas on his arms, that doesn't make Carl Venal a murderer."

David sat motionless on his bed with his gaze turned towards the light coming through the window at the end of the cell. He was completely certain that the information that he was giving was utterly correct and his nonchalant posture showed how positive he was. As he went about explaining his conclusion his voice was calm and clear.

"Carl Venal's father died when he was eight. He was too young to care at that point in his life. His mother went to every court case when he was being accused of his crimes and visits him every week. It's obvious that she is over caring by the way she even writes to him every other day."

"So?"

"Well, there was another person in history who led a similar life when he was young." David finally turned his gazed to Richard. "He was responsible for a lot of deaths, as well."

"Who?"

"Adolph Hitler."

Richard's expression became inquisitive.

"How was his lifestyle similar?"

"His father died when he was young and his mother was very over caring towards him."

"How will that affect Venal?"

"Although he needs others to stand by him he is still very independent in his thoughts."

"You can't think that Carl Venal will try the same thing as Hitler."

"Of course he won't."

"So what are you trying to say?"

"When Carl Venal finishes doing his time for robbery he will get in contact with the international far right extremist groups which he is still a member of. Only now, they've got stronger, Denmark and Germany in particular. When Venal sees this he will immediately want to move into a position of leadership. It's in his personality. He is not a patient person. The question you must ask yourself is 'How will he do this at speed?'"

"There's only one way." Richard answer was short, but sickeningly accurate. "By harming one of those he hates. It'll be an immigrant, a Jew or someone not of the Aryan race."

"Correct." David slightly nodded his head. "He will become a murderer."

Richard paused to think for a moment and then spoke in a quiet tone of voice.

"Your early life wasn't too dissimilar to Hitler's, either." He shrugged his shoulders. "Your father left when you before you were born and your mother didn't throw you out of the house at a young age. Has that contributed towards you having such extreme intentions?"

David sat back against the wall next to his bed and shook his head.

"My mother used to watch me get the hell knocked out of me by my stepfather. She was not the most caring of mothers." He was clearly unimpressed by Richard's wayward remark. "And as for my father, I didn't even get to see him. How can I possibly miss something that I've never even had?"

"Yes, but Hitler wanted to rule the world. Your intentions are just as..."

Richard was interrupted.

"Hitler wanted to rule the human race. I want to cure the world of it." David leaned forward and raised a finger. "There is a very big difference."

"Don't you think that there are some similarities?"

For a long moment David just stared at Richard with an acrimonious expression upon his face. He now found the psychiatrist's remarks to be quite agitating. Not only had the subject of Carl Venal suddenly been pushed aside and turned towards him he was also being compared to Adolph Hitler. As he went about getting the conversation back onto its original tracks he also made sure that the psychiatrist knew that his assumptions were extremely wrong.

"Hitler killed the Jews simply because of their religion. There are deaths all around the world which are brought about by reasons which are just as illogical." David stood up and walked towards the end of the cell with his eyes fixed upon the floor. "Have I ever spoken to you in a way which has suggested that I hated a person for their religion, their nationality or the colour of their skin?"

"No."

"Then surely you must see that I kill because of what people are, not because of their religious beliefs, the name of their country or what ethnic group they belong to." David turned to face the cell. "I see all men as being equal. Equal in their depravity, equal in their naiveté and equal in their imbecility. To compare me with someone like Adolph Hitler is just as ignorant as to liken me to the pope. They both rely on a mass of people to agree with their

190

views in order to gain power and then they have their aims restricted by the people who put them where they are. I have no such chains that bound me."

Richard sat with his head bowed and took a moment to let his mind absorb all that had been said in the conversation. He sometimes found that David could be way too far ahead of him for him to be able to comprehend the entirety of what he had to say. What his patient would think as being obvious he would consider to be way too intellectually advanced.

When Richard was sure that he had grasped the majority of the conversation he moved onto the next subject of the session.

"I have here the file of Julian Haymen." He took a folder from off of his lap and passed it to David. "He's been sent to Blackmoor for the indecent assault of his nine year old daughter and has been sentenced to six years imprisonment. He denied the charges, but claimed that he was provoked..."

Richard was interrupted.

"No more!"

"Pardon!"

"No more!" David passed the folder back to Richard. "I will not participate in this anymore. I will not give you anymore profiles and I will not take any more books."

"Why?"

There was a pause before the answer.

"Because I have finished."

Richard's eyes widened as he looked at David with a horrified expression upon his face. He knew that this day would come, but he had never been able to prepare for it. This was the moment that he had been dreading ever since he had started having the psychiatric sessions with his patient.

David was ready. He had finished his studying and was now going to do as he had promised. What he had said in the courtroom all those years ago was about to become fact.

Richard could not help but show his feelings.

"Bloody hell!" He shook his head erratically. "You're really going to try to do it, aren't you?"

David just stayed staring at Richard with an expressionless look upon his face. He did not need to answer. It was all really quite obvious. The time had come for him to do as he had foretold and it would be futile to try to talk him out of it.

Still Richard tried to get some reason from it all.

"But, you can't escape. They'll be watching you." He wiped his sweating brow with the back of his shirtsleeve. "No one's ever escaped from Blackmoor. I mean, do you think that they're going to release you?"

"Of course not."

"So how are you going to get out?"

David took in a deep breath and then spoke in a relaxed and assured manner.

"The same way I came in; through the front door."

Richard's brow became furrowed as he stared at David with an inquisitive gaze. There was something about that remark which for some reason seemed to ring eerily true. This man who stood before him was always a man of his word, but this was different. Not even *he* could just walk out.

As Richard spoke the expression in his voice was cautiously suspicious.

"Are you trying to play games with my mind?"

He received a wry smile in reply.

A dark depressing sky ominously enshrouded the prison as if it were a reflection on the gloominess of the lost souls it held within its walls. There had been a strong wind

191

blowing for the last couple of days now and anyone who had ventured out from the confinement of the walls soon found themselves being aggressively ruffled by the elements. The sombre weather seemed to be lugubriously akin to the harsh nature of Blackmoor.

There was a slight skid as a car pulled up in its allotted bay in the prison car park. As soon as the engine was turned off the driver pushed open his door and sluggishly stumbled out. Before he could even stand up straight the gusty wind immediately hit him full on, blowing his long coat around his body and knocking him off balance. After muffling a few expletives to himself he managed to get a hold of the wayward garment and regain his posture.

As Richard stood in the middle of the car park he gloomily looked around at the prison walls. He had always felt quite safe knowing that some of the country's most dangerous criminals were locked away in Blackmoor, but that had now all changed. It was almost as if they could all just get up and walk out without any hindrance whatsoever.

Richard had spent all night thinking about David and it was already starting to have an adverse effect his mind. He was sure that the walls of the prison did not seem to be as high today. It was almost as if they had sunken into the ground overnight. What had once appeared to be impossible to scale now seemed to be as passable as a stile on a country path.

Of course, Richard's thoughts were mostly unwarranted and he really did not have anything to worry about. No one had ever escaped from Blackmoor and there was a very good reason for it. Whether you were a guard, the warden or even the priest of the prison chapel, you were simply not trusted.

Every person who was allowed to pass in and out of the prison was subjected to a number of security checks. At every doorway which the inmates were not permitted to pass through there was a close circuit camera, a computerised switch card terminal and a personal identification number keypad. For someone to be able to enter or leave Blackmoor they would have to be a member of the authorised personnel, have a switch card and know their own personal identification number. If someone was without just one of these attributes then they simply could not pass through.

Even with all of the security measures that the prison had in place Richard still did not feel that it was enough to prevent David from trying to escape. It was obvious that he had been planning to do so ever since he had been locked up there in the first place. However, up until now no one knew when he was going to do it and after what had been said yesterday that time had now become apparent.

Any day now David would make an attempt to escape from Blackmoor prison. His time there had served its purpose and he was now ready to leave. He had stayed there for his convenience and just as if he was residing at a hotel he was now about to check out.

Richard knew this and was not about to let it happen. His main aim for coming in to work today was to talk to the warden of Blackmoor, Howard Fenton, and convince him to increase the security around David. How he intended to talk him into this he did not know yet and he knew it would not be easy. Funding for the prison was low and to try to get extra guards to be placed on just one person would not be an easy task.

On his way to the warden's office Richard had to pass through a number of security checkpoints. Each time he did so he had to look straight up into a close circuit television camera so that he could be recognised, run his switch card through a computerised inquiry terminal and type in his own personal identification number onto a numeric keypad. He had to complete each of these procedures at least half a dozen times before reaching his destination.

As Richard approached the door to the warden's office he paused for a moment to prepare what he was going to say. He wanted to make sure that he put his case over with the

192

utmost sincerity so as to make sure that his pleas were not ignored. If he did not succeed then there would be no telling what the price of failure would be.

Moments after Richard had knocked on the door a voice called out for him to enter the room. He did so immediately with an air of eagerness. As he closed the door behind him he forced a smile and uneasily greeted the warden.

"Hello, Howard!"

"Come in, Richard! I'm glad you're here. I wanted to speak to you."

"What about?"

"This psychological report on John Willis." Howard lifted a file off of his desk and waved it in the air. "He killed two people. One was his own father and the other his stepmother. How can you be so sure that he won't kill again?"

Richard sat down on the chair on the other side of the desk to Howard and then began to answer the question in a confident manner.

"John Willis used to get sexually assaulted by his father and stepmother on a regular basis." His brow furrowed as the topic of the conversation became quite grotesque. "Some of the tortures he was subjected to were really quite horrific. He has a number of scars on and inside his body. When he was arrested he was covered in his own blood and had several broken bones. He didn't tell it to the court, but when he killed them both it was without a doubt an act of self defence."

"He might've got a liking for it. What's going to stop him from killing again?"

"Well, this is what I thought at first, but David Cain told me..."

Howard interrupted.

"Cain! I thought he might get a mention." He shook his head. "I still don't like this murderer doing your work for you."

Richard breathed out an exasperated sigh.

"It isn't like that."

"What is it like then?"

"David Cain told me to ask John Willis if he ever intended to have children. When I did ask him he said that he could never do such a thing. I asked why, of course, and he told me that he could never risk himself doing to his children what had happened to him." He raised his eyebrows. "Does that sound like a ruthless killer to you?"

"It sounds like he doesn't trust himself."

"No, it's because he could never take the risk." Richard lowered his gaze in a forlorn manner. "In just one moment of sheer fright and frustration he lashed out and killed his father and stepmother. For one minute John Willis was a murderer, but since then he's simply been a lonely pain filled man."

Howard folded his arms and sat back in his chair as he went about trying to arrive at a conclusion of the discussion.

"So, you think he should be released?" The expression upon his face was scrupulous. "He's served seventeen years of two life sentences. Is that enough?"

Richard was adamant in his reply.

"Yes. He will never kill again."

"But has he been punished too little for his crimes?"

"John Willis served out his punishment before he had even committed the murders." Richard leant forward and raised a finger. "He's just got to be given the one thing that he's never had before, a chance in life."

Howard raised his eyebrows and took in a deep breath. He had full faith in Richard, but he did sometimes find himself doubting the psychiatrist's word. It was not so much that he did not trust the man, it was just where he got his information from that he did not like.

As Howard pushed John Willis' file to the edge of the desk he turned his gaze back to Richard.

"Well, I'll take your word for it, but I'm not entirely convinced." He creased his brow in an inquisitive manner. "What did you want to see me about anyway?"

Richard cleared a lump in his throat before answering.

"I need to talk to you about David Cain."

An exasperated expression immediately crossed Howard's face.

"Who's he hurt this time?"

"No one. It's more important than that."

"What is it then?"

"He's going to try to escape."

Howard immediately sat forward in his chair and leant his forearms on the top of the desk.

"What?" He nervously shook his head. "How do you know?"

Richard could now see that he had captured Howard's full attention and made the most of it by getting straight to the point.

"Well, since he got here I've been giving him the books he's wanted in return for the psychological profiles of the prisoners. He's been studying and learning every day since then. What for, none of us know. Nevertheless, he now says that he doesn't want any more books. Basically, he's learnt all he wants to." He raised his eyebrows. "It's because of this that I think he's going to try to break out. He simply doesn't need us anymore."

"Are you're trying to say that he's been using Blackmoor prison as..." Howard paused. "Some kind of library."

"Yes. I mean, think about it! It's the ultimate library." Richard waved a hand in an attempt to express himself. "Who's going to disturb him when he's locked up behind an iron door? Everything's done for him. He doesn't even have to cook his own meals. It's solitude in its extreme."

Howard started to become agitated.

"So what the bloody hell have we been giving him books for? Surely we should have never let him have access to them."

"It was agreed by both of us. You yourself said that he could have all the knowledge in the world, but he will never be able to use it in this prison." Richard shrugged his shoulders. "I mean, let's face it, some of the profiles we got off of him were exemplary. Derek Mowlam, for instance. I still think we were right to do what we did."

"But if you knew that he was going to try to escape after he had read all of those books why did you ever let him have them?"

Richard was not looking forward to hearing that question. He knew that it would be asked and up until now he had struggled to find an answer to it. Nevertheless, now that he was forced to confront it his honest nature took over and he came clean.

"The way I saw it at first was that David Cain was no different to any other prisoner in Blackmoor, but now I know that I was wrong. His intelligence is of a degree that I have never experienced before in my life. He can control people by words alone. The way you feel, what you think, even what you do." He lowered his gaze in a defeated manner. "I realise now that the first person he manipulated was me. I should've never of let him have the books."

Howard was more defiant.

"That just maybe, but we still have him and that's the main thing."

"Yes! Not even *he* could talk us into letting him go." Richard nervously paused for a moment. "But whether we like it or not he is extremely intelligent and there's no telling what he might've devised. I just don't think that we can keep him here with the same amount of security as the other inmates."

"And you're sure he's going to try to escape?"

"Yes."

Howard started to rub his moustache in an anxious manner and clearly appeared to be worried about the whole situation. Although he had full confidence in the security at Blackmoor he still did not like the idea of anyone even trying to escape. It was not so much their intentions that bothered him, it was more the fact that they might just have actually of found a way of breaking out.

Howard realised that he needed to solve the problem before it had a chance to even occur and in order to do that the first thing he would need would be information. There were a number of questions that would need to be asked and the only person who would have a chance of giving any answers was Richard. No one had spent as much time with David as he had and the psychiatrist knew more about him than anyone, at least he appeared to.

As Howard tried to make some progress he spoke in an apprehensive tone of voice.

"Do you know when Cain intends to try to do this or how?"

A contemplative expression crossed Richard's face as he thought about the question.

"I should imagine he intends to escape within a matter of days. I can't be completely sure though. As for how he's going to do it, I just wouldn't know." He shrugged his shoulders. "When I spoke to him about it he said that he was going to leave through the front door, but I think he was just trying to psyche me out. The thing is though; it wouldn't surprise me if that was how he was going to try to do it."

"Why?"

"That's just the sort of person he is. He's one hundred percent sure of himself all the time. So much so, that he would probably tell me exactly how he's going to escape simply because he's probably got such a flawless plan." Richard slowly shook his head in a constrained manner. "It's almost as if he thinks he's perfect and that everyone else is inferior."

Howard tapped a finger on the desk.

"That could be his problem. If he's over confident he'll make mistakes."

"Maybe, but we can't rely on that. We have to make sure he doesn't even get the chance."

"Indeed." Howard took a moment to think about it and then announced his conclusion. "We'll move him to a different cell. That's the first thing we should do. Then we'll make sure that we always have a guard keeping watch on him. I'm not going to take any chances. There's no way he's getting out of this prison."

Richard raised his eyebrows in a forewarning manner.

"Let's just hope so, because if he does escape we already know what he intends to do when he gets out."

There was a hint of derision in Howard's voice.

"You mean kill the entire human race. The infamous 'Omega' speech. You don't believe that, do you?"

As Richard spoke he lowered his gaze and shook his head in a despondent manner.

"I didn't believe it when I first met him, but now..." He looked up at Howard. "I'm not so sure."

"You look pissed off."

As soon as Jimmy heard the voice he immediately looked up with a startled expression upon his face. When he realised who had spoken he lowered his gaze back down again in a forlorn manner. He made no attempt to hide the miserable mood he was in and was not bothered about who saw him in it.

Jimmy seemed to be paler around the cheeks these days. It was mainly brought about by the fact that he had grown a thick ginger beard and had also not cut his hair for some time either. The two masses of bright red seemed to act as a frame around his face and at the same time diminished any colour that might have come from his skin.

As Paul Burrell stood in the doorway he stared at Jimmy with a perplexed look upon his face. He had noticed how the young Irishman had let himself go over the last six months, but up until now he had not said anything. However, today he thought he might as well find out what was wrong. After all, he had nothing else to do.

When Paul had finally finished expelling a large nonchalant yawn he spoke in an equally insouciant manner.

"You've been as miserable as fuck for the last six months." He took a few steps into the cell. "You were all right before. What's wrong now?"

"Nothing."

"Oh, come on! Don't give me that!" Paul picked up a magazine off of the bed and idly started to flick through it. "You were coping okay at first, but now you just sit in here all day doing nothing. I haven't heard about anyone being after you. So, what's with all this hermit shit?"

Jimmy now lifted his gaze again and stared at Paul in an irritated manner.

"It has nothing to do with you." He shook his head. "I don't mean to be rude, but could you leave me the fuck alone!"

"I only fucking wanted to know what's up."

"Yeah well, it's nothing you can help with."

Paul put the magazine down on the bed and then started to look around the cell.

"That's another thing." A puzzled expression crossed his face. "Where's that flute you made? You don't seem to play it anymore."

Jimmy suddenly stood up and glared at Paul with a fiery temperament.

"Just keep the fucking hell away from me, man!" As he pointed his finger towards the cell door he was visibly trying to calm himself down. "If you don't want what's happened to me to happen to you, you'll get the bloody hell out! As a friend, I'm telling you, keep the fucking hell away!"

Paul looked at Jimmy for a moment with a slightly agitated, yet confused expression upon his face. It was obvious that he did not know what was going on and it was with that in mind that he thought that it just might be a good idea to do what he had been told to. After a short moment of contemplation he turned to go. As he reached the door to the cell he stopped and turned around to say one last thing.

"I don't know what's up with you mate, but..." He shook his head. "I'm fucking well glad it aint happening to me!"

At that, Paul hurriedly left the cell.

The sound of voices suddenly came to a stop and was then followed by three loud knocks upon the iron door. At this, a wry smile insidiously crossed David's face as he stood in the centre of his cell. He had been patiently waiting for them to come to him for some time now and they had not disappointed him with the predictability of their ignorance. With an element of scorn he beckoned them to enter.

"Please, come in!" He whispered his next comment to himself. "I've been expecting you."

At that, the door swung open to reveal the prison warden standing in the doorway with half a dozen guards behind him. For a short while, Howard Fenton gazed around the cell

196

with an attentive expression upon his face as he assessed his surroundings. When he finally did walk in he stared at David eye to eye in a weak attempt at trying to show his authority. He then announced his orders.

"I want Cain taken to his new cell and I want this one thoroughly searched."

David just stared back at Howard with an expressionless look upon his face whilst the warden continued with his instructions.

"Take apart anything that might be able to hold even the smallest of objects; the mattress, the table, even the sink." He allowed himself a confident smirk as he stared at the inmate standing before him. "Leave absolutely nothing untouched."

There was a muttered reply from one of the guards and then the rest of them stumbled in to search the cell. Two of them approached David with wary expressions upon their faces and with nervous steps in their strides. Neither of them touched him. They just beckoned him to walk with them. This he did quite willingly and without saying a word. It was almost as if this was what he wanted and that they were doing exactly as he required.

As the guards led David out of his cell they turned to approach the east end of the prison wing. He followed in between them sharing the same pace without a hint of opposition. It was only when he had walked for about eight yards that he stopped and let the prisoner officers carry on going.

Whilst David had been walking with the guards he had started to pass Jimmy O'Neill's cell. When he had reached it he stopped in his tracks and stood staring through the open doorway. His eyes seemed to be intently fixed upon something that appeared to be of great importance to him.

Jimmy sat on a chair in the middle of his cell combing his long ginger hair. His expression was quite bland, similar to the thoughts that were passing through his mind. He was experiencing just another one of those same old days in Blackmoor prison when nothing ever seems to happen. That was until he suddenly felt a deathly cold rush over him.

It was almost as if Jimmy's soul had just been ripped from his body and had taken all the warmth of the flesh with it. At first, he sat in a frozen state not daring to move, but that did not last long. Turning his head to the left he looked through the open doorway of his cell. He had to squint at first because he was not wearing his glasses, but when he finally did focus all that he could see was David Cain standing quite motionless staring straight back at him with eyes like burning ice. The time had now come.

This was the moment that Jimmy had been dreading for the last six months. He did not want to get involved, but had been left little choice. There were times when he had wanted it all to be just a bad dream, but this was one nightmare that would not go away.

At first, Jimmy did not know what to do and he just sat on the chair staring back at the chilling light blue crystalline eyes. It was almost as if he was held in a hypnotic trance that had captured his mind, body and soul. Something had to break them from their statue like postures and then it did.

In one slow movement, David just slightly nodded his head. It was only a small gesture, but it had meant much more than it appeared to. The signal had been sent and it had certainly been received.

Jimmy lowered his gaze and closed his eyes. A cold sweat washed over his body as he took in a deep breath to try to keep control of himself. When he finally felt as if he was completely mentally prepared he stood up and closed the door to his cell. He then turned around to face a small mirror that was attached to the wall and sighed in a despondent manner.

The prison officers feverishly scoured the cell for anything that might be used as an implement for escape. Whilst they were doing this Howard stood intently watching their every move so as to make sure that they did not miss anything. It was while he was doing this that he noticed something in the far corner leaning up against the wall. Why he had not seen the peculiar object earlier he did not know, but now that he had he decided to examine it.

Howard weaved his way across the cell in amongst the prison officers until he got to the long wooden shaft in the corner. As he picked it up a perplexed expression crossed his face as he gazed upon its ornate sculpturing. This was certainly a beautiful piece of craftsmanship, but why it was in the possession of David Cain was beyond him.

After inspecting the object for a short amount of time Howard decided that he would take it away to study it a bit more closely. As he made his way out of the cell he kept his gaze fixed upon the twisted carvings along the shaft of the wooden implement. Just as he was about to pass through the doorway he stopped and spoke to the prison officers behind him without even turning to face them.

"Carry on searching the cell!" Still his attention was more fixed upon the object in his hands than the people who he was talking to. "I'll be in my office."

"Yes, Sir!" Came the reply.

At that, Howard went on his way.

A solitary figure stood in the middle of the cell staring out of the small window in the far wall. Although he could only see the cloudy sky above the prison it was the only thing that was worth looking at. The dull walls and bland furniture around him did not even merit a second glance.

Richard knew that David would be there soon and he had decided to wait for him. He was aware that he would not be very welcome, but there was something he just simply had to do. Whether it was for his own benefit or not he was simply not sure, but there was something he had to say to his former psychiatric patient.

It was while Richard was drifting off into a daydream that he heard a voice behind him.

"So, this is your attempt at clipping my wings?"

Richard turned around to face David and raised his eyebrows.

"I'd cut them off, if I could."

David smiled and took a couple of steps into the cell.

"Do you fear what I am capable of that much?" His expression turned to one of inquisitiveness. "You appear not to share the same views as the others do."

"Maybe I'm just a little more cautious. I fear what you can do, just as I do any other inmate in this prison."

"Liar!"

It was a blunt remark, but, nevertheless, very true. David knew that Richard was aware of what he would do if he were to escape and that was exactly why the psychiatrist was in his cell right now. This was his last attempt at trying to fathom out how this seemingly intellectually flawless inmate was going to escape. Not that he would ever be able to abstract the information directly from him.

Richard bowed his head and rubbed his hand across his face in an exasperated manner.

"It's true. I do fear what you could do if you were to escape from Blackmoor, but just because you intend to do something it doesn't mean you're capable of it." He shook his head. "Do you really think that you could wipe out the entire human race?"

"There are enough nuclear bombs on this planet to destroy it several times over, just as there are a number of individuals who are in a position to do it."

"But how could *you* do it?"

David laughed.

"Do you really expect me to answer that?"

"No, not really."

"So, let's get to why you're really here."

Richard turned away for a moment and sighed. He knew that he could not keep his real reason for being there a secret, but it was still very frustrating to be so easily read. As he tried to explain himself he stared at the blank wall to the side of him.

"I suppose what I'm really here for is just to make sure that you're here as well." He turned his gaze back to David. "I know that we haven't thwarted whatever plans you have made so far, but I'm going to make sure that I make it as hard for you as possible."

"Then the game is afoot." This was followed by a sarcastic smile.

"Games have rules." Richard raised an eyebrow. "And I have a rather deep suspicion that you won't be playing by any."

David nodded his head in agreement.

"Very true. But how do you intend to make it hard for me?" He shrugged his shoulders. "Are you going to check on me every hour of each day? Do you think that will be enough?"

"I will be as thorough as I need to be."

"And just how thorough is that? Will you just believe your eyes or will you draw upon one of your other senses to come to a conclusion? What will be enough to settle your mind?" He raised a finger up in front of Richard's face. "Will you need to touch me with your own hand just to make sure that I'm still here? Maybe what you see before you is an illusion?"

"You are not an illusion."

"Are you telling me that or yourself?"

Richard started to get quite agitated by what David was saying.

"Bloody hell! You're standing right in front of me." His face turned into a scowl. "You can't honestly expect me to believe it when you say that you're not actually here?"

"So, are you going to make sure?" David smiled in a sardonic manner. "Why don't you touch me to find out for certain?"

"I don't need to."

Although Richard was frustrated by the obvious attempt at trying to agitate him he could not help but feel that he wanted to do as David had said. He felt an overwhelming urge just to reach out and touch the man in front of him with his finger just to find out if he really was there. However, he could not let himself be so easily taunted and resisted the urge to make physical contact in order to confirm what his eyes were already telling him.

Instead, Richard put up a verbal barrier of defence.

"I know that you're trying to play games with my mind, but you're not going to manipulate me. I don't have to touch you to know that you're standing right in front of me, in this cell, in this prison." He turned to leave. "And that's where you're staying."

Just as Richard started to walk through the doorway of the cell, David made one last remark.

"And you achieved all of that with just your eyesight." A slight mocking laugh. "Congratulations!"

A man who no one recognised stood waiting in the middle of the prison wing. He watched intently as the psychiatrist left the cell that now held David Cain. When he was sure that no one was looking in his direction he inconspicuously walked up to the doorway and pulled a very sharp razor out of his pocket. As his eyes focused on the man standing in the cell, he took in a deep breath to prepare himself.

It was time to be rid of David Cain.

As Joseph McKinnie slowly and confidently paced amongst the inmates of the prison they either turned away or lowered their gazes. It was almost as if he was trying to reinforce his reputation by the way he permanently wore a sneer across his face and clutched hold of the handle of his baton in a forewarning manner. His imposing stature epitomised his ruthless nature.

Joseph had been the first guard posted to keep watch on David and he was now on his way to carry out his duties. He had only just been told which cell he had to go and stand outside of minutes earlier due to the information having been kept a close secret from everyone in the prison including the officers. There was not going to be a single opportunity of escape left to chance.

As Joseph reached David's cell he noticed that the door was ajar. Just to be extra cautious he gave it a slight push so as to take a look inside and make sure that the convict had not already gone. If this man was going to escape, one thing was for sure, he was not going to do it on this prison officer's shift.

Joseph peered into the cell as the door slowly swung open on its hinges. Much to his satisfaction standing there in front of him with his back to the door and his head bowed was David. The convict did not seem to be doing anything in particular and appeared to be totally unaware that he was being watched.

Just to make his presence known Joseph decided to make a forewarning remark.

"No one escapes from Blackmoor, Cain." He tapped his knuckles on the iron door just to show off its robustness. "And that includes you."

At that, David turned around to face the prison officer.

Howard stood in his office closely inspecting the flute that he had just taken from David's cell. As he studied its ornate shaft a slight look of admiration crossed his face. He was quite impressed with its ornate design and skilled workmanship. However, his expression became confused when he came to wonder how it had come into this particular inmate's possession.

David had never been seen in the prison workshop before, so there was no way that he could have made the flute himself. He was also not known for liking the beauty of music or art, so it was unlikely that he would have borrowed it off of another convict. In fact, as far as most people knew the only things that the killer ever associated himself with were violence and death. This was certainly an odd thing to have found in the mass murderer's cell.

After a while Howard gave up trying to work out why David would have such a thing as a flute. He had even tried blowing through the mouthpiece, but he had not been able to get much of a note. Although he had come to the conclusion that it could be used as nothing more than a plain piece of wood he decided that he would not give it back just yet. There would be no risks taken with this prisoner.

As Howard put the flute on his desk he turned away to walk to the end of the room. His office was situated on the top floor of Blackmoor and the view from the window looked out across the entire prison grounds. He would quite often gaze over the myriad of walls, barbed wire and iron bars that kept his convicts from the outside world. The inhibiting sight gave him a feeling of safety and satisfaction. It was with these comforting thoughts that he stretched out his arms and allowed himself a large carefree yawn

Richard slowly paced through the corridors of the prison with a raincoat folded over his forearm and a briefcase clutched in his hand. Although he appeared to be quite relaxed his mind was cluttered with insecure thoughts of David. It had been quite a distressing day and he was now glad that it was over. There seemed to be a voice screaming at the back of his mind which was trying to tell him that he and the prison warden had somehow overlooked something which was going to be very costly to them both.

As Richard approached a security checkpoint he pulled out his switch card from his top pocket. Just as he was about to run it through the card reader mounted on the wall he paused. He could not help it, but his mind kept telling him that he just had to make sure. There was no way that he could possibly leave the prison without checking on David one last time.

Turning on his heel, Richard slipped the switch card back into his top pocket and headed back down the corridor. All he wanted to do was look over David with his own eyes just to make sure that he was still in his cell. This was all he had on his mind as he made his way through cell blocks. Whether he was going to do this every time he left the prison at the end of each day he did not know, but he knew that he would not be able to rest his mind if he did not do it today.

Leaning up against the wall outside David's cell was a guard who had been posted there to keep watch on the inmate. When he saw Richard walking towards him he stood up straight and adjusted his cap. As the psychiatrist reached him he made a remark of reassurance.

"It's alright, he's still here."

"I'm glad to hear it." Richard half smiled.

"I can't see him going anywhere." The prison guard shrugged his shoulders. "This is the most amount of security we've ever given one inmate."

Richard did not find the last comment very encouraging. There was a very good reason for these extra precautions and it was this that was worrying him. This inmate's massive intelligence was only matched by his shrewdness when it came to doing the unexpected. It was these attributes that warranted the increased vigilance.

In an apprehensive motion Richard opened the peephole in the cell door and peered in. As his gaze went to the person on the bed a contented expression crossed his face. For now it appeared that he had nothing to worry about. Nevertheless, as he went to turn away a memory of a single sentence suddenly crossed his mind.

"Why don't you touch me to find out for sure?"

For a short moment Richard paused. His head suddenly became crowded with thoughts of what that sentence might have meant. However, it was only when he remembered what he had said in return to David that he finally disregarded the worth of the comment.

"I know that you're trying to play games with my mind."

It was with that dismissive thought that Richard contentedly turned around and left to make his way home.

The sun shone through a handful of clouds sending brilliant amber coloured rays cutting out across the sky. As the soft light rested upon the pastures below it lit up the hills with a warm glow. With all the different fields and their individual shades of crops the whole landscape seemed to resemble a large patchwork quilt that majestically covered the entire countryside. There was, however, only one true way to view this tranquil scene and that was from above.

A seagull effortlessly glided over the horizon and seemed to hang motionless against the backdrop of the scintillating blue sky. As the sun's soft rays glimmered off of its feathers it almost appeared to be made of a silvery metallic substance. With every gust of wind and flutter of its wings it gracefully soared higher and higher away from the ground below.

With its desire for solitude the seagull epitomised all that was unburdened by humanity. The further it rose from the landscape the more free it seemed to become. There were no buildings to block its path and no huntsmen to shoot it down. Nothing could deter it in its search for autonomy.

To be free from the world a creature needs a means of escape. For the seagull it was the power of flight provided by the agility of its wings. As for the lonesome figure that stood far below on the edge of the landscape it was his mind.

The hills of the countryside were cut off by a coastline of white cliffs that were constantly being stroked by the waves of the sea. Standing at the top of them staring out across the ocean was a person who seemed to share the same desire for solitude as the seagull. His mental wings were outstretched and he was in full flight. He had no walls surrounding him, no guards watching over him and no laws ruling him.

David Cain was as free as a bird. As he stood on the edge of the cliff looking out across the vast ocean he had a contemplative expression upon his face. Although his outward appearance was slightly altered, what with his head closely shaved, there was still no difference in the thoughts that were passing through the depths of his mind.

I am the one true god who shall reap vengeance upon you all.

The early start of a new day resulted in Howard rubbing the sleep from his eyes whilst he sluggishly paced into his office. As he hung his coat up onto a wall hook he turned to look at the flute on his desk which he had confiscated from David's cell the day before. He apprehensively eyed it with a thoughtful expression upon his face. There was something about it that suggested it might not be all that it seemed.

Howard walked across the office and put his morning newspaper on his desk. As he did so he picked up the flute and closely studied it. It, of course, looked no different from what it had done the day before and since he had not been able to get it out of his mind overnight he had not drawn any new conclusions on whether it had a secret use. If this was a clue to a mystery it certainly hid the answers well.

In a moment of exasperated frustration Howard hit the end of the instrument across the palm of his hand. There was a loud slap that was instantaneously eclipsed by a snapping noise. It was at that point that the flute gave away its sinister secret.

Lying on the edge of the desk was the broken mouthpiece end of the wooden instrument. As Howard picked it up he attentively studied it. The first thing that he noticed was that it had not initially been snapped off, but had actually been sawn in two. It also had three pins inserted into it to keep it connected to the main shaft, therefore, enabling it to be removed and replaced whenever necessary.

Now realising that he was onto something Howard started to study the rest of the flute. After pulling it around he found that the tail came off in just the same manner as the mouthpiece. The ends of the shaft had now been separated and all that was left was the centre section. Although a large amount of the instrument had been removed a good eighteen inches of hollow wood still remained.

Now that Howard had found that the flute had been tampered with he felt that he was getting somewhere. As his eyes scoured over it at every angle he became aware that both ends of the shaft had pieces of glass glued into them. With closer inspection he noticed that they appeared to be rounded and, therefore, must be some kind of lenses.

Howard soon came to realise that what he had in his hands was some kind of viewing implement, so he automatically raised it up to his eye. As he looked through the lenses of the hollow shaft he pointed it out through the window in his office. He was instantly taken aback by what he saw and numbly mouthed an obscenity in a surprised manner.

"Fuck me!"

On the other side of the prison yard was a watchtower. With the naked eye it was only just possible to see if there was anyone in it by the faint sight of movement within. However, Howard could now quite clearly see the guard, Jeremy Darwin adjusting his tie.

For some unknown reason, David Cain had somehow obtained a telescope. Although it was crude in its appearance, it was, nevertheless, very effective in its use. The only thing that bothered Howard was what the inmate had it for. It was while the prison warden was still gazing through the implement with a fascinated awe that he was suddenly distracted by a knock on the door to his office. He replied with in half attentive manner.

"Come in!"

At that, the door opened and Richard paced into the office. When he noticed Howard looking through the telescope he stopped in his tracks with a confused expression upon his face. As he stood watching the prison warden he spoke in an inquisitive tone of voice.

"What's that?"

"I found it in Cain's cell when we searched it yesterday." Howard turned around to face Richard. "It appears to be a telescope."

"What's he got that for?"

"I've no idea. I think we ought to find out, by going..."

Howard suddenly paused in mid sentence. Richard was standing by the doorway to the office whilst the prison warden was staring in his direction with a very worried expression upon his face. He then spoke in a very uneasy manner.

"Could you stand away from the door, please?"

Richard looked at Howard with a furrowed brow, but when he saw the look on the face of the warden he realised that something was amiss. Although he was not sure what was occurring he did as he was asked and took a step away from the doorway. The simple fact that all this had something to do with David was enough to make him seriously consider any abnormality.

Howard stayed facing in Richard's direction and slowly raised the telescope up to his eye. It took him a while to focus and when he finally did he kept the spyglass steadfastly still. He then gasped in a shocked manner.

Right down the far end of the corridor a prison guard was typing in his personal identification number into a security keypad and Howard could clearly see every key that he pressed. As he numbly lowered the telescope he turned to Richard and stared at him with a look of amazement. The shock upon his face was almost that of a person who had just seen his own gravestone, which as far as his career was concerned was not too far from the truth.

When Howard finally regained control of his mind he spoke in an astounded tone of voice.

"He's been collecting the guards ID numbers."

"What?"

"Cain! He's actually been doing it." Howard raised the telescope up in front of himself and gazed at it in disbelief. "He's been using this to get the guards personal ID numbers as they type them into the security keypads."

"Oh Jesus!" Was all that was said in reply.

Howard and Richard quickly paced through the prison wing towards David's cell. Each of them wore very concerned expressions upon their faces and said nothing to each other as they walked. They were both too numb for words.

When the two of them reached David's cell Howard instructed the prison officer who was standing outside to open the door. The guard instantly looked perplexed at why both the warden and psychiatrist of Blackmoor would want to see the same inmate at the same time. As he put the key in the lock he turned around and spoke in a reassuring manner.

"I looked in two minutes ago." He confidently nodded his head. "He's still in there."

Neither Howard nor Richard were willing to take this remark as concrete evidence and they did not even bother to offer a reply. As the door opened they both quickly paced into the cell not knowing what they were about to find. The first thing that they fixed their gazes upon was the head of a man with dark hair poking out of the top of the covers of the bed.

Richard went about trying to get the man's attention.

"David, wake up!"

There was no reply.

Howard then made another attempt.

"Get up, Cain!"

This time a muffled reply came from under the sheets. Richard and Howard both looked at each other with dumfounded expressions upon their faces. They did not really want to get too close due to their fear of getting within David's striking range. It was only when the person under the covers started to raise the sound of his muffled voice that one of them decided to act.

Richard stepped forward and slowly pulled the covers off of the person on the bed. Bit by bit the top of the head appeared, followed by the back of the neck. It then went silent.

Lying gagged and tied face down to the frame of the bed was the prison officer Joseph McKinnie. The ties that bound him were made out of cut up bed sheets that had been twisted around to make them stronger. He also had a neatly combed black wig on his head so as to make him look like David. However, what was more noticeable than anything was the physical state he was in. His jaw was twisted around to the side of his head making it almost impossible for him to be able to speak properly.

After getting over the initial shock Howard finally took some action and removed the gag from Joseph's mouth. As soon as the obstruction was cleared the Scotsman immediately started to cough to clear his throat of phlegm and blood. When he had finally relieved himself he managed to splutter out some words in a not too comprehensible manner.

"Cain! That fucking bastard!" A bout of coughing temporarily interrupted him. "Where is he?"

Richard replied in a pessimistic tone of voice.

"Right now, we don't know." He took in a deep-exasperated breath. "He could be anywhere. I just hope it's not outside the prison."

Even though Joseph was now being untied from the bed by the prison guard who had been standing outside the cell he still wanted more answers.

"He couldn't have just walked out. How the bloody hell can he escape?"

None of them knew the answer to this question, but if they had have realised what had been happening in the months leading up to this day they just might have been able to prevent what had happened.

It had all started just over a year before David had made his escape. He had heard the sound of a flute in the cell next to his and had gone to kill the person who was playing the instrument. However, just at the moment that he was about to garrotte Jimmy O'Neill a thought had entered his mind.

I need him alive.

Straight after that David walked into an empty cell and smashed its window. He then took two shards of glass from what was left and wrapped them in a piece of cloth which he had cut from the corner of a bed blanket. It was these objects that were going to be part of the main basis of his escape. This was just the beginning of his cunning plan.

A glint of light sparkled off of the shard of glass as David held it up to the window in his cell. After closely inspecting it for a short amount of time he half wrapped it in the piece of cloth which had been cut from a bed blanket and then held it against the wall to the side of him. With a precise and careful movement he slowly ran the jagged fragment along the bricks.

David repeated this action a number of times before stopping to have another look at the shard of glass. Where he had been filing it across the roughness of the wall it had been considerably worn down and had started to round off where there had once been a sharp point. It was already starting to take the correct shape.

For the rest of the day David kept doing the same to both pieces of glass until they were perfectly circular. This, however, was just the first in a number of processes that he would undertake over the following months. There was a much higher amount of precision required for what he was going to use them for.

Once David had made all of the correct calculations and measurements he started to work on obtaining the viewing accuracy that he needed. Everyday thereafter he went about filing the faces of the pieces of glass against the more smooth bricks of the walls to his cell.

Each lens was then meticulously rubbed with the thick piece of bed cloth until they became perfectly converged so as to reflect light to the exact requirements. Now all he had to do was obtain a shaft in which to mount them.

David stood in the centre of the cell staring at Jimmy with an expressionless look upon his face. His whole posture was calm and collected, yet at the same time he had an air of intimidation about him. When he had spent the required amount of time studying the man before him he spoke in a slow and easy tone of voice.

"You will do the following!" His words were mouthed almost as if he was simply making idle conversation. "And you will do it without question!"

Jimmy sat on the bed with a very gaunt complexion upon his face. His gaze just stayed fixed upon the person standing in front of him. He did not utter a word, because he did not dare to.

David carried on stating his orders.

"I have a number of tasks which you are to complete. They are quite simple and do not require too much intelligence. However, some will draw upon your carpentry skills." He reached into his pocket and pulled out a piece of paper. "I have here a list of instructions for you to follow and items which you will get for me."

Jimmy's expression started to become confused and as it did so David became more than aware of the fact. The calculated young man was not about to let his plans be thwarted by someone else's incompetence and as soon as he noticed that there was a sign that this just might happen he immediately went about eliminating any possibilities of failure. This he did by first trying to ascertain what the problem was.

"What is on your mind?" His brow furrowed. "Tell me now!"

Jimmy lowered his gaze and took in a deep breath. He did not want to cross this very volatile and dangerous man, but he could not help but hide his dissatisfaction. As he tried to explain himself he slowly shook his head in an apprehensive manner.

"Look, I don't want any trouble." He raised his head and nervously sighed. "It's just that if I get caught doing anything wrong I could get in..."

David interrupted.

"You have no choice." He handed Jimmy the piece of paper. "You will do everything I say and get me everything I need."

Jimmy reluctantly took the piece of paper.

"But why me?"

"Because I have chosen you."

"To do what?"

"To assist me..." David raised his eyebrows in a confident manner. "In my escape."

"Escape?" Jimmy's eyes widened. "But if I get caught helping you do that I'll be right up shit street. They'll throw away the bloody key."

"So you better make sure that you're not caught." David's expression now became viciously stern. "Because if you fail me, I'll rip your face off."

Jimmy was startled by the suddenness of the threat and as he replied the nervousness in his voice was quite evident.

"But what if *you* get found out?"

David knew exactly what Jimmy was thinking and it was already a contingency that he had been expecting.

"Are you thinking of informing on me?"

"No way! I wouldn't do that." A frightened reply.

"Am I to believe that?"

Jimmy tried to strengthen his plea.

"I honestly wouldn't..." He was interrupted.

"Do you doubt me?"

"What?"

"Do you think that there are limits that I will not go beyond when pursuing my means?"

"I don't understand!"

"Then watch as I show you!"

David did not say another word and just turned around to open the door to the cell. He then stepped outside and started to slowly pace across to the other side of the prison wing. As he walked off Jimmy intently watched him through the open doorway with a perplexed expression upon his face.

By the blasé manner in which David made his way towards his destination it was almost as if he was taking a stroll along a country lane. He did not seem to have any uncertainty in what he was about to do and there was not a single falter in any of his steps. His whole posture was calm, deliberate and unburdened.

Jimmy carried on watching as David finally came to stand outside of a cell that had its door wide open. Inside he could just see a large overweight man standing in front of a mirror combing his hair. How this particular individual was relevant to this he was not quite sure, but he had a feeling that he was about to find out.

David waited for a moment outside of the cell just to have a quick look around to see if he was being watched by anyone other than Jimmy. When he finally stepped inside he pulled the door to behind him. It was a good minute before he reappeared, but when he did the sight was as chilling as it was shocking.

The door to the cell was only open for a short amount of time before David closed it again, but it was just long enough for Jimmy to see the dead body of the large man lying on the floor in a heap. He gasped with horror at the hideous sight of the lifeless corpse. For the second time in his life he had witnessed a murder. Only this time was even more nauseating than when it had been him who had taken the person's life.

As David walked back across the prison wing he still had the same look of nonchalance about him. The expression upon his face was one of complete unconcern about the repugnance of what he had just done. He had just callously taken a man's life seemingly without any provocation whatsoever and he was clearly not troubled by it one bit.

David walked into Jimmy's cell and then closed the door behind him. He took a moment to consider what he was about to say just so that he could be certain of making himself quite clear. When he was ready he spoke in a steady and relaxed tone of voice.

"You see, if you don't do as I say then I will get someone else to." He raised his eyebrows. "And then I shall prove to them that there are no limits that I will go to."

It was an obvious hint and it was immediately understood. If David had to prove to another person that he was willing to kill anyone then Jimmy knew that it would be him who would be the next person to be made an example out of. The whole situation was so chilling it almost made his blood freeze. Although he had a very uncomfortable lump in the back of his throat he still somehow managed to get a sentence out.

"You've made your point."

David nodded his head just once and then started to list his demands.

"Everything I tell you to do you will do it straight away. If I need you to make something, you will complete it. If I need you to get an object for me, you will have it ready. And if I need you to complete a task, you will stop anything that you are doing and do whatever I tell you to. You will know when I am ready to receive all that I have requested when I give you a sign. That sign will be nothing more than a simple nod of my head in your direction." He looked at Jimmy with a suspecting gaze. "Is that totally clear?"

207

"Yes." Was all that was said in reply.

David carried on stating his orders.

"You will start by getting the following items!" He pointed at the list that Jimmy was holding in his hand. "A sharp razor for shaving, a roll of the clear plastic film which they cover the food with in the kitchen, a comb, an unused tea bag, a pair of scissors, a thin felt tip pen and a small pot of non-toxic transparent paper glue. You will then put all of these in a single plastic bag."

It was an unusual list of objects and Jimmy was not about to even start to think about what they might be used for. In fact, he found himself not wanting to know. Nevertheless, a perplexed expression did begin to cross his face as David proceeded with his instructions.

"You will also start growing the hair on your head and stop shaving your chin. This you will carry on doing until I give you the previously mentioned sign. At this point you will shave both your chin and your head and then put each of the collections of hair in two separate bags. Once you have done this you will bring both of those bags and the one holding the items to what will most likely be a cell which I would have only just been moved into." Jimmy's mystified expression had now been noticed. "I know that all of this may seem quite irrelevant to you, but your curiosities are no concern of mine."

Jimmy just sat on his bed staring up at David. Even if he did tell someone about the escape plan he would have a hard time convincing them that the items that had been requested would be of any use in a break out. Although his fear was now starting to subside it had been taken over by an intense feeling of inquisitiveness.

Still David continued with his commands.

"As for your carpentry skills, you will use them to convert your flute into a telescope."

"A telescope?" Jimmy shook his head. "I don't know how to make something like that."

"I can assure you I have no intention of trusting your intellect." David reached into his trouser pocket and pulled out the two lenses that he had made and a piece of string with four knots tied in it. "I have made sure that everything that needs to be calculated has already been done so. All you have to do is follow my instructions."

As Jimmy took the two lenses and piece of string he spoke with an unsure stutter in his voice.

"This could still be quite difficult."

David was not very pleased with the negative approach to his machinations. The idea of having this person making mistakes due to his ridiculous imperfections was not an option that he found to be acceptable. With each of his words now laced with a vicious fury he made sure that there would be no room for failure.

"Now, I will say this just one more time." David pointed a rigid finger into Jimmy's face. "You will make that the last time that you think about failing me! In future, every task I give you will be carried out with the utmost efficiency and without even a hint of incompetence! Do I make myself clear?"

"Yes!" A dispirited reply.

David just momentarily squinted in a scrutinising manner and then carried on explaining his plans of construction.

"The piece of string has four knots tied in it. When it is pulled taut it will give the exact measurements to where the two lenses are to be put and where the two ends of the telescope are to be cut off. The two knots in the middle are where the two lenses are to be placed and the two on the outside are where the ends are to be cut off." He raised a finger as if to show the validity of his next point. "Now, this is obviously not an item which I can leave lying around, so, therefore, you will make sure that the flute can be put back together

208

again when needed. It does not have to be playable just so long as it still looks like a musical instrument, therefore, enabling me to be able to keep it in my cell."

As Jimmy listened he inquisitively put the two lenses up to his eye. When he finally managed to get them in focus he realised just how well they had been made. His next remark showed his surprise.

"Mother of Jesus!"

David ignored this slight distraction and then gave his last order.

"When you have finished making the telescope I want you to bring it to me straight away. Other than that, I don't expect to hear from you until I give you the sign to bring to my cell everything else I have told you to get." He had now finally said all he needed to say and was just about to turn to leave when stopped in his tracks. "I suggest you get working right away. You have a lot do."

Jimmy just took in a deep breath and lowered his gaze.

"Very well!" Was all that he said.

It had been some time since David had left the cell and Jimmy had not moved from his position on the bed. He had been in deep thought about what he was going to do about the ultimatum and had still not made up his mind. Almost certain death or the risk of an extended amount of time in prison was not much of a varied choice. It was while he was still contemplating his options when he heard some voices coming from the prison wing just outside of his cell.

"Fucking hell! Call the screws! Jarrod Pike's dead."

This was followed by about an hour of shouting and people hurriedly moving about. Jimmy had been expecting this and just tried his best to shut the noises out of his mind. However, it was when he overheard two prison officers talking that he finally realised that out of his two choices there was really only one that he could take.

"It looks like Pike was screwing around with the light in his cell and got electrocuted. We found burn marks on his fingers."

"Was that all that killed him?"

"We're not sure yet. It looks like he also broke his neck when he fell off of the chair that he was using to change the bulb."

"Still, I suppose it's just one less scrote to think about."

"Yeah! As if we really give a fuck!"

It was the last comment that made Jimmy's mind up for him. If David were to kill him for whatever reason no one would give a damn about it anyway. The truth was, he might as well be alive and in prison than dead and forgotten. With a dejected expression upon his face he picked up his flute and started to measure out the distance between one of the ends and the point where he was going to make the first incision.

There was not a single word of thanks, but there had been no expectancy of any. Jimmy had just left the cell with his head bowed in a forlorn manner. He had now lost his mind's only means of escape from Blackmoor prison and there was nothing he could do about it

As David held up the flute he closely inspected it for any obvious markings from where it had been tampered with. He raised his eyebrows in an impressed manner when he realised just what a skilled job Jimmy had made with its alterations. The points at where it could be pulled apart were almost completely invisible to the eye and if he had not of known any different he would have probably have not even noticed the changes himself.

With a couple of slight tugs David pulled off both of the ends of the flute and laid them on his bed. He then stepped over to the door of the cell and slightly pulled it ajar. As he raised the telescope to his eye his gaze went to the front cover of a magazine which an inmate was holding up on the other side of the prison wing. A slight smile crossed his face as he confidently nodded his head.

The security doors which separated the cell blocks from the rest of the prison were set well back at the end of long corridors. None of the inmates were allowed to walk down these unless they were accompanied by at least two guards. This was done by one typing in his personal identification number into the keypad whilst the other stood well back with the prisoner by his side. By doing it this way it would not be possible for the combination to be seen by any prying eyes.

Since receiving the telescope, David had discretely followed Joseph McKinnie as he made his way around the prison. Every time the prison officer had typed in his personal identification number onto one of the keypads it had all been secretly viewed from what would normally have been a safe distance away. There had been a couple of times when the combination had been changed over the months, but it had, nevertheless, always still been seen, learnt and not forgotten.

A slight nod of David's head was followed by a rapid increase in Jimmy's heart rate. The sign had been given and it was now time to act. As soon as the initial shock had worn off he went about doing what he had been instructed to.

Jimmy slowly paced across the cell and came to stand in front of a mirror that was mounted on the wall. He took a moment to have a soul-searching gaze at himself as if to question what sort of person he had become. The fact that he did not have the courage to stand up to David made him feel weak and pathetic. If he really had have had a choice he would not have got involved at all, but unfortunately for him co-operation was the only option that would keep him alive.

Reluctantly diverting his gaze from the mirror Jimmy turned to open the top draw of the cabinet next to his bed. As he rummaged through the clothes he found a thick blue jumper. When he unravelled it, it revealed its hidden contents. There in front of him was every item that David had put on the list.

Jimmy carefully searched through all of the different objects until he finally found what he was looking for. As he cautiously picked up a sharp new razor he held it up in front of himself and then turned his gaze back to the mirror. With a distressed expression upon his face he put the blade to his head and started to shave.

A man who no one recognised stood in the middle of the prison wing attentively watching the door to David Cain's new cell. Where there had once been a long bright red beard on his chin and a mass of ginger locks flowing from his head was now just bare skin. This man looked so different to how he had done fifteen minutes ago even his own mother would probably have had trouble recognising him.

When the prison psychiatrist had left David's cell and Jimmy was quite certain that no one was watching him he started to make his way across the prison wing. As he approached the slightly opened door he paused and took in a deep breath so as to calm his nerves. It was at that point that he heard a voice come from within.

"Don't just stand around out there, come in!"

Jimmy did as he was told and quickly paced into the cell pulling the door to behind him. As he turned to face David he immediately saw those two blue chilling eyes staring straight at him. Even now there still seemed to be no warmth in this man.

In an attempt to get it all over and done with Jimmy handed David the plastic bags with the two lots of hair and various other items in.

"Everything you asked for is there."

"Did anyone see you come here?"

"No, I don't think so."

"Has anyone recognised you?"

"No. There's no chance of that."

"Very well, you may go."

Jimmy stood for a moment just to take one last look at David. There before him was one of the most volatile and dangerous men that he had ever come across. Although he had just largely contributed towards this psychopath's plans for escape he was actually quite pleased to be getting rid of him. It was a shallow viewpoint, but at least he would be out of harm's way. At least, that was what he thought.

David noticed that Jimmy was still standing in front of him, so with a slight frown he went about speeding up the static inmate's departure.

"If you're waiting for some kind of reward I can offer you just one thing."

"What's that?"

"A piece of advice."

Jimmy spoke in an inquisitive tone of voice.

"Advice? What advice?"

"It's nothing much, but you might find it useful. Make the most of the coming months." David turned away as he made his final decree. "Because it won't be long before you die along with every other human on this planet."

It was such a savage and callous remark that it totally took Jimmy by surprise. He did not know how David could possibly carry out such a threat, but, nevertheless, it had certainly sent a shiver down his spine. Although he felt a bit confused he was not about to try to find out what it had exactly meant and without saying another word he turned to leave.

As Jimmy went on his way he closed the door behind him and quickly started to pace through the prison wing. When he got back to his cell he sat down on his bed and breathed out an exasperated sigh. In a moment of relief he made his true feelings clear.

"Thank fuck I've got rid of him!"

It was now time for David to complete the last part of his plan. He had all of the tools that he needed and just simply had to put the final piece of the puzzle together. Although he had everything worked out there was still no margin for error. Not that it was at all likely that he would make a mistake.

David started by emptying out on his desk the contents of the plastic bag that had in it the various items that he had requested off of Jimmy. He then picked up the razor from the pile of objects and sat down in front of the mirror that was leaning on his desk. After taking a brief pause to look at himself he began to shave his head.

It was not long before David was completely bald and there was a pile of hair lying on the floor around him. After he had wiped himself down with a piece of cloth and had scooped up all the remnants of his scalp he put the handful of jet-black locks on the pillow on his bed.

Without a hint of indecisiveness David carried on with the next task. As he delved through the pile of assorted objects he took out the roll of cling film and the felt tip pen. Spreading out the thin transparent plastic across the desk he measured out fifteen inches and then cut it off with the razor. He then took hold of the two top corners of the separated piece with the tips of his fingers and put it up to the lower part of his face. After pressing down on the film with a piece of cloth the static electricity gradually started to make it stick to his jaw.

David's next move was to get the thin felt tip pen and draw an outline on the cling film of his mouth and all around his chin in the shape of a beard. When he was sure that his

211

markings were quite accurate by studying himself in the mirror, he pulled the transparent plastic off of his face. He then laid it flat down on the desk and once again started to sift through the pile of items.

This time David got the plastic bottle of paper glue and began to lightly squeeze a minimal amount of its contents evenly over the surface of the shape drawn on the cling film. When he was satisfied that he had covered every bit that was necessary he put it to one side. He then picked up the bag that had the remains of Jimmy's beard and poured the contents into a small pile on the edge of the desk.

David now reached over to the sink next to him and picked up a cup of water which he already had waiting. After he had dipped his forefinger into it he lightly shook it to make sure that it was not too damp. He then carefully pressed the tip against the pile of ginger hair so that it became evenly covered with the small strands.

In a calm and steady action David slowly brought his hand over to hover just inches away from the beard shape that had been drawn upon the cling film. He then lightly tapped the back of his knuckles, so that the hair fell from the tip of his finger and onto the glue. As he started from the bottom he slowly worked up so that he layered over every part of the surface. When he had finished he cut away the remainder of the uncovered cling film so that all he had left was the shape of the red beard.

After David had completed the first part of his disguise he made himself a wig for his head in exactly the same manner with the remainder of Jimmy's hair from his scalp. He covered his head with the cling film, outlined the shape with the felt pen and then applied the glue and hair accordingly. As he let the glue dry on the wigs he went about completing the final appliance needed for his transformation.

David, of course, was quite aware that there was one part of his features that he would have to alter in order for his plan to be successful. His eyes would have to change colour. The light blue would have to turn to a brown for him to be able to complete his masked metamorphosis.

For this David got the tea bag from the pile of items and dropped it into the cup of water. He then cut two half inch wide circular shapes out of the remaining cling film and put them into the now changing coloured liquid in the cup. When the clear bits of plastic had changed to being a light brown he took them out of the cup and put them on his desk to dry. After he had waited for a sufficient amount of time he in turn put each of them on the tip of a finger and then carefully stuck the dyed contact lenses to his eyeballs.

David was now ready to attach the wigs to his face and scalp. In order to make them stick to him he pasted the non-toxic paper glue to his chin and head. When he had covered every part of himself that was necessary he attached both of the hairpieces into the correct positions.

The only item that David had not used which was in the pile of objects that he had requested off of Jimmy was the pair of scissors. He used these to trim his new beard and haircut, so that they appeared to be well grown and attended to. His transformation was now just one feature short of being complete. A few slaps to his cheeks brought just enough blood to the surface to make them red enough to match those of the individual who he was going to impersonate.

David now had to make sure that he would have enough time to get clear of the prison after he had escaped. He therefore had to get someone to replace him so as to make it look as if he was still there. This was not something that he could ask someone to do for him, so he was simply going to give the person who he had chosen to do the task absolutely no choice in the matter.

David had to make sure that his replacement looked like him and would not be able leave his cell. In order to achieve this he made another wig using the same procedure as

212

before, but with his own hair which he had cut off earlier. So that he could keep his victim from going anywhere he began to make his bed into a bondage rack. This he did by removing all of the covers apart from the top one and then ripped them up into strips. He then tightly twisted them around so that he ended up with several pieces of very strong rope. After he had tied each one to the metal frame of his bed he put back the top cover to hide its sinister alternative usage.

Now all that was left to do was for David to wait for his unknowing and unwilling impersonator to arrive. He put the black wig on his head and stood patiently facing the light of the window at the end of the cell. Soon he would be on his way to freedom.

It was not long before David heard the door behind him open, closely followed by a voice.

"No one escapes from Blackmoor, Cain." The sound of knuckles being tapped against iron interrupted the forewarning statement. "And that includes you."

David turned around and then gave his reply.

"You could not be more wrong."

This was followed by an extremely accurate and hard punch to Joseph McKinnie's chin. As the fist made contact there was low crunching noise as his jaw got pushed out of its socket. His head immediately lulled back and his eyes dizzily went in alternative directions.

Before Joseph McKinnie's limp body could slump to the floor David grabbed hold of him and threw him onto the bed. He then made his way over to his desk and picked up the razor. Sitting down next to the unconscious man he started to shave the hair off of the prison officer's head and chin.

As soon as Joseph was completely bald David took his security switch card and started to undress him. He then tied him face down onto the bed and gagged him. The prison officer's neck, arms and legs were all tightly tied to the metal frame so as to make sure that when he awoke he would not be able to move. For the finishing touches the wig with the black hair was glued onto his head and the top cover to the bed was pulled over his body so that he could not be recognised.

David now took off all of his own clothes and started to put on the prison officer's uniform. Just before he put on the peaked cap he got the razor and cut a small split down the back just so that his head could fit into it. He was now ready to leave.

For a couple of hours David stood outside the front of his own cell as if he were guarding against his own escape. As soon as the next prison officer approached from a distance to take over the watch he immediately turned and opened up the peep hole in the door as if to make it look as if he was being thorough in his duties. When he heard the footstep of his relief pull up close to him he spoke in a voice that perfectly mimicked Joseph's highland accent.

"The bastard's still in there." He nodded his head. "Aye! He won't be going anywhere."

There was an unenthusiastic reply.

"I'm pleased to hear it."

At that, David turned and left. As he walked through the prison wing he started to follow another guard up ahead of him so that he would know which way he would have to go in order to leave. Every now and again he reached a security point where he had to use the switch card and type in Joseph's personal identification number. This did not once cause a problem.

David soon reached a room that was full of lockers where there were a couple of guards who were putting their coats on. Without even pausing for thought he simply just reached into his trouser pocket and pulled out a bunch of keys. After sifting through them he came across one which had the number seventeen on it. He then casually walked up to the corresponding locker and opened it. Acting as if he was doing something that was quite normal to him he pulled out a coat that was hanging inside and put it on.

Once the prison officer who David had been following went on his way again he once more started to follow him all of the way out. When he reached the main gate he turned to have one last look out across the prison grounds. As he gazed around his eye was caught by a figure standing at a window on the top floor of one of the blocks. He slyly smiled to himself as he saw Howard Fenton stretch out his arms and yawn in a carefree manner.

David then walked out of Blackmoor prison never to return again.

A lone figure stood on the edge of a cliff looking out across the vast ocean. The sun shone against his pale skin making it glow a dull amber colour. There was a contemplative expression upon his face as thoughts of what was about to be passed through his mind.

It was no one's fault that he was there. There was little that anyone could have done to stop it. The plain truth was that David had simply contrived the perfect escape plan and the fact that he was now free from Blackmoor prison proved it beyond any doubt. He had just done exactly what he had said he would do and casually walked out of the front entrance. This may have seemed like an act of mockery, but the truth was that making the exceptionally difficult look extremely easy was just his way of doing things.

The heads of the people in the room all turned around to face the front as the detective superintendent paced into the office to announce the current state of affairs. There were police officers in plain clothes and uniform all gathered around with their attentions cast towards the man who was about to address them. This was not a meeting for the public or press alike, but was just for those who had the distasteful job of trying to put right what was wrong.

The tall greying detective superintendent coughed to clear his throat before starting his announcement.

"Good morning! You have all been called here for this meeting today to be informed that yesterday there was a breakout at Blackmoor prison. The inmate who escaped is known to be David Cain, the 'Starrow School Slaughterer.'" The depressing news was followed by some muffled remarks of disapproval. "We have informed the press and it'll be put out on the midday news today. We decided that it would be proper to let the public know due to the nature of the person who has escaped."

A stocky uniformed chief inspector took over.

"As some of you are probably aware, David Cain is considered to be extremely dangerous. This is a young man who apparently holds no value in human life and should only be approached by any of you when aided by back up. I'm sure that you've heard of the 'Omega' speech that he gave at his trial the moment before he was sentenced. This is a person who will have no qualms about killing if he's confronted."

The detective superintendent carried on.

"I'm sure you can appreciate how important it is that we catch him as soon as possible and put him back behind bars. We are going to start by putting twenty-four hour stakeouts on his mother's old house and his old school. We are also going to contact Blackmoor prison to find out if we can get any extra information about where he might go to." He pointed to a white board on the wall behind him. "We'll write down on the roster who will be doing what and you'll be given whatever surveillance equipment that you might need. OK, has anyone got any questions?"

A plain clothed officer raised his hand and when he received a nod off of the chief inspector he spoke aloud so that everyone in the office could hear him.

"Is it at all likely that he might go abroad?"

The detective superintendent answered.

"We don't know for sure, but it's quite likely he will not go too far away. There are few places that he can go to where he will know his surroundings."

A number of plain clothed and uniformed police officers now started to ask various questions each in turn and were alternatively answered by the detective inspector.

"Have we got any recent photographs of him?"

"Yes. The prison is providing those for us."

"Have we got any background info on him?"

"We're going to be sending some of you to conduct interviews with various people who might be able to help us in finding him, including members of his family and people who he used to be associated with."

"I thought Blackmoor prison was meant to have the highest security in the country. How did he escape?"

"We aren't informing the press of this, but apparently he just walked straight out the front gate wearing a prison officer's uniform."

"Is there any indication of what he is intending to do now that he is out?"

This question could not be answered.

215

A lone figure slowly paced along a winding country lane that was flanked by high dewdrop soaked grassy banks that rose above either side of the road. The fields beyond were freshly ploughed and created a rough colourless backdrop to the scene. As for the sparse amount of trees that were loosely scattered around the countryside their leaves had long fallen leaving just the skeletal twigs and branches which had once held the lush green hue that had adorned them.

The solitary young man who was steadily strolling along the lane seemed not to be in a hurry to get anywhere. Time was on his side, just as the odds were in his favour. Soon he would start the final part of his plan and all that he had ever dreamed of would come into fruition.

As David reached the top of a hill that peaked above the uneven countryside he took a moment to study his surroundings. The weather was typical for the middle of autumn and a strong wind immediately caught hold of his long black coat sending it fluttering about his body. This did not bother him due to having other things on his mind, so he just stayed facing head on into the full force of the gust regardless of its biting chill.

It was what David could see straight ahead of him that was what he had been searching for. In the distance towards the bottom of the road was a small farm with a number of barns and sheds. This was his destination and would be the starting place of his machinations. After a quick glance around at the surrounding countryside to make sure that nobody was watching him he intently went on his way.

The usual sounds of livestock could be heard as David strolled onto the courtyard of the farm. There was a small bungalow, a chicken house, horse stables and two large barns which were probably used for holding machinery with various other aids for tending crops. It seemed as though everything that he needed was there, so he went about putting his plan into action.

David shouted just loud enough so that anyone in the surrounding buildings could hear him.

"Hello! Is anyone here?"

After a short while the front door to the bungalow opened and a middle-aged woman stepped out. She was short and had quite a stocky frame. Her appearance was rather scruffy, probably due to previously being involved in various tasks in and around the farm. She wore a dress that was stained with mud and a dull coloured cardigan that had its fair share of holes.

The woman spoke with a strong countryside accent.

"Hello! Can I help you?"

David forced a slight welcoming smile.

"Good morning! I'm looking for Mr Henley. Is he around?"

"No, he's in the fields gathering in the sheep." The woman started to walk towards David. "Is there anything I can do for you?"

"I hope so. My lorry broke down just up the road and a passerby said that Mr Henley or one of his workers from his farm would be able to help. Are they here?"

"I'm afraid not. We only have one other hand here and he's with my husband."

"Well, that's alright." A wry smile crossed David's face. "In fact, that's perfect."

The middle-aged woman sat in an unconscious state, tied by a long piece of rope to a straight backed wooden chair in the centre of the kitchen. Her head was flopping down to one side and a trickle of dribble was seeping from her mouth. There were no bruises on her head or body and it appeared as though she was asleep.

David had simply pushed his fingers into the pressure point of the woman's neck so as to cut off the circulation to her head and knock her unconscious. He had no wish to make her go through any unnecessary pain even though it was his full intention at a later date to take her life along with every other human being on the planet. Death was not a sport for him to enjoy, it was just something that he had to do every now and again. So, for now he would just keep her out of his way by bounding her as opposed to prematurely killing her.

After waiting for about thirty minutes whilst sitting next to the unconscious woman in the kitchen David heard a tractor pull up outside of the house in the courtyard. He immediately stood up and went to stand by the hinged part of the door so that when it opened he would be hidden behind it ready for whoever was to walk in. The wait did not last long.

As the door swung open the rough voice of a middle aged man called out.

"I'm home, Harriet. Could you put the kettle..." The sudden realisation. "What the hell...?"

David's agility was quick enough to take the already stunned farmer completely by surprise. He grabbed hold of the side of the middle aged man's neck with his fingers and squeezed. After approximately three seconds there were now two unconscious people in the kitchen of the bungalow.

With the knowledge that there was only one person left to subdue, David made his way out into the courtyard and approached a young man whose back was to him whilst knocking the mud off of a tractor with a stick. At first, he just kept on quickly walking towards his victim making the most of the fact that his presence had not yet been noticed. It was only when he was within feet of the target that his footsteps were heard.

The young man slowly turned around thinking that it was his employer who was approaching him, but when he saw a person who he did not recognise a slightly perplexed expression crossed his face. He seemed as though he was just about to speak, but he never got the chance. David grabbed hold of his neck and dug his fingers deep into the sides. There was a slight struggle at first, but it did not last long and soon there were three unconscious people on the farm. Everything was, of course, going to plan.

David now had to make sure that he had somewhere to put his hostages where they would not be able to escape from. There was a cellar under the bungalow that could be got to via a trap door that could be locked on the outside with a large block of wood. It seemed to be a suitable enough place to keep them and had no other routes of escape. One by one, being careful not to be seen, he dragged them in and tied them up.

It took David about an hour to search around the farm and make sure that it provided him with just about everything that he needed. In one of the barns he found a truck for carrying a small amount of sheep and in a reinforced metal shed a large stockpile of industrial weed killer. The main bedroom of the house had a metal cupboard that he had got the key to from the farmer's pocket and had opened it up to reveal two shotguns and several boxes of ammunition. Other instruments which he had acquired included a dark blue rubber chemical proof suit with breathing apparatus used for spraying insecticides, a collection of small cages for transporting chickens, a reel of cable and an old fashioned alarm clock which had two bells and a hammer on top.

David now had the tools as well as the machinations to complete his plan.

A voice called out from the entrance of the police station canteen.

"Derek, the detective super' wants you!"

"Yeah, cheers!"

"Find Louise Walken as well, will you! He wants to see the both of you."

Detective sergeant Derek Hickey looked up from reading his newspaper and smiled.

"Walken! That's a marriage made in heaven, isn't it?"

"Well, they say opposites attract." A sarcastic reply.

With a muffled grunt Derek got up out of his chair and started to make his way out of the canteen. He was quite pleased to be partnered with Louise Walken due to his liking for the inexperienced police officer who had just come straight out of training college. It was nothing lustful. He just liked the attitude of the feisty young recruit. The two of them got on well together and they often shared a joke about their lack of sexual compatibility, what with him having a distinct lack of physical fitness and her youthful good looks. Besides, he was happily married and was the proud father of two children.

A veteran in the police for over fifteen years, Derek had joined in his early twenties and had left a career in estate agency well behind. Since then he had learnt virtually everything there was to know about the job and was considered by his colleagues as being one of the more valuable members of the criminal investigation department. Although he had never progressed beyond the level of sergeant his methods and opinions on procedures were well respected amongst all of the ranks.

To look at, Derek appeared to be more like the office worker that he once was what with a large belly that protruded over his belt. He did not go much on exercise and his diet rarely consisted of all of the required food groups. All this did not matter to him though, as long as he could smell out a criminal and chalk up a conviction, he was quite happy with his physical state.

As Derek made his way through one of the station corridors he came to pass the rest room. There were windows that he could look through to see who was in there and he noticed Louise Walken sitting talking to a uniformed woman constable. With two knocks on the glass he called out to her in a playful manner.

"Constable Walken, the detective super' wants you to water the plants in his office. Best you get along there!"

He then went on his way without waiting for a reply and with a smile upon his face. Louise turned to see who had spoken to her just to catch a glimpse of the person walking off. When she realised that it was Derek who had called out in such a way she turned to the woman constable next to her and grinned

"Cheeky sod!" A showing of her true feelings for him then followed. "Bless him!"

Louise was quite aware of Derek's dry sense of humour, as it was very akin to her own. She enjoyed working with the middle-aged man and found it very productive what with his years of experience rubbing off on her. Although she took her job very seriously, she still, nevertheless, managed to keep her sense of humour.

After leaving school it was Louise's first ambition to get a degree at university in order to become a physiotherapist, but with the want for a more exciting line of work she chose a career in the police force. Her family and friends had repeatedly questioned her over her seemingly ridiculous decision, but she had been recalcitrant with her choice and stubbornly went through with what she wanted to do with her life.

At six foot tall and having quite a muscular physique, Louise was quite a daunting site for most of the criminal elements she encountered. She had been doing gym work for a number of years now, but had still managed to keep her femininity. With medium length brunette hair and captivating blue eyes she could also quite easily arrest a man's heart.

With the request to go to the detective superintendent's office Louise realised that she was obviously going to be given something quite important to do. After a quick smile to the female officer who she had just been talking to, she went on her way.

"I need you two to go to Blackmoor prison tomorrow and talk to the psychiatrist there about David Cain. His name's Richard Lewis and he'll be expecting you."

Detective superintendent Gareth Hillier sat with an expressionless look upon his face as he spoke to the two plain-clothes officers in front of him. He wore a dull grey suit and a dour coloured tie. His tone of voice did little to excite as well, but, nevertheless, Derek and Louise sat listening intently as the he gave them their orders.

"What I want you to do is, see if he has any idea of where Cain might be or if he knows what he's trying to do. You also better tell him that we might need him here at the station at a later date if anything else occurs that we'll need his advice on." He sat back in his chair and gave a slight nod of the head. "That'll be all."

At that, the two of them got up and left.

Richard had met the two police officers at the front entrance of Blackmoor prison and was now walking with them to his office. Derek and Louise both had to show their warrant cards in order to gain access and had then been given temporary security cards so that they could pass through the security check points at the ends of each of the corridors. Police officers were not even trusted in this place. Not that it now had the same faultless reputation for the detainment of prisoners that it had once boasted.

As Richard led the two police officers through the corridors of the prison he tried to inform them of the magnitude of the task ahead of them.

"You've got your work cut out for you. He'll be about half a dozen steps ahead of you by now."

"What do you mean?" Derek replied.

"Well, he won't be staying in just one place. He'll be constantly travelling around doing whatever he needs to do and then move on."

Louise spoke inquisitive manner.

"Do you think that he's planning on doing something in particular then?"

"Very much so." Richard turned to face her as he walked. "He won't be moving around from place to place just so that he doesn't get caught. He'll be doing it so he can do whatever he needs to do."

Derek made a scornful remark.

"I see. He wants to carry out that 'Omega' speech, does he? He's contriving our demise."

Richard did not make any reply and just wore a forlorn expression upon his face as he came to stop outside of his office. He knew that the person who they were talking about had every intention of wiping out all of humanity and he did not feel like treating the matter with anything less than the recognition that it deserved. As he put the key into the lock and turned it he spoke in a forewarning manner.

"When David Cain was in this prison he took full advantage of our biggest weakness. We underestimated him. And believe me, we paid for it." He pushed open the door and stood back to let both of the officers in. "If you also make the same mistake as us then it won't just be you who regrets it."

As Derek stepped into the office he made it clear that he was less than convinced by Richard's excessive opinion of David's capabilities.

"You can't really think that he's capable of killing off the entire human race?"

After the two officers had made their way into the room Richard closed the door behind them and then answered the question.

"Even though it sounds quite unlikely, I simply don't know for sure whether he could accomplish something like that." He stood with a thoughtful expression upon his face whilst he contemplated what he was about to say. "But what I am sure of is that he will try to do what he has threatened to. He will make a concerted effort to bring about the genocide of the human race."

Whether Louise wanted more answers because it was her job to get them or through her own fear was not totally apparent.

"How can you be so sure that he really meant what he said in that 'Omega' speech?" She shrugged her shoulders in a dumfounded gesture. "I know that he killed three people when he was a schoolboy and some inmates since, but I still find it hard to believe that he would even attempt to do something that seems so impossible."

As the three of them sat down at the desk in the middle of the office Richard recalled the conversation he had with David when he had asked the scheming inmate why he wanted to annihilate the entire human race.

"I once spoke to him about the 'Omega' speech. I must confess I wasn't at all prepared for what he said to me. There I was expecting him to say that he was going to do something totally impractical, like go around murdering everybody one by one, but then he came out with something that made me felt like someone had just danced on my grave." As he bowed his head a distant expression crossed his face. "Cain spoke as if he had some kind of godlike powers. It was almost as if he thought that he could kill a billion people and then create his own new race afterwards just by will alone. He really was convinced that he could wipe the human race out of existence. It was at that point when I realised that regardless of whether it was possible or not, he was still going to try to kill us all regardless."

Derek made his scepticism clear.

"David Cain might be a mass murderer, but there's absolutely no way that he could just cause some kind of holocaust."

Louise was a bit less incredulous.

"Well, he doesn't seem to be putting in any lack of effort into attempting whatever he intends to do. He's already escaped from the highest security prison in the country and now he's seemingly disappeared off of the face of the Earth." She passed on the opportunity of assumption to the psychiatrist. "Do you really think that Cain is that dangerous?"

Richard felt that there was nothing that he could do but to let his true feelings show.

"David Cain is the most intelligent person that I have ever met and because of that I have more fear of him than any other man that I've ever met. He has what can only be described as a super intelligence." He looked Louise straight in the eye. "You see, the truth is that we will really struggle to find him and in the mean time while we're looking for him he will take the lives of innocent people. It's something that we simply can't do anything to prevent."

Even Derek was taken aback by the stark reality of this remark. All he wanted to do was play down the possibilities of David being as big a threat as everyone else seemed to think that he was. However, not even he could doubt that there would be lives lost if this particular psychopathic convict were not caught as soon as possible.

A shroud of silence had now covered the office as the realisation of just how grim the situation was that they were in. As the three of them sat there with gaunt expressions upon their faces none of them made any attempt to ease the now morose atmosphere. They had just been talking about a person who wanted all three of them, their families and everyone else they knew dead. It was a conversation so dark and seemingly without solution that it was more horrifying than their worst nightmares.

Concrete chimneys reached up to the sky as if they were pillars holding up the clouds, huge iron gas containers stood like tower blocks amongst the diminutive buildings that stood below and a myriad of twisting metallic pipes wound themselves around each and every one of the structures imposing a unity amongst them all.

This was Tarbon Incorporated Chemical Plant where the seeds had seemingly been sown for it all to have somehow begun and it was now about to harvest the culmination of the end. It was a fitting piece of irony that humanity would see the source of its destruction start at the same place where the cause of David's disfigurement had been bestowed upon him. His deformity had inadvertently led to the impending mutilation of society.

The people in the surrounding streets of the chemical plant carried on with whatever they were doing with an understandable lack of realisation of what was about to be unleashed upon them. It was a cold calm before the storm. A red autumn sun was setting on the horizon and above it an almost clear sky that was adorned with a handful of grey clouds that were tinted with a warm shade of orange. Such a tranquil scene seemed somehow fitting. The last normal day of life as humanity knew it was a beautiful one coloured by the paintbrush of Mother Nature.

David stood looking at the chemical plant through the wire fence that surrounded the outskirts of the grounds. The small truck that he had stolen from the farm was parked on the road next to him. Inside it were all the things that he needed to accomplish his machinations. After his mind went over the entirety of his plan for one last time he took a single deep breath and then went about fulfilling his destiny.

A van pulled out of the front entrance of the chemical plant and drove down the road that went along side the edge of the grounds. The driver was an engineer who had just finished his day at work and was now on his way home. It was while he was wondering what his wife had cooked him for his dinner that a man walked into the middle of the road in front of him and hailed him to stop.

Thinking that something could be wrong and that he might be able to help, the engineer pulled up at the curb just in front of a muddy looking truck. As he wound down the window of the van the man in the road started to walk towards his side of the vehicle. After turning down the radio he spoke in a polite and approachable tone of voice.

"Are you alright mate?"

There was no answer.

David sharply opened the door of the van with one hand and grabbed the driver around the neck with the other. Dragging the choking man out of the vehicle he held him down to the ground until the blood supply was cut off to the brain resulting in unconsciousness. He then carried the limp body over to the passenger side of the farm truck, opened the door and then unceremoniously shoved him in. After a quick glance around to make sure that nobody had seen him he got into the driver's side and then immediately started to strip the engineer of his work overalls and security pass. The necessary disguise had now been attained.

As soon as David was dressed in the correct attire in order to enter the plant he started to unload some of the things out of the truck that he had taken from the farm and put them into the back of the engineer's van. He then got in himself and drove towards the entrance of the chemical plant. When he reached the barrier at the checkpoint most of the other workers were leaving due to it being the end of their working day. It did not take long for a member of security to approach him and ask for his identification. The photograph on the pass that he handed over did not look too similar to him, but he had correctly anticipated that the guard would pay little attention to detail and after a carefree nod of the head in response he was allowed to continue through the gates.

As David drove through the grounds of the chemical plant he passed a number of very large cylindrical containers that were all labelled with danger signs warning of toxic chemicals. It was only when he came to one that was about thirty metres high and wide that he finally found his target. This one had all kinds of warning notices attached to it including one that read 'Poisonous Flammable Liquid'.

David parked within inches of the side of the large cylindrical container and then opened the engine bonnet of the van. Using a spanner that he had taken from the engineer's toolbox he unscrewed the bolts that held in the car battery and then removed it. He then went around to the rear of the van and opened up the double doors. In the back were most of the things that he had taken from the farm.

At a steady and measured pace David proceeded to put on the rubber chemical suit and the breathing apparatus used for the spraying of fertilisers on crops. As soon as he was fully covered up he got a screwdriver and started to split open the six large sacks of industrial weed killer which were already blended together with a large amount of sugar and the gunpowder from the several boxes of shotgun cartridges. After unwinding the reel of cable he put one end of it into the spillage of the volatile mixture which was now pouring out into the van and split the other end so that one part of it was connected to the negative bolt of the car battery and the other tied to the hammer of the old-fashioned alarm clock. He then laid it on top of the battery with one of the bells resting upon the positive connection. The fact that it was already set to go off in two minutes time was a declaration of how well he had even calculated the timing of his plan.

Adorned with the dark blue chemical proof suit and the breathing apparatus David made his way towards the grounds on the edge of the chemical plant. When he got to the fence that surrounded the whole of the proximity he clasped his hands upon the wire and bowed his head. He then braced himself.

Three seconds later it turned six o'clock.

Derek strolled into the criminal investigation office on the third floor of the police station after returning from the visit to Blackmoor prison. He immediately made his way over to the coffee percolator and proceeded to pour some of the thick dark liquid into a mug. After putting in three large spoonfuls of sugar and giving it a stir he turned to speak to Louise who was now sitting at her desk.

"Well, what do you think about all that then?"

"I think Cain's set quite an impression on Mr Lewis." Came the reply.

"He did seem to overrate his capabilities, didn't he?" Derek wore a thoughtful expression upon his face. "I'm not saying that Cain isn't dangerous, but he's not the next Adolph Hitler."

Louise sat back in her chair and sighed.

"I think Mr Lewis was just trying to tell us not to underestimate him."

Derek had other ideas.

"You don't believe all that about him having a super intelligence, do you?" He walked over to stand by a window that looked out over the town of Starrow and carried on talking with his back to Louise. "These escaped convicts are rarely out there for more than a week anyway. He'll be lucky if he gets to swat a fly, let alone kill the entire human race."

It then turned six o'clock.

As the hammer hit the bell on the alarm clock it immediately produced a fizzing spark. This burst of energy was then instantaneously dwarfed by a massive eruption as the van that was packed with the explosive burst into a ball of flames. However, it was what followed next that really shook the town of Starrow. The large cylindrical container that held the poisonous flammable liquid got caught in the blast and within a fraction of a second created a mountain of raging fire that engulfed almost a quarter of the chemical plant.

Flames shot into the air like talons clawing at the sky, whilst an ominous dark green cloud instantly rose up about them. The searing heat caused a number of other liquid and gas filled canisters to erupt creating a dominoes effect of explosions. It was almost as if hell had come to the town of Starrow and had brought its dark evil with it.

The shock wave from the blast had hit David full on the back, but due to him being a reasonable distance away and having a firm grasp upon the wire fence in front of him he was only slightly shaken. When he was sure that the main impact of the blast had subsided he lowered his arms down by his side and took a step back. He then went to leave the chemical plant.

All around David was pure pandemonium as he steadily paced amongst the chaos that he had bestowed upon Tarbon Incorporated. Whilst he was leaving via the security gate there were numerous thunderous explosions accompanied the screeching noise of sirens sounding out like a chorus of high pitched screams. As he got into the farm truck and drove off he took a look back to see what he had left in his wake. The scene was exactly what he had hoped to see. Towering flames engulfed buildings, whilst an ever enlarging dark green cloud hovered above like a swarm of demonic wasps.

Success had been the only acceptable outcome of David's machinations and it had certainly been obtained.

Derek stood gazing out of the window across the town when a large flash in the distance suddenly caught his eye. He squinted at first to shut out the bright light and then looked across the horizon in an attempt to verify where it had come from. It was at that point when a thundering clap hit the police station.

Derek instantaneously dropped his coffee mug and let it smash against the floor.

"What the hell was that?"

The sudden roaring explosion had now gained the attention of Louise and the rest of the police officers in the room. There was a clattering of chairs and tables as they clambered across the office to look out of the window. In the distance there was a bright glow which had lit up the streets all around it. However, after a while the light slowly began to be smothered by a dark cloud that had started to rise up over the town. As the setting sun slowly lowered down to rest upon the horizon it shone through the mist and bathed the whole of Starrow in a ghostly green hue.

Louise just uttered one sullen word.

"Cain!"

No one knew what the high pitched sound meant. Some of the people shopping in the streets just paused for a moment and then carried on going about their business. Office workers hardly even noticed the extra sound what with the abundance of computer induced noises that they experienced on a daily basis. The children in the playgrounds gave no thought to the distant noise that was virtually being drowned out anyway by their screaming as they were playing games.

It was only when it became visually clear that the danger became apparent. There was not a person in the town of Starrow who did not realise that something was now very wrong. As the dark green cloud slowly hovered above them the inevitable panic set in.

Cars swerved into each other as the drivers looked up to the skies. People ran aimlessly as their senses guided them in no particular direction. It seemed like the chaotic confusion would never cease until ever so gradually the screaming and shouting suddenly started to subside. The toxic cloud that had been hovering above had now started to lose its heat and was slowly lowering down onto the occupants of streets below.

As the bemused people started to gag and cough their hysterical cries became less audible. Some covered their faces with their clothing, whilst those who were near buildings rushed inside closing the windows and doors behind them. After about five minutes every street in the near proximity of the chemical plant was enshrouded with the phantasmal green mist. It was those who were still caught up in its vapour that began to pay the price.

A woman who was pushing a pram with one hand and was leading her young son with the other had been walking along a quiet suburban street which was lined with houses both sides. As the mist lowered about her she had at first tried to run away from it in an attempt to get back to her own home. This, however, was a futile effort and the toxic vapour immediately started to take an effect on her.

The woman started to drowsily stumble about and unintentionally let go of her son's hand without knowing. When she realised what she had done she let go of the pram and went to stagger back to get her child. In a weary and delirious state she made her way along the path knocking into a number of garden walls along the way. It was when she reached her son that she found him slumped down on the edge of the curb in an unconscious state.

The grim sights that followed moments later were almost as if it were a scene from a war zone. Even in her confused state the woman had somehow managed to summon what senses of survival she still had left and was now making her way along the street with her children in tow. As she uncontrollably stumbled with each faltering step she unwittingly held her unconscious son upside down by one of his legs whilst dragging the scraping pram along on its side behind her with her baby half hanging out.

This was just one of many horrific casualties that the inhabitants of Starrow Town endured that day. Those who were old and frail choked to death, whereas as others who had only been within the clutches of the mist for a short while received severe burns to their skin. However, what the people did not know was that they had only witnessed just the beginning of David's wrath.

As the news program on the television set showed live footage taken from a helicopter of the devastation a correspondent described the pictures in a voice over.

"The scenes at the Tarbon Chemical plant the day after the explosions that rocked the local area are ones of total destruction. Most of the company buildings have either been totally levelled or have at least been rendered completely inoperative. Fires are still burning out of control and there's a thin green mist sitting on the streets of Starrow Town. The police have instructed everyone within a five-mile radius of the plant to either leave the town or stay inside their homes and make themselves makeshift gas masks out of handkerchiefs or cloths. I must say, that in all of my twenty years as a correspondent I have never witnessed such a horrifying sight of obliteration."

The footage was replaced by a newsreader sitting in a studio.

"So far there are no confirmed reports of how this could have happened, but what with the recent escape of David Cain, 'The Starrow School Slaughterer', from Blackmoor prison, some people are suggesting that this could be him carrying out the threat of his now infamous 'Omega' speech."

The television set was turned off and a silence immediately swept over the office. There were at least two dozen uniformed and plain clothed police officers waiting to hear their latest instructions on how to deal with the dismal situation. With the lull seemingly to be his cue, Detective superintendent Gareth Hillier paced up to the front of the office and addressed those gathered before him.

"Early reports have revealed that a man hijacked a Tarbon Incorporated company vehicle and entered the chemical plant. The description of the person matches that of David Cain, but we cannot be certain yet if it actually was him. We believe that the van that was taken was used to transport a large amount of explosive into the grounds of the plant that was then detonated next to a large container of a poisonous flammable liquid. We've called for extra police support from five of the surrounding counties to deal with the catastrophe. We can't send anyone into the plant yet due to the toxins that are still in the air, but protective clothing is now on its way. That's the situation so far." He made a gesture pointing to a man standing to his left and then changed the course of his oration. "Right, we have Richard Lewis here who is the psychiatrist of the prison which Cain escaped from. He has some ideas of why the chemical plant was targeted and what we should expect next. So, if you could give him your attention please!"

Richard had been leaning up against a wall, but when his introduction was made he stood up straight and went about explaining his own theories to everyone in the room of why all this was happening.

"Good morning! I'd like to start by saying that I am just about certain that this is the work of David Cain. It definitely fits his modus operandi. Everything was planned to perfection. His entrance into the plant was completely undetected. The quantity of explosive he used appeared to be the exactly right amount, and his choice of which chemical container to target for the maximum amount of destruction was faultless. He has without a doubt succeeded in accomplishing the first thing he has set out to do." He sighed in a conceding manner. "He's taken us completely by surprise."

The sudden realisation that David Cain had been successful in the first part of whatever he was trying to achieve made the police officers on the room starkly aware of the fact that he was already at least one step ahead of them. Those of them who had been expecting him to be just another ex-convict on the loose who would in time be caught with the minimal amount of damage caused had now been bluntly educated in the reality of the situation. As the true seriousness of the predicament became apparent the expressions upon their faces turned quite gaunt.

As Richard carried on giving his grim views on the matter he felt the mood of the people in the room become increasingly uneasy.

"In case any of you thought that the problem of David Cain was not that great or would not be around for long you could not be more wrong. Make no mistake; we are now playing catch up. He's spent a long time planning all of this and everything that he does now he has already meticulously thought about time and time again before. This is all simply putting in action what he has previously practised in his mind probably a thousand times before. Whilst he was in Blackmoor he used his time to educate himself in a number of different academic subjects, including chemistry. This is probably why he was able to make such a large explosive device and choose exactly the right chemical to ignite." He took a moment to pause for thought. "As for why David Cain targeted the chemical plant, well I believe that he did it to use up our resources, so that we can't afford to use the manpower looking for him. Although this may seem to have worked for him it has, however, helped us ascertain one thing. If he wanted us to concentrate on something local to Starrow Town then we can be quite sure that whatever he is about to do next will be in this area. Unfortunately, the most important question that still remains is what he plans to do next. To this, I'm afraid I have no answer."

The last sentence earned a stony silence throughout the office.

All of the offices in the building looked as though the inhabitants had left in a hurry. Computer screens and lights were still on and all of the doors had been left open. The only thing that stirred was the constant wailing noise of the security alarm system.

David was still wearing the rubber chemical proof suit as he walked through the offices at a steady pace whilst constantly searching for the entrance to the section of the building which held the necessary pieces of equipment that he would need for the next part of his plan. After passing through a number of corridors he came across a sliding glass door. There was a sign above it that signified what was in the room beyond and on the wall next to it was a security switch card port. He took a moment to read what was written on the sign and then walked back into an office nearby.

225

A short while later David came back holding a chair in both hands. With one almighty hurl he threw it straight at the glass door immediately shattering it. He then turned around and left in the same way as which he had come. Such an act would normally have triggered the security alarms around the building, but as they were already going off it did not make much of a difference.

As David strolled out of the building and into the car park he went to the back of the farm truck and opened it up. Stored in it were about twenty cages which all held three chickens in each, some of which had laid eggs. One by one, he collected each of the cages and took them into the section of the building which he had just gained access to.

Yet another phase of David's plan was now about to be completed.

Richard sat at the same desk as Louise and Derek in the criminal investigation department of the police station. He uneasily supped at a cup of tea whilst he stared at a map of Starrow Town on the wall to the side of him. A wistful expression crossed his face as he spoke in a contemplative manner.

"He's out there somewhere." He glumly bowed his head and breathed out a deep sigh. "He's just got the whole bloody thing worked out."

Louise tried to throw some light on the situation.

"Well, we know he's local. We've just got to eliminate all of the places where there would be no point in him going." She gazed at the map with a pensive look upon her face. "He might even be right under our noses."

Some ideas now started to enter Richard's head and as he began to make a less defeatist approach to the problem he sat up straight in a more exerted posture.

"You're right. We can start by cancelling out all of the average shops and houses in the town. There would be no point in him staying around here for something which he could find anywhere else in the country."

Derek now started to join in.

"There are still a lot of places which he might be able to find some use of." He gave a short list. "Schools, factories, banks and anywhere else that any average thief would find something worth stealing should all be considered."

Louise nodded her head in agreement.

"It would probably be best just to work out which of all of the places in Starrow would store the most dangerous things that he could get his hands on."

There was a tone of plain obviousness in Richard's voice as he spoke.

"Well, he's already been there, hasn't he?" He pointed to the edge of the map on the wall which had a large red ring drawn around it. "The chemical plant's got the most dangerous chemicals for miles around, but he's already hit there."

Louise made a grim suggestion.

"He might've gone back there to get some chemicals for making some kind of dangerous gas. Do you think we should find out if they keep anything there that could be made into a nerve gas?"

Derek instantaneously picked up his phone and began to dial a number.

"It'll take a while to find out, but it's all we've got so far. I'll contact the emergency line and start making inquiries."

It was not a massive step, but by the three of them trying to think in the same way as David it seemed like a good way to start. What with Louise's young vitalised mind, Derek's years of experience and Richard's psychoanalysis, they could well become a good team. All they needed now was a bit of luck.

226

The blackness of night seemed to be darker than normal around the buildings near the chemical plant. No lights were on and nothing stirred. It was now a desolate part of town where no one dared to stray. That is, of course, apart from one person.

It was a lonesome sight as David sat in the middle of a large room with just a couple of small lamps shining in his direction to give him light. There were no windows to allow in any extra illumination and the skylights were filled in with concrete. Although the atmosphere was dim and cheerless it was also quiet and free from any disturbances.

David had dispensed with the rubber chemical proof suit, but was still wearing the breathing apparatus. For the last eighteen hours he had been hard at work and had not allowed himself a single break. He was now carrying out the most important part of his whole plan and was executing it with his usual decisiveness. Every calculation he made was determined without error and every action he carried out was skilfully undertaken to perfection. Not a thought was wasted or a corner cut.

These creations would be the greatest of David's achievements yet.

It had now been four days since the destruction of the chemical plant and the police had still not got any nearer to catching their main culprit. Masses of uniformed officers had carried out searches of the streets that were considered to be safe, whereas those who had protective clothing scoured the danger zone. It was, nevertheless, all in vain. David was nowhere to be seen.

Derek had made a number of phone calls to try to contact some of the managers of Tarbon Incorporated so that he could get some details of whether there were any chemicals stored at the plant which could be used for making nerve gas. Unfortunately, most of them were either dead or were still in hospital. It was only after trying every hour for a whole night and morning that he had finally been put through to the home of one of the engineering managers. As he was speaking on the phone the tone of his voice revealed the nature of the news that he was hearing.

"We were wondering if there was anything kept there that could be used in the production of nerve gas." A dejected expression crossed Derek's face as he slowly bowed his head. "I see. Thank you for your help."

Louise approached with two cups of coffee in her hands.

"What did he say?"

"There's nothing there that could be used to make any kind of nerve gas."

"That's good news, isn't it?" Louise put one of the cups of coffee in front of Derek. "At least we know he hasn't got hold of anything that dangerous."

"I suppose so, but it just means that we still haven't got a clue what Cain's up to."

Louise sat down and then passed a piece of paper across the desk.

"I've got a list here of the companies that were abandoned due to the explosion at the plant." She opened the top draw of her desk and pulled out a packet of biscuits that she began to open. "It's got what they produce as well."

Derek took the piece of paper and had a quick glance down the list of products of the companies.

"Children's toys, hi-fi equipment, contraception manufacturers... I hope they weren't doing a quality control check at the time." A smile crossed his face, but was then suddenly replaced by a look of inquisitiveness. "The last one on here is a microbiology laboratory."

Louise had just taken a bite of a biscuit and was now trying to lick the crumbs from around her lips.

"That's where they do things with viruses and diseases, isn't it?"

Derek looked up from the list and gave just a low spirited, one word answer.

"Yes."

227

There was a loud knock on detective superintendent Gareth Hillier's door, but he responded with an unenthusiastic and sullen reply.

"Come in!"

Derek did not waste any time in entering and immediately started to report his findings.

"I think we might have an idea of where he is, Sir!" He passed the list of company names across the desk. "If Cain is planning on doing what I think he is then he will be at Virbac Limited Microbiology Laboratory which is in the Haven Farm Industrial Estate, just three hundred yards from the chemical plant."

"How do you know?"

"It was abandoned at the time of the explosion. We got in contact with the owners and they said that they have not sent anyone back there since, not even to feed the chimpanzees and rats that they keep there. We also spoke to Richard Lewis, the psychiatrist from Blackmoor Prison. He told us that David Cain read a number of books on microbiology when he was locked up. That means he knows about such things as the AIDS virus, influenza and all kinds of killer diseases." Derek leant forward and pointed a finger at the name on the bottom of the list. "If he's going to be anywhere, it's there."

Gareth immediately stood up and spoke in a determined tone of voice.

"I want every officer who's out on the streets called in, I need breathing apparatus for as many them as possible and the armed response units as well." He paused for a moment and then gave a slight nod of his head. "Let's hope that this is a start."

The twilight dusk was lit up with a sea of flashing blue lights and searching torch beams. A helicopter hovered overhead and shone a spotlight on the entrance to the Virbac Microbiology Laboratory. There were over a hundred police officers, some of which were armed, all surrounding the building ensuring that there would be no escape for anyone who was inside. This was one operation that there would be no unnecessary chances taken.

Derek and Louise had been joined by Richard at the station and were now sitting outside of the laboratory in an unmarked squad car watching what was happening. They were all wearing face masks so as not to breathe in any toxic vapours that might still be in the air. Before they had come out they had been told that there was now no need for them to wear any protective clothing, so they had just rushed out of the station as they were. As they waited patiently for things to get going there was suddenly a call on the radio.

"Alpha Romeo Uniform is go, go, go!"

A number of the police cars then started to move aside just as a black transit passed through the middle of them and pulled up outside the laboratory. Six armed officers who were all wearing gas masks and bullet proof jackets filed out of the back of the van and immediately surrounded the entrance. After some shouting amongst themselves they ran in and disappeared out of sight.

About five minutes went by before anything else happened. When it finally did the six men walked out of the laboratory in dejected postures and with their guns lowered by their sides. There was then another call over the radio.

"The area is clear. Repeat! The area is clear."

This was then followed by a multitude of downhearted murmurs amongst all of the police officers surrounding the building.

After the laboratory had been announced as being empty, Derek, Louise and Richard had been allowed in to investigate. They had been told that the air inside the building was breathable so they had now removed their face masks. It appeared as though someone had

228

been there and it certainly looked as though something had been going on, but they simply did not know what. However, something they were sure of was that whoever had been there knew the nature of place they were in and what they were doing.

A glass door had been smashed which lead to a restricted area that had a sign at the entrance that read 'Viral and Bacterial Department - Authorised Personnel Only - Dangerous Biological Agents Within'. This was a particularly large room used for laboratory work that had no windows and had the skylights filled in. Kept in a number of other rooms attached to it were caged animals for the usage of experiments. These included chimpanzees, rats and also some chickens that seemed to have only just been recently added to the collection.

It appeared as though something very peculiar had been occurring, so in an attempt to throw some light on the situation the doctors who worked for the company had been called in to see if they could make sense of it all. Two of them had come to the laboratory and for the last three hours had been trying to ascertain what had been going on. They had checked all of the animal specimens to see if they had been subjected to anything unusual and they had examined a number of viral and bacterial samples that had been left lying around on the worktops.

One of the doctors was in his mid-fifties and the other had just turned thirty. Henry was the older of the two and was almost entirely bald. He spoke at a very slow pace and had a permanent unhurried disposition. Edward had a look about him that suggested that he was just out of university and he appeared to be somewhat over enthusiastic. His hair was neatly combed into a quiff and his clothes under his white coat were of the latest fashion.

Whilst the two doctors had been searching around they had regularly stopped to confer with each other about their findings and every time they had done so they had negatively shaken their heads in a disapproving manner. It seemed as though they were either just as dumfounded as everyone else about what had been going on or that what they had been discovering was making them rather anxious. Whatever it was that was seemingly worth so much of their attention was certainly of a malevolent nature.

Whilst all this was happening Richard, Louise and Derek had been instructed by the detective superintendent to wait around in the laboratory. As soon as any findings were made they were to gather the information and if need be get extra clarification on any details that might be considered too vague. It took some time for anything to happen and when it did it was the older of the two doctors, Henry who approached them with a less than clear theory of what had been going on.

"What has happened here is without a doubt very ominous." He looked at his partner and shook his head. "We think that whoever has been here has, among other things, been trying to cultivate viruses and bacteria."

Derek stepped forward and tried to get the doctor to elaborate on his claim.

"I don't understand." His brow furrowed inquisitively. "Do you mean that if it was Cain who's been here, he's been trying to grow viruses and bacteria?"

"Not exactly. He's been trying to alter the biological structure of current viral and bacterial samples that we already had here. Unfortunately, it looks like he's succeeded." Henry walked over towards his partner. "Edward will explain in greater detail."

Derek, Louise and Richard paced over to a table at the centre of the room that had a large microscope and a number of chicken eggs on it. It seemed odd that these should be at the centre of their attention, but there appeared to be little else worth starting with. After all, there did not seem to be a lot around here making much sense anyway.

Edward was sitting on a high stool and turned to face them as he started to give his version of events.

"All of these embryonated eggs that have been left here have been coated in iodine to disinfect them and have then had small holes drilled into them. It appears as though someone has been injecting viruses into them. We've also managed to get some samples of the viral cells from inside the eggs that were left and have put them under a microscope. This is where we found something really strange. They've all been injected with the influenza type 'A' virus, but in different cavities of the egg. There were some which we found injected in the amniotic and the chorioallantoic cavities, but it was what was in the allantoic cavity that really caught our attention." He put his hand on the microscope. "The viral cells have somehow been made to mutate. Not only have they grown by at least forty nanometres in size, but the hemagglutinin and neuraminidase envelope spikes have also increased in length as well."

Louise was just as perplexed as everyone else who had been listening and she did not try to hide her understandable ignorance.

"I'm sorry, but I haven't got a clue what you're talking about."

Henry realised that his colleague was being rather over descriptive, so he tried to clarify their findings in more laymen's terms.

"I'll explain. The changes that have been made to these influenza viral cells are massive. If it is Cain who's been cultivating the viruses here he could not have chosen a more incurable one to alter its structure." He nervously rubbed two of his fingers against the side of his head. "Influenza has killed more people than any other virus known to man. Although it is only deadly to people who have a low immune system, such as elderly or young people, it is still a major killer. There just isn't a way of ever completely eradicating it. The reason why it is so hard to find a cure for is because it constantly goes through changes in its antigenicity, which basically means that it regularly alters its make up so that the body's immune system doesn't recognise it. You see, what's worrying is that if Cain has managed to somehow make changes as significant as the overall size of the cells and the spikes on the wall of the influenza virus, then there's no telling what he might've been able to do to its lethalness. He could've created something which is more deadly than AIDS and even more contagious than the common cold."

Although Richard was sure that David was behind all of this he still just hoped from the bottom of his heart that it was actually not the case. He knew that if this young man who he knew to be so extremely intelligent was involved that not only would he be willing to attempt to make such a lethal virus, but he would also have the capability to be successful in its creation as well. The whole prospect of something so terrifying sent a shiver down his spine and as he spoke to the doctors he made no attempt to hide his fear.

"I think we can all be quite sure that it was Cain who has been here and it seems as though his intentions are just as clear." He uncomfortably gulped. "We just basically now need to know if this virus is deadly."

Edward answered in a solemn tone of voice.

"That is true. That is our first concern. But I'll warn you now, if it is deadly, I think that it will all be far too late." He nervously glanced at his colleague and his shoulders slumped in a defeated manner. "If there are more of these eggs and they hatch then we could well experience an epidemic or even a pandemic."

Derek still wanted more answers.

"But wouldn't that mean that we would have to catch the virus off of chickens?" He looked at the others with a hopeful expression upon his face. "That's not possible, is it?"

A regretful expression crossed Henry's face as he put a damper on Derek's suggestion.

"A number of years ago there was a cull of chickens in China. There was evidence that some people who died of influenza had actually caught it off of the birds."

Although things were looking rather grim, Louise still tried to search for a solution.

"Let's just say that Cain has made some kind of lethal virus. Surely he's also got a cure?"

With a shake of his head Edward discounted Louise's attempt at trying to solve the problem at hand.

"The only way that could happen would be for him to create the ultimate cure, because that would be the only way to destroy the ultimate virus." He picked up one of the chicken eggs and examined it with an optimistic gaze. "Our best chance is to just still hope that he hasn't been successful in creating the latter."

Derek summed up all of their feelings with a profound remark followed by slapping his hand on one of the worktops.

"Fuck it!"

Although Henry had already been an ill laden harbinger he still had some more bad news.

"Well, I'm afraid that it wasn't just the influenza viruses that were tampered with. We found that changes had been made to a number of different types of bacteria, some of the bacteriophage and four of the chimpanzees have been subjected to something very peculiar." He walked over to a table at the edge of the room and picked up a small vial. "We looked at the bacteria in this vial under the microscope and noticed that it had also been mutated. Its normal effect is to bring about unconsciousness, but only when it is inhaled at a close distance. What it can do now we just don't know. We'll have to do further tests to find out. As for the bacteriophage that he's altered, well he seems to have everything worked out. You see, a bacteriophage is a virus that kills bacteria. The word 'bacteriophage' means 'bacteria-eater'. He could well have made it to counteract the effects of the other bacteria that he's created that brings about unconsciousness."

Derek had a look of disgust upon his face as he tried to fathom out what the point of it all was.

"So, what the hell did he do to the chimpanzees?" He looked at the others with a worried expression. "Does he hate every living creature?"

Edward started to walk over to a room in the corner and beckoned the others to follow him. Inside were several cages with a chimpanzee in each. Some of them seemed to be quite normal, yet three of them had their heads shaven and appeared to be quite docile.

As Edward began to explain he picked up a child's ball that had been left on a table.

"Some of these were subjected to something really strange. They seemed to have had injections in their heads and have lost all of their mind control. They don't respond to any kind of action." He handed the ball to one of the chimpanzees, but it just totally ignored it and gazed into open space. "She would have grabbed it before, but now she doesn't even appear to know it's there. Very odd. Very odd indeed."

Although Derek and Louise now had something to call back to the police station with they still had very little that was conclusive. They would inform the detective superintendent of the viruses and bacteria that had been altered, but they could not sound any panic alarms due to the lack of confirmation of the capabilities of the new mutated cells. As for what had happened to the chimpanzees they just seemed to be the most peculiar of all of the occurrences. The fact that some of them could not play with a child's ball anymore seemed to be of an insidious insignificance which made it all the more worrying.

Whatever was afoot was certainly going to have dire repercussions at a later date and at a very large scale.

Whilst the police were searching through the scraps of evidence which David had left behind after his visit to the microbiology laboratory he was elsewhere carrying on with his machinations. The warehouse that he was now breaking into did not have any security

231

guards and had just a mediocre alarm system that he had already dismantled. This lack of precautions, however, was not very surprising considering that the building only stored various types of wholesale food.

It took David a while to search through some files in the administration office and when he found the ones that he required he quickly read through them before putting them back. He then paced into the main storage area of the warehouse and opened up a large door to a walk in freezer. There were a number of boxes of ice cream, which were stacked up inside and labelled with serial numbers. After taking a while to scour amongst them he came across the ones that he had been looking for. With a small knife that he had taken out of the office he cut open one of the boxes and took the lid off of one of the tubs inside.

David now went about completing one of the major parts of his plan. He pulled a bag of ice out of a rucksack which he had over his shoulder and then removed a fist size vial from out of it. After unscrewing the lid, he poured its liquid contents into the tub of ice cream and mixed it around with the knife before using it again to smooth it over.

To make sure that there was no trace of David ever being in the warehouse, he closed up every box, shut all of the doors and repaired the alarm system. He then slipped off into the night, like a breath in the wind, leaving no hint of his visit. However, the tasteless mixture that he had just added to the ice cream would dramatically affect the lives of all those who would unknowingly consume it.

Only the tops of the tall bushes could be seen above the low mist that had rolled in from the hills and swept across the moors. There was a frost that sat upon the grass that added an extra unforgiving greyness to the bitter surrounding countryside. Even the amber glowing sun seemed not to be as hot as it shone across the icy morning landscape. It was almost as if Mother Nature had woken up in a sullen mood.

David took a moment to gaze across the moors before turning to go into the country cottage that he had just recently claimed for his own. He had travelled out west, changing his vehicle on a couple of occasions and had finally come to finish his journey in the middle of an almost barren land which had no other buildings for miles around. The choice of destination was quite deliberate due to its isolation and lack of dependence upon the outside world.

David had searched through a local map and had chosen the cottage due its lone standing in the depths of the moors. It was totally self sufficient with a large fireplace in the living room and a diesel powered generator in a shed outside. The kitchen was fully stocked with food and there was even a selection of clean clothes. There was a stable in the large back garden that held two horses and the oats to feed them. This was the perfect place for a person to stay whilst they prepared to bring about the genocide of a whole race.

The results of the experiments that David had performed at the microbiology laboratory had played a great part in how he had acquired the cottage with such ease. Most of the theories that the two doctors had come to were actually quite correct, especially when they had said that he had mutated the bacteria which rendered a person unconscious when inhaled. He had enhanced it enough so that all he would have to do was pour a small sample of it on the floor of a room in order for it vaporise and render the entire inhabitants unconscious. The samples that he now had would have to be kept in a cool place so as to prolong their life expectancy, but that was not too much of a problem due to the cold time of year. To protect himself from its potency he had also created a bacteriophage that he could apply to his nostrils and respiratory tract so that it would kill off the bacterial cells that he would also breathe in.

The old couple who owned the cottage were now both unconscious in a spare room. David had released the sleeping bacteria into the house and had regularly been applying it to them to comatose them for a very lengthy period of time. Although it would have been easier just to kill them straight off, he decided that there was no reason why they should not die in the same manner as everyone else on the planet.

Out of all of David's recent achievements his masterpiece was the creation of the virus that would rid the world of the human race. The doctors had found samples of mutated influenza type 'A' viral cells in the embryonated eggs and they had been right to be nervous about their discovery. He had chosen the most incurable virus known to mankind and had turned it into an unstoppable killer. Whereas before it had only taken the lives of the very weak it would now bring about death to even the fittest and healthiest of people. It could be passed on from person to person just by the release and inhalation of the viral cells in their breath, the incubation period was less than two days and after a fortnight the entire respiratory tract of the host would deteriorate to the point of being totally decimated. Every aspect of it was perfect.

As for the cure, this was just as faultless in its inception. David had created a viralphage that could kill off any viral cells of the orthomyxovirus family which were acquired via the respiratory tract. It was simply a virus that ate other viruses. A genius had bred the ultimate killer and it just so happened that he had also developed the ultimate protection from it. Where he had hidden it was just as intellectually brilliant.

Over the last few weeks David had let the eggs hatch that he had infected with the virus and had then bred the chicks into chickens. He did not need to test his creation on any humans due to his confidence in his own success. Failure was simply not a contingency that he had taken into consideration.

In order for David to spread the virus amongst the human race he was going to infect himself and then go forth into society. He would go to a number of airports, train stations and wherever people gathered together. It would then be a formality as his victims inhaled the airborne droplet nuclei from his breath. Death would not only be undetected as it spread, but it would also be totally unexpected until it finally came about after the two weeks.

Before David had infected himself with the virus he had taken a suppressing drug which slowed down the incubation period. He had got a thick flu medicine from a simple chemist shop and had altered its chemistry by extracting and adding new chemicals to it. The new liquid would coat his throat and increase the amount of mucus that covered the line of the windpipe so as a result it would slow down the deterioration process and increase the amount of time in which the respiratory tract would decay. Constant application would only prevent his own death for about a month-and-a-half, but by that time a large amount of humanity would already be dead and he would then be able to apply the outright cure to himself without the risk of being caught with it by the authorities.

Everything was now in place for David to bring about the genocide of humanity. The entirety of his plans had so far worked out to perfection and it would simply be a matter of time before everything was complete. All that was required now was for him to unleash his super virus into society. The final Armageddon was about to begin.

People wearing suits and work overalls poured off of the trains and shuffled through the station. With every carriage-full that arrived the more the crowd increased in size. The rush hour was in full swing and, of course, everything was moving at a snail's pace. There was, however, one amongst the masses who did not have a destination, but certainly did have an ambition.

David stood in the middle of the station doing nothing more than just breathing. Those who walked past him could not have possibly known what he was passing on to them and they just went on their own way unwittingly knowing what they had just contracted. It was all so systematic and yet at the same time it seemed all so casual. A person could have been doing nothing more than simply making their way to work and two steps later they would be infected with a fatal virus. This was the beginning of end for them all.

Over the last few days David had visited a number of major coastal ports and airports so as to pass on the contents of his deadly breath. He had deliberately spoken with as many foreigners as possible just to make sure that the virus would be passed on worldwide. Whilst he was in prison he had learnt a multitude of various languages and had also developed their accents to perfection. The conversations he had conducted were only short and would usually involve him asking the people a simple question about finding out the times of flights or ferry departures, but it had always taken up enough of their time to complete the infection.

So, as David stood watching with a knowing eye as the people walked past he had just one thought in his mind.

Breathe and die!

At first there had been just a small amount of reports on the news and in the papers about a flu virus that was going around. People had been advised to visit their general practitioners so as to get a vaccine. It would, of course, be to no avail, but the media simply did not know what had been unleashed into the population.

Although the public were treating the outbreak of the virus as just another bug that was going around the authorities were starting to give it the attention that it deserved. The state intelligence department had been informed and they had immediately begun to take blood and saliva samples from people who had been infected with the virus. It had taken just days for them to notice that there were signs of large-scale cell destruction in the respiratory tract. A number of laboratories had all drawn the same conclusion and it now appeared as though their worst fears were realised. There was a deadly virus on the loose and it was spreading fast.

With little choice now but to take the highest level of action required it was decided that the Prime Minister should be informed. The head of the state intelligence department and the chief superintendent of the Starrowshire police force were now at Downing Street ready to announce their findings. Whilst they were waiting in the cabinet meeting room they sat with nervous expressions upon their faces as they pondered how each of them were going to word their version of accounts. It was not going to be easy to tell the leader of a country that the inhabitants of it were all possibly going to die.

As the door opened to the room the two men immediately stood up and turned to face the Prime Minister as he paced in. He seemed to have an air of relaxation about him as he approached them, but that would not last long. His manner would surely change dramatically the moment he was told about the killer virus.

In a composed posture the Prime Minister reached out to shake hands with the two men in front of him and spoke in a calm tone of voice.

"Good morning, gentlemen. What is it that requires this meeting at such short notice?"

The head of the state intelligence department answered in a calculated and professional manner.

"It's not good, I'm afraid, Sir. I trust that you've read about the outbreak of flu that's going around right now?"

"Yes. I hear it's affected a number of people."

"Well, I'm afraid it isn't just flu." He gave a blunt account of the situation. "It is in fact a deadly virus which is spreading across the country and will soon start to kill whoever contracts it."

The chief superintendent of the Starrowshire police force confirmed the serious nature of the news.

"It's as bad as it sounds, Sir. The country and even the whole planet could well face its biggest disaster since either of the world wars."

The Prime Minister stood rigidly aghast and uttered just one sentence.

"Bloody hell!"

A number of dragging hours went by as the meeting went on into the afternoon. The Prime Minister just sat there at the large conference table with a gaunt expression upon his face whilst the two men opposite him explained all. They told him about how David had broken into the microbiology laboratory after clearing the surrounding area by destroying the chemical plant and had then cultivated the killer virus. They told of how he had got the explosive, what he had done to the embryonated eggs and simply just went over every other detail that was deemed necessary to mention. It was almost as if they were describing the end of the world, which as far as the human race was concerned, they were.

Duncan Young had been the Prime Minister of Great Britain for just over two years and had so far enjoyed a reasonably successful term. The polls showed that he was still popular with the public and that they still trusted him. Up until now, he had never really had a major incident to deal with, but that was just about to change on a massive scale.

Compared to most of his predecessors Duncan was quite young at the mere age of forty. He had an average size build and a quite photogenic appearance about him. Although his job required him to be regularly seen with a smile upon his face to show that all was going well within his government, he actually had quite a cheerful disposition anyway, so he never really needed to put on an act. What with a full head of hair, without even a hint of grey, his whole appearance suggested that he was quite capable of carrying out the requirements of the high position of state which he held without ever showing any signs of wear and tear.

As Duncan heard the final descriptions of how the virus destroys the respiratory tract he could not help but show his feelings of disbelief.

"I just can't see how it could possibly happen. It seems just so unbelievable." He let out an exasperated breath and shook his head. "Are you sure that people are going to die?"

There was a feeling of unwillingness to answer in the chief superintendent's voice.

"In the south there's a middle-aged woman who has got half of her windpipe missing. The doctors have tried to replace it with plastic piping, but they say that it's just not going to work." He raised his eyebrows in a hopeless manner. "There are about another forty-five cases which are heading the same way."

Chief Superintendent Giles Knighton was known for being a rather pessimistic person and the frame of mind that he had adopted on this occasion was understandably of no exception. What with his grey hair and heavy bags under his eyes, the years of job pressure had obviously got to him. His melancholic attitude was the exact opposite to the Prime

Minister's abundance of optimism and his outlook on life had visibly taken its toll on his appearance.

In a defeated tone in his voice, Giles gave the prime minister his grim view of the situation.

"Unfortunately, we have to make the choice of whether or not to inform the public. If we do we could cause utter panic and if we don't we could be accused of hiding something of national importance." He shrugged his shoulders. "There just simply isn't a right decision to make."

The head of the state intelligence department was more conclusive in his approach as he gave his own suggestion.

"People already know that a bug is going around and are taking precautions not to catch it. That's good enough. We can't make it public yet. There'll be riots, looting and all kinds of lynch mobs going around hunting for people to blame. We'll have to keep it quiet for now." He nodded his head in a self-assured manner. "If too many people start dying and the media start asking questions then we'll have to let it out. Until then, we'll put a complete blanket over it."

It was quite normal for Simon Sheridan to make an approach that was direct and assertive. Although he was coming to the end of his career within the intelligence department, he still had lost none of the drive that he had entered the profession with. His body might have had the years taken their toll upon it, but his state of mind was as sharp as ever. In a confident tone of voice he prompted the Prime Minister to agree with him.

"Do you not agree, Sir?" He sat back in his chair and crossed his arms. "It is the best choice we have."

Duncan sat thinking about it for a moment and then gave his answer in a not too positive manner.

"It does seem to be the best thing to do for now, but as soon as anything changes we'll have to review our decision. Until then, we'll keep it under wraps." He stood up and turned around to face a large painting of the queen on the wall. "I'll have to inform Her Majesty and the president of the United States, but other than that, I dare not even speak to my own family about it."

The three of them had just participated on the most traumatic meeting of their lives and the strain showed. There was not a face that was not pale and a palm that was not sweating. They were all now just taking a moment to try to cope with the stress of the situation, whereas at the same time they all secretly spared a thought for their own loved ones. It was not easy for any of them.

As Derek pressed the button a high pitched buzzing noise sounded out and was then followed by a woman's voice coming out of a speaker in the wall.

"Reception. Can I help you?"

Derek answered.

"Yes. It's detective sergeant Hickey and detective constable Walken from Starrow police station, and Mister Lewis from Blackmoor prison. We phoned Warden McCoist earlier to inform her that we were coming."

After a brief wait a door within some large gates to the left of them opened and a woman dressed in a prison officer's uniform beckoned them to enter.

"Come in! We've been expecting you."

Derek, Louise and Richard walked through the doorway and found themselves in the main entrance area of the Lithrow Town Women's Correctional Facility. They had been sent there by the detective superintendent to question an inmate there who they thought might be able to give them some information about David's future intentions or even give them some idea of his current whereabouts. Their instructions were to have a very high amount of discretion and that they were not allowed to give any reasons to why they were asking the questions that they were.

The three were led through a number of corridors which were partitioned by Iron barred gates and were each opened with a key by the women prison officer who they were following. They soon came to an office that had a table with four chairs around it. After sitting there, waiting for about three minutes, the inmate who they had come to see appeared at the entrance of the room and immediately made it clear that she was fully aware of what they were there for in a less than cordial manner.

"I suppose you're here because of him." She paced into the room and sat down at the opposite side of the table to the three of them. "It was just a matter of time before you lot turned up."

Marilyn sat there for a moment just ignoring those in front of her whilst she ate a small tub of desert which was obviously the latter part of a meal that she had just been having. With one last scooping spoonful she finished the remainder of it and then shoved it away from her in a disgusted manner. It appeared as though she was none too impressed by the prison's culinary offering and she made her feelings more than clear.

"That was the fucking worst that they've served up yet!"

Marilyn then pulled a lighter and a cigarette out of her top pocket and then proceeded to light it. Her whole attitude was utterly apathetic and she made no attempt at trying to hide the fact that she did not want to be there. She had a permanent sneer upon her face and she eyeballed each of them in front of her in turn.

Since Marilyn had left on that fateful morning her whole life had crumbled to pieces all around her. It had not taken her long to succumb to the stress of it all and she had soon turned to drugs. In an attempt to pay for her addiction she had become a dealer, which had then resulted to her receiving a number of convictions. This was her fourth and she was now a quarter of the way through a twelve month sentence.

Even Marilyn's appearance had dramatically changed. She now had a number of earrings in each ear and her nose was pierced too. Although she still had some of her good looks from before, her face had fallen in due to chain smoking, whereas her drug habit had badly affected her once clear complexion.

Derek started by introducing who they were.

"Hello, Mrs Cain. I'm detective sergeant Derek Hickey, this is..."

Marilyn interrupted.

"Look, I've got better things to being with my time than sitting here getting to know you. Just tell me what you want to know about him!"

Derek frowned and then conceded to her demands.

"All right then. You obviously know that your son has escaped from the prison where he was being held and that we haven't found him yet." He momentarily waited for a reply, but when he saw that he was not going to get one he continued. "Well, we were wondering if you might know where he's gone?"

"How would I know? I'm in prison if you haven't noticed." Marilyn blew smoke across the table into their faces. "I'm not a bloody clairvoyant."

Louise was less than impressed by the lack of co-operation being shown by the inmate and she made her feelings clear.

"We didn't think you were. It's just that most mothers have at least some idea where their sons are." She leant forward across the table and spoke in a caustic manner. "We thought that you might remember anything about where he used to go when he was young. That's if it isn't too long ago for you to remember."

A reprising scowl twisted Marilyn's face as she glared back at Louise and deliberately gave an unhelpful response.

"Yeah! He used to go to school, his bedroom and sometimes to the park for a walk."

Richard could see that they were not getting anywhere with the interview, so he decided to use some of the information about David's life that he had gained when they had spoken to each other in Blackmoor.

"Whilst I was working in the prison where your son was I spent a great deal of time talking to him. He told me a lot about his life leading up to..." He paused. "What he did. We discussed a lot of things, such as his schoolwork, his family and all of the other things that he loved, but there was one thing that we never talked about. In fact, the only reason why I know about it is because he asked me to do something for him one day that involved it. I believe there was a girl called Sally?"

This had obviously taken an effect upon Marilyn by the way that the expression upon her face had just become somewhat pensive. There almost seemed to be a hint of sadness in her eye, but it disappeared as quickly as it had come into view. With her emotions in check, she returned to her previous derisory state of mind.

"She was just some old tart he used to knock about with. There was nothing between them. They were too young to know about that sort of thing." A disdainful expression crossed her face. "She was probably as glad to see the back of him as I was."

Richard did not believe Marilyn and tried to press her further on the issue.

"Nevertheless, he did have feelings for her, didn't he?"

"Maybe, but I doubt it. He was indifferent to most things." Marilyn took a deep lug of her cigarette. "The little bastard never gave a toss about anything."

"We just need to know if it is at all likely that he would try to see her." Richard put his hands flat on the table and leant forward to stress the point. "Do you know if he would do something like that?"

There was a pause as Marilyn thought about the question and when she answered it seemed to be with an element of reluctance.

"Yeah. He might do." She shook her head in a condemning manner. "I can't see why though. The little Yank bitch aint worth the time of day."

The rest of the interview yielded very little in the way of progress. Most of the discussion was taken up by questions being rebuffed with unenthusiastic replies. It was only when Marilyn got up to leave that she said something quite peculiar.

"He had a good life at home. I just left him alone so he could get on with whatever he wanted to do." She raised her eyebrows. "In fact, I'm surprised that he even escaped from the prison."

Derek looked at Marilyn in an inquisitive manner.

"Why is that? Did you think he wasn't capable of doing it?"

"No. He was always a devious little sod. Too clever for his own good." Marilyn made a gesture towards the iron cell door. "I just would've thought that a place like this would suit him. He preferred being away from everyone else. The unsociable wretch used to do nothing but read books and learn about a load of old shit. I sometimes wondered what was outside that he hated so much. At least in somewhere like this no one in the world gives a toss about you. We're all just ignored."

With that, Marilyn lethargically threw her cigarette butt on the floor and left. Richard, Louise and Derek just sat with pensive expressions upon their faces staring into the empty space that she had left. They were not really that interested in her views, but what she had said about David being too clever and the fact that he hated what was outside had certainly left its mark upon their minds.

Marilyn appeared to somehow know very little about her son, yet at the same time she had seen things about him that many others had blatantly missed. No one had known just how intelligent he was or that he had such contempt for the outside world. Unfortunately, it now looked as though society was just about to pay the price for its ignorance.

A dark outline of a man's figure stood in front of the window as a dull moonlight shone through the curtains into the room. The expression upon his face was hidden within the darkness as he stood watching over the young woman who was asleep in the bed in front of him. In a rucksack over his shoulder were some of her clothes and other belongings ready to be taken away with him.

In a careful and steady motion, David slid his arms under Sally's body and lifted her into the air. After a taking a brief moment to study her he bent down and lightly kissed her on the forehead. He then took her out of her home and away deep into the countryside where no one could find them.

Derek, Louise and Richard were too late. As soon as they had thought of it, David had already visited Sally and taken her away with him. He was not just a number of steps ahead, but leaps and bounds.

The fax machine made a whirring noise as it unloaded the message and then sliced the paper off as it finished. On the top of the facsimile was the name of the sender and the exact time at which it had been sent. It only had a few lines on it, but the words would bring the darkest of tidings.

The message was for the eyes of only one person, the Prime Minister, Duncan Young. As he pulled the piece of paper out of the fax machine he took a moment to read what it said. A look of despair immediately crossed his face and he slumped down into the chair behind his desk. It was what he had been expecting, but it had still taken him aback and had knocked a large chunk out of him emotionally.

After taking a while to get a hold of himself, Duncan picked up a telephone off of his desk and pressed just the single red button which was on it. It took about five seconds for someone to answer on the other end of the line and when they did he spoke in a low-spirited tone of voice.

"Hello. I'd like to speak to the Mister Sheridan, please."

There was a brief wait and then Duncan began to pass on his message.

"It's bad news, Simon." He paused to hear what was being said at the other end. "Yes, I'm afraid so. I got a fax from Chief Inspector Knighton. It says that a Mrs Linda Poldark died today of a mystery virus, aged just thirty-two, and that the death was caused by the total decay of the respiratory tract. I'm calling a meeting to be held here at Downing Street to be attended immediately. We'll discuss what we're going to do and then I'll contact Her Majesty and the President of the United States. I'll see you in half an hour."

At that, Duncan put down the phone and dejectedly rested his face in his hands.

After the first death, the toll had started to rise quite steadily in a number of countries. One turned into seventeen, which then became forty-nine, and then that increased to one-hundred-and-sixty-two. It was not long before deaths were being reported all around the globe. As soon as it appeared as though it was getting out of control and that the authorities would not be able to hide it any longer, all the other world leaders were contacted to inform them of how the virus had come about. It was then up to each world leader to deal with it how they liked.

Some of the newspapers had already printed stories about people dying of a mystery bug a number of weeks before, but the public had dismissed these as being just isolated illnesses. It was only when people started to catch colds which were more uncomfortable than usual and that the doctors surgeries were now starting to get full of what were seemingly otherwise healthy men and women that people began to worry. There was a silence from the authorities and it appeared as though society was being kept in the dark about all of the facts. The people were now suspecting that something could be drastically wrong.

It finally took a message from the Prime Minister to the media that he was going to make a national address when it was finally confirmed that something of a national importance was occurring. This, however, was not going to be announced in just one country, but worldwide. All the leaders of all the nations were going to reveal the grim news to their people all at the same time.

Every living room and public place that had a television set was tuned into the same footage. People stared at the screens with an air of dreaded anticipation brought about by not knowing the nature of what was about to be announced. It was when the sight of the prime minister sitting at a desk, staring at the camera with a gaunt look of terror upon his face that a stone cold silence swept across the entire country. It seemed as though the worst fears that everyone never knew that they even had were now about to be realised.

Duncan nervously began his message in a broken voice.

"I am here today as it is my duty to inform you all that I have the gravest news that any Prime Minister has ever had to announce to his or her people. No death of a monarch or news of a war has ever matched what I am about to say to you all today. I must first ask that you all remain calm and that you do not do anything that is not befitting of the people of this great nation. I have an immense pride in all of you and I praise the character of each and every one of you." He quickly wiped away a tear that was welling in his eye before it got the chance to fall roll down his cheek. "David Cain, the 'Starrow School Slaughterer', has kept the promise that he made in his infamous 'Omega' speech at his trial. He said that he would attempt to wipe humanity from the face of the Earth and it appears that is exactly what he is trying to do. He has somehow created and released into society a killer virus that is sweeping across the country and the world. Some of you will probably already be aware of the fact that there are people who have already contracted a so-called bug and have, thereafter, died. Well, this is more than just a bug. It is an extremely deadly virus. The worst of what I have to inform you is that we do not yet have a cure for it. However, we do now have our top doctors working on it. I advise you all to wear masks so as not to spread the virus if you have got it or not. In the mean time, I am going to announce a countrywide state of emergency and martial law. The army is already being deployed into the streets to maintain order and a nine o'clock curfew is going to be put in place. Whilst we are trying to solve this problem and get the cure for every single one of you I want to ask you all just to remain calm. As far as food and energy is concerned it will be rationed to each family. You can obtain these necessities at your usual shopping centres without cost, but you will have to accept the fact that there will not be a lot to go around and that you will have to queue for whatever you do get. I again ask you all just to remain calm and act in an orderly manner. Finally, I have one last request. This is not, however, to the people of this country, but to one individual."

Duncan now took a long pause so as to gain enough self-control to carry on with the next part of his announcement.

"Mr Cain, I ask you, man to man, if there is a way that you can stop all of this, please do it for all of our sakes! I beg of you, have mercy upon us all!" He could now visibly be seen to be holding back his tears. "I give you my word, you will not be harmed if you co-operate. Please stop what you have started and give us a second chance!"

There was more to Duncan's announcement, such as how he was going to run the government and that anyone who had caught the virus should just stay at their home and not spread it around. As he bravely continued with the rest of his speech he occasionally had to pause to wipe away his tears and gain his composure. There was little advice that he could give to the people and he was really just trying to do his best to install some morale into society. It was all really just a lost cause and he knew deep down that there was not a lot that could be done for anybody including himself.

The sound of people crying could be heard in every public place and living room across the country. Workers downed their tools, families cuddled together and those who were too terrified to do anything just crumbled on the spot. There was not a person in the whole world that had seen the leader of their nation's broadcast who did not feel a grotesque sense of fear at the announcement of their impending demise. Humanity had been given its last rites and the apocalyptic battle between good and evil was now going to be fought.

As Richard stood amongst the officers in the Starrow Town police station watching the screen with reddened eyes he spoke just one sentence aloud for all to hear.

"The end of the world truly is nigh!"

The neural chemicals slowly disappeared out of the syringe and through the needle into the cerebral cortex. A number of vital food nutrients were pumped through a thin plastic tube that travelled down the windpipe and into the stomach. Ultrasonic pulses were passed through electrodes attached to the temples of the cranium and deep into the brain.

After taking all the time that he needed to complete the operation David stood back and just gazed upon Sally. She lay there upon the makeshift operating table in the middle of the kitchen with her hair closely cropped on the top of her head and at the sides. It would take a while for her to come round after the operation, but it would be worth the wait.

David had injected Sally with various chemicals to help the recovery of her cerebral cortex. He had then sent carefully measured ultrasound pulses, similar to those that are emitted by a dolphin, through her cranium in order to repair any damaged brain tissue. It was an operation that he had already carried out on the chimpanzees in the microbiology laboratory in Starrow Town after first putting them into a coma and then waking them. The experimental exercises had been a complete success and now that there was so much more at stake he knew that failure would simply be an unthinkable outcome. Nevertheless, out of all of his machinations he considered this to be one of the simplest to complete.

With his usual careful tenderness, David slowly lifted Sally up off of the table and carried her to the main bedroom. There was a look of longing upon his face as he gazed upon her delicate features with each step that he took through the cottage. Although the super virus was his greatest creation, bringing his loved one back to the land of the living would be without a doubt his most perfectly beautiful achievement.

At first there was a blank darkness, and then the black slowly turned to grey. Soon there were visible shapes of colours starting to emerge, followed by a collection of restful noises. It was not long before everything became clear; sight, sound and mind.

Ever so gradually, Sally slowly sat up in the bed and peered around the strangely unfamiliar room. This was not a place where she had been before. The wallpaper, the pictures on the walls and all of the furniture were totally unrecognisable to her. Even the sounds of the birds singing outside were different to what she was used to hearing in the built up area where she was from.

A sudden uncomfortable feeling of fear now began to sweep over Sally as she came to realise that not only did she not know where she was, but also that she was alone. Her dumfounded expression now turned to one of anxiety. In her state of despair her breathing became irregular and her body started to uncontrollably shake.

It was at that moment when Sally felt an uncomfortable numbness in the right side of her head. She suddenly became aware that she also seemed to have little control over the side of her face. As she instinctively rubbed her hand against the part of her skin where she felt no sensation she realised that she could only feel a small amount of hair upon her head. Nothing was making sense and the feeling of isolation had now started to make her fear escalate beyond her control.

It was not long before the harrowing mental strain of the situation became far too much for Sally to cope with and she began to lose a grip of herself. Her eyes were already filled with tears and she now began to unashamedly sob. In an attempt to shut out the stress of her predicament she covered her face with her arms and rolled up into a protective ball.

With her fragile state of mind, all Sally could do was just sit there on the bed with her head snuggled into her body whilst hoping that it would all just sort itself out. It seemed as if she would never be freed from her anxiety when suddenly a dark figure rushed into the room and sat next to her on the bed. In an effort to comfort and reassure her, the person embraced her with his strong arms, immediately putting a stop to her sobbing and erratic shaking.

Sally was now not sure if her situation had become better or worsened. Her crying had at first stopped due to the surprise of suddenly being held by someone, but now she was feeling a sense of warmth from the person's touch. As she slowly looked around to see who was seemingly trying to comfort her she felt a multiple of emotions. Shock, happiness and relief all washed over her at once as she gazed upon the face of the person who was sitting next to her. She then spoke her first word in many years.

"David."

Sally now started to cry again. This time, however, it was not due to being scared. The overwhelming magnitude of the situation had completely taken over her and she again let her emotions take control of her. She did not have a clue of what was happening, but what she did know was that she was safe, happy and once again in her lover's grasp.

David had waited for so many years for this moment. To hold Sally in his arms just one more time was the most wonderful thing that he could ever imagine. There had been times when he was in prison when he had thought that his studying and planning were the only important things to him in his life, but now that he had his truelove in his embrace he suddenly realised just how much he had missed her.

How fitting it was that Sally's first spoken word after all this time was the name of her lover. It was, however, hardly surprising considering her last intelligent thought before having her brain mutilated was of David, and now after being healed by his very own hands it was again her first. She did not know it, but she had pleased her beloved immensely just by uttering that one word. It was only a small thing really, but it had meant so much.

It had not taken long for David to start to assess whether the operation had been a complete success. He needed to know if it would be necessary for him to carry out any further surgery. As he carefully studied Sally's actions a number of calculating thoughts passed through his mind.

She seemed to be quite worried at first. This was obviously due to being scared at not knowing where she was. Good. That means she's aware of her surroundings.

It appears that she has control of her upper body. She seems to be clutching me quite firmly. That must mean she remembers what I meant to her.

She doesn't appear to have any speech defects. Her first word was to say my name.

Bloody hell! That felt so good. I remember how much I love her now.

My beautiful darling!

For a long time the two of them just sat unmoving on the bed in the warmth and reassurance of each other's arms. Neither of them wanted to break the comforting tenderness of the moment and they were both quite content to stay as they were. The pleasure of knowing that they still had the same unequivocal love for each other after all these years was felicity in itself. Heaven was not a place, but a state of mind.

There was a low humming noise as David switched on the stereo and turned up the volume. As he opened the window in the room which faced onto the back garden of the cottage he took a moment to watch Sally as she stood in the middle of the lawn gazing up at the stars in the night sky. She wore an all in one white dress that he had taken from her wardrobe when he had snatched her from her home. The pale moonlight shone straight through it making it glow in a beautiful blue hue. After all these years she still looked as beautiful as she always had done and even now it sent a flush of electrifying pleasure flowing through his veins.

The sheer sight of Sally brought back all of the memories of how life used to be when David and her were young and in love. It almost seemed impossible that everything could

243

have changed so dramatically and become so tragic. Happiness, adoration and sensuality had turned to anger, hate and violence.

With an increased sense of longing, David quickly walked out of the back door of the cottage and into the large garden where Sally was waiting for him. As he put his hands out she lightly grasped hold of his fingers and pulled him in closer. With an inquisitive expression upon her face she spoke to him in a soft whisper.

"I have so many questions I want to ask you."

"I know, my love..." David smiled and slowly nodded his head in a reassuring manner. "And I shall answer them all."

"Where are we?"

"In the west of the country."

"How did I get here?"

"I brought you here."

"Why is everything so clear, yet it used to be so..." She was interrupted.

"I promise I will tell you everything, but tonight is the first time in years since we last held each other." David's expression became almost pleading. "So, let's have one more dance, just like we used to. Just like when we were young. Just as we should have never have stopped doing."

At that, Sally conceded and passionately put her arms around David whilst resting her head upon his shoulder. Even though there were a thousand more questions that she wanted to ask him she did not want to lose the desirable sentimentality of the moment. She had not known it whilst in her vegetative state, but she had been waiting for this dance for just as long as he had.

Classical music from the stereo now started to flow out of the open window from the cottage at a slow and easy pace. It seemed to reach into the two lover's hearts as their emotions for each other entwined through their sensual embrace. In exact time with the tempo of the overture they started to waltz across the lawn.

As the damp grass stroked against the underneath of their bare feet it felt soft and gentle to the touch as if they were treading upon a carpet of rose petals. The whole moment was one of calmness and subtle desire. However, after so long apart there was going to be more to tonight than just an unhurried dance around a garden.

Just as their hearts wanted more passion the tempo of the music speeded up almost as if to answer their unspoken request. The two of them started to quickstep across the lawn in a wide circle in rotation after rotation. Their swaying turned to swinging and their close embrace turned into a clasping of the hands at arm's-length.

As they effortlessly danced across the lawn they kept their gazes fixed upon each other's eyes. Although they were both still in their twenties they were both very much ingenuously innocent in their ways. They had, after all, been apart for a large part of their young lives and, therefore, had some catching up to do as far as their sexual maturity was concerned. However, they did not feel as if they were doing that badly or that they had ever let themselves down before.

It was as if they had never been separated as they majestically swayed around in circles across the lawn without either of them once stepping out of time. Their faces were alight with the joy and happiness of being in physical contact with each other after so long apart. This was not just a prelude to foreplay, this was good fun.

Everything just felt so damn good. No violence, no hatred, all the dark sides to life were just distant thoughts to be left at the back of the mind whilst more pleasurable emotions took over. It was just like all those years ago when they had first started to begin a romance with each other. Life was once again giving out the things that made it worth living for. So much so, that David had even forgotten that he was still living in the cruel world that he hated so much.

Sally lay down on the thick fake fur rug in front of the crackling fireplace. The glowing light from the flames made her naked skin gleam like a soft golden silk. As she took in a deep breath and closed her eyes she waited in anticipation for the long missed ecstasy of her lover's touch.

David slowly paced into the room and took a moment to gaze upon Sally's naked body. Even now she still had the same smooth skin that had always driven his senses to immediately excite and send him into an overwhelming feeling of exaltation. With an abundance of uncontrollable instincts that he dared not to repel he knelt down beside her and went about feeding his impassioned cravings.

At first, David just ran his hands over the smooth flesh of Sally's body and then lowered himself down to rest himself on top of her. Slowly kissing her on the lips and then the neck he worked his way around her body. Every move was made at a slow and lingering pace so as to make the moment of tenderness last.

It had been a long time since either of them had experienced any sexual pleasure, but that was still no reason to hurry. They had all night and hopefully the rest of their lives. Time was on their side for now, but fate had a habit of being cruel.

The thudding sound of hoof against soil added to the sense of naturalism that only the purity of nature could provide. Every stride that the two horses took seemed to be in perfect timing with the beating of the pounding hearts of the riders that were upon them. All the adrenaline that life could produce was merged into one overwhelming feeling of exhilaration.

A blissful breeze blew softly against David and Sally's faces as they rode across the colourful flowery meadow upon horseback. The golden rays of the sun made the dew on the green grass sparkle like the stars in the night sky. All the beautiful sights that the countryside had to offer seemed to be akin to the affectionate moment that the two lovers were sharing.

As David and Sally galloped across the soft pallet of colourful meadows without any intended destination they approached a stream which idly flowed through the grassy landscape. It felt like a good place to stop, so they dismounted and took a moment to stand together in each other's arms. The expressions upon their faces were blissfully relaxed and seemed to reflect the tranquillity of the idyllic serenity of the view around them. This was a truly heavenly place that had thankfully remained untouched by the destructiveness of human hands.

Although the surroundings were peaceful Sally's mind was full of turmoil. A number of awkward questions were clawing at her consciousness, while at the same time they were accompanied by fears of what their answers might be. She had a dreadful feeling that something horrible had happened after she had had her accident. It was almost as if there had been a dark cloud looming over her from the very moment that she had woken from her vegetative state.

As Sally and David stood by the stream, holding each other tightly in their arms she studied him attentively. She could sense an indifferent aura radiating from him that felt bitterly cold and heartlessly unfeeling. He still seemed to have the same loving emotion in his touch, but she noticed that he somehow lacked the caring sparkle that he used to have in his eye. In an attempt to get some explanations to the questions that were plaguing her mind she went about trying to pry some answers out of her lover.

"You're not the same person as you used to be David. Something happened, didn't it?" Her expression was sad, yet at the same time it showed a deep amount of concern. "What was it? What made you change?"

245

"The world." His voice was void of expression as he spoke. "One minute I was with you and the next I had nothing."

Sally rested her head on David's shoulder and whispered to him in a reassuring manner.

"Yes, but we're back together now." She dreamily closed her eyes. "And nothing's going to ever tear us apart again."

"Yes, my darling." David's voice suddenly became chillingly temperamental. "And this time I'm going to make sure of it."

Sally's eyes instantly opened wide as a despondent and startled look crossed her face. In that moment she felt the entirety of the coldness that she had sensed coming from her lover. Even in the days when someone had beaten David up she had never heard him talk like that. As she pulled away from his side she spoke in a hurt tone of voice.

"My god!" She slowly shook her head with despair. "What's wrong with you?"

"There's nothing wrong with *me*. Not anymore." David's lips tightened and he took in a deep breath before continuing. "I used to be feeble when I just stood there and took the beatings that everyone else gave me, but not now. Things have changed. I'm now the one who is strong and it's them who are weak."

"What do you mean? That was years ago when you were hurt by those people." Sally looked confused. "Surely you don't live with Norman anymore, and it must have been years since you last saw those other two who used to cane and bully you. What were their names again?"

"Cutter and Dent."

"Yes, that's right. You don't have to worry about them anymore."

"I don't."

"Exactly!" Sally half smiled. "They can't harm you now."

David looked deep into his lover's eyes as he enlightened her of what he had done.

"I made sure that they can't hurt me." He raised his eyebrows in a carefree manner. "I killed all three of them."

That was it; confirmation of Sally's worst fears. She had suspected that something dreadful had happened and unfortunately she was right. There was a time when she would have thought that David could never be capable of such a thing as murder, but now as she looked at the unrepentant look upon his face she knew that he had just spoken the truth.

Sally did not want to admit it to herself, but she had to face the fact that the man who she had loved for so many years had now become a cold blooded killer. She could not understand how a person who previously had been so caring and loving could turn so savage and cold. It hurt her immensely to think that things could turn so sour, but what was worse was that there was a time once when it looked as if everything was going to be so good.

As David continued with his explanation Sally stared at him with a look of horror chiselled into her face.

"I smashed in my stepfather's head with a ball hammer, I cut the teacher's throat with a kitchen knife and I broke the boy's neck with my bare hands." He spoke about the killings as if they were menial tasks that he had carried out. "They got what they deserved. They paid for their crimes with their lives."

Tears now started to flow from Sally's eyes as the full impact of the truth settled in. She felt hurt, disappointed and sorrow for what could only have been. Although there was now clearly nothing that she could do about what had happened in the past she could not help but feel sorry for her lover. Deep down she knew that even though what he had done was wrong she still thought that he almost had a valid reason for doing what he had.

David could see that Sally was now shocked and scared, so he decided that he ought to tell her about what his full intentions were.

246

"Do you remember what we used to talk about? The wars, the greed and all of the other things that we hated, but were forced to live with." He sneered and shook his head in disgust. "It's still going on. The leaders of the governments have changed, but their ways have not. They line their own pockets whilst at the same time others suffer as a result of it. Well, now is the time for it to stop."

Sally was clearly distressed and as she spoke her words almost incomprehensibly stumbled.

"But killing those three won't have made any difference." She breathed out an exasperated sigh. "What good will killing people do? That's not going to help the human race."

"I quite agree. That won't help humanity at all."

"So, why did you do it?"

David took a moment to make sure that Sally was ready for what he was about to tell her and then went about informing her about exactly what his full intentions were.

"Five days ago I released the ultimate virus into the human race. I infected myself and then passed it on to people at major airports, trains stations and all other kinds of crowded public places. Within a matter of months every person on the planet apart from you, a handful of chosen ones and myself will be dead." He spoke slowly and precisely so that he would be completely understood. "In order so that I can live to see them all die I gave myself a chemically altered flu medicine to slow down the effect of the virus. The reason why I have not yet completely made myself immune is because I don't want to risk them catching me and finding the real cure. So, even if they were to get a sample of the medicine in me they would all still die anyway. There is no escape from that."

Sally looked amazed as she tried to get some logic from it all.

"What's the point in killing the entire human race?" She raised her hands in an almost frantic manner. "There has to be some intelligent life left."

"And there will be."

"What, just you, me and few others?"

David looked up to the sky as he spoke.

"No. Not just a few, but a whole new race. I have developed a way of mass creating a new life form whose intelligence is similar to my own." He spoke in an informative manner. "I have designed a drug which alters the DNA in a woman's reproductive cells so that when she is pregnant the food supply sent from the placenta to the unborn baby's brain is increased considerably. This will enlarge the brain of each new born and will bless it with a massive intelligence. A whole new superior master race will be created."

Sally was aghast at what she was hearing. The man standing before her was not only thinking of taking over the whole world, but what made it even more frightening was that he was actually in the process of doing it. This was not the person who she had fallen in love with all those years ago.

As Sally started to think about the immense mass destruction of life that David was planning on carrying out she started to get angry at his ruthlessness. She felt a hot fury boil up inside her as she looked at him standing before her as if he was about to do something no more significant than step on an ant. This was not something that she was going to let him continue doing without him giving her a full reason of why. She immediately went about trying to get a worthy explanation in a demanding tone of voice.

"So, what gives you the right to take someone else's life just because they're less intelligent than yourself?"

"Humans do." The reply was short and was well practised.

"Well, who gave you the right to decide who should live and who should die?"

247

"The answer to that is exactly the same answer as any human would give you just before they intended to kill a living being." David raised his eyebrows in self-assured manner. "I gave myself the right."

Sally was finding it difficult to produce a valid argument and her last question would also be her final attempt at coming up with a way of reasoning with David.

"So, how can you justify becoming a god?"

"Because every religion up until now has failed. None of them have ever put a stop to the suffering around the world. With a new super intelligent race that does not understand the logic in killing for fun, harming another being for greed or depriving their own kind for their own benefit, Earth will be a much better place. So, now you answer a question for me! Why should the human race carry on living on this planet with all their wars, hatred and crime, when a more peaceful, caring and productive race can take over?"

Sally just stood staring at ahead of herself with an expressionless look upon her face. She felt numb after hearing the apocalyptic words that she had just been subjected to. It was only after thinking about it for a while that she finally decided to answer David's question with one of her own.

"So, you're really going to do this?"

"Yes."

"And I have the choice of whether I can live with you in this *new* world or die?"

"Yes. It is up to you."

"When do I have to make this choice?"

"You must decide now. The time is drawing near for the judgement day of mankind. You can either live with me in a peaceful and intelligent civilisation or..." He paused. "Perish with the rest of humanity. The choice is yours."

Sally bowed her head and took in a deep breath before continuing.

"In that case, promise me just one thing, David?"

"What?"

"Just before you take the lives of my family and me." As she raised her head she revealed a look of heartbreak and despair upon her face. "Have the decency to come to me, look me in the eye and tell me if you ever really did love me. Just look me in the eye!"

David waited for a moment before giving his answer. His mind carefully went over all that Sally had said and then what his response should be. When he finally did speak it was in his usual cold and unfeeling fashion.

"What would be the value such a pointless act?" He shook his head in an arrogantly indifferent manner. "I have better and more important things to do with my time."

It seemed as though David's dance with Sally was going to be the last that they would ever have. For all of the time that he had loved and adored her he finally remembered the one fact that meant they could never be together. She was *human*.

Realising that Sally could now be a costly liability David reached into his pocket and pulled out a small canister. He put it up to her face and unscrewed the lid. The bacteria immediately vaporised out of the top and into his lover's lungs.

It did not take long for Sally's body to go limp and collapse forward onto David's muscular chest. Although he now had no intention of sparing her life from the virus that he had infected her with he still could not help but impulsively catch her in his arms to stop her from falling to the ground. With one last moment of compassion for anything that was human he gave her a slight kiss on the forehead.

Love is a star that can shine through even the darkest of skies, but like all things it can eventually fade away.

There was an almost surreal atmosphere that stretched from being what could only be described as complete elation to one of an almost tearful sadness. Sally was back with her parents with what now seemed to be a perfectly normal mind and yet with her she had brought dour news of great sorrow on her return. David had released her from her mental imprisonment and had then locked her up in an even darker conscious cell. It was a multitude of emotions that only he could have brought to their family.

Mike and Melanie had been utterly ecstatic when they had seen Sally appear at the front door seemingly unharmed. She had been missing for five days and although they had had a good idea of who she had been with they had still feared for her safety. The shock of seeing her even made them momentarily oblivious to the fact that she was conscious and it was only when she spoke that they finally realised what had actually occurred.

Sally had found herself at a train station not too far from where she lived and had gone straight home as soon as she had got her bearings. The joyous situation had, however, all turned sour after about fifteen minutes of her return when Mike and Melanie had asked her what had happened. She had told them about what David had done and what he planned to do. Although she had somehow regained the entirety of what life had to offer, she had also been informed that she was about to lose it all. It had been a big rise to the absolute heights of happiness, followed by an even bigger fall to the dark depths of sadness.

Mike and Melanie had immediately called the authorities when Sally had turned up and within minutes the police had arrived at their house. Although they had wanted to be alone with their daughter they had realised what she could offer in the way of information, so they had decided to do what was the right thing. As they sat in the living room either side of her they did their best to comfort her and support her.

Derek, Louise and Richard had arrived at Mike and Melanie's house and were at first unaware of what had actually happened to Sally. They had not known about the accident that she had been in years ago and it was only when she had explained about how she had been healed that they had realised the enormity of what had occurred. Their original thoughts had been that David had just kidnapped her due to some kind of deranged act of obsession, but now they had no choice but to believe that there was another reason for her disappearance. He had tried to save her from the fate he had bestowed upon the rest of humanity.

After everyone had been introduced to each other Richard did his best to talk to Sally in a comforting tone of voice so as not to put too much pressure on her.

"There must have been a reason for why he healed you. He wanted you to live through it all with him, didn't he?"

"Yes. He wanted me to be a part of his new world." Sally bowed her head in a saddened posture. "It was almost as if he was proud of what he was telling me."

Derek spoke in an astonished manner.

"You mean he's pleased about what he's doing?"

Sally peered up at them without raising her head and revealed the redness of her eyes.

"I'm afraid so. It's almost as if David thinks that he's helping the world by killing everyone. I just don't know how he could've become so cruel." She sniffed. "He used to be so caring. There was a time when he wouldn't have harmed anyone, but now that's all changed."

A puzzled look crossed Louise's face as she tried to shed some light on what was being said.

"I don't understand why he would want to wipe out the human race." She lifted her hands up in a bewildered posture. "What could he possibly achieve in this 'new world' that he talks about without humanity?'"

Richard answered part of the question.

"He once said something about that to me. It was almost as if he thought that he could replace the human race with a whole new ultra intelligent life form." He despondently shook his head. "I never did quite see how he could expect to do something which is so nigh on godlike. We know that he's a genius, but to do that is even beyond him."

It was with feelings of regret that Sally enlightened them.

"David can do it." This was greeted by some very scrutinising stares in her direction. "He told me how, as well."

Mike was now so taken aback by what he had just heard that he too joined in with the questioning.

"How could he do such a thing?"

After taking in a deep breath, Sally's eyes seemed to go off into a distant world as she spoke of what David had told her.

"He said that he was going to manipulate the DNA in the reproductive cells of some selected women so that they would give birth to children who will all have massive intelligence's like his own." She briefly paused. "As he called it; 'the perfect race.'"

Derek made a grim observation.

"He really is going to attempt to be a god. The replacement of humanity with a whole new race." A look of grotesque horror crossed his face. "We're actually being eradicated to make way for another life form."

The last sentence summed up all that David was bestowing upon Earth's so called master race. It made them feel inferior, just as it made them also realise exactly how humanity was simply not needed on this planet anymore. Their demise would be brought about so as to make way for a new improved version of living being.

Some families stayed at home in an attempt not catch the now rampant virus off of anyone, but in some cases it had been too late to avoid it and they had simply brought the contagion to the people who they had least wanted to be its victims. Those who were free from contamination found that they could not live in solitude forever and would soon have to venture out to the shops that they would now find to be empty. There was simply no escape from death, whether it was caused by the infection or through hunger, it just could not be avoided. Over a hundred thousand lives had already been lost worldwide, which really made people realise how inevitable their demise was.

Some of the people who had caught the virus were now making the most of their last hours by fulfilling their sexual needs with their loved ones or finding new partners to share their urges. There were also those who still found solace in religion and stayed at their places of worship in an attempt to pray for their lives, if not their souls. It was, however, the streets of the towns and cities that drew most of the people as they attempted to find some answers to it all.

There were places which seemed to be magnets for gatherings as people came to spread their views whilst others came just to listen to them so as to try to shed light upon it all. Some preached about their religions, others taught ethics and the remaining people inevitably spoke about politics. Although they all had different things to say, they all had one thing in common. Each of them blamed the imperfections of society.

An old frail vicar stood on a wooden box and called out to the passersby.

"Jesus said that 'the meek shall inherit the Earth'. We were naive enough to think that he meant us. Now that we look upon the dusk of humanity's existence I realise that he spoke about the other creatures of the planet that have for all these years been kept in captivity by us. It is they who will survive and it is us who will perish. We were the pretentious ones who thought that we deserved the Earth and it was Mother Nature's other creatures that were the meek." He raised his arms and shouted his last words. "God save our souls!"

There was a young couple who appeared to be new age travellers and they were both stripped to the flesh. As the man spoke they hugged each other closely for comfort and reassurance.

"It took the end of the world to finally make us want to save it. After all these years of teaching our young we forgot that there was so much more to learn ourselves." He affectionately wiped a tear from his lover's eye. "All this time that we've been taking from Mother Nature we were never giving in return. She's just curing herself of us."

A young man wearing a neat suit stood holding a placard that had the word 'Fools' written in large letters upon it.

"We deserve it. We've spent billions of pounds on wars and the weapons to fight them when we should have been buying our lives. How many bombs is a cure for cancer worth. What could the cost of a tank buy for a man with AIDS? This virus that is killing us all was bought with the lives of every soldier that has died in all of the wars that we've ever had." He laughed in an ironic manner. "We are such fools we even paid our own money for the privilege of our own deaths."

A young boy and his father were standing hand in hand on the edge of the crowds watching the spectacle with saddened faces. They were both infected with the virus and they had come out to the streets to find some answers just like everyone else had. It was only after a short while of listening to the people who were shouting out their views that the son summed up what she saw in a simplistically innocent manner.

"Why are they all talking Daddy? It's never helped before."

His father agreed.

"That's right, son." He shrugged his shoulders as a tear ran down his cheek. "The teachers, preachers and politicians have all had their say and now that it's too late they've finally learnt what they should have years ago. It was action we needed, not words. We should've helped each other and not ourselves."

The plight of mankind summed up to its entirety.

Duncan Young, the prime minister, stood at the entrance to number ten, Downing Street with Jeffrey Hannah, the president of the United States and a number of other world leaders of various countries. They had gathered to have talks about the crisis to try to establish a way of how to put a stop to it all. Although they knew that time was running out and that their chances were extremely slim, they had, nevertheless, tried to show the public that they were actually making an effort.

There was a podium in front of the waiting press and Duncan Young, the Prime Minister, approached it to make his announcement. As soon as he took his position a number of reporters started to ask him various questions about such things as the death toll of the virus, a possible cure and the whereabouts of David Cain. With all of the shouting, he found that he could not make himself heard, so he made a lowering motion with his hands in an attempt to obtain some silence. When all of the noise finally did die down he began to speak in a morose manner.

"Good afternoon, ladies and gentlemen. This won't be a long statement as we have a lot of work to do. I'll first give you an account of the current situation and then the president of the United States, Mister Hannah will also have a few things to add about how we intend to take action." He put the palms of his hands on the podium and took in a deep breath before continuing. "We can now confirm that the virus that is currently infecting our society will probably bring about the deaths of close to a million of the world's population within the next two months at the very least. It had entered numerous countries and there are few places on earth that it hasn't reached. It has come to our attention that the reason why David Cain is doing this is because he intends to replace the human race with a whole new species that he will himself create. We believe that he will do this by artificially inseminating a number of women with his own sperm who have previously had the DNA in their reproductive cells altered by him with the use of some kind of drug that he has created. It appears that this is the reason for the crisis that we are now facing. I'm afraid that is all I can say for now."

At that, Duncan stepped away from the podium and was replaced by Jeffrey Hannah. The president was a tall man with neatly combed grey hair and well-tanned skin. He did his best to appear calm and adjusted his suit jacket in a steadfast manner as he spoke.

"Good afternoon. My statement will also be short for the same reasons. We have obtained information that leads us to believe that there is actually already a cure for the killer virus that is sweeping across the nations of this world. Although all of our top doctors are currently working on finding their own solution, we feel that our best chance of getting a cure is by ascertaining the whereabouts of David Cain. Only he can give to us the remedy to this problem as we believe he must have created a cure for himself." His expression became almost pleading. "So, if there is anyone who can give us the information which will lead us to him, please could they call the emergency lines straight away and tell us everything that they know."

After waiting at the podium for a short while, Jeffrey turned and walked away. As he left the press started to call out a barrage of questions, none of which he answered. He just followed the rest of the world leaders through the doorway of the Prime Minister's residence and then went about starting the most demanding meeting that any of them would ever be a part of in the whole of their lives.

Louise, Richard and Derek were sitting amongst a number of uniformed and plain clothed police officers in the atmosphere of a very sombre briefing room in Starrow police station. Chief Superintendent Giles Knighton was standing at the front of the room and was clearly suffering from sleep deprivation brought about by a worry induced lack of rest. He had given up trying to appear upbeat, but as he addressed his colleagues he still tried his best to be professional.

"I've called this meeting because we've got to discuss where Cain is going to go next. We've got to start thinking up some possibilities. It's our only chance of catching him. We know some of the places where he's been so far. There was the chemical plant that he blew up, the microbiology lab which he used to cultivate the virus, his ex-girlfriend's house where he kidnapped her, then a cottage somewhere in the West Country where he performed an operation on her to cure her brain damage. Every time he goes somewhere or does something we find out about it afterwards when it's too late. We've got to try to predict where he's going to go next." He shook his head and exhaustedly rubbed his hand against his forehead. "He's leaps and bounds ahead of us. The public know it, he knows it and, worst of all, we know it. So, we need suggestions where he might go next so that we can get there before he does."

A plain clothed woman constable tried to give a constructive proposal.

"There may be an old school friend he wants to visit?"

Derek abated her suggestion whilst reading from a file he had held out in front of him.

"Cain didn't have any friends at school. He was a loner." He shrugged his shoulders. "Not that it's surprising."

Another female uniformed officer gave her view.

"If he is going to genetically engineer a new race of beings there might be a hospital where he needs to go, one with a maternity ward?"

Louise now discounted that offering.

252

"It's a good idea, but it's unlikely he'll choose women who are already pregnant. He'll want ones which he can artificially inseminate himself."

The chief superintendent, Giles Knighton, was now starting to realise that their options were running out.

"I believe that all Cain is going to do now is just hide out in the countryside away from everyone and wait for the virus to finish us all off? It shouldn't be that hard to find him."

There was a stony silence that was so cold that it was almost as if it had frozen everyone to the spot. No one moved. They all just stayed where they were like rigid statues. It was only when Richard spoke and people turned to look at him that there was finally some movement.

"I have a suggestion where he might go." He looked around to make sure that he had everyone's attention. "I think I know where David Cain might just go over the next few days. It's just a hunch though."

The chief superintendent prompted Richard.

"Go on!"

"Up until now, Cain has been about a dozen steps ahead of us all the way through this by making every one of his decisions using his intellect. I mean let's face it, he's a lot more intelligent than any of us are. He knew which virus to cultivate and how, he pioneered and performed corrective brain surgery on someone and that's just some of the things we know about. But when he kidnapped Sally Moore to ask her if she would live with him in his new world, it was a decision made by his emotions and not through reasoning. It wasn't a logical step to take. It didn't even help his overall plan." He gazed around room in an assertive manner. "So, with that in mind, even with his superior intelligence, I think he's just as controlled by his emotions as any of us. I believe he's going to make the same mistake again. After all, he is only human."

This had not enlightened many of the people in the room and most of them just sat staring at Richard with perplexed expressions upon their faces. Giles Knighton was not fully aware of the psychiatrist's point either and he made no attempt at showing his ignorance.

"What mistake do you think he's going to make again?"

"I think David Cain is going to make another attempt at trying to get in contact with Sally." Richard felt slightly embarrassed by what he was now about to say. "Simply because he's in love with her."

The chief superintendent was not too convinced.

"Up until now he's only ever gone to each place he's been to once and then he's moved on within days. If he's as intelligent as you say he is, then surely he won't do anything as stupid as to go somewhere where he knows that we'll have people watching?" He shook his head. "I'm not going to waste officers needlessly by putting them somewhere where he's not going to go."

"That's exactly what he's expecting you to say." Richard folded his arms in a confident manner. "He'll know that you'll have no more than a handful of officers keeping watch on Sally Moore's house. This is our last and best chance at catching him."

Louise was now starting to see Richard's reasoning and tried to help him in his plea.

"I think he's got a point. We haven't been able to guess what Cain was going to do because none of us thought that he would be capable of doing something as implausible as creating a super virus or healing someone who's got brain damage." She pensively ran her fingers through her hair as she pondered what she was saying. "But we know that this Sally Moore meant something to him. He made his original first three kills on the day after she got run over by a car and put in hospital. There was no reason for him to kidnap and heal her

253

other than because of what they had together. There's no way she was part of his 'Omega' plan."

Derek was now also beginning to understand the logic in it all.

"It does seem like the only chance that we've got. Cain has succeeded in everything that he's tried so far, apart from one thing. He asked Sally Moore to live with him after everyone else was gone and she declined. In other words, he failed. I don't think that he will accept that." He looked at Richard with a pensive gaze. "I think he will go back and get her whether she likes it or not."

Giles looked at Derek, Louise and Richard in turn and then spoke to all three of them in an almost doubtful manner.

"And you think that he'll go back to this Sally Moore's house and try to take her again?"

Derek and Louise assuredly gave their replies.

"Yes, Sir."

"I do, Sir."

Richard also gave his opinion in a similarly positive fashion.

"I spent a number of years trying to psychoanalyse David Cain to try to find out who he is. I found out that he was cold, callous and calculated, but I also came to realise that he wasn't always that way. He used to the complete opposite and he was actually caring, kind and considerate." He raised his finger in a resolute manner. "And it's that part of him that will make him go back to Sally Moore's house and take her away with him. She may not be part of his plan, but she's certainly part of his life."

Giles nodded his head in understanding and then gave out his orders.

"Right, I want Sally Moore's house surrounded for a half mile radius. Every officer is to be armed and to wear plain clothes. I don't want Cain knowing that we're on to him. This is our last chance, so let's get it right." He turned to face Richard with a sceptical expression and spoke to him in an almost inaudible voice. "That's if he turns up."

"Well, if he doesn't…" Richard paused and half smiled. "We're all fucked!"

Undercover police officers were hidden at each end of the street where Sally lived. They were sitting in the top bedrooms of the houses with the best views looking out of the windows in the hope that they might catch the one man who could hand them back their lives. The whole operation was considered to be a bit of a long shot, but at this point anything was worth the effort. With the death toll rising by tens of thousands each day worldwide, even the slimmest of chances would be worth pursuing. It was just a matter of whether their target was going to turn up.

It was now three o'clock in the morning and most of the street was covered in a blanket of darkness. There was the occasional cat that wandered about the alleyways and gardens, but no one could see anything that resembled a fully-grown man. That, however, was because the person they were looking for was far more cunning than they had given him credit for.

David was, of course, fully aware of the presence of the police officers that were watching out for him from across the street. He had expected as much and had already prepared a plan for dealing with the situation. As they were looking out for him, no one was doing likewise for them.

Keeping in the confines of every shadow, David had made his way along a number of back gardens leading to one of the houses which had some of the policemen hiding in it. When he got to the back door he quietly turned the handle and stepped inside. He then walked to the foot of the stairs in the hallway and started to slowly make his way up them.

As he got to the top he looked through the doorways of two of the bedrooms and noticed an armed officer in each of them.

David now pulled a vial out of his pocket and carefully unscrewed the lid. He then poured some of the contents on the floor at each end of the landing making sure that the gaseous vapours would waft into both of the rooms which had the policemen in. There was no chance of it taking any effect upon him because he had already applied some of the bacteriophage to his nose and throat so as to nullify the potency.

It took a short amount of time for the bacteria to takes its effect, and when it did, David made his way into the room at the front of the house to investigate. There was now an unconscious police officer wearing a bullet-proof jacket slumped on the floor with a pistol and radio lying by his side. He removed the gun out of its holster and took a moment to study it. After a short while he shook his head and muttered a few words in soliloquy.

"Damn things!"

Before David went on his way he took the police officer's radio with him so as to have the advantage of being able to listen to what the police were saying. He then left the house by the same way in which he had entered and started to climb across the gardens that led towards where Sally lived. When he reached the patio at the back of her house he noticed that there was a light coming from inside. Ever so slowly, he leaned around to see who was inside.

Sally was sitting on the settee in the middle of the living room just staring at the blank screen of the television set. She seemed to be in a world of her own and the expression upon her face was one of a total emptiness. It appeared as though she was deep in thought, but it was also quite obvious that she had nothing but turmoil in her mind.

David took a while to gaze at Sally, just as he used to when they were a young couple. It still somehow felt good. He then knocked on the glass of the patio doors and waited. At first there was no response, but after a short wait, which seemed like an eternity, she slowly looked around to see what the noise was.

Sally was instantly taken aback at the moment that she had seen David standing looking at her. However, what she did next was something that he had never seen her do before. She closed her eyes in an attempt to shut him out of her life and dispel him from her thoughts.

David had noticed Sally's reaction, but he did not let it affect him. He had expected his reception to be very cool and he was under no delusion that she might change her mind and come to live with him in his new world. With an air of arrogance, he just waited at the patio doors for her to open them.

Sally realised that she had to do something, so she opened her eyes and got up to let David in. As she moved across the living room she uncomfortably kept her gaze averted from his. After sliding one of the patio doors open, she spoke in an uninviting manner.

"You had better come in."

David did not say anything in return and just stepped inside the house. Sally closed the door behind him and still did not look him in the eye. The stony silence that loomed over them just made the uneasiness of the moment even worse than it already was.

It was David who finally broke the deadlock by announcing his intentions for being there.

"Well, you asked me to come to you." He raised his chin in a stalwart manner. "What do you want?"

Sally could now not help but finally succumb to the temptation of looking up into David's eyes and gazed upon them with a vexed expression. It had been weeks since they had last seen each other and with every day that had passed she had been yearning for him to come to her and answer the final question that she had put to him. She then spoke in a harsh tone of voice.

"You know exactly why I asked you here. I wanted you to tell me if you ever really did love me." She shook her head with disgust. "Well, did you?"

David stood staring at Sally for a long moment with a thoughtful expression upon his face. He carefully prepared the words in his mind that he was about to say and took his time as he did so. When he was finally ready to give his answer to her plea, he took in a deep breath and started to speak in a tone of voice that seemed to have no emotion in it whatsoever.

"Sally, all I have to say to you is..."

Before David could finish his sentence he was interrupted by a loud crash, as the living room door was kicked open. The room was immediately filled with police officers all wearing bullet proof jackets and pointing guns in his direction. Bright torch lights had been switched on outside in the back garden, which were now shining through the patio windows into the house. Whilst all this commotion was going on, he just stood in the midst of it all still staring at Sally.

Now that David was surrounded a police officer called out a command to him.

"We've got you trapped, Cain. There's no way out. Get down on the floor!"

"I don't think I will lower myself to do that." Came the reply.

"Get down on the floor or we will shoot you, Cain!"

David was quite aware of the fact that he had walked into a trap, which had also probably been set up with Sally's consent. He found it quite understandable that she would do such a thing and was not very surprised that it had happened. However, he still stared at her straight in the eye as he rebuffed the police officer's command.

"Killing me would not be a very good idea considering that you need me alive to give you the whereabouts of the cure."

The police officer that had been calling out the commands now realised that he would need this man alive, so he decided that a different approach was needed. He put his gun into its holster and pulled out a pair of handcuffs from a pouch in his belt. As he slowly moved towards David he spoke in a stern tone of voice.

"Now you listen to me, Cain! I'm going to put these cuffs on you and if you try anything my officers *will* shoot you."

Sally still stayed looking deep into David's eyes, almost as if she was searching through his soul for one last ounce of goodness. It hurt like crazy to think that they could have been so much in love and yet now all that there was left between them was the darkest of hatreds. Nevertheless, she simply could not let it end like this and she just had to make one last attempt at trying to get back the lover that she once knew. The last thing on her mind was now the first thing on her mind.

Just as the police officer was pacing forward with the handcuffs at the ready, Sally darted towards him and grabbed his gun out of its holster. She immediately cocked it and pointed it straight at David. Although she was also now surrounded by a number of guns aimed at her, she shouted a command in a demanding tone of voice.

"Get back or I'll kill him!"

The police officer spoke in utter amazement.

"What are you doing?" He went to take the gun back. "Give me that!"

Sally just raised the gun up in the air and let off a single shot. This immediately made the surrounding police officers realise that she was not faking and they wisely started to pull back. With an overwhelming expression of resolve upon her face she spoke in a determined manner.

"There's no point in taking him. He won't ever give you the cure. You're all just wasting your time." Sally stared straight at David eye to eye. "There's only one way that we're going to do this."

The police officer whose gun had been taken tried to make some sense of it all.

"What are you going to do?"

Sally did not answer him directly. Instead she just spoke to the man who she was looking at down the end of the gun barrel.

"David, I know that you are doing this because you think that it is right and I know that you don't care if we all die, but I also know that if you were to die then all that you've done would be for nothing." She gritted her teeth with a fierce vehemence. "So, I swear to you, if you don't tell me where the cure is I will kill you. If it comes to it, none of us will live."

The expression upon David's face was calmly relaxed and his posture was almost arrogantly composed. He appeared to be totally unmoved by the threat as he just stayed staring at Sally with the same unfaltering gaze. His tone of voice was just as laid back as he spoke.

"Then we shall all die."

A tear started to roll down Sally's cheek as she shouted her final plea with so much passion that she shook with emotion.

"David, please give us the cure!" She aimed the gun at the centre of his body. "I promise, if you don't I will kill you."

Just one word was uttered in reply.

"No!"

The trigger was pulled, the pin slipped forward and the gun was fired. After the initial bang there was a thud as the bullet hit David in the stomach, which was then followed by the sound of smashing glass as his body was pushed through the windows of the patio doors. All of the expressions upon the faces of the people standing around were of utter shock and there was not one among them who had it in them to do anything but to just freeze to the spot. The living room was now just a chilling scene that was adorned with horrified statues and was cast over with an equally stony silence.

David had at first found himself laying on his front with his face in the broken shards of glass. There was an excruciating pain in his stomach and he did his best to hide his discomfort by not uttering a single agony induced murmur. All he could do was just roll over onto his back and grasp his midsection with both of his arms.

David now found himself staring straight up at the night sky and gazing at the stars that littered the heavens. The blood that gave him life was pouring out from between his fingers and onto the bricks of the patio floor that he lay upon. He could now do nothing more than just wait for the inevitable.

Sally took a few steps towards David and then stopped. She had obliviously dropped the gun to the floor and it had already been picked up by the police officer that she had taken it from. With the realisation of what she had just done she bit her lip and began to weep.

As Sally again began to stumble forward she came to stand over David as he lay amongst the broken shards of glass. There were so many things that she wanted to say and yet with all of the anguish that she felt there was not a word that she could get out of her mouth. With all her grief stricken guilt she could not help but fall down onto her knees amongst the broken glass and bow her head over the man who she had just decided to kill.

David could now see Sally kneeling next to him out of the corner of his eye and he turned his head to face her. Every now and again he coughed up some blood, whilst at the same time the thick red fluid oozed down his cradling arms. Even though his expression was clearly one of utter pain, he somehow managed to let out an ironic wheezing laugh just before he spoke.

"Well, I know how to make a cure for influenza, I know how to wake someone from a deep coma and I know how to create a super intelligent race, but I did not know that you were going to do that." A blood soaked smile crossed his face. "You always could floor me within an instant."

Sally just momentarily closed her eyes and then quietly whispered her words in a suppressed manner.

"I'm sorry, David!" She lightly grasped hold of one of his hands that was holding his stomach. "But I just couldn't let you..."

Sally was prevented from finishing her sentence.

"I know. You did what you thought was best. I understand." David slightly nodded his head. "There was no other way for you."

"I just had to. I can't let you do this. There's no point in us all dying. We need that cure David." There was a hint of playful mockery in Sally's broken voice. "I would've hated to have wasted that bullet for nothing."

This resulted in another spluttered laugh from David, followed by him pausing to steady himself before he began to speak.

"Very well. The cure is a viralphage that is capable of killing any orthomyxovirus. It is in a couple whose farm I used not long ago. I poured it into their mouths after I had rendered them unconscious." He turned his head to look at one of the police officers. "They live five miles south-west of the town of Charlow on the outskirts of a village called Thornhampton. The cure can be mass-produced by simply applying it to a host and then taking a sample of their saliva five minutes after. Act quickly! There is no time to waste. Your kind is dying as you stand there."

This was immediately followed by one of the officers making a call on his radio to the emergency headquarters informing them of the news. There seemed to be a sudden wave of relief wash over all that were there and the expressions upon their faces clearly showed their alleviated content. The atmosphere had now become relaxed all round and the only people who were not sharing the feelings of elation were those who were now upon the broken glass on the patio floor.

All Sally could do to thank David was to bend down and kiss him on his blood soaked lips. She then said something that she had been hiding at the back of her mind from the moment that she had first let him into her house that very night.

"I suppose now that this has happened there's something that you should know." She satisfyingly smiled. "Not everything you tried for is lost, my darling."

"What do you mean?" David lifted one of his bloodied hands off of his stomach and looked at it with a hopeless expression. "I can't see me getting out of this one."

"Yes, that's true, but you will live on." Sally lightly bit her lip and her eyes opened wide with anticipation. "I'm pregnant with your child."

As the news slowly sunk in a look of calmness and fulfilment gradually crossed David's face. He wore a smile of utter pride and happiness at Sally's and his accomplishment. As he softly spoke each of his words his gaze did not turn away from his lover's eyes for one instant.

"Thank-you! Thank-you so much for letting me know that." He blissfully sighed. "And in return, it looks like there is something that I should tell you."

"What's that?"

"You wanted to know if I ever really did love you." David paused, just to see the expression upon Sally's face turn to one of desperate expectation. "My sweet, sweet Sally, I have never ever stopped loving you with all my heart from the moment I first met you. You have simply always been the strongest and beautiful love of all my life."

At that, tears started to flow down David's cheeks and mingled in with the ones that had also fallen from Sally's eyes. The two of them just stared at each other with the same undying devotion that they had always had in the depths of their hearts. Once again their lost souls had found one another and had melted together forged by the heat of their compassion. Yet again, two had become one.

The door swung open, heads rose and a silence swept over the room as the announcement was shouted out by one of the prime minister's political aids.

"We've got Cain." A deep breath. "And the bloody cure!"

A raucous cheer immediately followed this from those who had understood what had been said and the muttering of interpreters as the foreign leaders were told of the news. The heads of states were all gathered for a meeting in the crowded cabinet room at Downing Street and were now all standing up shaking each other's hands in jubilation. When the elation finally died down the Prime Minister, Duncan Young cleared his throat to make a short speech.

"Ladies and gentlemen, this is a great day for all of us and our nations at the end of some very torrid times. I can assure you that not only will all of your countries get the cure straight away, but I will also promise that David Cain will be given the appropriate punishment for his crimes." He nodded his head in an assured manner. "I give my word to you all."

The ambulance carrying David had arrived at Starrow hospital accompanied by a massive police escort of speeding squad cars and motorbikes. On the way the paramedics had taken samples of his blood just in case he did have the cure in him. Although this would prove to be unsuccessful, they would, however, find the traces of the medicine in his respiratory tract that would slow down the incubation period of the virus.

David had been rushed into an operating theatre and was now surrounded by a number of surgeons and armed police officers. His whole chest and stomach was now covered in blood and his mouth was grotesquely splattered with the scarlet fluid. Although he had been responsible for thousands of deaths there was still a humane urge to save his life. This, however, was not something that he was going to allow.

David saw one of the surgeons approach him with a breathing apparatus ready to give him an anaesthetic, but with what strength he could muster he pushed him away and shouted out a forceful command.

"No! You keep your hands off of me! The last thing I want is to spend my last moments having you prod me around." He coughed out a splutter of blood. "Leave me to die in peace!"

A high-ranking police officer stepped forward and spoke to one of the surgeons.

"Is there anything that can be done for him?"

The reply was spoken in a subtly quiet manner.

"Not with a bullet wound to the stomach. He's lost a lot of blood already and by the way he's coughing it up there must me an enormous amount of internal damage."

"Then leave him!"

The police officer bowed his head and then took a step back. This was followed by a lull around the operating theatre as the inhabitants looked upon the broken man that lay before them. There was no remorse, just the habitual respect that such humans as these gave towards the loss of any life.

David's breathing had now started to slow down and become shallower. His eyes seemed to grow more distant, just as his eyelids appeared to become increasingly heavy. The blood that was teeming from his mouth and midsection now began to halt its flow. In one last movement, he sluggishly reached his arms out wide with his palms facing upwards in an almost divine posture as if he were attached to a crucifix.

Just as one long breath came out of David's mouth, his eyes closed and at last shut out the outside world which he had hated so much. Death was inevitable.

The waiting room at Starrow hospital was packed with the usual amount of patients and an excessive amount of police officers that had been posted there to guard against any acts of revenge against the latest submission to the accident and emergency ward. Sally was sitting in one of the corners and was understandably in a state of devastation after shooting her lover. Although she was surrounded by police officers and a crowd of people, she was, nevertheless, very much alone.

After about ten minutes of waiting, a rather morose looking doctor entered the waiting room and began to look around. When his gaze went to Sally, he uncomfortably paced across the room and got her attention by bending down in front of her line of vision. He then spoke in a whisper so that the people around could not hear what he had to say.

"I'm sorry! David has just passed away. There was nothing that we could do for him. He wouldn't even let us touch him."

Sally let out a heart-wrenching cry of mental pain and burst into tears.

The news of David's death was greeted with an indifferent atmosphere by the collection of world leaders who were crowded into the cabinet meeting room at number ten Downing Street. Now that they had the cure for the virus it was of little significance that this person had died. Although they would have been demanding retribution for him at a later date they were now more interested in distributing the viralphage amongst the people of their countries.

The political aid that had informed the leaders of the news was now bending down and talking quietly into the Prime Minister's ear.

"Sir, I suggest that in order to assure the public that it is now safe to walk the streets and that we have the cure you might want to go to the hospital where Cain is and give a statement. We can get there in minutes by helicopter." He straightened himself up. "You will be able to inform them all where to get the viralphage and suggest that the weakest are to be seen to first."

Duncan nodded his head in agreement and then stood up at the centre of the table that was surrounded by the world leaders. To get their attention he knocked a teaspoon against a glass tumbler and readied himself to address them all. After a brief wait for silence, he began.

"I will go to the hospital where Cain has died and make a statement to the public from there. I have been informed that the cure for the virus will be obtained within the next few hours, so by the time that I get there I should be able to announce to the world that we definitely have it and that he's dead." He took a moment to look around at all the nation leaders. "As soon as our doctors have started to mass produce the viralphage I assure you that you will all be provided with it in the quickest amount of time possible."

At that, Duncan turned to leave the room. On the way to the hospital he would make a concerted effort to pen what would yet again be one of the most important speeches of his life. This would be one of the better moments of his career, especially after recent events.

A muffled cheer came from the waiting room of the accident and emergency ward as Sally slowly paced down the steps outside the entrance. She paused for a moment and closed her eyes in an attempt to shut out the sounds of the jubilation brought about by her lover's death. It was no good though. She could not keep the heart wrenching sounds or the excruciating pain at bay.

Sally was lost in turmoil. There seemed to be no escape from the overwhelming grief that laid siege to her mind. She wanted to get away from it all, but she knew that what she had done would stay with her for the rest of her life. It seemed that the pain would only finally cease when her life came to an end as well.

This was once such a beautiful world. Mother Nature's gift to us all was herself. She used to be so much.

The air was clean, each of the seven seas was a pure blue and every landscape was of an untouched majestic beauty. There was once a time when all of the creatures that lived upon this planet were at one with nature. It was such a beautiful place.

And yet now the air that we breathe to keep us alive is actually starting to do us harm. The seas are so polluted that they barely sustain the life that dwells within them. There are cities with towering buildings that are almost akin to concrete gravestones put there to commemorate the loss of the beauty that they replaced.

Mother Nature evolved her creations so that they could adapt to their surroundings, however, she's been so devastated by her supposedly greatest piece of work that she has lost her control over the monster that she created. The human race has replaced her as the giver and taker of life. So, now that they have taken her place it appears that they are not able to take the responsibilities that come with it. There must be one more step in the cycle of evolution.

Humanity must be joined by a being that can fulfil the obligations that such a position as being the master race demands. They have no choice but to share their position of being the sole rulers of the world and let another more advanced living being take some of the burden that they have laid upon the shoulders of the gods that they pray to. The process of human evolution must not be waited upon any longer.

It is time for the human race to stand side by side with a new life form that will evolve from them. A race that can take on the responsibilities that humanity cannot fulfil. A people who can create, cultivate and cure.

The time of the Geni is nigh.

With that final thought, David opened his eyes and the life once again flowed through them just as strongly as it had ever done. This was his world and he was not going to let it waste away from being the once beautiful place that it had been. As for the human race, they could live, learn and adapt; for they were about to get a second chance.

David was still lying on the operation table in the middle of the theatre with his arms stretched out at his sides surrounded by the surgeons and police officers. With a flick of the wrists two small glass vials rolled out of his sleeves and fell to the floor. They instantly smashed releasing the vapours of the sleeping bacteria into the room and out into the corridors beyond. Within seconds he was the only person who was awake within the accident and emergency ward of the hospital.

As the young man stood over the unconscious body of the police officer he held the revolver in his hand and muttered a few disapproving words.

"Damn things!"

David had never liked guns and he had always considered them to be one of mankind's most efficient, yet destructive creations. His views were a grim testimony to their inventiveness and depravity. With a sneering scowl upon his face, he put it back down onto the floor.

The unconscious police officer lying before him was wearing a thick bullet-proof jacket and David decided that this would provide a good piece of protection, so he put it on underneath his coat. After making sure that he had everything that he needed, he turned to leave. As he left through the back door of the house he looked around at the surrounding gardens. There were a number of sheds and, although it was late, there seemed to be rather a lot of them with dimmed lights coming from inside. Those who inhabited them obviously had a reason for being there.

David now switched on the radio that he had taken from the police officer so that he could listen to what was being said by those who were watching out for him. As he climbed over the fences of the back gardens on his way to Sally's house a number of messages started to sound out that he had been spotted. This did not bother him and he simply just kept going towards his destination. He had already planned his escape, by releasing a massive amount of the sleeping bacteria which was heavily compressed into a canister which he had taped to his back, therefore, anything that they did now would be to no avail.

"David, please give us the cure!" Sally aimed the gun at the centre of his body. "I promise, if you don't, I will kill you."

Just one word was uttered in reply.

"No!"

The bullet hit David in the midsection and sent him crashing backwards through the glass patio doors. He had not expected Sally to attempt to kill him and for some strange reason it felt good that she had done such a thing. It reminded him just how strong she was and it had simply brought back all the memories of why he had ever loved her.

When David had walked away from one of Norman's tempers, Sally would plea with him to beat the hell out of his stepfather. There were times when he had been doing homework for hours without a rest, but in an instant of passion she would wrestle him to the floor and ravish him. So now that he was going to bring about the genocide of an entire race, she was willing to kill him for it.

Sally simply balanced everything out in David's life. She had always been able to bring about a level of equilibrium if there had ever been too much of an extreme. Good and evil, light and dark, pleasure and pain, all bled into one.

David had found himself laying face down amongst the broken glass on the patio floor with the bullet lodged into the metal plate of the protective jacket. Acting quickly, he picked up a large jagged shard and ran it across his wrist. He then grabbed the forearm of the cut arm with his other hand so he could speed up and slow down the flow of the bleeding. He then held it across his stomach to create the illusion that he had been shot in the midriff. Just to make it even more convincing he also bit into his lip so that he would be able to cough out blood in order to show fake signs of internal damage. The new plan of escape had all been thought out within a few seconds, but its level of efficiency was exceptional.

There had been a countrywide announcement that the Prime Minister was going to make a declaration at the Starrow Town hospital. Although the nature of the statement had not yet been disclosed it was, nevertheless, expected to be of some significance to the current worldwide crisis. People had already started to gather in the surrounding streets in their thousands and were now being kept at bay by a mass of police officers and army soldiers. Anyone who was not there was either at their homes watching the news on television or already dead.

Duncan Young stood at the top of a wide set of steps that led up to the entrance of the hospital. As he looked over all of the people who had gathered around to hear the declaration he wore a contentedly proud expression upon his face. He was just about to announce that the state of emergency was over and that he, their Prime Minister, was about to give them the cure that would save their lives. If there was ever a vote winner, this was it.

There were a number of microphones and news cameras pointing in Duncan's direction, but he delayed making the announcement so as to wait for confirmation that the cure had been obtained. The delay was too much for some of the members of the media and their impatience resulted in them shouting out questions to the Prime Minister. Nevertheless, their calls for answers fell on deaf ears and they were just ignored. They would simply have to wait, just as the millions of television viewers across the world watching the impending live statement would also have to.

The confirmation of the acquirement of the cure was going to be relayed to the Prime Minister via one of his political aides who was standing next to him holding a mobile phone. Every now and again, Duncan would turn to him and prompt him for the all-important information, but he had so far received no more than just a morose shake of the head in every instance. There was now not a person who was not starting to feel the stress of waiting and, of course, the not knowing if they were going to survive.

Up until this point the political aid's main duties of employment had been to see to any of the Prime Minister's direct needs and to take messages for the other members of the cabinet. He was a short thin person with neatly combed hair that stood over his brow into a quiff. Although he was small in stature, he was proud of the big responsibilities of his job. Today's task would certainly be one to tell his grandchildren about.

At first, most of the people standing around dismissed the noise as just another sound that could be heard amidst all of the talking and shuffling about of the gathered crowd. It was only when the bleeping tone of the mobile telephone stopped and was then followed by the prime minister's political aid answering the call that everyone realised that the moment had come. There was now a hush as the conversation on the steps in front of the hospital entrance took place.

"You've found the couple in the farm? Excellent!" This was followed by some murmurs of approval from the surrounding onlookers. "They were at their home and you've taken samples of their blood. OK, thanks a lot."

A broad contented smile crossed Duncan's face as he walked over to stand in front of the political aid and waited for the inevitable good news to be passed onto him. Everyone standing around could also now sense the feelings of relief and the eased expressions upon their faces showed their gratification. It was only when the telephone conversation continued that the atmosphere began to change.

The political aid's tone of voice started to become apprehensive, just as his complexion became gaunt.

"What do you mean it won't work? How do you know?" There was now a look of utter horror etched into the features of his face. "They've already died of the virus."

At that, he unintentionally dropped it to the floor and bowed his head.

Duncan just muttered a remark to no one in particular.

"He lied to us. Cain knew that he was going to die, so he lied to us."

Families sitting in their living rooms watching the live coverage on the news sat patiently waiting for the Prime Minister's announcement. People gathered in public houses, staring at television sets, too nervous to even lift their drinks to their now dry mouths. The crowd that had gathered outside of Starrow Town hospital hushed down into a lull in expectancy of the statement that would declare that there was to be mercy upon their lives. It was all so nerve wracking.

Sally walked through the empty streets without any particular sense of direction. She had given up trying to wipe away the tears from her eyes and had just let the constant flow of the salty liquid stream down her cheeks. Nevertheless, her feelings of grief would not last long. This was something that she was going to make sure of.

Although Duncan was surrounded by thousands of people, he felt as though he was the loneliest man in the world. The expression upon his face was one of utter horror and as he nervously swallowed he could feel his throat painfully constrict. He just simply did not know what to do. As he shook his head in disbelief he turned to face the hospital that now held the supposedly dead body of the man who had brought about the devastation of mankind and stared at it with utter desolation.

It was at that point when something caught Duncan's attention. At first his brow furrowed and then as he tried to focus on what was beyond the glass doors of the entrance to the hospital his eyes twisted into a squint. Although it all seemed utterly impossible, he was sure that he was now looking at David Cain, who in return was also staring straight back at him whilst surrounded by a mass of unconscious people laying on the floor.

For one long moment, Duncan just stood there gazing into the reception area of the accident and emergency ward. Sweat had been pouring out from all over his body, but now it felt as if it was freezing to his flesh. What was also unfathomable was that he appeared to be the only person who had noticed the lone man standing there so seemingly out of place. The implausibility of the whole situation felt so surreal that he almost wondered if he was dreaming.

It was, of course, all very real. David stood in the middle of the hospital entrance staring straight at Duncan with his sharp light blue eyes. The top half of his body was still soaked in his blood, but the self-inflicted wound to his wrist had now been stitched up and wrapped in a bandage. He held the canister of compressed sleeping bacteria which had previously been taped to his back in his other hand whilst the contents hissed out of the valve at the top. All of the people who had been standing in the ward when he had entered were now lying on the floor at his feet.

In a slow and steady motion, David started to pace towards the exit that led out into the streets where Duncan and the crowds of people had gathered. As he approached the glass doors he pushed both of them at the same time and took one long stride outside so that he was now at the top of the steps where the Prime Minister and the reporters were standing. He then took the valve off of the compressed canister sending the entirety its contents out across the hospital grounds and the surrounding streets.

Whilst all this had been happening, Duncan had just stood there unmoving with an expression of complete disbelief upon his face. In just one day he had witnessed the reprieve of life for humanity, the sudden realisation that it was actually still going to be eradicated, the death of the person who had caused it, and now the resurrection of that same man. This was the stuff that the most terrifying of nightmares was made out of.

As if all that was happening was not strange enough, Duncan had now for some reason started to feel light headed. He had already noticed that the people who were standing closest to David had fallen to the ground seemingly unconscious and he was now starting find it hard to stay upright himself. With what few bewildered thoughts that he could bring to his mind he simply just wondered what the hell was going on. One deep breath later he was lying face down on the concrete steps without ever having been aware of what had just happened to him.

Sally now found herself walking through the entrance gates of the park where David and she had spent so much of their time when they had been together. She had not deliberately made her way there. It had just happened. With the same unintentional sense of direction, she kept on pacing towards the bench next to the large oak tree where they used to sit.

265

At first, Duncan slowly opened his eyes and when he realised that he was not waking up in his bed his face became bemused. It then hit him. The memories of not getting the cure, David standing there staring at him and the people falling down unconscious all entered into his mind. As he quickly sat up and turned his head to try to get his bearings he noticed that he seemed to be the only person who was waking up. This day got more and more unbelievable as it went on.

Slowly getting to his feet, Duncan stood up and gazed around at the hospital grounds. What he saw was a sight that seemed almost as unreal as it was shocking. The whole place was littered with nearly a thousand unconscious bodies of the people of Starrow Town. It was, however, the person who was still standing amongst them who had now caught his attention.

David stood staring at Duncan with his hands clasped behind his back in a relaxed posture. There were people all around him slumped in various positions where they had fallen in their unconscious states. He was about thirty yards away from the Prime Minister and when he called out to him his words were spoken in a seemingly respectful manner.

"Good afternoon, Mr Young." A slight smile crossed his face. "I think you and I need to talk."

David had taken a small vial of adrenaline from the hospital laboratories and injected it into Duncan so as to wake him up and had then poured some of the bacteriophage down the Prime Minister's throat so as to keep him from falling back to sleep. He had then waited patiently amongst the unconscious bodies of the people in the hospital grounds for the unconscious man to wake. Just for the sake of privacy he had also switched off the news cameras which were lying on the ground that had been filming the event live to the homes of the people.

Duncan just stood there with an expression of utter bewilderment, which was quite warranted considering the inexplicable nature of the scenario. He was at first quite stupefied by the fact that everyone around him was lying on the ground and yet he was completely conscious and upright. It was only when it had finally sunk in that he had just been spoken to that he reacted by replying to David's statement in an agreeing yet vexed manner.

"Yes, I agree. I think we do need to talk." Duncan started to carefully step over the bodies of the people as he made his way across the hospital grounds. "There's a lot that needs to be said."

David just stayed where he was and continued the discussion in the same almost pleasant tone of voice.

"I suppose you would like to know what is to become of the human race and the whereabouts of the cure for the virus?"

"Well, of course I'd like to know." Duncan wore a riled expression upon his face. "You've slaughtered about a million people just for this so called intelligent race of yours. I'm sure that there's absolutely no way that you could justify being a murderer, Mr Cain."

There was a time when David would have been more than furious at being spoken to in such away, but nowadays he simply was not going to let it bother him. He would just explain himself in a clear and precise manner so that this ill-educated person could learn from him. Therefore, in a steady and elucidated tone of voice he made the reasons for his actions plainly clear.

"You call me a murderer?" David shook his head in a disagreeing manner. "I would have thought that you would call me normal. You see, your people consider humanity as being the master race and, therefore, you think that it is your prerogative to put your own interests above that of any other creature. Such as, if there were wild animals that fed on people and roamed the streets they would be exterminated due to being a danger to society. Your excuse would be that you are looking out for the interests of your master race. The way

I see it is that humans create weapons of mass destruction, they have wars, they obliterate important rain forests, they deplete the ozone layer, and they basically do more harm to every creature on this planet than all of the other species put together. I simply decided to exterminate the problem. That doesn't make me a murderer. It just means that I'm looking out for the interests of the new master race that I am going to create."

Duncan was not so convinced by the statement.

"What about all of the innocent children that have died, because of the virus that you created?"

David answered the question with a well considered reply.

"That can also be asked about all of the harmless creatures whose habitats have been destroyed by humanity and all of the innocent children that have died in your wars. You have always considered it to be justified when you have eradicated life for your own means on the grounds that the life you have destroyed would one day be a hindrance to you. But now that this philosophy of 'death to all that is inferior' has been turned around and used against humanity you now decide to call it murder. You just do not like the fact that your race is not at the top of the food chain anymore."

The discussion was not going in the direction that Duncan had originally expected it to. He thought that there could not possibly be an excuse for taking the lives of human beings, but now that he was hearing that it had been done using the same ideologies that society had always lived by it was all becoming rather too harrowing. His main aim had been to quote a number of reasons for why he should be given the cure, but it now seemed as though he had failed at his very first attempt at trying to argue his case.

Nevertheless, Duncan still kept trying to plea for an act of clemency.

"Not all humans are that bad." He put his hands flat on his chest. "Most of us never kill."

Still David had plenty of answers to justify his actions.

"I quite agree that not all humans are killers, but every single one of you is still responsible for the way that the world is. After all, you do all pay for the taxes that finance the armies and their weapons. Without all of you paying in the money together you would not be able to have wars. You all think that it is acceptable to pay for the unacceptable. What should cause an international outcry of descent is actually deemed as quite tolerable."

Duncan now realised that he was never going to justify to David that the human race deserved to live on this planet ahead of an ultra intelligent species that just might be able to make the world a better place. Although he felt like giving up, he still, nevertheless, knew that he was the last chance for the whole of humanity. He simply had no choice but to once again beg for mercy.

"Well, it looks like I can't change your mind. So be it! If that's the way you want it." Duncan nodded his head in a subdued manner and then started to lower himself down to the ground. "I'll get down on my knees if I have to. I can be that strong."

David was less than impressed by the show of diminution and went about correcting the Prime Minister's lack of judgement of the situation.

"Get up! That's not what this is all about. You may like people to beg to you, but I don't find that sort of thing acceptable." The expression upon his face was almost one of pity. "You really do not understand, do you?"

As Duncan started to straighten himself up he slowly shook his head as he spoke.

"No, I don't."

"Then I'll explain. I always used to consider myself as being a victim of the ways of society, but the fact is that I was not the only one. I was one of many." David wistfully paused for a moment before completing his statement. "You see, humanity's most pained victim is itself. And to punish those who have already suffered enough would only be the

267

easy way of doing things. It's that kind of philosophy that has destroyed this planet. So, that is why I want to help you."

Duncan's expression now became bewildered, but before he could say anything, David broke the all important news.

"I'm going to give you the cure."

Sally approached the large oak tree next to the bench in the park. What she saw before her made the pain feel even worse. Inscribed into the bark of the tree were the words that had been carved by her own hand a long time ago.

David

4

Sally

The suffering was simply unbearable.

Those who had been watching their television sets had seen the crowds gathering outside of the hospital fall to the ground unconscious, only to then lose the reception on their screens. In desperation they had flowed out into the streets in an attempt to maybe find a neighbour who could tell them what was going on. However, it was to no avail and they simply realised that they would just have to wait to find out if there was going to be a reprieve without even knowing how they were going to be informed of it.

Duncan just stood with his jaw dropped and with a shocked expression upon his face. A minute ago he was almost accepting the fact that he was not going to be able to obtain the whereabouts of the cure for the virus, but now it seemed as though it was simply going to be given directly to him. Even though he was grateful for the news he, nevertheless, could not help but ask why the change of mind had come about.

"But why? If you're so sure that the human race is so evil and that the world would be a better place without it, why let us live?" He bowed his head for a moment and then spoke in a perplexed tone of voice. "Are you not going to create your ultra intelligent race?"

An assured expression crossed David's face as he spoke.

"Oh, I will create my ultra intelligent race. You can be sure of that." He now began to smile. "And I am going to make sure that humanity is not the master race of this planet anymore."

"But you said..."

Duncan was interrupted.

"I said that I was going to give you the cure, and I am. But instead of bringing about the genocide of the human race, I am going to speed up evolution so that it is joined on Earth by an ultra intelligent species. The two will live side by side." A thoughtful expression crossed David's face. "Humanity has devised many different political, ethical and religious philosophies, all of which have so far failed. Well, this is mine. The philosophy of 'Genism'."

"You mean you're going to try to alter the genetic make-up of the human race."

"I have already started."

"How?"

"To explain that, I will have to start by telling you where the cure for the virus is."

Duncan had unwittingly forgotten what his main priority was and now that he had been reminded he went about taking full advantage of the opportunity to save his race.

"Of course, where is it?"

David took in a deep breath and then spoke in a manner that was almost as if he were discussing the whereabouts of the nearest bus stop.

"The cure is in the Lithrow Town Women's Correctional Facility."

Had Richard, Derek and Louise of heard that last sentence they would have realised just how obvious a place it was to have hidden the cure.

Marilyn sat in the small interview room lethargically ignoring those in front of her whilst she ate a small tub of ice-cream which was obviously the latter part of a meal that she had just been having. With one last scooping spoonful she finished the remainder of it and then shoved it away from her in a disgusted manner. It appeared as though she was none too impressed by the prison's culinary offering and she made her feelings more than clear.

"That was the fucking worst that they've served up yet!"

Richard, Derek and Louise just sat staring at her with blank expressions upon their faces. They could see that the woman sitting in front of them was deliberately trying to show them a lack of respect, but they just did their best to show that they were not affected by the display. Nevertheless, had they have realised that Marilyn Cain, David's mother had just finished eating the cure for the killer virus right in front of their very eyes then they probably would have reacted in a more erratic manner.

In days to come, Richard, Derek and Louise would find out where the cure was hidden and they would no doubt see the calculated obtrusiveness in the choice of place of where it had been hidden. David would have needed to put it somewhere where he would be sure that he would be able to find the hosts at a later date and, of course, he would also be able to use the women virtually as reproduction factories to create his new master race. It was all so obvious, yet so ingenious.

There had been a break-in at a food wholesale warehouse a number of weeks ago, but it had not been detected by the police or even by the owners of the business. Nothing had been taken and there had not even been a trace of any forced entry, but, nevertheless, something of a great importance had been left behind. A single box of ice cream had been laced with a concoction that included the cure for the virus and a drug that would alter the reproductive cells of any woman who consumed it. The reason why this particular type of foodstuff had been chosen was because the less than zero temperature that it was kept in would be able to sustain the life span of its new added ingredients.

David had broken into the administration office of the warehouse and had searched through the filing cabinets for the relevant information that he required. He had soon come across a list of customers and the food consignments that were to be sent to them. Within the list was the serial number of the boxes of the ice cream that would be sent to Lithrow Town Women's Correctional Facility. It was just one more masterminded plan among many.

"Ironic really." David half smiled. "It is the only thing that I have ever entrusted with my mother."

A part of Duncan wanted to go and get the cure, but he could not bring himself to leave. The man before him was just about to explain to him how the human race was about to be genetically altered into a whole new species. He simply just had to find out how this was going to be achieved.

As David described the events that had taken place and what they would lead to he spoke in an explanatory tone of voice that was akin to that of a schoolteacher.

"You see, it was not just the cure that the women in the prison consumed. They also took a drug that alters the DNA in their reproductive cells. After a matter of months of any of them becoming pregnant their unborn baby will have a massive amount of the food supply from the placenta sent to the growing brain. This will not only increase its size, but also its efficiency." There was a look of calculated thought upon his face. "I should imagine that the average overall increase of intelligence will be about seventy percent per person. That should be just enough to enable the new race to be able to define between the absurdity of making a weapon of mass destruction, and wisdom of the creation of a non-toxic ultra proficient fuel. I call the new race 'Geni'."

"But that's playing at god." Duncan raised his hands and shook his head in a forewarning manner. "Absolutely no one should do that."

A disagreeing expression crossed David's face as he replied to the comment.

"Playing at god. How can you say such a thing? The human race is almost godlike in its abilities as it is. Everything on this planet is in some way affected by your actions. The problem is that it is normally in a negative way. The climate, the air that you breathe, the land that you live on and the welfare of every living being is ruled by humanity." He paused for a moment to consider what he was about to say and then when he began to speak again he pointed up to the sky. "Imagine a god up in heaven, looking down on Earth. He sees a city where the people who inhabit it are evil and depraved. After careful consideration, he decides that he wants to wipe them off of the face of the Earth. He, therefore, points his finger at the city, a bolt of lightning shoots forth and every building and person is eradicated."

The discussion was now becoming quite confusing for Duncan, but, nevertheless, he continued to listen as the young man before him explained his views.

"Now imagine that same city with the same evil people, only this time the god is replaced by a single human being. One man sits in a part of the world and also decides to obliterate them off of the face of the Earth. He also lifts a finger, but this time presses a button and a nuclear warhead drops on the city, and, of course, eradicates every building and every life within it." David paused to make sure that what he was saying was being understood by the Prime Minister and when he was sure that it had all sunken in he continued. "Now imagine the same god as before sitting on his cloud, looking down upon a village of starving people in a third world country whose crops have failed. He concludes that they are worth saving, so he decides to feed them. He again points his finger at their fields, a wave of miraculous power shoots forth and then suddenly the crops begin to grow. Everyone is then fed. But now consider a human sitting somewhere on the Earth who knows about the plight of this village and its starving people. He could send them some packages of food that will last only so long or even send some farming equipment in the hope that they can become self-sufficient, but he is not capable of changing the weather and making their land fertile. And the reason for this is quite simple."

"Why?" This was all that Duncan could say.

"Human beings make bad gods. You can destroy, pollute and kill on a massive scale, but you cannot create, cultivate and cure in the same magnitude." David explained it all as if he were giving a gift from the gods, which in a way he was. "The new race that humanity will be joined by will not see the logic in the evils that you are currently capable of, but instead will only strive to create its own morally superior achievements."

Duncan was not sure whether he liked what he was hearing or not. There would normally be a vote in parliament or a nationwide referendum to decide on such a policy, but it did not appear as though that was going to happen in this instance. He even now found himself wondering how something so dramatic could be carried out and his inquisitiveness forced him to enquire if it would be at all possible.

"But how do you intend to accomplish this throughout the entire world?" He shrugged his shoulders. "You couldn't have injected that many women in the prison so that they alone would create this new race."

David nodded his head in a conceding manner.

270

"This is true." He pointed a finger at Duncan. "But that is why I am telling you this. In due time, I will send the formula for the drug altering gene to you. You will then make sure that every leader of all the nations in the world will have the drug."

"What makes you think that I will do that?"

David confidently smiled.

"Because you can see the good that it will do for every living being on this planet, you are wise enough to know that this is the best thing ever to happen to this planet and..." He raised his eyebrows. "You must be just as sick and tired of all this suffering as much as I am. Why wouldn't you do it?"

Duncan nodded his head and spoke in a yielding manner.

"Yes, you're right." His expression then became cautious. "But what if the other world leaders refuse?"

"Indeed, some of them will refuse, but not all of them will and those who do accept will soon reap the rewards." David glanced around at the unconscious bodies that were surrounding him. "It will actually be beneficial to rely upon the shallow ways of peoples thinking. Some countries will want to make the ultimate soldier or efficient money maker out of the new beings, but those that they try to manipulate will see beyond the superficial goals that have been set for them and refuse their wishes."

"What about religious countries?" Duncan shook his head. "They won't accept the presence of the new intelligent race."

"So, what do you think will happen when economies start to collapse because the oil fields that they relied upon have become obsolete because of new more efficient fuels, and when people in small open minded countries have the cure for AIDS and large countries do not? Just look at what one of me has done. Imagine what ten of me could do or even a thousand." David assuredly nodded his head. "Everyone will want what has made the successful countries thrive. They will all want geniuses to improve their economies, resources and, essentially, their lives. It will simply be a case of relying on the greed and needs of humans."

Duncan raised his hands in a submissive manner.

"Alright, let's just say that I do send the formula for the drug to the leaders of the world." His expression became forewarning. "You know that people will come looking for you. They will want to punish you for what you have done."

"Let me worry about that." David's tone of voice became sardonic. "I think I've proved that I can evade your search parties."

"That's true."

"Well, that will be all then."

Duncan suddenly appeared to be rather bemused.

"What, you mean that's it?"

"Is there anything that you do not understand?"

"Well, I just can't believe that you've told me that you're going to take the course of evolution into your own hands and advance the human race, but are now just going to walk off like it's nothing."

David just nodded his head and then went about summing up all that was going to be in an encouraging manner.

"I used to ask myself, 'what is this world?' Well I now know the answer to that question. The world is whatever each of us wants it to be. The new race that will join humanity will just widen that choice. The genetic alteration of the human race will give to the world a being that will put a stop to the wars that kill so many, the constant pollution that poisons the planet and the suffering that is caused by the arrogance of the species that once ruled the world. It will be the true master race." He wore a contented smile upon his face

271

and wistfully looked around at the world in which he now lived in. "Genism is the philosophy that will finally bring us peace on Earth. We cannot deny our planet that."

At that, David just gave one slight nod of his head in the Prime Minister's direction and then spoke just one more sentence.

"Goodbye, Mr Young!" He then turned around and walked off.

Duncan now found himself just standing amongst the mass of unconscious people staring at the back of the person who was slowly pacing away from him. It was the most subdued of exits from someone who had just singlehandedly sown the seeds that would bring about the evolution of a race and would change the face of the Earth forever. Nevertheless, as he watched David disappear off into the streets of Starrow he could not help but feel good about all that was going to be. Deep down, not only had the human race just been given a reprieve, but he also knew that he had just received something that was better than a gift from the gods. It was a gift of the gods.

So, the years passed by and all that had been spoken of on that day came to be. At first there were only a few countries that adopted the formula of the drug and even they only experimented on a small number of births. The women who were at the prison also had their babies and they too were cautious of what their offspring would become. However, with the attention of the world turned to all of the newborn ultra intelligent children the miracles began to happen and humanity started to realise that it was time for change.

The new race became known as Geni, just as David had wanted. They lived side by side with humans in a very cordial existence. Just their being there put a stop to such intolerances like racism, sexism and homophobia, simply because no one could look down on anyone else anymore knowing that they themselves were so inferior.

Positions of importance in society were willingly handed over to those who were clearly superior at filling them. Control of medicine, science and education was given away with an eagerness that yearned for all the answers to the greatest of questions. Ever so slowly, the human race became aware of what was good for them and they gave up their position of master race to those who could do better.

The first breakthrough came in Sweden when a married couple of Geni who were doctors found a way of preventing certain types of cancer by halting the abnormal cell division within the body caused by carcinogens. They sold their findings to the countries of the world for guns and ammunition that they then had scrapped. Their fame did little to change their lives and they kept on practising medicine regardless.

A number of years later, a Canadian man pioneered a fertiliser that required just a third of the water normally required by a crop and which also speeded up the cellular growth of the plants. This all but put a stop to the planet's famine problem and the third world just simply ceased to exist. He accepted a small house in Quebec for his troubles.

By this time the political philosophies of capitalism and communism were becoming distance memories and the world's leading parties mainly adopted green based issues. New ecologically friendly fuels and nuclear fusion were providing most of the planet's energy, until a female Lithuanian university student invented the first ever gravity powered generator. Two generations after she had given her creation away for free there were no other forms of power production in usage. When she graduated she ran a large landscape gardening company and spent her days replacing the now mostly unused motorways with lush greenbelt.

The phasing out of currency became the next big accomplishment. People were simply given whatever they needed in the way of food, utilities and medicine whenever they needed it. Central banks closed, the funding for war became obsolete and corruption was starved out. It was all quite simple really. Money was the route of all evil, so they got rid of it.

The greatest achievement that came about happened just one hundred years after the cessation of the existence of currency. It was not, however, brought about by scientists, doctors or inventors, but instead by the world's politicians. Every border of every country was wiped off of every map and all of the nations became one. Earth was now not a place of division separated by religion or political persuasions, but was one of a utopian unity.

The Geni and human race soon came to look back on the dark times as an era of malevolent contempt. Wars, pollution, genocide, corruption and other human induced suffering were concepts that had no place in contemporary life and were just things that were read about in the history books out of a matter of interest. None of that ever happened in Genopia.

However, with all the achievements of the new race there was still one mystery that they had not tried to solve. Some said that it was best left unanswered, as there are some things that simply did not need to be known. This was one subject that all the intelligentsia agreed that ignorance towards was acceptable. No one ever knew what became of David Cain, and they did not want to know.

Sally stood in front of the large oak tree looking at the words cut into the bark that she had long ago inscribed herself. They had meant so much then, but they held no value now. David was gone and with him he had taken their love. There was nothing left for her now.

Reaching into her pocket, Sally took out her keyring which had the penknife attached to it. As she pulled the blade out of the handle, she held it out in front of herself and studied it to assess its effectiveness. Its sharp edge would undoubtedly slice through the flesh with ease. Rolling up the sleeve of her left arm, she muttered a few broken last words in soliloquy.

"This pain just has to stop."

Sally did not even look at her wrist as she raised the knife up above her head. An expectant grimace crossed her face as she steadied herself for the searing agony that the blade would bring when it cut through the pulsating vein. She then brought it slashing down, slicing deep into the flesh. It immediately sent a splash of blood up into her face making her grit her teeth as she braced herself for the end of her life.

There was, however, no sensation of pain in Sally's arm. An expression of bewilderment crossed her face as she opened her eyes. Ever so slowly, she looked down towards the knife that was still held tightly in her grasp.

Instead of seeing the blade cut deep into her wrist, she saw that it was imbedded into the palm of someone else's hand. The incision had produced a lot of blood, but the person did not seem to be in any hurry to remove the object that was slicing into their flesh. It was almost as if they could take the pain.

David carefully pulled each of Sally's fingers away from the handle of the blade with his free hand and then removed the knife from her grasp. He already had his gaze fixed upon her and as she turned to face him their eyes met. With a hurt expression upon his face, he slowly shook his head almost as if to suggest that she should have known that he would have been there for her. As the realisation that they were once again going to be together sunk in they passionately embraced each other, kissed ecstatically and clung together for dear love. Heaven was once again a state of mind.

Hearts pounded, tears flowed and emotions ran amok. After kissing for what seemed like an eternity, David pulled away from Sally and looked deep into her eyes just to witness the happiness in them. In return, she lightly bit her lip in anticipation for him just to finally confirm that this time their love was for real and that it was going to last. So that is what he did.

David got the penknife that he had in his hand and turned around to face the large oak tree that already had their previous carvings in it. Whilst he cut some new words into the bark, Sally grasped him around the waist and closely watched over his shoulder as he inscribed the last piece of the message. When he was finished, they both took a moment to just gaze upon what was now written in front of them and contentedly smiled to themselves.

The rest of their lives were now ahead of them and the two lovers finally felt as though they could actually be together in the beautiful world that they had always talked about. With a satisfied expression upon his face, David put his arm around Sally's shoulder and started to lead her across the park towards the future of pure happiness that they had sacrificed so much to gain. As the two of them wandered off into the distance they left just one reminder of them ever being there.

The words that were carved into the large oak tree were simple in their text, but they were passionately full of love in their meaning.

David
4
Sally
4
Ever

The end.

I accept that genetic engineering is a contentious subject, so I feel I ought to explain how I arrived at the philosophy of Genism at the end of the book. To be quite honest the hardest part of this book was to write the ending. How could one human being, as in me, think of a way to achieve what classical philosophers referred to as 'the good life?'

There were a number of possibilities that I considered as a finale for the story of which some were more obvious and/or better than others were. One was, of course, that David would just forgive the human race and allow it to carry on the way it was and just hope that it would get things right on its second chance. This, needless to say, would be an extremely far-fetched and unlikely ending. Two world wars, two nuclear bombs, people starving in the third world, etc... How many more chances and slaps on the wrists do we need?

A more attractive ending that I contemplated was to have David live the rest of his life like a god, and that every time a country or society did something immoral he would punish them with a lethal bacteria or virus. The problem I had with this ending was that nothing would come from it, in respect to the fact that it faced the same problem that the first idea came across. Would the human race ever learn by its mistakes? It is a sad fact that there would probably never be a punishment harsh enough that would make us change our ways.

It was whilst I was trying to work out a suitable philosophy that I attained the most important piece of knowledge that I have ever learned in my life. I realised that I simply did not know the answer and that I never would. This is how we learn in life. It is only when you realise that you do not know it all you can set about learning it all. So, it was at this point that I realised that there was only one person who could conceive a philosophy that could even come close to being perfect. David Cain. Like any writer I had to get into the mind of my character and find the answers there.

Genism is, of course, like any other philosophy in that it has its positive arguments as well as its negative criticisms. I actually found it quite pleasing that it had such a large amount of pros and cons. It left me with an ending of which its substance is enjoyably debatable.

The first criticism of Genism is that just because a person has an ultra high intelligence does not mean that they would use it for the good of all. There is the possibility that the individual could become the ultimate criminal instead of a pioneering doctor. Such a person might see the value of hurting others for their own gain instead of considering psychopathic behaviour as unacceptable. This is not something that we can ultimately arrive at a conclusion about because none of us could even begin to imagine what would go through our minds if we were to have such an intellect.

There is also the factor of human imperfection. If humanity were to attempt to speed up its own evolution there would be the chance that it would make mistakes. It would not be too unlikely that it would pursue an ultra intelligent race for the financial rewards. This would certainly be an inviting factor for such investing companies, but when profit is a goal costs are always minimised. Cutbacks could lead to mistakes and disastrous consequences would surely follow.

The human imperfection factor also brings forth a question that is akin to that of the chicken and the egg conundrum. To create something so advanced might require an intellect as evolved as the end product for it to be an attainable goal. Can something imperfect create perfection? Obviously, an ultra intelligent race would not necessarily be faultless, but it would be extremely more advanced than that of which created it. Up until now, we have only created computers that are fractionally as efficient as that of the human brain. Assuming that it is possible, David already had the necessary intellect to create an ultra intelligent race, whereas we do not.

One of the strongest criticisms of Genism is the defective parenting factor. It does not matter how intelligent a child is, if they are brought up by one or more inadequate parents there is a strong possibility that they will not fulfil their full potential. There is, however, the likelihood that they might not be effected by such parental shortcomings as violence, lack of love, not enough education in the home, withdrawal of attention, etc., but all of us are a product of what we are subjected to by our guardians. A child who is a victim of society's blindness to their lack of a good upbringing at home normally grows up to eventually make society their victim. Everyone needs a chance in life, no matter how intelligent they are.

The creation of a super race has, of course, been tried before. Hitler's way of trying to achieve it was nothing short of sick, but at the same time not too different to David's first attempt. Get rid of the weak and replace it with what he thought was stronger. There is a big difference, however, between doing away with one race to make way for another and evolving a species into a better version of it. Whether a more intelligent master race would be better or not is yet to be proven, but most of the cures found and inventions created have been given to society by those with the greatest intellects.

So, would Genism work? This is something we will never know unless we try it, that is, if we should. I certainly do not know the answer, but I have a feeling that one day we might all find out.